"PLEASE KISS ME," TONI WHISPERED

A smoldering passion possessed him. "You're flirting with fire," he murmured, "but I think you know that."

And then, unhurriedly, his lips met hers. For exquisite moments his mouth brushed lightly back and forth — taunting, tempting, deliberately arousing....

She closed her eyes as a great wave of wanting flooded through her. Her hands crept unbidden around his neck as her lips parted more fully and she sought his mouth with a betraying ardor.

Luis stopped at once, breaking away with a suddenness that left her dazed. "Odd," he said derisively, "I have a feeling that you didn't want to stop. Would you have preferred more?"

"Of course not." Toni feigned lightness. "I don't deny I enjoyed the experiment. But that's all it was."

His low amused chuckle did nothing to calm her seething excitement.

ABRA TAYLOR
is also the author
of these SUPERROMANCES

1—END OF INNOCENCE
5—CLOUD OVER PARADISE
12—A TASTE OF EDEN

These titles may be available at your local bookseller
or by writing to:

Worldwide Reader Service
1440 South Priest Drive, Tempe, AZ 85281
Canadian address: Stratford, Ontario N5A 6W2

ABRA TAYLOR

RIVER OF DESIRE

A SUPERROMANCE FROM
WORLDWIDE

TORONTO · LONDON · NEW YORK · SYDNEY

Published, June 1982

First printing April 1982

ISBN 0-373-70021-0

CHAPTER ONE

"A MISOGYNIST? You're kidding. This should be fun to watch."

The amused drawl came from a tall thin man with a puckish professorial face and prematurely thinning hair. Like his two companions, he was seated on the edge of a large packing crate, part of a miscellaneous collection of baggage and film equipment that rested on the riverbank near a complex of enormous docks. The black waters of the river teemed with a variety of picturesque craft, just as the shoreline swarmed with humanity of every skin color from light to dark, and wearing every manner of clothing consistent with the tropical heat of the day. Elsewhere along the riverbank Portuguese was being shouted, but this trio spoke English—a matter that set them apart, as did the store-fresh jungle gear they all wore.

"Fun to watch what?" puzzled a second, somewhat younger man with an open ingenuous expression. "You're one up on me, Ty. I can't even remember what the word 'misogynist' means."

"I doubt you ever knew, Barney," laughed the third and only female member of the group. Her pleasant husky accent, like those of the two men, was

American. "It means the very opposite of you—in other words, a woman hater. So don't look for any pretty little nurses at this place we're going to. I don't expect there are any."

"No women! Now she tells us. My God, Toni, what the hell are we supposed to do?"

"Take cold showers," suggested the young woman equably.

The three were a team: Ty Chisholm, director and cameraman; Barney Evans, soundman and sometime assistant cameraman; Toni Carruthers, producer. Together they formed a stripped-to-the-bone film-production crew, the machinery of their small operation well oiled by more than a year of working together. The independent New York production company that employed them specialized in travel and wildlife documentaries, and it was for this reason that the trio was now in Brazil: a twelve-part television series on South America had been sold to an educational network. The first six shows, focusing on South American cities, had already been put in the can. Still to be filmed were those segments dealing with the remoter parts of the continent: and first and most important of these was the great Amazon basin, a complex, exciting, challenging area almost as large as the United States.

While Ty and Barney concluded some scheduled shooting in Venezuela, Toni had come on ahead to the Amazon to lay the groundwork for the month-long expedition about to begin. For her, most of this past week in Manaus, main city of the Amazon interior, had been spent in attending to the considerable shopping required for an expedition into the jungle. At the moment, surrounded by the crates and cartons containing Toni's purchases, the production team was waiting for the weekly supply plane that was to ferry them into the Amazon hinterland, and for the Brazilian official who was to escort them to their destination.

"Good Lord! A month without women," grumbled Barney, looking at Toni accusingly. Although several years past his student days, when he had learned sound-recording techniques at the Eastman School of Music in New York State, Barney was still a bachelor—an eligible and enthusiastic one, who reveled in the appeal his boyish good looks held for most women. Barney was unused to being deprived of the fair sex.

Toni merely smiled serenely. "If this man Quental can manage without women for eleven years, surely you can manage for a month."

"Eleven *years*," whistled Ty. A Midwesterner, Ty was a dedicated womanizer twice divorced for his sins. He had trouble abjuring women for eleven days, let alone eleven years. In that respect, he and Barney were two peas in a pod.

"What's with this Dr. Quental?" asked Barney. "A Schweitzer complex? Save the Amazon Indians and that sort of thing?"

"Maybe a bit of that," Toni acknowledged lightly, "but I hear his main aim was to get away from the female of the species. He buried himself in the jungle when he was quite young—the year he became a doctor, in fact."

Ty shook his head in disbelief. "It takes all kinds. Does Quental know that one of the species is about to land in on him?"

"As Senhor Garcia made all the arrangements by letter," Toni replied, "I really can't say. When Garcia arrives, perhaps he'll fill us in on the details. Dr. Quental knows we've been given government permission to film the Xara Indians, and he knows we'll be staying for a month. That much he agreed to under duress, on condition we don't try to film him. And I suppose he knows there are three of us. But whether he knows about me...,"

"As I said, it should be fun to watch," Ty grinned, giving his shapely female teammate a knowing once-over.

It was not the first glance Toni Carruthers had attracted on this busy waterfront. Hers was a cool serene beauty. One could only guess at the elegant shape of long legs hidden beneath drab and unflattering trousers, but all her other assets were visible enough, and they included some very feminine curves. Her hair, a warm subtle caramel color, was cut in a shoulder-length swing with a straight fringe across her brow. She wore it looped casually behind her ears, with not so much as a single curl interrupting its satiny well-groomed smoothness. At the moment lipstick, a hasty slash of pink, was her only concession to femininity; and little of that was needed to enhance a face with just the right touch of independence to the chin, just the right curve of humor to the mobile mouth, and just the right hint of stubbornness to the straight well-shaped nose. Toni was too much of a career woman to indulge in any excess of feminine froth. Perfume was her one weakness, and at the moment, clad for an expedition to a remote Amazon tributary, she had not even indulged in that.

"After a year of living with the two of you," Toni retorted imperturbably, "I've had plenty of practice with difficult males. He won't give me a moment's pause."

"Does anyone?" snorted Barney Evans.

"Who told you all this stuff about Quental, Toni?" asked Ty.

"That pretty girl at the airport—the blonde you were both ogling yesterday afternoon. We started to chat while I was waiting for your flight to come in. The name Quental was familiar to her; she's dealt with him from time to time. Evidently he does come out of hiding once in a blue moon, and when he does he usually flies to Rio. She thinks he must have business interests there."

Barney put on a puzzled expression. "Girl at the airport? I don't know what girl you're talking about."

"Neither do I," Ty echoed innocently.

"The one at the Varig desk." Amused, Toni looked at the two other members of her film team without revealing that she had overheard both of them, at separate moments, trying to make a date with the attractive Varig employee for next month, when the crew would be returning to Manaus after their filming in the jungle was completed.

Ty pursed his lips and pretended to think. "Mmm, yes, I vaguely remember catching a glimpse of some exotic-looking female."

"In passing," agreed Barney, feigning idleness. "What else did you learn from...what did you say her name was?"

A humorous gleam touched Toni's wide-spaced gray eyes. "I didn't say her name at all," she returned placidly.

"I think you're holding out on us," grumbled Barney.

"So do I," sniffed Ty. "What else did you *not* find out?"

Pensively, Toni cast her eyes heavenward and wrinkled her attractive nose. "Well, she said he's the lean, mean type. Tall, dark and arrogant as sin. A *macho* South American male, to hear her tell it."

"Hell, Toni," complained Ty, "you know that's not what we mean."

"What else do you want to know?" asked Toni with bland innocent eyes. "I think she said he was over six feet tall, with a trace of Indian blood—"

"Knock it off, Toni," Barney growled. "Luís Quental isn't the topic under discussion."

"The Varig girl," urged Ty, giving up efforts at subtlety. "Tell us about the Varig girl."

"She says he's the type who knocks women flat," mused Toni as if she had misunderstood, taking some small revenge for the teasing so often inflicted on her.

"With you around," Ty said disgustedly, "it's more likely *he'll* be the one who gets flattened—without even knowing what hit him. I've seen you do it too many times to doubt your ability. Now give, Toni; tell us all."

"You two are sex fiends," Toni sighed. Absentmindedly she twirled the plain gold band on her ring finger. "Do I have to set you up wherever we go?"

"Yes! As producer it's your duty to keep us happy. And as you're still not in the open market yourself...."

"How can we head off for a womanless month in the jungle without some reward at the other end?"

"Not exactly womanless." Toni's warm unflirtatious laugh reflected her comradely relationship with the two men. "You'll have me."

"As I said," Ty came back grumpily. "Womanless."

"Thanks for the compliment," said Toni dryly. Then she smiled and gave in, reaching into the breast pocket of her shirt to extract a small piece of paper. "Here's her name, her phone number and all the vital information. She has a friend, reputedly stunning. I've made a double date for the two of you for a month from now. She thought you were both very sweet, trying to pick her up in bad Portuguese. There was a sign on her desk saying she spoke seven languages. Didn't you see it?"

"No," said Barney.

"We were too busy looking at her," explained Ty.

"What a twosome you are," sighed Toni.

Barney slapped her playfully on the back with the ease of familiarity. "We're not a twosome, we're a threesome."

"About time we became a foursome," Toni remarked with a glance up the high riverbank, toward the city that lay at its crest. Manaus was an extraordinary place to find in the heart of the jungle. On the great Rio Negro only miles from its junction with the Amazon itself, it was a modern sprawling city with a rich and fascinating past, where unusual old architecture existed side by side with tall contemporary structures. From the riverside little of this was visible. It was near the end of the dry season, and the inky waters of the Rio Negro were at their lowest, fifty or sixty feet below the coming high-water mark, an annual rise and fall that necessitated huge floating docks and caused the present enormous height of the riverbank.

"Just like Garcia to make a last-minute entrance," grunted Ty Chisholm, who had little love for the Brazilian official assigned to deal with the film crew's needs. "I don't care what his position is, assistant to the minister, special adviser or whatever. He's a pompous little man with red tape running in his veins."

"Oh, he's not so bad," soothed Toni. "Considering he's a fairly high official, he's putting himself out to deliver us to Quental's compound personally. What's more, it was Garcia who prevailed upon Dr. Quental to put us up for the month. He has some kind of pull with Quental because of family connections.''

"They're related? Now I know I won't like Quental!''

"They're only brothers-in-law,'' Toni revealed. She herself had learned of the connection just days before, in her last official communication from the Brazilian government. "I gather Diogo Garcia must have married one of Quental's sisters—he has six of them. I found that out at the library, when I was looking up background material and happened to run across a Quental family tree. Some years ago someone did a study on the descendants of the old rubber barons, and the name Quental caught my eye.''

"I don't know how you ever found time to go to the library,'' remarked Barney, eyes roaming over the numerous packing crates among which they were waiting. "You must have bought everything but pith helmets.''

"Nobody wears a pith helmet in the Amazon,'' smiled Toni. "Besides, most of that isn't for us. Gifts for three hundred Amazon Indians don't fit into a nutshell, no matter how you pack 'em.''

"Can't think how you found time to scout locations, too,'' Ty marveled. "From what you told us about the Manaus Opera House, Toni, it should make quite a—''

"My God,'' interrupted Barney in a stage whisper. "There's Garcia. And wouldn't you know it? A pith helmet!''

THE QUENTAL COMPOUND was no more than an hour from Manaus by air, but it was an hour that took the cargo plane over hinterland so remote that it seemed few men could ever have penetrated these parts. Like an endless green bouquet the jungle stretched beneath, threaded here and there with ribbons of rivers that were a mere handful of the eleven hundred tributaries pouring their liquid offerings into what was beyond a doubt the mightiest river in the world. Each tributary seemed to have its own hue: blue, turquoise, green, gray—the shades separate and distinct, and easily distinguishable from the broad mud-yellow flow that was the Amazon itself.

First of the tributaries seen by air was the Rio Negro, on whose banks they had been waiting not so very long ago. It was a river that in the wet season would become as wide as the Strait of Dover. Even now, in the dry season, its flow was so great that many minutes after the plane had put the confluence of the two rivers behind, the Rio Negro's inky-black stream could be seen coursing alongside the mocha-yellow waters of the Amazon, not intermingling for many, many miles. And the Rio Negro was not even the largest of the Amazon's tributaries.

But then, reflected Toni, everything about the Amazon seemed larger than life. And perhaps it was only to be expected of a river that coiled across the South American continent like a great sleeping snake four thousand miles in length, with its tail almost touching the Pacific in the high reaches of the Andes, and its mouth opening into the Atlantic in a two-hundred-mile-wide yawn. The Amazon's flow equaled that of twenty Mississippis, and in the season of flood it could spread out to create swamplands as big as the state of Texas. No wonder the earliest Spanish explorers had mistaken the river for a fresh-water sea!

Senhor Garcia sat beside Toni during the flight. He pointed out the occasional patch of brown unforest-ed land where settlers were attempting to create agricultural cooperatives in the middle of the jungle, but for the most part the sea of greenery was uninter-rupted by signs of human habitation, except on the very fringes of the riverbanks.

"Ah, if the plane were flying lower," he said, "then you would have some idea of the size of the Amazon! Halfway up trees a hundred feet high there are mud lines from last year's flood. Many of the houses are built on stilts, and when you see a settle-ment of any size it is likely perched high on a cliff-side." Although Garcia spoke excellent English, he was using Portuguese at the moment, largely because Toni had started the conversation in that language, having found that practice was the key to fluency.

"Travel by water and then you will be impressed!" Garcia went on. "I would do so myself, but I am always in a hurry. When a man has many responsibil-ities...."

Garcia *was* a bit tiresome, reflected Toni; but unlike Ty and Barney she had some appreciation of the considerable cooperation received from the Bra-zilian government in general, and Senhor Garcia in particular. An important part of Toni's job was to handle the sometimes delicate negotiations with various governments as they traveled from country to country, and in other parts of South America she had dealt with many officials less obliging than Diogo Garcia. The fussy pompous little man was not her favorite person, either, but he had been helpful to the film team months before, during the filming of Brazilian cities. In fact, during the segment shot in Rio de Janeiro he had loaned his own house—a large secluded home in a better district, which was used by Garcia and his wife only on those occasions when they were able to take time away from the rounds of officialdom in Brasília.

Toni's tolerance for human foibles had stood her in good stead in the years since she had become a film producer. Young for the job but totally dedicated, she had thrown herself into her work after the death of her husband nearly five years before, according to him a loyalty that had long since discouraged Ty and Barney from directing their romantic attentions to her. Now, nearly the age of twenty-seven, she had been a producer for three years—first when she had filled in on a stopgap basis because of someone's sudden illness; then on a permanent basis when that particular assignment, a special on Aztec ruins, had been completed with dispatch, tact and budgetary restraint.

Toni's knowledge of Spanish had helped on that occasion in Mexico; it had also led to her current assignment in South America. Her fluency had been

attained during her teenage years, after her parents—
an elderly couple for whom Toni had been a late,
only and much wanted child—had taken an early
retirement and moved to Spain. With Spanish already at her fingertips, it had been easy enough for
Toni to bone up on Portuguese, the language of
Brazil. Earlier, during the filming sessions in Rio de
Janeiro, São Paulo and Brasília, she had developed a
command of Portuguese nearly equaling her grasp of
Spanish. And a good thing, too: Ty and Barney were
hopeless with languages.

"Considering what a busy man you are," Toni interjected as soon as a pause came in Garcia's mono-
logue, "it's good of you to come along in person to
introduce us to Dr. Quental. I thought you would
send one of your aides."

"Ah, but I have business, personal business—a
matter that can hardly be attended to by letter. There
is a message to deliver, and as Luís—that is Dr.
Quental's name, did you know?—as Luís has not
visited Rio de Janeiro for several months...well,
someone had to speak to him about this matter, and
as time was running short...."

Garcia's words trailed off, and he spent some
moments fidgeting with the buttons of his white
linen suit, as though somewhat apprehensive about
his approaching encounter with Luís Quental. Perhaps the message regarded some sensitive subject,
Toni speculated, since it could not be entrusted to
the mail.

"I hear you're related to Dr. Quental by marriage," she remarked. "Your aide mentioned it in his last letter."

"Ah, did you not know?" Garcia looked surprised. "But I am sure I mentioned it many months ago, when we last met. To be connected with the Quental family, it is not a thing to be kept secret, like a skeleton in the closet, ha, ha!"

Although the witticism escaped Toni, she smiled diplomatically. "Perhaps you did talk of your family connections, Senhor Garcia." In truth, during their earlier acquaintance Garcia had talked of little else. "However, at the time the name Quental meant nothing to me."

Garcia puffed his cheeks importantly. "Ah, but now that you know the name you can appreciate what it means. I think I do not exaggerate to say that the Quentals are bluebloods of the Amazon. Yes, indeed—bluebloods."

"I gather the first Quental was a rubber baron in Manaus. I presume he went bankrupt after the turn of the century, like all the others?"

"Bankrupt?" Garcia appeared to be taken aback for a moment. "On the contrary. Oh, quite the contrary! The first Quental was a man of vision. He saw what was coming when cultivated rubber began to appear on the market, about seventy years ago. He had sold his interests long before the crash of the wild-rubber market. By then he had invested in other things—coffee, real estate, mines. In his later years he sold these, too, and created a family foundation— a charitable foundation, headquartered in Rio de

Janeiro. As if he had anything to repent, ha, ha! The Quental Foundation is well known in Brazil. I myself manage a small part of it, which is why I have had to visit Luís at his clinic on a few previous occasions.''

"Oh? Dr. Quental maintains some connection with the foundation?'' That, then, would explain the occasional trips to Rio.

"Connection? Yes, assuredly, as Luís is now head of the Quental family. But he has little love for boards and subcommittees. He prefers the life of a recluse.''

"Why?'' asked Toni, deciding on directness.

Garcia frowned, harrumphed and shuffled his feet beneath the seat before answering. "Luís is...a bitter man,'' he said carefully.

"I hear he doesn't like women. Why is that?''

Garcia ran a finger under his shirt collar, as though her question caused him to sweat a little. "Perhaps it came about in violent reaction to his youth. Because of the Quental fortune, women were always eager to put themselves in his way. Perhaps he grew sick of his own success. Myself, I can think of nothing else that would have caused him to walk out on his responsibilities.''

It was possible, Toni reflected, that such a set of circumstances might turn a man into a cynic. But enough of a cynic to remove himself from the world and bury himself in the jungle?

"When we were in Brasília I didn't meet your wife,'' Toni remarked pleasantly, in hopes of finding out more about the Quental connections. "I believe

Senhora Garcia was in delicate health at the time.''

Garcia sighed and laced his pudgy fingers. ''Yes, I remember. A matter of exhaustion. She had taken the staff and returned to Rio for a time. You understand how it is when a man has important duties such as mine: there is little peace even for a moment. There are ceremonies, openings, ribbons to be cut, official visitors to entertain, and a man cannot delegate everything to his aides. . . .''

Toni's detour had been a mistake, for it unleashed a barrage of information of the type she had no wish to know. She was relieved when the plane began its descent a few moments later, allowing her to return her attention to the plane window. Below, the carpet of multihued green resolved itself into individual treetops, some touched by gold or flame colors. And just at the moment when she was certain the plane was aiming for disaster, it banked slightly and a twisting green river snaked into view.

As the pilot closed in for a landing, frothings of white spume signaled the presence of rapids in the swiftly flowing river. For heart-stopping seconds the plane seemed to skim danger, only a few feet above the tumble of water over jagged rocks. Then the *Catalina* touched down with a hiss and began to taxi along safely clear of all obstacles, in a site where the river was broad, level and deceptively calm. Its goal was a huge raft moored in the center of the river, and it was here that the passengers deplaned while the crew started to unload the weekly supplies for the area, along with the bales of gifts for the Xara Indians. As the plane could land no closer to the place where Luís Quental had founded his clinic, the party was to be met here and transported by rivercraft for the balance of the journey, a matter of a few miles.

From a clearing where thatched roofs could be seen peeping over the high riverbank, a number of dugout canoes now pushed off toward the raft. As the paddlers sat well forward in the bow, the sterns of the boats rose high—an effect strange to the unaccustomed eye. But their somewhat clumsy appearance was belied by the grace with which the odd circular paddles of bright red and green flashed into the water, bringing the canoes swiftly toward the *Catalina*. Two *lanchas*, dugouts different only in that they were powered by ancient outboard motors, also joined the traffic in the river.

"They come from the village of *caboclos*," Garcia explained, using the word Toni knew to mean halfbreeds—the hardy and heterogeneous river dwellers of the Amazon who were part Indian, part European and part a mixture of almost any other race imaginable, reflecting the many nationalities who had attempted to wrest order out of the jungle through the course of the centuries.

"Why is Dr. Quental's clinic so far from the settlement?" she asked.

"Because there are other villages along the river," explained Garcia, adjusting his stiff pith helmet. "Luís chose a place central to all of them, and to the Xara village, too. A nuisance, this river journey! Let us hope we do not have to wait long for Getulio."

"Getulio?"

"Getulio O'Hara, a man who works for Luís. Although Getulio is only a *caboclo*, he has some education. He speaks Portuguese very well, unlike some of the *caboclos*, who are more at home with the Indian dialects spoken in these parts."

"O'Hara? That's a very Irish name to find in the depths of the Amazon."

"But not so very unusual," claimed Garcia. "I believe Getulio is descended from Americans who settled Santarém after the Civil War. Certainly his ancestry includes more than Indian and Portuguese! I think you will understand when you see Getulio's hair."

With that forewarning, when a motorized *lancha* appeared around a riverbend to pick up the film crew, Toni had no doubt as to the identity of its occupant. Long before she could define the features of the face she could discern the hair—an astonishing rich paprika red that was the legacy of some unusual racial mix. Although it was graying now, putting Getulio's age at something well more than fifty, it was still his most distinctive feature, and doubly incongruous because it topped a weatherbeaten face the color of a Brazil nut, with dark Indian eyes, high cheekbones and a grin as dazzlingly white as his shirt.

"*Bom dia*, Senhor Garcia," he called in Portuguese as he maneuvered alongside the raft, avoiding the wingspan of the plane. "We did not expect you to arrive today, in person!" As he stepped from his *lancha* he noted Toni for the first time, and his eyes widened. Unaware of Toni's grasp of his language, he murmured tactlessly, "She is one of those who will be making this film? *Meu Deus*, when the doctor finds out—"

"Never fear, Getulio, never fear," Garcia soothed hastily. "There will be no objection. In a little time you will understand."

Getulio started to voice more concerns, only to be overridden by Garcia, who performed hasty introductions and conveyed the information that Toni spoke fluent Portuguese. Getulio's alarmed protests petered to an embarrassed halt, but the doubt in his eyes remained unchanged, a reaction that added to Toni's growing apprehension.

At last Getulio gave up his wary inspection of Toni and her associates and turned his full attention to Garcia. "Have you any news of Braz?" he asked eagerly.

"Ah, yes, indeed, because I have just come from Rio de Janeiro. I have news of the very best sort for you." Garcia beamed at Getulio, his manner considerably warmer than it had been with the roughly dressed *caboclos* from the village, many of whom were still standing about on the raft. "Braz and Ana are well, and you will see them one week from now."

Getulio's eyes lit into sunbeams. "Braz and Ana are coming to visit?"

Garcia's smug smile suggested that Getulio's hopes were not in vain. "No more questions now, Getulio; we'll talk later." He turned to the film crew and ex-

plained in English, "Getulio's son is a doctor in Rio
de Janeiro. Braz O'Hara is a very clever lad and well
educated. You will meet him next week, and his wife,
Ana, too—a schoolteacher."

With an unaccustomed touch of cynicism, Toni
wondered if Braz O'Hara's professional standing
had any bearing on Garcia's warm manner toward
Getulio. But the thought was unkind, and she thrust
it swiftly from her mind.

Moments later the supply plane departed with
assurances from the pilot that he would return after
his daily rounds to pick up Senhor Garcia, who was
to remain for a few hours only. With the help of
others on the raft, Getulio attended to loading crates
and luggage into his *lancha*. When his dugout could
carry no more, he prevailed upon a villager with a
similar motorized boat to transport Ty, Barney, the
film equipment and the bales of goods still remaining
on the dock. And so it was that Toni set out for the
Quental compound in Getulio's laden craft, with
only Senhor Garcia at her side.

Mud and trailing debris clung high on the trunks of
the enormous trees that pressed in upon the riverbanks, a tangle of impenetrable green. It was a beautiful, deceptively placid scene, with the blue of the
sky and the green of the river and the multihued
forest fringing the brick-red banks. With the plane
now gone and the village put behind, the river seemed
eerily lonely. Its silence was broken and yet at the
same time strangely accentuated by the steady put-
put of Getulio's outboard motor, an invader in an
alien world where anything might lurk. A sensation

that was half appreciation and half apprehension shivered across Toni's skin.

In the gloomy lower shadows necklaced by creepers, no life was visible, but high in the treetops vivid birds rested, silent in the growing heat of day. One green umbrella of a treetop was so laden with great still herons that it seemed to have burst into bloom with enormous white blossoms; parakeets and other gaudily colored specimens also inhabited the high branches. One large red-wattled creature looked comically like a turkey, and perhaps was.

Toni caught herself on the verge of impulsively trailing her fingers in the cool green waters and instead asked Getulio the sensible question.

"Certainly there are piranha," Getulio said cheerfully. "But there is no need to worry. There are piranha in nearly all the rivers, and people travel them all the time. Most who live in these parts bathe twice a day, although they pick their spot carefully. It is safe wherever the river runs swiftly enough. There are things more troublesome than piranha—the *piums*, for instance."

"Piums?" questioned Toni, who had not come across that particular word in her study of Portuguese.

"Inventions of the devil," warned Garcia, who had extracted a can of aerosol insect repellent from his briefcase and was in the process of applying it to every exposed part of himself. He offered the can to Toni. "Believe me, you will need it when we reach the bend where the river narrows. There is a sandbank there where the *piums* breed."

Even before she had managed to finish applying the spray, a few minuscule insects materialized and began to make themselves at home in the folds of Toni's garments. But that was only the advance contingent. Moments later a swarm descended, each insect so tiny it was almost invisible, each seemingly with a homing instinct for the vee of Toni's unbuttoned collar, and other places where the insect repellent had not reached.

"There are no *piums* at the camp of the doctor," reassured Getulio, noticing Toni's distress. He himself seemed immune to the bite of the devil's inventions. "We have been fighting such things for years by making war upon their breeding places."

"And I think they've decided I'm one of those breeding places!" Toni claimed wryly, plucking at her shirtfront.

"Do not scratch or the bite will be much worse," Getulio warned; and Toni obeyed the sensible command. After all, what harm could be done by a tiny insect like that, however bothersome?

Several minutes passed before the *lancha* rounded another bend in the river and a tall flagpole came into view, its flag drooping listlessly in the hot breezeless air. By then the cloud of insects had almost disappeared, but that was of little consolation to Toni, whose skin was already aflame from their pernicious love affair with her neckline. *Piums* had found their way up her ankles, under her shirt sleeves, down her back; and by now it took a decided effort of will to avoid scratching.

The *lancha* pulled in beside a floating dock constructed of whole logs and attached to the shore by rough fibrous ropes. For the moment, because of the height of the steeply sloping red riverbank, no buildings were visible. Lush grasses and a stand of bamboo rimmed the rise, and crude steps had been cut into the earth to create a path to the higher level. Getulio cut the motor, leaned over to grab the dock and clambered out to make the boat fast.

Toni accepted his helping hand and stepped out onto the bobbing dock. Where the bark had decayed off the damp logs, the rounded surface was smooth and slippery, but thanks to the rubber soles of her practical new laced boots, balance was not too difficult. Garcia managed the feat with somewhat less dexterity because of the city shoes he wore. He started at once up the rise, leaving the unloading of the boat to lesser mortals.

Toni was already crouching to heave a duffel bag to the dock, her back turned to the shore, when she heard a deep masculine voice greeting Garcia at the top of the rise, its timbre harsh and somewhat impatient, with the ring of one accustomed to plain speaking.

"I didn't expect you, Diogo," said this rough resonant voice. There was an abruptness to the sentence, as if the man who spoke did not have much love for his visitor. Curious, Toni turned her head without rising to her feet. Perhaps because she was accustomed to hearing Senhor Garcia addressed with a certain amount of deference due to his government rank, it seemed to her that the words bordered on rudeness, something that augured ill for her own reception.

The man greeting Garcia was standing at the very crest of the riverbank, a factor that contributed to the impression of a sinewy height even greater than Toni had expected. She was in no doubt as to his identity: every bone in her body vibrated with the instant intuitive knowledge that this was Luís Quental. There was an aura of power to his presence, a purely physical impact due no doubt to his size and his lean muscular frame. He was not looking in Toni's direction, and for the moment she could see only a part of a profile—enough to determine the strong delineation of the jaw, the jut of high cheekbones and the black swath of hair that curved carelessly over the collar of a rumpled, sweat-stained khaki shirt. His thumbs were hooked casually into the beltline at his flat waist, but his stance was otherwise aggressive— long legs planted firmly apart, sleeves rolled to reveal muscular forearms, head thrust at an angle that suggested something less than pleasure.

"I had reason to come in person," Garcia said in a voice nervous with apology. With her good understanding of Portuguese, Toni had no trouble following the conversation; already its nuances had put all her warning systems onto full alert.

"That much I can see for myself," came the sarcastic and somewhat ungracious retort. "Were you afraid I might change my mind about allowing this film nonsense?"

"No, no, Luís, of course not," Garcia denied hastily. "I know that when you agree to something you always keep your promises." His sudden obsequiousness put a bad taste in Toni's mouth; it also gave her some insight into the power wielded by this cynical doctor who had chosen to lead the life of a recluse in the Amazon jungle. "I assure you, Luís, I appreciate the favor."

"I don't do favors," Quental returned curtly. "I consented only because it might help people understand the Xara Indians and other tribes like them."

Garcia hastened to agree. "Exactly what I told the minister," he said, mopping his brow beneath the pith helmet.

"However, if these foreigners cause any trouble they'll be out on the next plane. I won't stand for having the Xara upset."

"The *americanos* have agreed to all your terms," Garcia assured him. "They realize they can film the Xara only once a week, and that they are to undertake no expeditions to the Xara village on their own. They also know they must not attempt to include you in their documentary."

"I hope they're not expecting luxury accommodation. The only available sleeping space is in the clinic itself."

"So they were told," Garcia hastened to say. "Believe me, Luís, there will be no problem."

"That remains to be seen," returned Luís Quental with an arrogance that made Toni's hackles rise. Although she usually reserved judgment until after she had known people for a time, she found herself already disliking the doctor's abrasive manner. And as yet she had not even sighted his face.

Quental went on, now with a streak of deep sarcasm, "And to what, Diogo, do I owe the honor of *your* presence here in the jungle? Surely you didn't come just to introduce me to some Americans too ill-mannered to learn Portuguese, when you know I speak their language perfectly well. Usually you avoid this backwater like the plague, unless you're in need of more funds for some charity ball."

For an awkward moment Garcia did not answer. In spite of the thirty or so feet between herself and the pudgy government official, Toni had the distinct impression that he was swallowing, trying to work up courage to say something.

"Well?" said Luís Quental scornfully. "Out with it, Diogo. And while you're at it, take off that ludicrous hat. In the eleven years I've been here in the jungle, I've never once had to treat a case of sunstroke."

As the hat came off, Garcia's eyes shifted toward the dock where Getulio was unloading cartons unhelped by Toni, who remained too riveted by the scene at the top of the riverbank to lend a hand as she had intended to do. "I think you would rather hear my news in private, Luís," Garcia suggested apologetically. "If I could speak to you alone for a moment, at once...."

"Always the diplomat, eh, Diogo?" came the ironic answer. "There's no need now to tell me what your mission concerns. If you've come to ask me to change my mind about anything—'' he hesitated perceptibly ''—the answer is no. I still plan to proceed.'' Then, with an abrupt change of topic that seemed like a deliberate cruelty to his sweating brother-in-law, he asked, a little too derisively, "And how is Constância? Still in the social whirl?''

"Luís...'' implored Garcia, patently upset by Quental's sarcasm, which seemed to extend even to one of his own sisters, a matter that added to Toni's sense of foreboding. Dr. Quental, it appeared, had little use for social pretensions and even less for politeness.

Quental's cynical mockery went on, like a scalpel probing at his brother-in-law's weaknesses. "Well, Diogo? Aren't you going to tell me about Constância's latest exploits?''

Sweating profusely, Garcia mumbled, "She sends her love, and a letter that I have in my briefcase.''

"Touching,'' derided Quental.

Recovering a small portion of his dignity, Garcia said, "There is no need for mockery, Luís. Now if we can talk in private—''

"So impatient, Diogo?'' mocked Luís Quental. "I admit you make me curious.''

"Then let us have a few minutes alone, Luís. It is important, believe me, and it can hardly be said with others listening.''

This time, when Garcia's eyes skated toward the dock, reminding his host that others were present, Luís Quental also turned. For the first time Toni could see his full face—the lean cynical features, the high ascetic cheekbones that denoted some trace of Indian blood, the scornful twist of the mouth, the dark eyes. If she had been riveted earlier she was immobilized now: it was a face she had seen briefly once before.

But where?

At sight of Toni, thunder deepened the line etched between those black brows, where the furrow was already so deep that it could only have been put there by years of pain or concentration. The black eyes blazed with a disbelief and fury Luís Quental made no effort to conceal.

"What is *she* doing here?" he exploded, his voice trembling with a rage frightening in intensity. "Why in the devil's name have you brought that *woman* to my place?"

CHAPTER TWO

"WAIT, LUIS; I can explain—"

"I gave permission for no woman to come here!" Luís Quental at last dragged his storm-and-lightning eyes away from Toni's bent figure. As he did so she rose to her full slender height, finding more dignity in standing on two feet, despite the slipperiness of the dock. She had not expected to be greeted with warmth; even so the depth of this instant antagonism dismayed her. There was something purely primitive about Luís Quental—a savagery that reminded her of a hungry, angry jungle animal snarling at some natural enemy.

"You said you would explain, Diogo. Start explaining at once!"

Diogo Garcia's sweaty apologies included the admission that the news had been deliberately concealed from his brother-in-law by the simple expedient of misspelling Toni's first name. "But, Luís, you do not yet know the whole story," he urged in a decidedly upset voice. "Wait—do not say more until we have talked in private. There are things I must tell you, important things—"

"Who is she?" snapped Quental, cutting through

Garcia's protests authoritatively. Even from this distance Toni could see the muscles working in deep hollows beneath those high cheekbones.

"She's a member of the film crew—the producer, in fact. But I swear you will not mind under the circumstances. Usually, Luís, you are prepared to listen to reason."

"Not this time!" came the curt reply. Every bone in that long lean body was rigid with hostility, and Toni felt an answering antagonism bristling along her spine—a violence of reaction she could remember feeling for no other person in her life. Perhaps he didn't expect her to understand his Portuguese, but that was no real excuse.

"Tell her she'll be flying back to Manaus with you," Quental snapped. "I might stand a woman around this place for a few days, but for a month— never!"

"You've had women here before," Garcia reminded him. "Patients, guests. I thought—"

"I don't want that one!" Quental exploded with no lessening of the forbidding determination in his face.

"Luís, please, we must talk in private."

"I'll give you one minute, Diogo, but don't expect me to change my mind." Luís Quental shook himself free of his brother-in-law's importunate hand. Imperiously he turned on his heel and started to stride away, the set of his broad shoulders boding no good, followed by the pudgy figure of the shorter man hurrying to keep up. "Holy mother of God, you of all people, Diogo, should know not to bring a woman here for a month's stay. In the city women are trouble enough. But here in the jungle. . . ."

The harsh voice diminished into the distance as the rise of land intervened in her vision, so that Toni could no longer see the two men. She directed a quizzical glance at Getulio, who like herself had long since abandoned all pretense of unloading the boat. Getulio shrugged and looked apologetic, but said nothing.

And then an icy shiver raced through her veins as she heard that unprepossessing voice once more, in an angry explosion of one word: *"What?"*

The word had blasted out from some distance, for the two men were by now far out of view. Nonetheless Toni knew the exclamation could only have been uttered by Luís Quental. It was spoken with a deep commanding ring, devoid of the heavy, oily nasal quality that characterized Garcia's tones; and it sounded scarcely less encouraging than any other syllables he had uttered during these past few moments. Only long habits of composure kept Toni's face from expressing the apprehension that curled in the pit of her stomach. First the *piums* and now a hornet's nest!

After that there was only a raging of voices from the distance, close enough to determine the strong emotion but too far to understand the content of the conversation. And yet it seemed that Luís Quental was now listening to whatever his brother-in-law had to say. Toni darted another sidelong glance at Getulio and was surprised to find him grinning uncertain-

ly. Perhaps, thought Toni grimly, Getulio had enjoyed the spectacle of his employer's temper and was
now amusing himself with the contemplation of the
fireworks still to come.

She smiled at Getulio with the surface calmness she
always adopted under stress, and remarked with an
attempt at pleasantness, "That was quite a reception.
I have the distinct feeling I'm less than welcome."

Perhaps Getulio's embarrassed grin had only been
one of encouragement, for now he shrugged and
said, "Do not worry, *senhora*; perhaps it will be all
right. Listen. . . ." He cocked his head toward the top
of the riverbank, where all sounds had now ceased.
"The doctor has taken Senhor Garcia to his own
bungalow to talk, I think. And he would not have
done that if he did not plan to listen. When the doctor listens, he is a reasonable man."

That was a statement with which Toni could not at
this moment agree. "Does he always welcome women
this way?" she asked, the wry twist of her mouth indicating a feeling that fell somewhere short of amusement.

Getulio pursed his lips and turned back to his task
of unloading supplies. "He is not always so very
bad," he said mildly. "Mostly he just turns the back.
And to some women he can manage a little politeness,
if he does not dislike them too much. He has been very
good to my son's wife, Ana. When she came here to
visit four years ago, just after she and Braz were married, Dr. Quental did not even turn his back on her."

As a definition of being good to someone, it lacked

in credibility. What a boorish, domineering, unlikable man their host had turned out to be! And where had she seen that grimly carved, cynical face before? She could not entirely agree with the Varig employee's assessment of Luís Quental's looks and masculine appeal. He had a commanding physique, to be sure, and an unusually strong character, if the messages defined in that granite-hard mouth and those extraordinarily high slanting cheekbones were to be believed. It was a decidedly memorable face, for she herself remembered it although she was absolutely certain she had never so much as exchanged two words with the man. Where could she have seen him? In Manaus last week? No, some instinct told her it had been long before that....

To quell the feelings of foreboding that had been in no way diminished by Getulio's words of reassurance, she turned once more to the boat and set about heaving such luggage as she could manage onto the bobbing dock. Toni was not one to run from trouble, and she had no intention of running now. Already she was firming her resolve to deal patiently with what appeared to be some difficult days ahead. She knew that she must not give in to the very human temptation to return rudeness for rudeness, antagonism for antagonism, cutting word for cutting word. To do so would be to jeopardize the success of the venture that lay ahead: and after the difficulties of acquiring permission to film the remote Xara Indians, she had no intention of undermining the arrangements in any way. For Toni, her job took precedence over all instincts for childish retaliation. As long as Dr. Quental allowed her to stay, let him do his worst!

Getulio paused in the act of removing Toni's personal carryall from the *lancha* and looked at her uncertainly. "I have removed everything but the *senhora*'s things," he said.

"We'll remove the *senhora*'s things, too," Toni said firmly, hoisting her suitcase onto the dock. At this point she was not about to plan for defeat. She had always known the Amazon expedition would be no soft, safe sinecure—but she had not expected a hazard like Luís Quental, next to whom a pack of wild boars would look tame. Deep down she was far less confident than her manner to Getulio suggested. Nevertheless she had all the proper government permissions tucked into her pockets, and she had no intention of leaving now unless forcibly evicted.

Several minutes later, no sounds of the second *lancha* bearing Ty and Barney had yet been heard. "Perhaps I should go and see what is the matter," suggested Getulio, looking anxiously along the green river. By now all the luggage was on the dock and awaiting further disposition; Getulio had carried some of the cartons to the top of the rise. "There might be engine trouble, perhaps? Not all motors are as dependable as ours."

As Getulio climbed once more into the boat and started the powerful new outboard motor, Toni pondered with a touch of humor that, engine trouble or no, Ty and Barney could not possibly be facing more flying sparks than she herself was likely to face within the next few minutes. Too bad they wouldn't be here to help her through the coming debacle with Quental!

Shortly after Getulio's craft pulled away from the dock, voices from the top of the rise advertised that Diogo Garcia and his unmannerly brother-in-law were now approaching once more. Tucking her suitcase under one arm and slinging a duffel bag over one shoulder, Toni glanced upward, her face already schooled into a cool, pleasant, unrevealing smoothness in expectation of the battle that was to come. Toni had her own ways of dealing with trouble, and losing her temper was not one of them—except in extreme cases.

Her first sensation was one of surprise, as she noted that there were elements of decided relief in Garcia's expression. Had there been a change of heart on Luís Quental's part? His face was still set into grim unprepossessing lines.

"Come along, then," he commanded roughly, looking down the hill from his disdainful height. He had switched to English, and Toni had the distinct impression that the change was dictated not out of politeness but as a deliberate insult—as if he expected her Portuguese to be so poor that he did not wish to sully his own language by listening to Toni's efforts. The serene smile she had donned for the occasion was totally wasted on her host. Quental's eyes were directed at a point several inches to one side of Toni's face, as though she were transparent, she thought wryly; or as though by pretending she was not there he could will her out of existence. His scowl was no more welcoming than before.

And yet it seemed that Senhor Garcia had managed to convince Luís Quental of the desirability of allowing her to stay. How had Garcia succeeded in that? The chubby official had seemed so obsequious toward his daunting relative that Toni had been sure the battle would not be so easily won.

Quental stooped and scooped into his powerful arms the largest of the cartons Getulio had already transferred to the top of the riverbank. Where his sleeves were rolled, Toni became unwillingly aware of the easy flexing of muscles accustomed to strenuous exercise. Quental then turned to his brother-in-law and issued a crisp arrogant order in Portuguese. "And you, Diogo, start carrying your weight. Get down there and relieve that bitch of her luggage."

Toni's eyes widened; she could not believe her ears. For a moment of deep shock she was too paralyzed even to pretend surface composure; and so, it seemed, was Diogo Garcia, who had the grace to look thoroughly mortified on behalf of his brother-in-law.

"Luís, she speaks Portuguese," whispered Garcia at the end of the awkward moment, in a voice just audible to Toni's ears.

"In that case I take back the epithet," Quental said, so derisively that Toni knew he did no such thing. "I'm sure she's a perfect...lady." There was no apology whatsoever in his manner, and although he had switched back to excellent English he did not even look in Toni's direction. He transferred his sarcasm to Garcia. "Well, Diogo, where are your manners? I have seen you leap to Constância's side when she is carrying nothing heavier than a hatbox! I suggest you take the woman's suitcase."

Toni fought down the very human instinct to speak sharply, knowing she must not dignify his earlier insult by commenting on it. If Luís Quental wanted to call her a bitch on no evidence whatsoever, there was very little she could do to defend herself; but that did not mean she intended to let his churlishness pass altogether unmarked. She would mark it in her own way.

"So good of you to make me welcome, Dr. Quental," she said with admirable serenity as she climbed up the rise unaided. She came to a halt on the uppermost level where thick grasses spiked at her ankles, and defied that cruelly chiseled face with cool gray eyes. "It isn't necessary to put Senhor Garcia to any trouble on my behalf. Really, his manners have been perfect in every way."

Her pleasant inflections put no emphasis on the "his," but the emphasis was there all the same. And yet Quental could hardly take exception without admitting that he himself had been less than polite. The unspoken comparison seemed to trouble him in no way: his lip merely curled with scorn.

"It's a man's job. Besides, women are too soft for such burdens," he said contemptuously, without bothering to look Toni in the eye.

Toni's placid smile remained perfectly in place, and nothing disturbed the millpond surface of her eyes. Although no women's libber, she would have liked to defend her gender. But she knew it would be immature to rise to Quental's bait, and she was too much of a diplomat to do that. "Appearances can be deceptive," she said lightly. "Really, I'm tougher than I look."

Quental half turned his shoulders until he was facing Diogo Garcia. To the point of rudeness, the movement underscored his continuing antagonism. "No doubt you are," he muttered sarcastically. "Nevertheless, Diogo will carry your luggage. The exercise will do him good."

Toni's fingers tightened over the suitcase, the only gesture of defiance she allowed herself. "Perhaps Senhor Garcia could carry something else," she suggested levelly, although her smile was by now a trifle too fixed.

Garcia hesitated, uncertain what to do. As if impatient with the delay, Luís Quental deposited his own load into his brother-in-law's pudgy fingers and reached for Toni's burdens, wresting them firmly from her grip. For one brief moment of contact, her flesh seemed to sizzle, no doubt due to a well-concealed flash of annoyance at his overbearing attitude. She burned inwardly, but she did not protest; to argue with her host over such a trifling matter would further no particular cause.

"Why, thank you, Dr. Quental," she said with perfect possession. "That's very considerate of you. Nowadays one so seldom meets a real gentleman."

Garcia now performed belated introductions, during which Quental's eyes remained for the most part directed somewhere behind Toni's head, flickering only once toward her mouth with the most scornful of expressions. But Toni did not need to see into the black burning eyes to sense the overpowering heat and hostility that emanated from that tall virile body. Despite Garcia's successful intercession on her behalf, it was all too clear that Luís Quental resented her presence there with every fiber of his forceful body. If he had a dislike of women, it seemed to be doubled in her case. Getulio's comments suggested that her reception was even less auspicious than most; but why? Had she offended Luís Quental at some point in the unremembered past?

"I have the odd feeling I've seen your face before, Dr. Quental," she said with all the pleasantness she could muster, once Garcia had finished his nervous introductions. Having had a few moments to reflect on the situation, she had decided it was best to confront matters head-on: if Luís Quental had some particular reason to dislike her, she wanted to know it now. "Possibly I've seen you in Rio de Janeiro? I understand you sometimes go there."

"Much to my regret," came the discouraging retort, which provided no particular insights.

The answer, Toni noticed, caused Garcia to look as uncomfortable as she herself was feeling beneath her uncracked exterior. "I was in Rio myself about eight months ago," she persisted equably, "when we were filming in the city."

Her exploratory remark was greeted by a dauntingly unfriendly silence from Luís Quental. If he recognized her, nothing in the brooding darkness of his face gave any indication. Garcia filled the awkward moment, turning to his stone-faced brother-in-law. "It might be possible, Luís," he said half apologetically. "The film crew was staying at my house for a matter of a few weeks. And as you yourself were in Rio for a few days about that time. . . ."

Bitterness curled down the corners of Quental's mouth, and a brief emotion that Toni could not understand touched the dark eyes that had fastened themselves somewhere in the neighborhood of her collarbone. The direction of his gaze served to set her flesh on fire in that very region; it took fully five seconds before she realized this was due not to his attentions but to the *pium* bites. Forgotten for the past unsettling minutes, the discomfort of those bites now returned with a raging intensity, contributing to the difficulty of maintaining her usual poise.

Quental dragged his eyes away. "So you've already reminded me, Diogo," he said tightly. "But I have enough to remember from that trip without recalling every face I may have seen in passing." A derogatory note entered his voice. "I was quite busy in Rio, as you yourself pointed out not long ago."

Garcia looked taken aback. "Yes, I—"

"Come along, both of you," Quental cut in. He then turned abruptly on his heel to stalk across the grasses of the clearing, leaving the others behind him.

Garcia whispered to Toni encouragingly, "Things will improve, you will see. Luís is a gentleman at heart. Oh, a little bitter, but now that he has agreed you can stay, you need have no fear. Luís always keeps his word.''

And then, balancing the carton with more spryness than Toni would have expected, Garcia huffed off in the wake of those long impatient legs toward a large low white building that occupied the central position in the clearing.

It was, she could see from here, the only sizable structure in the clearing; she surmised at once that it was the building used as a hospital—or perhaps "clinic" would be a more exact word, for if it was a hospital it was certainly not a very large one. Flanking it, against a backdrop of tangled jungle vegetation, were a few small utilitarian-looking buildings. One open-sided structure clearly served as a kitchen; a building adjacent to that appeared to be a storehouse, if the packing crates visible through the open windows meant anything. Another tiny edifice set at a small distance appeared to house a generator, evidenced by the drums of fuel standing alongside its outer wall. Electricity: that was more than Toni had expected. Perhaps she could hope for proper plumbing, too?

Set apart from this grouping of buildings, in a location somewhat more favored only because some person had taken the time to grow profuse masses of multihued flowers to soften the impact of stark whitewashed walls, stood an L-shaped bungalow of moderate dimensions. The doctor's own quarters, Toni concluded: it was the only habitation in the compound that looked as though it might be intended for that purpose. Perhaps Getulio was the gardener who had trained the fragrant flowering vines until they almost enclosed the tiny shaded veranda set into the L of the building? At the moment, as Toni stood in the hot direct sun of noon, taking a moment to survey the place where she would be spending this next month, that veranda was the only nook that looked cool, private and appealing. The rest of the clearing looked bleak and brown against the lush green forest; the hospital building itself was uncompromisingly stark.

Her quick appraisal of the scene took seconds only, and she had almost caught up to Garcia by the time he reached the whitewashed main building, a dozen steps behind Luís Quental.

Quental entered the clinic by only two paces, his broad-shouldered frame effectively preventing the others from walking through. Standing in the doorway, Toni had a good view of the small, sparsely furnished entrance area. A very old half-breed clad in hospital white sat at a wooden table, dozing. He woke with a start when Quental spoke a few words to him in the Tupi-Guarani dialect of the region, addressing him as Manoel.

Garcia whispered to Toni, "That old man speaks no Portuguese. So if you need anything while you are here, you will have to ask Getulio, or Luís himself."

To the left of the entrance area was a heavy curtain shutting off a space that served some indeterminate purpose. To the right was a wide double door,

screened to permit cooling breezes to penetrate, and
this revealed what appeared to be a ward. At the far
end there were two proper hospital beds, but these
were not in use; the several patients in view used
hammocks. They stared at the newcomers with dull
incurious eyes, too ill or too apathetic to stir in their
beds of string or grow self-conscious about the near
inadequacy of the white hospital gowns that covered
them. There was a good deal of medical equipment,
I.V. stands and other gleaming stainless-steel para-
phernalia, not all of which Toni could identify, but
which surprised her by its very variety and modernity.
Certainly, for a medical facility in such a remote location, the clinic appeared to be very well equipped—
except for beds. But then, Luís Quental was by all
accounts not a man who needed to reckon the cost of
anything; and she already knew that few people in this
part of the world slept in beds, hammocks being
preferred by most inhabitants of the Amazon.

She presumed there were other small rooms out of
range of visibility—an operating room, no doubt,
and outpatient facilities, as well as the rooms where
the film team would be sleeping. But from her vantage point these could not be seen.

There were no nurses, nor had Toni expected any;
and not just because of Luís Quental's misogyny. In
this sparsely inhabited part of the world it was unusual enough to find a doctor, let alone a clinic where
patients could sleep. In any case, Getulio and possibly the old man Manoel fulfilled the nursing func-
tion; and no doubt that was enough.

Quental deposited his own load of baggage in order to relieve Senhor Garcia of his burden. After setting down the carton he straightened, almost colliding with Toni, who had been leaning forward to satisfy her curiosity about the building where she assumed she would be sleeping. For the briefest of moments their eyes connected, and his flicked away at once; but in that moment Toni realized that he did recognize her, that he had probably recognized her from the very first moment he had seen her. Beneath the deep tan a dull red color appeared high on those craggy Indian cheekbones, the only sign of humanity she had seen in the man since arriving in this remote outpost.

Where had she seen him before? The mystery occupied her mind for the next few seconds while Luís Quental checked the luggage label on the suitcase and ascertained that that particular piece of baggage belonged to Toni. He picked it up once more and turned to his brother-in-law. "While I settle Senhora Carruthers you can wait for me in my bungalow, Diogo," he directed. "Pour a drink if you wish. No doubt, now that you have the promise you came for, you will feel you have something to celebrate." His whole demeanor suggested that he himself did not.

"Is that yours, too?" he asked Toni coldly, prodding the duffel bag with his foot. "If so, you've brought too many personal effects to the Amazon. You'll have little need for provocative clothes in this place."

The scorn in his voice triggered a wave of heat that

rose up Toni's throat and this time had nothing to do
with the aftereffects of her encounter with the
wretched little pests along the river. She firmed her
lips and reminded herself that there was no point in
taking exception to every veiled insult that came her
way. The only halfway feminine piece of apparel in
her luggage was a sheer tailored silk shirt, and that
had been included on a last-minute thought only because it took up very little space and might be useful
if circumstances called for something slightly dressier
than the baggy and thoroughly unprovocative clothes
she had purchased in Manaus. But why bother protesting?

"No, only the suitcase is mine," she returned in a
deliberately level voice.

"Come along, then," he directed brusquely. Leaving the entrance of the clinic, he strode off without
looking at Toni, this time in the direction of a stand
of heavy bushes where a thatched roof could be seen
barely peeping through the greenery.

Uncertainty caused Toni to hesitate briefly before
following. "I thought I'd be sleeping in the hospital
with the rest of the team," she murmured in some
surprise, with Garcia her only audience. She shielded
her eyes against the pervasive sun to watch Quental's
long rapid stride.

Diogo Garcia spread his hands in a gesture that indicated he understood his difficult brother-in-law
very little more than she did. "With some men," he
reassured her in a conspiratorial voice, "the bark is
worse than the bite. Luis is not always the tyrant he

appears to be today. Perhaps he thinks you will want to sleep in a private place, out of sight of the men.''

"More likely out of sight of him," Toni returned dryly.

"Do as he says. It is best to obey, if you wish to stay on his good side."

"You mean he has one?" Toni's mobile mouth curved into the beginnings of a smile, and Garcia responded with a soft intimate chuckle, as if he privately shared her opinion. In that moment she found herself quite liking the little man, pomposity and all. *He* at least was human, with a whole host of human failings. . . and probably a few redeeming facets, as well.

"Go now," Garcia said, leaning close and squeezing her arm encouragingly. "Luís is growing impatient."

Toni turned her eyes back in Quental's direction to find he had come to a halt not forty feet away and was watching the small scene with deeply brooding eyes and a disapproving mouth that promised nothing but trouble. Serenity intact only to outward appearances, Toni nodded a brief wordless farewell to Garcia and started across to where that tall imperious figure waited.

In the distance Toni could hear the vibrations of Getulio's returning outboard disturbing the hot quiet air. Well, with Ty and Barney about to arrive, it was a good thing the worst of the reception was over. Surely if she managed to keep her cool in the face of Quental's outright insolence his attitude would start to improve. And perhaps if she could remember where she had seen him once before she would start to understand the reasons for his immediate and unusually deep antagonism.

Luís Quental had already moved into the small shelter by the time Toni arrived at its entrance. She stood speechless, struggling for composure, as a wave of dismay washed through her at its wretched appearance. It was little better than a hovel. Slivers of daylight appeared through the thatched roof and through the walls, where the mud packing had fallen away here and there to reveal the bamboo construction beneath. There was no furniture whatsoever on the beaten earth floor, except for one rickety table and chair and a couple of dusty hurricane lanterns standing in one corner.

Was this an attempt to humiliate her? To force her to complain, so that he might have some excuse to ask her to leave? If so, Dr. Quental had sadly misjudged her!

"You'll have to use a hammock," he said, putting her suitcase down. He straightened then, his muscular height very imposing in the dim confined space.

Toni was sure that his words had been intended as a taunt; she answered them with a smile as cool and enigmatic as Mona Lisa's. Her gray eyes, however, wore a mirror sheen that reflected no emotion at all. "I expected that," she said in a level voice. "I brought a hammock with me."

But then, to her surprise, Quental frowned at a particularly large chink in the wall. "If I'd expected a woman I would have done something about this," he muttered. "As it is, I'm afraid you'll have to put up with it for a night or two, until something better can be arranged."

Toni stared at him, wondering if she could have been mistaken. Could it be that she had misjudged his intent in assigning her to this hovel? "I could move into the main building with the others," she suggested, somewhat heartened by the apparent relaxation of his rudeness.

But that only brought a return of that tight taut anger to his lean features. "Absolutely not," he snapped, directing his gaze toward the curve of her hip. "There's only one empty room in that building, and it's not designed for separation of the sexes. Moreover, I won't have a woman upsetting my patients. If you want to share quarters with your friends, do it somewhere else, but not on my property! While you're around here you'll sleep alone—like it or not!"

Toni tensed, wondering what could have caused such a ferocity of feeling about something that seemed a very simple suggestion to her. She felt her face coloring, an uncommon occurrence for her, and was glad that his eyes seemed intent on avoiding that part of her anatomy. Her lips felt stiff with the effort of keeping her temper, but she could not let his innuendo pass totally unremarked. Meeting trouble calmly was her style, not sidestepping it altogether.

She forced a note of reasonableness into her voice. "You've made several remarks, Dr. Quental, that suggest your opinion of me is not very high. Am I correct?"

"Yes." The single flat word, directed at her feet, dripped scorn.

Toni swallowed deeply; despite all previous happenings she had not expected such rude directness. Pride sent her chin tilting higher and curled her fingers into her palms so tightly that she could feel the nails cutting at her skin. "Why?" she asked mildly, still maintaining control, but with effort. "If you have some reason for passing judgment, Dr. Quental, perhaps you should tell me what it is."

His lips were twisted in a bitter line of disdain as his eyes now traveled to the plain gold band on her ring finger. "You're a married woman, *senhora*. And your surname suggests to me you're married to neither of the men with whom you do your traveling. Does your husband have nothing to say about your traipsing around foreign countries, living with other men?"

Stunned, Toni could only stare at the cynical set of his mouth. Unnerved, she licked her lips, knowing she must not attempt to answer until she had controlled the involuntary tide of indignation that was sending ripples down her rigid spine. It was becoming apparent that Quental wanted her to lose her temper—and that was something she absolutely refused to do.

By the time she spoke none of her internal battles registered in her cool even voice. "Let me set your mind at rest, Dr. Quental. As it happens, I'm a widow and have been for nearly five years. And as it also happens, since my husband's death I haven't been interested in the type of arrangement you mention. I work with my associates—I don't *live* with them, at least not in the way you seem to be implying."

He was only briefly thrown off stride, his eyes flickering only to narrow again, all without abandoning their studied and somewhat insulting contemplation of her hip. "You're too young to be a widow," he observed in curt unflattering fashion. "What did you do—marry an elderly man?"

"No," she answered quietly. "My husband was only twenty-four when we married, and I was nineteen. He died in an accident a little more than two years later."

"Your husband must have been an extraordinary man," Quental noted with a sarcasm so deep it verged on a sneer, "to command loyalty so long after his death."

For a moment painful memories tightened Toni's throat. "I loved my husband," she stated levelly, without taking offense, "and I still do."

"Spare me the protestations. After five years I find that too hard to believe, especially in this day and age."

Toni breathed deeply and slowly, reminding herself that to quarrel with this man was to bring trouble tumbling down on the heads of the entire film crew. Quental was spoiling for a fight, and she would not give him the satisfaction—certainly not over a matter as personal as this.

"Believe it or not, as you please," she said. "In any case I assure you I'll cause no trouble while I'm staying in this place."

"I should hope not," he grated, swiveling away from her and going down on his haunches to inspect the hurricane lanterns. The movement was clearly intended to put an end to the train of conversation. "I'll have Getulio refuel your lamps before dark. Leave one lit tonight, all night."

"I'm not afraid of the dark, Dr. Quental."

"Nevertheless, do as I say," he snapped, coming to his feet once again and moving toward the exit.

Toni maintained silence, outwardly compliant but inwardly in a state of turmoil over his abrupt dictatorial manner. Perhaps to relieve some of the emotions that had been suppressed during the encounter, a fingernail gave in to a long-standing impulse at the collar of her shirt.

"Don't scratch!" Quental ordered, turning in time to see the momentary lapse. His dark eyes probed the shape of her shirtfront for a moment, and then he wrenched his eyes away and turned his back, but not before Toni saw the beads of moisture start to gather on his brow. Without looking at her he said, "*Pium* bites, I imagine? Or is it something else?"

"*Piums,*" she conceded, wondering why that sheen of sweat on his brow seemed to trigger some haunting ghost of memory.

"Are they bothering you much?"

"No," she lied, sure that to admit the truth was to lay herself open to a sarcasm more biting than any *pium* she had encountered. "I was covered with repellent. I only have one little bite."

For once he made no cutting remark. "Come to

the dispensary and I'll give you some salve. The curtained area at the front is the outpatient section.''

"No, thank you. I came prepared; there's ointment in my suitcase.'' And then, still in a reasonable voice, "I've never found it necessary, Dr. Quental, to seek medical aid for a fleabite.''

"I wasn't planning an examination,'' he retorted caustically, and started toward the door.

"Dr. Quental!''

He halted on the threshold without turning to face her again, his sinewy shoulders drawn in dark silhouette against the lush bushes beyond the doorway. It almost hurt Toni's eyes to look at that tall frame backlit by sun, tension in every tendon, as if he had already guessed what she was about to say.

"Yes?'' he said, but in such a discouraging tone of voice that Toni almost regretted having stopped him. It had been on an impulse, after all; she was not yet sure whether her memory was correct.

"Are you allergic to perfume, Dr. Quental?''

His body, already tense, stiffened even more, and his hands came up to brace themselves on the door frame. He did not turn around. With some part of her mind Toni noted the long, strong, capable fingers; the blunt cut of well-kept fingernails; the muscular forearms where a crisp dusting of hair darkened the firm tanned flesh.

"No,'' he denied flatly.

"But you were in Rio about eight months ago?''

"About that time,'' he admitted with evident reluctance.

"And you went to a restaurant in a converted colonial home? I don't remember the name, but it was decorated with Brazilian antiques and some relics of the conquistadores."

"I really don't remember," came the cold answer.

Toni noted, with some long-awaited satisfaction, that her forthright approach had put him on the defensive, as it had been intended to do. "You ordered deviled crabs," she stated pleasantly.

"Did I? It seems, *senhora*, that your memory is superior to mine."

Toni wished she could see his expression. With her eyes fastened on the back of his head where dark thick hair curved over the khaki collar, she willed him to turn around, without success. "I remember what you ordered only because you walked out before it arrived," she said. "I don't think I caught more than one glimpse of you, although you were sitting very close to me—not two feet away, on a banquette seat. You were alone."

His silence seemed to confirm the correctness of her hazy memory, so she continued. "You went off in a hurry, leaving a large bank note on the table to pay for your meal. Later I overheard the maître d' tell the waiter that you had said you were allergic to my perfume. The restaurant was very crowded, and he hadn't been able to give you a different table."

Again that pregnant silence, during which Luís Quental neither confirmed nor denied her statement. At last Toni went on, determined to get to the root of the matter, "If you're not allergic to perfume, doctor, perhaps you're allergic to something else?" *Me, for instance,* she added in her mind. "I should hate to think I had driven you from the restaurant that day."

"You flatter yourself," he responded in chilling fashion.

"But you were in the restaurant," she persisted amiably, with the kind of assurance that suggested that fact had been established beyond a doubt.

"I was there," he admitted curtly, "but if you happened to be sitting next to me, I assure you it escaped my attention. Perhaps I gave the maître d' some foolish excuse for leaving. Really, I don't recall."

"Were you not feeling well?" asked Toni, still curious. "From the one glimpse I had, I remember your face looked quite gray beneath the tan." And there had been that sheen of moisture on his brow, too—the thing that had triggered her recollection of an occasion she might have forgotten altogether by now had not the day been memorable in other ways.

"Perhaps you were imagining things," he said. "I left for other reasons altogether."

"A forgotten appointment, Dr. Quental?" Toni asked, not in order to invade his privacy but to put the incident into perspective once and for all. Certainly, from her memory of the long-ago occasion, she had done nothing in the space of the few minutes involved to earn the kind of reception that had awaited her here eight months later. And if Luís Quental had misunderstood anything that had been happening at an adjoining table, between two absolute strangers—well, that was his fault, not hers.

"Something like that," he agreed tersely, and walked away without a single backward glance. Unsettled, Toni watched until he vanished beyond the bushes that sheltered the crude shack from other buildings in the compound. To her annoyance, she found her fingernails misbehaving once again at the site of the *pium* bites. Scolding herself, she came to her knees and opened her suitcase to search for the salve that would offer a less illusory relief than scratching, which no doubt only aggravated the trouble. Drat those little monsters!

Moments later she confirmed her suspicion that there were several of the minuscule creatures still at work beneath her shirt, each a maddening torture to her flesh. Coin-sized swellings had risen on every available inch—bypassing, fortunately, her hands and face and all the exposed parts that had been protected by repellent. Clearly the *piums* were as vengefully inclined to women as was Dr. Quental himself. She slathered the salve over her throat, over her midriff, over the valley of flesh unprotected by her brassiere, and over her ankles, too. By the time she finished, the contents of the tube had been used up to the very last squeeze. The ointment helped, but not much.

As she rebuttoned her shirt preparatory to leaving the hut in search of Ty and Barney, she reflected that that day in Rio might have been memorable to both of them, too—and for reasons that had nothing to do with Luís Quental. Why had the embittered doctor been so evasive about that fleeting encounter months before? She sensed he was not telling the whole truth. For one thing, intuition told her that despite his denials he had recognized her today; she had been sure of that earlier, and she was still sure of it.

Why had he left the restaurant? Had he really vanished to keep some suddenly remembered appointment? It was possible; but she recalled now that she had been conscious of his whitened knuckles forming fists against the tablecloth for some minutes before he had left. That, in fact, had been what had caused her to glance sideways and catch that one glimpse of his face. It might be true that his behavior had had nothing to do with her; but he had been in a state of tension for some time before his abrupt departure. Whatever had driven him from the restaurant, it had been neither sudden nor forgotten!

No more than half an hour had passed since her arrival here, and already she had confronted a host of unexpected uncertainties. What, for instance, had Senhor Garcia said to Luís Quental that had caused him to come to terms with Toni's unwanted presence?

And what was her own reaction, her real reaction, to the disturbing doctor? She disliked him intensely; but she was honest enough to admit to herself that she was affected by him in a purely physical sense, with a sexual awareness of the kind that had been shut out of her life for many years. But no, she must not think like that; it was disloyal to Matthew.

And what unexpected difficulties would this next month bring?

Well, there was no use puzzling over questions to which there were no immediate answers; it was time to return to the others and start laying plans for the schedule of shooting that lay ahead. She frowned at the finished tube of salve, gave it a last angry and unrewarding squeeze to vent some of the excess emotion awakened by Luís Quental, and thrust it aside along with her introspective and oddly troubling thoughts. She would not let Luís Quental get under her skin like. . . .

"Like a pesky *pium!*" she muttered out loud, and then gritted her teeth as the thought set up a new wave of unbearable itching that seemed to assail every millimeter of skin, all the way from her neck to her safely booted toes. Oh, Lord, what misery! What purgatory! Her fingers hovered two inches from her neckline, caught in a tug-of-war between maddening insufferable instinct and ordinary common sense.

Was she going to be able to bear it in the Amazon? Was she going to let herself be licked by a little insect so tiny it could hardly be seen? Was she going to give in now?

"Damn, damn, damn!" she proclaimed wildly, as her fingernails flexed over empty air.

CHAPTER THREE

SHORTLY AFTER THE ARRIVAL of Ty and Barney, the
noon meal took place. It was eaten in the shelter of
the open-sided edifice that also served as a cooking
shack, around a large, crude picnic-style table
flanked by benches. As Garcia's return flight would
not leave for a few hours yet, he joined the group;
and so did Getulio, swelling the numbers at the table
to six.

If Luís Quental still had strong reservations about
Toni's presence in his jungle retreat, he managed to
keep them largely to himself during the first part of
this meal. Aware now of her command of Portuguese, he uttered no more disparaging remarks, at
least not in Toni's hearing. But if he was not actively
rude, neither did he in any way encourage communication. He simply treated her as though she were not
there. If he had anything to say, he said it to one of
the men, even if it affected Toni directly.

"Did you bring mosquito nets?" he asked Ty Chisholm near the end of the meal.

"Toni?" asked Ty, his eyes skating in her direction.
As Ty had taken no part in the purchasing or packing
of supplies, he was unable to field the question.

"Yes, we did," she said, her level voice effectively concealing any resentment she might feel. Previous parts of the conversation must have made it crystal clear to Luís Quental that she had been in charge of provisioning for the trip.

By now she was only toying with her meal, a concoction of some kind of fish along with black beans that were filling but hardly a gourmet treat. She had little interest in the meal except as an excuse to keep her fingers clutched firmly around knife and fork. It was the only way to fight the overriding desire to scratch, a desire that had by now become a fire to her brain and a fever to her flesh.

"Desculpe-me," murmured Getulio apologetically, wiping his mouth and coming to his feet at the far end of the table. He cleared away most of the dishes, Toni's excepted, and deposited them elsewhere in the cluttered cooking shack for later attention.

No wonder Getulio wanted to excuse himself, thought Toni. Although he had smiled and nodded his brick-topped head politely throughout the meal, he could not possibly have understood a single word of the English that was being spoken around the table. Yet he seemed to be enjoying the company, so clearly he was a social animal at heart, with none of his employer's instincts for self-immolation. How lonely he must be, buried in this remote spot with only a bitter brooding doctor and some sickly patients for company!

"Excuse me, also," muttered Senhor Garcia hurriedly. "I wish to speak with Getulio about a little matter." He mopped his mouth and hastened after the old *caboclo*, who had gone off in the direction of another small shelter that was evidently his own abode.

So there was to be yet another private conversation, reflected Toni with a return of curiosity. That Garcia's news concerned Getulio's son, Braz, was something she already knew; but some nuance in the earlier conversation had also suggested to her that the message Garcia was about to impart was connected in some way with the news he had already told Luís Quental. Whatever that was!

But with her flesh enflamed by *pium* bites she could not concentrate on that line of speculation, and so she turned her attention determinedly back to the conversation at the table. Luís Quental was speaking again. The slant of the roof protected most of the table from sunlight, but a single shaft fell on his face, emphasizing the harsh high planes of his cheekbones and the deep valleys of his eyes.

"You won't likely need mosquito nets tonight," he said, still to Ty, whom he seemed to have selected as official spokesman for the group. "Except for Senhora Carruthers, of course—because of the chinks in the walls of that particular building."

"Chinks in the walls?" questioned Ty, looking at Toni again. "Are you sure you wouldn't be better off bunking in with us, Toni? There's room for another hammock in the room Barney and I are sharing."

"Tiny chinks," said Toni with a serene smile, taking a backhanded revenge in the knowledge that

Quental knew she was lying. She was damned if she intended to voice a single complaint about anything for this next month. She crossed her fingers, mentally at least, and went on, "My quarters suit me very well, and I'd much rather sleep where I can't hear the rest of you, in case you snore."

"Aw, c'mon Toni," objected Barney. "In all the time we've known each other, have you ever heard me snore?"

"Sure she has," Ty stuck in, "because you snore like the proverbial man from Calcutta. Now, on the other hand, she's never heard *me*. Isn't that so, Toni?"

The dual response caused Toni to cringe inwardly, for she knew it could be interpreted as meaning she had reason to know their snoring habits. "As I haven't had the opportunity to hear either of you," she said with feigned lightness, "I'm not taking sides." She darted a swift glance toward the end of the table to surprise Luís Quental's eyes trained in her direction. His gaze shifted at once, but nothing softened the skeptical scornful lines etching his mouth.

Ty and Barney engaged in some further friendly banter during which each accused the other of world-class snoring. Under other circumstances Toni might have joined in the good-natured ribbing, but today she was in no mood—whether because of Quental's cynicism and disapproval or because of the fiery discomfort of the *pium* bites. Aware now that some part of his attention was directed to her, she clutched her knife and fork even more resolutely, redoubling her efforts to keep her fingers from wandering inadvertently toward her shirt.

"You'll all need your mosquito nets tomorrow night," Quental interrupted abruptly after a few moments, evidently tiring of the meaningless conversational nonsense at the table. "Tomorrow we go to the Xara village."

Ty and Barney halted their repartee at once and turned toward their host, as did Toni. "Wednesday is the day I call on the Xara village," Quental explained. "Sometimes I return the same day, but usually I camp overnight. And naturally, that's what we'll do this time. As it's six miles each way, I hardly think some of you—" here he paused almost imperceptibly, punctuating the sentence "—I hardly think some of you will be capable of making the return trip without a night's rest."

Toni needed no prompting to know exactly which member of the party he considered incapable. She was grateful when Barney groaned, "Twelve miles! I certainly couldn't do it. I've never walked that far in my life. My God, do we really have to carry our equipment that far?"

"Getulio will arrange for several *caboclos* from along the river to serve as bearers. He would come himself, but he stays here to run the clinic while I'm away. He's had paramedic training and he's well equipped to deal with simple emergencies." Quental laced his fingers and leaned forward, propping his elbows on the table and taking over the center of at-

tention much as if he were at the head of a boardroom table instead of in an Amazon backwater. In an
effort to keep her mind from her tormented skin,
Toni found herself paying rapt attention to the way a
dark lick of foreclock fell over his brow, the way the
muscles moved in his throat when he talked.

"Getulio's cousin Fernão will likely be chief bearer
for the trip. Like Getulio, he's part Xara Indian. He
speaks Portuguese and he also speaks the dialect of
the Xara, so he can help with translations if necessary, should I be busy elsewhere."

"Only if Toni helps, too," commented Barney.
"Ty and I haven't mastered your language yet."

Quental's hard lips tightened briefly as if he did
not like to be reminded of Toni's competence in any
way. "There's also a young Xara girl who speaks
Portuguese; I'll tell you about her in a minute, after
we've covered the travel arrangements." He looked
at Ty pointedly, half turning in his seat so as to ex-
clude Toni altogether. "The Xara aren't really
equipped to handle so many overnight visitors. As I
generally go alone, they manage to put me up. But
with your film crew, and bearers, too...." He nodded in the direction of the hut used as a storeroom.
"I have a tent the bearers can use. I believe you were
told you'd have to provide a tent yourselves. Did you
remember to bring one?"

"I brought two." It was Toni who responded with
the full outward semblance of coolness, ignoring the
fact that the words had not been aimed in her direction. "One for Ty and Barney, and a smaller one for

me. You see, Dr. Quental, I prefer to sleep alone.''

If that small but pointed comment made any impression on Luís Quental it did not register in a single flicker of his face. Inadvertently Toni thought about a silly desk sign Matthew had bought her years before, in the month before their marriage: My Mind Is Made Up; Don't Confuse Me With Facts. And because that memory brought a lump to her throat, she turned her mind determinedly back to the business at hand.

''We'll need quite a number of bearers to carry our gifts to the Xara village,'' she pointed out, straining for a tone of reasonableness that seemed at this moment very difficult to maintain. As producer it was her task to deal with the matters that Quental persisted in addressing to Ty. Not that she would have minded, if it were only a matter of personal pride involved; but Ty's job as director was going to be unnecessarily complicated if he had to start serving as intermediary for all of Toni's administrative functions, too.

''We'll leave the bales of gifts here,'' Quental decreed to an air space somewhere in the middle of the table. ''The Xara chieftain will send runners to pick them up, when I give him the word. I assume you were told to bring machetes for the men and cooking pots for the women?''

Ty and Barney looked to Toni for the answer. But this time she maintained silence, curious to see if Quental could be finessed into addressing the question directly to her. She watched him covertly from behind a sweep of lashes, her polite pleasant expression the very antithesis of his.

When no one responded, Luís Quental's nostrils flared briefly in a way that told Toni her strategy of silence was having its effect. Ty and Barney, who knew Toni well, watched with intent interest, their mouths totally expressionless but their eyes now on full alert.

Quental did not repeat his question but instead said with a frown, to that same neutral air space, "What kind of machetes did you choose? Some makes are inferior."

In the extending silence Toni could see Ty and Barney sliding amused glances in her direction, until Ty at last prompted laconically, "Tell him, Toni."

"Oh, were you talking to me, Dr. Quental?" she asked innocently. "I'm so sorry. I didn't hear your question."

She could practically hear his teeth snapping with exasperation. "I don't imagine you remember the make of machete you bought," he said sarcastically.

"Collins," Toni answered promptly, confident after the thorough investigations she had made that no fault could be found with her choice.

None could, but that did not produce any relaxation of those dark lowering brows. Lines of irritation bracketed the harsh mouth, and he laced his lean fingers tightly together as if he would like nothing better at this moment than to close them around her throat. Toni hid a smile behind a bland expression and a smooth swing of hair, her usual sense of humor reasserting itself at this visible proof that she had managed to sliver her way under his skin. For one blessed millisecond of time, the *pium* bites were forgotten.

Luís Quental changed tack slightly. "Even with Fernão and one or two other bearers along, each of you will have to carry your own load tomorrow. As we're staying overnight, it would be unforgivable to impose too many extra visitors on the Xara."

This time Toni answered without hesitation, satisfied with having made her point once, even though Quental was still not looking at her. "That will be fine," she said evenly. "I'm sure I speak for my teammates, too. All of us are prepared to carry our share."

"I'm speaking to the men," snapped Quental. "Naturally I wouldn't expect a woman to carry a load. You wouldn't have the strength."

"You're very considerate, Dr. Quental," Toni came back promptly, "but perhaps you put women on too much of a pedestal."

Across the table she could see Ty and Barney wearing the exaggeratedly straight faces they always wore when they were highly amused by something. Well, they might think she was handling Quental, but she wished she had the same confidence. The temporary reprieve of a moment ago had passed, and now her self-possession was once again suffering from the aftereffects of a hundred—no, a thousand—long-vanished *piums*. A flood tide of itchiness that was almost a pain flowed upward from her ankles. She locked her feet together so that she would not give in to the desire to rub her legs against the supporting crosspiece of the table, like a bear scratching on a tree after hibernation.

If she simply ignored the bites, they would surely go away in their own good time. But she must not scratch. *Must not scratch.*

"Don't scratch!" snapped Quental, and Toni almost jumped in the moment before she realized he was not talking to her. Ty Chisholm, who had been caught with one fingernail worrying at a reddened patch behind one ear, lowered his hand guiltily.

"It's those little devils that attacked me on the river," Ty said in self-defense, winning Toni's immediate and heartfelt sympathy.

"I'll give you some special salve," Quental promised. "Any problem like that, it's best to attend to it at once. The rest of you might remember that, too. In this part of the world parasites can be a problem. If there's a square inch of raw flesh, they'll find it. And infections of all kinds like nothing better than a hot damp climate. So please, no scratching." His eyes skirted the table and came to rest on Toni's slender fingers clenching the knife and fork as if her life depended on it. "I suggest," he added with deep irony, "that anyone who can't cope with today's troubles certainly shouldn't head back into the interior tomorrow. Some people are simply not cut out for the jungle experience. Is anyone else still suffering from the *piums*?"

Toni's lips remained sealed, while Barney said

cheerfully, "Not a bit. Toni provided us with some ointment that fixed me up right away."

"Me, too," said Ty. "I just forgot to put it on that one spot."

Toni's sympathy evaporated. If the ointment worked for them, why didn't it work for her? But at this moment she would have bitten off her tongue rather than admit her deficiencies to the sarcastic and unlikable doctor.

"That brings me to my next point," Luís Quental went on dictatorially, his dark scornful eyes still trained on Toni's fingers. She had the distinct feeling that he could see her face perfectly well out of the corners of his vision. "If any one of you has so much as a sniffle, I want to know about it before we start for the Xara village. Under no circumstances are you to keep your medical problems to yourselves. Is that clear?"

"Perfectly," Toni replied with a cool smile that she hoped was not going to waste on Quental's half-averted gaze.

He frowned. "Are you all well supplied with anti-malarial pills?"

"Thanks to Toni, yes," Barney said, and Toni knew he was doing his small part to further her cause. "She made us take our chloroquine before we even left Manaus."

"She's a whiz," Ty drawled, tugging at his ear as if to relieve the site he could not scratch. Then he added, somewhat ruining the effect as far as Toni was concerned, "She looks after everything, even our love lives."

Toni's smile became somewhat glazed. She crawled inwardly, but knew she must not dignify the two-pronged remark by protesting. Quental would misconstrue it, she was sure; but Ty's intentions had been good. All the same, couldn't he have praised her in some other way?

Quental merely nodded, his mouth austere. "Now let me tell you a little bit about the Xara...."

Toni tried to concentrate as he proceeded with a short description of various Xara customs and ceremonies. Since she had read many facts about other Stone Age tribes in preparation for this expedition, very little was news to her except for the given names of some of the tribe's members. Her attention was riveted, however, when Quental turned directly to Ty and Barney and said in an impressively authoritative voice, "And whatever you do, stay away from the Xara women. That's a direct order. The Xara are very possessive, much more so than other tribes. And although their new chieftain is a man of some intelligence, even the smallest lapse might result in serious trouble—for all of us."

To emphasize the gravity of his statement, he added, "I won't even examine a woman except in the presence of others, preferably her own husband. I avoid talking to the women, too. I suggest you do the same—if you value your hides."

Barney made a low whistling sound through his teeth. "What do they do, shrink heads?"

Quental smiled, but grimly. It was the first time Toni had seen him smile, and although it was not an entirely heartwarming expression, it did soften the harsh lines somewhat, making her wonder what this man might have looked like if he had not been so embittered by life. The smile, however unpropitious, drew attention away from the gaunt cheekbones and imperious nose, redirecting it to a strong mouth and chin that on closer examination turned out to be remarkably well formed. In the lips were underlying hints of something other than cruelty: sensuousness, perhaps? All at once and against her will, Toni recalled what Garcia had said about Luís Quental's womanizing in his youth, and for one moment of disloyalty to her dead husband she found herself wondering....

"No, the Xara don't indulge in head shrinking," Quental replied in response to Barney's question. "But they do go in for curare-tipped spears. You gentlemen do know about curare, I imagine?" The word "gentlemen" needed no emphasis to make its meaning felt.

"Toni refreshed our memories before we came here," Ty nodded, earning Toni's undying gratitude and even some forgiveness for his earlier blunder. "Nowadays it's used as a tool of modern medicine, isn't it?"

Quental scowled for reasons known best to himself. "Under proper conditions," he said. "Needless to say, the Xara spears are not the proper conditions. One scratch can finish a man, and the Xara can be very hot-tempered. I don't want to alarm you unduly, but I should warn you that it's only a matter of fifteen years since a party of *garimpeiros*—prospectors—were killed off because one of them tampered with a Xara woman. Rape... or so it was claimed at the time. The truth will probably never be known, for no one was left to testify to the story. Not even the woman."

Another low whistle of alarm was sounded. "What happened to her?"

"The Xara killed her, too," Quental said in an uninflected voice.

"That's horrible," Toni burst out, breaking a private vow not to intrude into the conversation except in matters that pertained to her own duties. "It wasn't her fault if she was raped."

Quental's brooding gaze was directed at his own steepled fingers. "It's equally horrible that the other prospectors were killed, too, for they had done nothing," he said harshly. "Justice is swift and primitive in these parts. The Xara are a Stone Age tribe, and they're a very particular lot. They don't like their women being touched, perhaps because they saw it happen too often back in the days of the rubber boom. Then, Xara women would be seized and taken at gunpoint—Getulio's grandmother is a case in point. That's how he acquired his strain of Xara blood."

"But the woman—" Toni started to protest, putting aside caution for the moment because she was angered by his callousness.

"The Xara won't stand for infidelity, no matter what the circumstances," that peremptory voice cut in, "even when it happens among members of their own tribe. They're completely monogamous—even the chief himself takes only one wife, and he takes her for life. Adultery is punished severely, and so are other sexual offenses. Unfortunately, the Xara sometimes proceed on the wrong evidence. The birth of twins, for instance."

Several pairs of eyebrows remained raised, until Ty spoke for all the listeners. "Twins? What does that have to do with it?"

Quental's deep-set eyes remained shuttered, as though he did not particularly like this topic of conversation. Some quality in his voice, perhaps its very harshness, began to suggest to Toni that he was not as unmoved as he pretended by the fate of that unfortunate woman who had died fifteen years before. She subsided, listening with less antagonism as Quental went on.

"I have no sure way of knowing whether this still happens, but in the past, when a Xara woman gave birth to twins—something that's done in private, in the jungle, even today—she would kill one baby and hide its body. If she had gone back to the village with two babies, everyone would have been certain she had slept with two men."

A fit of nausea gripped Toni's stomach. Barney looked a little pale, too, as he said, "That's sick. Twins are twins."

Quental nodded in grim agreement. "Unfortunately, I believe there's a particularly high incidence of twins among the Xara. Perhaps it would be better if they had never figured out that men are involved in the making of babies—a thing some Stone Age tribes have yet to deduce.''

"Can't they be taught the truth about twins?" Toni asked, still too horrified by what she was hearing to think of holding her tongue. "Surely you must have tried!"

For once the scowl on Quental's face had nothing to do with his reaction to the presence of a woman. "Of course," he said, his voice flat and hard. He, too, seemed to have forgotten their vendetta for the time being. "But genetic lessons aren't very well received by a tribe whose system of counting is so simple that the word for the number ten is *amaikrutamaikrutamaikrutamaikrutamaikrut*—in other words, the number two repeated five times. The Xara are very clever in many ways, but they simply haven't the logic systems or even the vocabulary to understand some concepts. The Xara believe what they see with their eyes—no more, no less. They've never seen twins.''

"But you said—''

Luís Quental interrupted forcefully. "Perhaps you misunderstood me, *senhora*. I said no twins had been seen—I didn't say no twins had been born. I also said, if you remember, that no Xara woman would dare return to the village with two babies. Nor would I dream of suggesting to the Xara males that their wives might be producing twins, or there could be wholesale slaughter. The tribe is depleted enough as it is.''

A dreadful silence fell over the table as others

assimilated the full horror of these harsh revelations. Pale and for once shaken to the very core, Toni sensed that despite the stoniness of his expression, Luís Quental was as affected as anyone by the facts he had conveyed.

At last he continued, his voice forcibly controlled. "I'm not sure of the exact incidence of twins in the tribe, but my guess is that it's remarkably high. Inbreeding over the years may have increased the genetic probabilities. The men may not understand what's going on, but I believe the women do. There's a lot of whispering among them every time there's a pregnancy; in fact I think the Xara females are joined in a conspiracy of silence. I'm sure I could teach the women how twins are conceived, but really, it's the men who have to be convinced. And without evidence I can't convince anybody. In my first year here I made the mistake of predicting twins for one woman, before I knew the tribal customs. Since then no pregnant woman has allowed me to examine her."

"Then how can you be sure of all this?" asked Ty.

"Because over the years a sizable number of women brave enough to do so have walked through the jungle after giving birth and left one of their newborns here—including that first woman, the one for whom I predicted twins so many years ago. She nearly died from the effort." A brooding darkness crossed Quental's face, and Toni wondered if there were not at least a few women he admired in this life. As she watched his granite-hard mouth, so ascetic now, a terrible tightness seized her throat.

"Perhaps all of the Xara babies have been saved in recent years," he said heavily, "but I can't be certain."

"What happens to the babies you take in?" Toni asked quite gently, finding all thoughts of hostility petty at this moment.

"When the infants are old enough to travel, Getulio makes a trip to a convent downriver, where the nuns will care for abandoned children and educate them, as well. In fact, it was that same religious order that educated the one Xara girl I mentioned earlier—the one who speaks Portuguese. The nuns told me she was a Xara twin, too, saved by chance when a missionary priest happened to be in this neighborhood about nineteen years ago. So you see this sort of thing has been going on for some time."

"Those Xara men sound like a dreadful bunch," Toni remarked unthinkingly.

Her observation seemed to anger Luís Quental, restoring the man Toni disliked intensely and putting her back on the defensive at once. "They've had to put up with a lot, too, over the years." His voice was curt, his manner once more so abrasive that it was clear he was putting an end to the temporary truce. "They're a fine people, brave in war but peaceable under most circumstances. The Xara have more good qualities to recommend them than most people who call themselves civilized." Here his lip curled with a contempt directed solely at Toni, on whose throat his eyes had come to rest. "In private they're gentle, loving—and unfailingly loyal to their chosen partners."

Ty Chisholm coughed and changed the subject slightly, sensing uncomfortable undercurrents. "Your hospital seems very well equipped," he observed. "Why do you make the round trip every week to the Xara village? It seems to me they should come here when they're in need."

"Sometimes they do, for urgent complaints." Quental's eyes turned to Ty again. His voice became level, if somewhat discouraging in its tone. "They come to the edge of the clearing and call out. But they won't stay in the hospital, and they won't come at all if the problem can wait."

"Well, at least it keeps your hammocks empty," Barney mused with an unsuccessful attempt at lightness that only caused Luís Quental's face to shutter over completely.

"That," he snapped, "is not the purpose of a hospital."

Toni put in a quiet and seemingly innocuous remark, thinking to take some of the pressure off Barney and fill what had become an awkward lull in the conversation. "If the Xara won't stay in the hospital," she said, "I suppose it's because they're suspicious of modern medicine?"

"As you don't know the whole story," he lashed back with a rancor that seemed out of all proportion to what she had said, "I suggest you keep your conclusions to yourself. They used to stay in the hospital, until I decided it wasn't safe to allow it. Now if you'll excuse me, I have some urgent matters to attend to." He pushed himself away from the table, bringing the talk to a flat and final conclusion. Several pairs of eyes watched as his long limbs strode impatiently away, feet crunching the grasses flat and dark head thrust forward at an angle that suggested some belligerence, or perhaps just haste to leave a conversation that had become distasteful.

"Touchy fellow," murmured Ty once Quental had vanished into the large building. " 'Misogynist' is putting it mildly. I get the feeling, Toni, that he hates your guts."

Toni forced a smile. "You've just won a gold medal for the understatement of the year," she said lightly. "I have a distinct premonition that he has plans to feed me to the piranha." Or to the *piums*, her ankles screamed back up at her.

"He doesn't seem to like us much, either," Barney noted, making a wry face. He mused silently for a moment and then added, "When he was getting us settled into our quarters, I happened to wonder out loud what a lone man would do for women if he had to stay here very long. 'Do without,' he snarled. My God, he practically took my head off."

"Frustration does terrible things to a man," sighed Ty. "You know, I have this odd feeling that I've seen the man before, but I can't think where. You have a good memory for faces, Toni. D'you think we might have run into him before—perhaps in Rio?"

"That would be too much of a coincidence," Toni equivocated lightly, managing to avoid a direct lie. She was certain that Ty and Barney, for reasons of pride, would both wish to forget that long-ago day in

Rio. And she did not want to remind them of it—at least, not in each other's hearing. Working almost in tandem as they did in virtually everything, Ty and Barney had both chosen that particular day to make serious passes at her, without the other's knowledge. Barney's attempt, the more difficult and also the more physical of the two, had come during the afternoon; Ty had made his move in the restaurant that evening, a meal at which Barney had not been present because he had been nursing a black eye.

It was entirely likely, Toni mused, that Luís Quental had overheard some of Ty's blandishments on that long-ago night. If he had, that could account for his low opinion of her morals. No doubt he thought she had given in to the seductive suggestions, possibly because she had listened to Ty's outright proposition without turning a hair. Conceivably her smile and her easy manner had given Quental the wrong idea: certainly something had.

And yet, after his attempt that night, Ty had been quite as demolished as Barney—although in Ty's case the only injury inflicted had been to his ego.

"Quental seems to think you're too soft for the trip tomorrow, Toni," chortled Barney, who had good reason to know otherwise. "I can hardly wait to see him eat his words."

"I'll try not to let you down," Toni responded with a grimace, adding in the privacy of her mind that she would die a thousand deaths before complaining to Luís Quental about anything. Even if they encountered a million *piums* along the way! Odd;

before coming to the Amazon she had been some-what apprehensive about the big creatures she had read about: anaconda and jaguars and caiman and wild boars, and a few other things, too. Had she come all this way just to be defeated by a flea?

"No," she muttered aloud, reaffirming her grip on the knife and fork.

"I beg your pardon?"

"Er, no, I won't let you down. Or myself!" She pushed some black beans around her plate simply to justify her continued possession of the knife and fork, but the very thought of swallowing another mouthful revolted her. The eating implements came to rest at attention, like sentinels, beside her plate. "Tomorrow I don't intend to give Dr. Quental a single reason to look down his disapproving nose," she stated.

Ty spent a contemplative moment measuring Toni's hands and their immutable grasp around the eating implements. Thoughtfully he probed at the reddened spot behind his ear and then stopped as if he had suddenly remembered Quental's injunction. "Perhaps under that abrasive surface of his, Quental's attracted to you," he suggested, lifting his eyes and smiling at Toni blandly.

"Not a chance," said Toni.

"You certainly got under his skin," said Ty.

Toni managed a light laugh. "His armor plating, you mean," she corrected. Now why did Ty have to phrase himself that way? Just the thought of skin sent a new flood of torture to every nerve ending in her body.

"It doesn't seem to take much to rub him the wrong way," Ty went on idly, "but sometimes friction is a sign of attraction."

"That's nonsense," Toni said with something less than her usual good temper. Why did he have to keep using words that reminded her of the ills her flesh was heir to?

Ty mused on as if he had not heard. "Why, after eleven years in the jungle, any red-blooded male might get an itch he couldn't scratch. It's quite possible you tickle his fancy...why, Toni, love, whatever are you doing with that fork?"

Toni snatched the offending fork tines away from her right-hand sleeve, where they had crept inside the cuff placket, propelled—although she could hardly believe it herself—by her own left hand. Disgusted with herself, she dropped the fork on the table and pretended insouciance. "Just fidgety," she said.

"Odd," said Ty, rubbing lightly at his earlobe once again, "I had this funny impression that my complaint might be catching. Tell me, Toni, love, do the *piums* hate you, too?"

"They don't hate me at all," she returned as casually as possible under the circumstances. "It's all in your imagination, Ty. Why, I don't think I got a single *pium* bite today."

Lies, lies, lies! Well, except for one piece of truth. The *piums* didn't hate her. They loved her!

"Then what were you doing with the fork?" asked Barney with a lazy smile, joining into the exchange to which he had been merely an interested listener until this point.

"I...was fiddling because I felt like having a cigarette."

Ty and Barney, who knew she almost never smoked, exchanged glances totally devoid of expression, then turned as one to look at her again.

"Then why didn't you just put a flea in my ear?" murmured Ty, drawing a mutilated pack from his pocket and throwing it across the table, along with a book of matches. Both men watched with intense interest as she struck a match and held it with unsteady fingers.

"Antonia, my love," drawled Barney, "you look as though you're in the throes of withdrawal. I never thought I'd see you bitten by the tobacco bug."

My God, thought Toni wildly, without needing an answer, *are they doing it deliberately?* After the close camaraderie of a year, she was in no doubt. And she knew they would persist. She drew deeply on the cigarette once, without inhaling, and threw it on the ground, rubbing it in well with the heel of her boot. "I guess it's not a cigarette I want, just an afternoon siesta. Will you please excuse me?"

"Not feeling up to scratch?" inquired Barney, his wide eyes far too ingenuous.

"Oh, I imagine she's just itching to get away from here in case Quental comes back," furthered Ty.

"That wouldn't faze Toni," Barney said seriously. "She can face any kind of ticklish situation."

Gritting her teeth, Toni stooped to collect the

shoulder-strap carryall she had placed on the ground before the meal, conscious that Barney was concurrently making his way around the table with some foul intent. Even knowing this, she could not stop her reaction when he passed light tantalizing fingers down her spine. She scissored to attention, rigid with rage.

"Will you please stop it, you two? You're like a bad vaudeville act!"

"Why so prickly, Toni?" asked Barney innocently.

"Is something eating you?" Ty said.

Temper now beginning to fray badly, Toni glowered at the two men warningly. "Look, I don't need you two clowns to tell me when I need to consult a doctor. One little bite on my wrist and—"

"That bad, is it?" asked Ty laconically.

She slung the bag over her shoulder in a defiant gesture, much to the detriment of the shoulder in question. "What makes you think it's bad at all?"

"You're the one who mentioned a doctor. We didn't."

Toni sagged and sighed; there was no use trying to hide everything from these two. "Well, I am a trifle uncomfortable, but only because my ointment's all gone. I was too generous with the supply, and it ran out before I reached my arms." Not true at all: her arms had been as well anointed as anything else. But for her the ointment simply hadn't helped all that much. "There's more salve in the luggage somewhere, but I haven't had time to look for it. And at this point I'd rather tie my tongue in knots than ask Dr. Quental for anything.''

"Why didn't you say so in the first place?" Barney reached into his breast pocket and extracted a tube that was hardly used, reminding Toni once again that others must be much less susceptible to the *piums* than she herself seemed to be. "Here, catch. I can do without.''

"I'll look in the luggage for more," offered Ty.

Toni caught; and blew both of them a kiss. "Thanks," she said with heartfelt gratitude, remembering that there were reasons she counted these two as friends. In that moment she became aware of another presence in the distance, and turned swiftly to go.

"Sleep tight and don't let the bugs bite," drawled Ty, with no more than a slight suggestion of a guffaw. And when that seemed to put a firecracker under Toni's feet, causing a sudden spurt that took her several paces away from the table in record time, he called out, "Something bugging you, sweetheart?''

She swiveled long enough to hiss, in a low voice, "Quental!" and then resumed her headlong progress.

Barney must have misunderstood her warning, which had been intended only so that the pair would not say anything to give away her state of discomfort. "Don't worry, love," he cried too audibly, "we won't let Quental bite!''

"We wouldn't want the bastard to eat you alive!" crowed Ty.

As she hurried away to the infuriating sound of their sniggering, she wondered how long it would take Ty and Barney to discover that Luís Quental had emerged from his dispensary only seconds ago and was watching from a shadowed corner of the building with a dark brooding expression.

In MIDAFTERNOON the distant drone of the plane returning to pick up Senhor Garcia brought Toni out of her hair-shirt hiding, from the supposed siesta during which she had not slept at all, nor even tried to. A mild shortness of breath had added itself to her other complaints. She made her way to the riverside to find the others already gathered to say goodbye. Among them, expectably, was the tall forbidding figure of Luís Quental. She firmed her resolve and descended the slope, determined to reveal none of the afternoon's sufferings in his presence. He turned his back before she reached the gathering on the dock.

"More comfortable now?" Ty murmured in the quietest of voices, his question covered by the noise of the outboard motor coughing into life. "Or are you still suffering?"

Something in the way Quental's shoulders stiffened told Toni he had overheard. Damn his fine-tuned ears. "No problem," she answered Ty evenly. "I had a wonderful sleep." And she turned away quickly to make her farewells to Garcia, giving Ty no chance to incriminate her with further questions.

At last Garcia climbed into the rivercraft where

Getulio already waited. The *caboclo*'s nut-colored face was so wreathed in contentment that Toni could only conclude that Garcia's news had been excellent, as promised.

"*Adeus*, Luís!" called Garcia as the craft finally pulled away into midstream. "*A próxima semana!*"

Until next week? Was Garcia planning to return in a week? He had made no mention of that to Toni. But perhaps he considered it his duty to return and check up on the situation, after the unpromising reception earlier in the day. As she turned to leave the riverbank, a hand caught at her sleeve from behind, the brown lean fingers curling around her sleeve for seconds only—just long enough to prevent her from following her fellow filmmakers up the slope. Toni halted without turning to face her interceptor. At her side Ty paused for a moment, raising a quizzical brow to ask if she needed moral support; Toni signaled an imperceptible negative.

She stood quietly but tensely, awareness like electricity charging the afternoon air. Without seeing Quental's face, she suspected that from his unseen vantage point he was scrutinizing her more closely and openly than he had ever done before—probably assessing her physical state because of the small remark he had overheard. She had the peculiar sensation that every nerve ending in her body was betraying her by flashing its own coded message through the air.

Luís Quental waited until the two American men were well out of hearing and the river quiet but for the distant burr of the motor that had long since vanished around a riverbend. By the time he spoke Toni was sure he was scornfully aware of every prickling impulse in every hair on the nape of her neck.

"The usual course of action when one is suffering is to consult a doctor. I presume you weren't listening when I said that all troubles, even minor ones, were to be brought to my attention prior to tomorrow's trip."

His manner was dampening. Much as she would have liked to respond with some cutting remark, Toni knew she must not do so; Luís Quental's cooperation was vitally important in the venture that lay ahead. She remained silent, waiting for him to continue.

"My personal prejudices, I assure you, do not extend into my professional life. As the person in charge here, I have some responsibility for your welfare, and even more for the welfare of the Xara. Now tell me your problem."

"It's unimportant," she said. "Really, Dr. Quental, I don't think—"

"I insist."

There was tempered steel in the words, and Toni knew she could expect no peace until she gave him a satisfactory answer. And yet if she admitted to her present discomforts, might he forbid her to undertake the expedition to the Xara village? She had been looking forward to the adventure with some eagerness, and insect bites were not exactly a medical emergency—or shouldn't be. By tomorrow hers

would most certainly be better. And the slight shortness of breath she had been experiencing could be
due to the humid air. "It's not a medical problem at
all," she claimed, "so please don't trouble yourself
about it."

"A stomach disorder, perhaps? I noticed you
toyed with your lunch. And you must have spoken to
your friend about something, for him to be aware
you were suffering. What was your complaint?"

"I...happened to mention to Ty that I felt hot
and sticky and uncomfortable." Well, as a version of
the truth that was not too far amiss. "I meant to ask
Getulio if he could arrange a bath, but I didn't have a
chance before he took off. I'll ask him when he
comes back."

There was a small silence, compounding that
strange air of tension between them. At last Quental
spoke, a derisive note now ringing in his resonant
voice. "Getulio will be stopping off at the village to
visit his cousin Fernão, in order to arrange for
tomorrow's bearers. As he's already prepared supper, I doubt he'll be back until shortly before the end
of the day. Would you care to put the question to
me?"

She did not; but she could see no other option.
And truthfully, visions of immersing herself in cool
water, preferably laced with baking soda, danced in
her head. "What does one do about a bath in this
place, Dr. Quental?" she asked pleasantly, still without turning to face him.

"Our plumbing is very limited. There are no

plumbers in this part of the world, and besides, any patient well enough to graduate from sponge baths considers he's well enough to go home." He paused, and a mocking condescension entered his voice. "Personally I use the river. But if you're nervous about piranha, you probably won't like that suggestion. I can arrange some other contrivance for you, I suppose. I imagine you'd be happier with a small basin of the type Getulio uses to give sponge baths. It has its limitations, but at least you won't get...eaten alive."

So he had overheard Ty's parting shot. Not that it really mattered; except that it meant Quental probably thought she had been complaining about his treatment of her. And she would prefer him not to know that his arrogant disdain had reached her in any way.

Forewarned and forearmed by Getulio's chance words, Toni was able to reply calmly. "The river would be fine, Dr. Quental. I'm sure you'll show me a safe place." Unflustered, she turned and bestowed on him a cool smile, taking some spiteful delight in catching the brief surprise in the dark eyes before they dropped away from hers.

"I'm not sure the river's a good idea for you," Quental said with a scowl, confirming Toni's guess that he had been certain she would refuse the suggestion. "The only parts safe from piranha are where the waters run very swiftly, as they do off this dock. Piranha avoid swift currents. But one has to be a strong swimmer to cope."

"I'll cope," she responded with more equanimity than she felt. "I'm a good swimmer."

The dark coals of Quental's eyes were fastened on Toni's collarbone, barely visible above the shirtfront she had fastened high enough to conceal the topmost of the *pium* bites. She had the odd sensation that he could see right through the fabric, that he was imagining the flesh beneath, looking for weaknesses, discovering all secrets.

He tore his eyes away. "You can't bathe without a partner nearby," he said gruffly, frowning at the surface of the green river. "That I absolutely forbid. Do you have a bathing suit with you?"

"No." It was a need that had not occurred to Toni, and now she found herself wishing she had accepted the offer of a small basin. But pride would not allow her to back out at this point; to do so would be to earn more of Quental's contempt. And in any case, a month of sponge baths was not a thrilling prospect.

"Perhaps you'd care to change your mind," he taunted.

"No, thank you; river it is." Well, she thought grimly, she could always bathe in her underthings. They were unerotic and practical garments, a far cry from the dainty lingerie she had chosen for her honeymoon so many years before. Since Matthew's death, the ache that still lay in her heart had always forbidden the choice of provocative lingerie, and the neat piles of bras and panties in her suitcase would hide far more than most bikinis. She turned away from Luís Quental and started the short climb up the riverbank.

"Where are you going?" he called.

She turned and took a last look at the glowering man on the dock, taking some joy in having won a small moral victory in the conversation of the past few minutes. "To get soap and towels—and to ask Ty Chisholm to stand guard!"

Ty agreed, and aimed on down to the river while Toni went to her wretched hut to fetch soap, shampoo and towels. With no chest of drawers to hold her things, she had not unpacked, and the search through her suitcase took a few minutes. When she reached the river again, she was startled to see that the brooding figure seated on the red clay bank was not Ty but Luís Quental. Although his back was resting against the stout flagpole and his elbows were propped loosely against bent knees, there was a tension in the long limbs, a coiled and waiting awareness as he stared moodily into the swift emerald eddies of the river.

"Where's Ty?" she asked as she descended the steps hewn into the bank.

Quental did not even spare her a glance. "I sent him away," came the dry sarcastic retort. "A nonswimmer is a very poor choice for a partner to save you in case of trouble. I told him I would make other arrangements for your bath."

"Then I'll ask Barney," she said evenly, although a faint warmth in her cheeks might have betrayed some consternation if Quental had been looking at her.

"Don't bother. Neither of your friends is available. I gave them a bottle of my best brandy to share and warned them to drink it in the cooking shed, where my patients can't see."

Nothing Ty and Barney would like better, reflected Toni with a trace of exasperation. Although they claimed otherwise, they both had an occasional weakness for the grape. This time it took a great deal of effort not to react to Quental's high-handed tactics. Toni was no masochist, and his every move seemed calculated to drive her to the brink of confrontation. Nevertheless she guarded her temper. "Why did you do that, Dr. Quental?" she asked mildly. "I happen to know Barney swims, and very well, too. Have you some reservations about allowing him to act as my partner?"

"Yes," Quental told her with brutal frankness, "because I've decided that if you're going to strip for a swim, you can do it in front of me."

Toni stared, hardly believing the words that had issued from those hard lips. He had neither risen to his feet nor turned his hooded gaze from the water—quite as if he had decided on a good vantage point for the striptease he expected. All her usual efficient thinking processes deserted her for the moment. Outraged at his arrogance, she was too angry to bother protesting that she had not planned to undress at all.

"You can't mean that!" she exploded, taking no trouble to conceal the tremble of fury in her voice.

The edges of his strong mouth took on a deeper curl, indicating scorn and perhaps a twisted satisfaction that he had at last drawn some emotional reaction from Toni. He shifted his position against the flagpole until he had her beltline in view, his gaze traveling no higher and no lower. His attention to her belt buckle was insolent. "I am a doctor," he reminded her. "I *have* seen naked women before."

"Do you think Barney hasn't?" flashed Toni, before she took time to realize how that sounded.

"I'm sure he has, many times." The bitter biting words left her in no doubt as to how her own question had been taken. "Nevertheless this is one occasion when he won't. I have no reason to trust his swimming abilities, and this river is swift. I'm responsible for your safety as long as you're in my domain. I assure you that of all the men within miles, I'm the only man who will be totally unaffected by the sight of your nakedness. A doctor gets used to such things. Now undress, and hurry about it."

Toni bit back a gasp at the brutal directness of his command. Fists clenching so tightly that her knuckles hurt, she struggled to regain her shattered poise, with some degree of success. "I have no intention of doing any such thing," she claimed coldly.

His black brows drew together into a forbidding scowl as his eyes swept from her waist to her ankles with slow searing contempt. "In other words," he concluded with bitter irony, "you don't care what man you undress for, as long as it's not me. Shall I try to guess why? There is no thrill, is there, is undressing for a man who will not respond!" A deep obsessive expression began to darken the gaze fixed on her ankles. "No, you want a man who will grow aroused, who will perhaps be unable to hide his arousal, who will be driven to want you, at the risk of everything, even his own sanity—"

"Dr. Quental!" Toni's outraged interruption brought an immediate halt to the driven words. It had a strange effect on the embittered doctor, much as if she had slapped him forcibly in the face. Jarred for a moment, he seemed almost as shocked as she. And then his eyes left her ankles, where they had been mesmerized, and fastened on a blade of grass. His face became closed and wooden, as if the vehemence of moments ago had never been. Only a dull suffusion of color high on the slanted cheekbones betrayed his state of mind in any way.

"Naturally, if you prefer I shall keep my back turned while you disrobe," he said stiffly.

Toni could not so easily dismiss the laden emotions she had so recently witnessed. "I think perhaps I'll forget the bath-altogether," she said, deciding her tortured skin would simply have to do without the cool immersion until some other time.

His lips drew back briefly, revealing white teeth gritted into an expression that was not a smile. "If you prefer, I'll promise to remain turned away even while you're in the water—unless you call for help. And although I suppose you may not appreciate the fact, I am a man of my word."

As her rational powers returned, Toni recalled that even Garcia had said this was so. And yet under the circumstances she did not feel entirely comfortable with the idea of stripping to her underwear, despite its lack of eroticism. Quental's emotional vehemence had left her feeling vulnerable enough, even fully clothed in unfeminine jungle fatigues. She spent a moment contemplating the cool green water while she decided what to do.

"All right, then," she said finally, with remarkable self-possession under the circumstances, and even managed a faint smile behind a thick veil of lashes while she watched Luís Quental make good his promise. He rose to his feet, the length of him unfolding to its full authoritative height, and then he swiftly swerved so that his face was turned to the flagpole and his strongly muscled back to the river. He squared his shoulders and waited.

Toni moved onto the slippery dock, well out of his line of vision. She took her time, placing her soap dish, towels and shampoo bottle where they could be easily reached from the water. Without taking her eyes off Luís Quental's tense spine, she removed her leather belt, drawing it free of the loops that confined it around her waist. And then, with a deliberate lack of speed, she sat down to loosen her bootlaces, still facing the spot where he stood.

"Please hurry," he directed gruffly a few moments later.

"I'm having trouble with a stuck zipper," Toni said, noisily manipulating the slide fastener at one hip pocket. "I'll let you know if I need help." With slow deliberation she removed the contents of that pocket, and then another, and another, until all her perishable personal effects had been removed from her clothes.

Toni intended to have a small moment of revenge; and Luís Quental's promise to keep his back turned had suggested the means.

"I take it you managed with the zipper," he remarked in a somewhat bleak voice after listening to the soft thud of a small notebook landing on the dock.

"Yes, I managed," she returned coolly, making a mental note that the signs of strain that had crept into his voice were confirmed by the rigid set of his shoulders. "I won't need to trouble you after all. Are my things likely to be safe here on the dock?"

"Yes."

"Good," said Toni calmly, looking at the minuscule pile of personal possessions she had removed from her pockets. "I shouldn't want a wave to come and wash them away."

Her mouth curved upward when that remark caused Luís Quental's fingers to flex once at his sides. "Are you going in now?" he asked tersely.

"No, I'm not quite ready yet. I have a few more things to remove."

"Then do it," came the grim order.

"I'm doing it as fast as I can," Toni responded, unperturbed. "The dock is a little slippery, and it slows me down."

And with that her socks, too, came off, again with a lack of speed that allowed her all the time in the world to study the way Quental's hands had reached forward and gripped the flagpole for support. She smiled to herself. So much for his claim to be unaffected by a woman's nakedness!

If he but knew it, the only naked thing about her was her toes! For a short time she sat watching him, arms crossed and hands sliding up and down over her sleeves, partly because it was the next best thing to the scratching she was trying to avoid, and partly because it made noises very much like those of someone removing clothes.

When she could prolong this part of the torture no longer, she said with a studied trace of nervousness, "I'm about to go in now. Are you sure you'll hear me if I need help?"

"Absolutely sure," came the thick answer.

"Is it safe to swim out into the river?"

"As I won't be watching, it would be safer to hang onto the dock." His voice was muffled, his knuckles whitening over the flagpole to an alarming degree.

"And you're certain there are no piranha here?"

"Certain. *Meu Deus*, must you stand there questioning every little thing? Get in the water at once!"

Toni hesitated for another moment and then asked ingenuously, "Do you have a patient waiting for you, Dr. Quental?"

"No," he grated.

"Good," she breathed. "I was afraid you were in a hurry. And really, I'd like to wash my hair."

"Get in," he snapped. "Have you no sense? Some boat might come around the riverbend at any moment."

Amused, Toni glanced down at her fully clad body and then looked back at those rigidly held shoulders not a dozen feet away. Without seeing his face she could practically feel the clench of his teeth and the tight closure of his eyelids.

Deliberately she pretended to misunderstand his warning. "Please don't worry, Dr. Quental. I won't let myself be run down in the water. If a motorboat approaches, I'm sure I'll hear it in time to climb out."

"Get in," he repeated, and this time it sounded very like a curse.

By now dark patches of sweat had taken possession of the armpits of his shirt, and cords of effort stood out along the back of his neck, visible on either side of the lick of black hair that brushed against his damp collar. Quental's imagination was doing its very worst—and after what she had suffered at his hands, Toni was human enough to enjoy it thoroughly.

Coming to her haunches, she clung to the side of the dock and lowered herself with a light splash into the swiftly flowing green, feeling its coldness like a shock against her heated flesh. For an instant, with the rushing speed of the river dragging against the heavy weight of her clothes, she almost lost her grip on the log. Involuntarily she gasped, and then glanced upward to make sure Quental had not looked around.

He tensed but did not turn, merely raising his head for a moment, like a jungle animal sniffing the breeze. "Are you all right?"

"Fine," she assured him quickly. "It's cold, that's all. Like ice on my skin."

She saw a small shudder travel over the sweat-drenched shirt, as though emanating upward from those flat, male, muscular thighs. Just as if someone had put an ice cube down *his* spine, she thought with amusement. Keeping a guarded watch on him, she clung to the side of the dock and washed as well as she could—swiftly loosening fastenings, refastening them even more swiftly, soaping her arms directly through the cloth and her legs by pushing the baggy trousers high on her legs. At last, reasonably certain she had cleansed every part of herself except her hair, she replaced the soap in its dish and decided that sweet revenge could be a little sweeter yet.

"Oh, dear," she said forlornly.

Quental reacted instantly and with a rigor that did her vengeful heart good. "What is it?" he demanded, his head jerking back upward from a determined bend that had suggested contemplation of his feet.

"Nothing," she said at once, so that he would not turn. "I'm not sure I can reach my shampoo, that's all. But I don't think I need your help. Wait a moment...." She indulged in some minor splashing, as if raising the top half of her body out of the water. In truth, the shampoo bottle was only inches from her fingertips.

Her cool gray eyes took in Quental's long bronzed fingers, clenching and unclenching over the flagpole, putting the tendons of his shoulders and tanned forearms into a state of perpetual tension.

"It's all right, I have the shampoo," she announced, deciding the cruel game had gone on long enough. After that, she shampooed quickly, ducking several times and working her fingers through her scalp to let the swift currents of water rinse away the lather. At least her perverse pleasure in baiting Quental had taken her mind off piranha and even *piums*: during the chilling plunge she had quite forgotten her former discomfort. Inflicting torture, she concluded wryly as she at last clambered out on the dock, was far superior to suffering under its slings and blows!

"All finished," she said calmly, pushing her sodden hair from her eyes and giving her waterlogged clothes a quick shake, like a dog after a swim. As a few drops of water shaken loose by Toni splattered against Quental's clothes, he reacted as if stung.

"Get dressed," he rasped.

Toni took time only to towel down the shirt that clung too revealingly, attempting without much success to pluck it away from her skin so that it would not delineate the contours of her breasts. There was no need to draw this scene out to the point of sadism. Toni had proved very much to her satisfaction that Luis Quental had a weakness all the willpower in the world could not conquer. By now she had a very good idea of why he might have left the restaurant on that long-ago night: perhaps her perfume had been at fault after all. It was evident that the years of frustration had aroused in him a dangerous need, a need that reached deep into the very roots of his being. He might hate women, but after this day's events let him try to pretend he could do without!

And yet she saw no need to humiliate him completely; she had no wish to see his face. She could guess very well that it would be bathed in perspiration and suffused with the dull flush of desire; that his forehead would be creased with effort and possibly anguish. And many years had passed since she had been naive enough not to know what other signs of arousal might mark a man's body under such circumstances.

Hurriedly she shook out her boots and slipped her damp feet into them, without taking time for the laces. With no ado she gathered together her socks, belt, bathing necessities and other possessions and at once started for the rise, where she would soon walk into Quental's line of vision.

"You can't go up there until..." came a tortured command as she began to brush past the place where he stood, in such short order that he must know she had not had time to dress. When the rest of the sentence was swallowed she knew he had seen. She came to a halt near the top of the riverbank, without turning to confront him. She wanted him to be in absolutely no doubt; there was no point vanishing before he had taken a good look at her waterlogged clothing. And perhaps one more taste of triumph was not too much to ask.

"You bathed like that?" he demanded in a strange, shocked, strangled voice.

"Why, Dr. Quental," she said, mustering her

very coolest air, "surely you didn't think I was naked?"

And to a silence with the impact of a thunderclap, she trailed the rest of her damp victory march up the slope.

CHAPTER FOUR

IF THE PREVIOUS AFTERNOON had seemed like victory of a sort, this afternoon seemed very like defeat. As Toni trudged along single file with the men, she told herself that the severe shortness of breath and the pains shooting like guided missiles through her legs and her arms were imagination, all imagination. After all, the *pium* bites had looked much better this morning. The swellings had subsided. Only tiny dots remained at the site of each bite, although a pale even rash—more of a flush, really—had appeared here and there.

If only the dratted itch hadn't kept her awake last night! If only she had been able to accustom herself to sleeping in a hammock! If only Getulio had not warned her that the reason the lantern must be left burning all night was to keep vampire bats from coming through the chinks in the walls! If only the moths and other insects had shunned the light in like fashion! If only the skies had not released a torrent of rainfall, one of the first of the wet season, sometime during the night! If only the rain had not come dripping through the roof of her very inadequate shelter!

And if only that horrid cacophony of sound hadn't awakened her just when she had finally managed to drift into a wretched sleep!

The din had exploded through the jungle at about four in the morning. Toni's first terrified instinct had told her that a hundred furious bulls were charging her hut, vying for the privilege with a hundred enraged lions. It had been a monstrous, mind-shattering roar that shook the very earth, and some minutes had passed before she was rational enough to remember the warning Luís Quental had issued over the dinner hour the previous evening. By that time his self-control had been fully restored, his face more formidable than ever. After her moment of triumph at the river, Toni had been much too sensible to continue her baiting in any way; in fact, with the success of the film venture at stake, she had made extra efforts not to antagonize him further.

"Howler monkeys," he had warned, directing his words pointedly away from Toni, "are really quite gentle and innocuous-looking. They have enormous vocal cords, though. Their Adam's apples are the size of tennis balls, and they enjoy using them. It takes an old Amazon hand to sleep through the din."

After the howler monkeys ceased their uproar, Toni had not been able to sleep again. By then every bird in the entire jungle seemed to be celebrating the approach of dawn, making up for their midday silence. There had been a noisy symphony of trills, chatters, squeaks, drumbeats, cackles, whistles, flutings, booms, groans, cooings, chants and chimes covering every note in the scale and then some.

But last night's tortures seemed tame by comparison with the discomforts she was facing now. The Xara village might be only six miles distant, but it seemed like double that. It had rained again in the early afternoon, and the jungle still dripped, turning everything to mud and misery. The dripping wetness had not discouraged the insects, clouds of whom seemed to be thriving on a diet of one part insect repellent and ten parts Toni Carruthers—or so it seemed to Toni.

At least there were no *piums* in the jungle; it appeared they preferred the river and other open spaces. Not that the *piums* could have found a place to roost, with sweat bees taking up every available inch of skin not claimed by mosquitoes. Oddly, though, the mosquito bites affected her less than the *piums* had done; and the sweat bees didn't bite at all, although their nuisance value was considerable.

Toni's troubles were not confined to insects. The laced waterproof boots she wore—a necessity for tramping through the jungle—had been bought in Manaus on a day when her feet had not been swollen with heat and damp. Now the boots felt at least a half size too small. Oh, misery!

The path to the Xara village penetrated a green dank world composed of rotting vegetation underfoot and rioting vegetation overhead. There was less undergrowth than Toni had expected, but more overgrowth—orchids exploding on high; creepers as thick as a man's arm supporting trees long since dead; and every growing thing fighting upward, upward, upward to seek its own hard-won space in the sun.

Few creatures seemed to inhabit the lower spaces, or if they did they stayed out of sight. But at times the air seemed full of fluttering giant butterflies—glittering morphos and other species, iridescent in shades of cobalt and emerald and orange and yellow, like huge shimmering flowers freed from their earthly confines. It was a world with many beauties, but with physical discomfort distracting her Toni was too miserable to appreciate any of them: she felt as though she had suffered mutation into one gigantic insect bite.

Although Luís Quental had indicated that he traveled this route every week, and that the Xara Indians often covered it, too, already green things—vines and creepers and strangler figs—had put out tough twisting tentacles along the way, like giant fingers reaching out to reclaim the path for the jungle.

"They say nature abhors a vacuum, but I didn't know they were talking about a little path in the Amazon!" grimaced Ty Chisholm as the party came to a brief halt while Getulio's cousin Fernão, who was leading the file, hacked away at a tough foot-thick liana that had fallen from its aerial support.

Toni's exhausted response was closer to a grunt than a laugh. Her sense of humor had plummeted to something below zero on today's march, and only Luís Quental's intimidating presence bringing up the rear forced her into any kind of pretense at all.

"Are you going to admit your weakness now and let me carry that pack?" came a scornful voice from behind, and Toni half turned to find that Quental's eyes had settled on the rucksack strapped to her back.

She squared her sagging shoulders and tilted her chin stubbornly. The rucksack scratched against her skin, contributing to her earthly hell. "No," she said, and faced forward again as the file resumed its progress. The unaccustomed shallowness of her breath prevented her from elaborating on the single word.

"Could it be," derided the man behind her, "that you're being purely stubborn? I warned you to carry nothing. This is no trip for a woman, especially one who is as soft as you."

Toni clenched her teeth and trudged on, unwilling to dignify his sarcasm with an answer. At the moment it was difficult to remember that Luís Quental had weaknesses, too. He was certainly displaying none at the moment. The burden on *his* shoulders would have swayed the back of a pack mule, and he was carrying other things, as well—a medical kit and a heavy caliber rifle.

The contemptuous murmur at her ear continued, so low that the others marching ahead could not hear it. "When you turned I noticed a few bites at your throat," he commented, causing a moment of numb wonder because Toni had not noticed his eyes leaving her rucksack. "I suspect you've been scratching. Perhaps you should let me have a look at you."

"Not necessary." Toni was passingly pleased that her voice did not sound too much like a wheeze. No doubt nothing would please Quental's twisted mind more than the proof that her physical state was far from good. And as for the sight of her tormented feet—how that would amuse him! "I'm fine," she said throatily.

"Really?" He sounded skeptical but made no further comment on what he had observed. "The Xara village is still a half mile from here. Are you sure you have the stamina?"

"Sure," she averred, once more wasting no words. And if anything kept one foot slogging after the other for the next half mile, it was a gritty determination not to make a fool of herself in front of Luís Quental. Damn his rawhide skin and his stinging sardonic tongue!

"At last," groaned Ty directly ahead of her, and Toni came out of a haze of exhaustion to note that they were at last emerging from the jungle. Directly ahead lay a small twisting stream known as an *igarapé*, a tributary too tiny to be dignified by the name of river. Across it lay a structure too rickety to be dignified by the name of bridge: it was a flimsy concoction of saplings shakily balanced over trestles resting on the mud bottom, with lianas strung across to serve as handrails. Several totally naked youngsters who had been fishing from the bridge stopped what they were doing and watched with a mixture of curiosity and hostility as the party approached. Handsome, sturdy and very light of skin, they all had short bobbed hair and bangs, a cut that looked as though it had been done with a bowl and made no distinction between the sexes. Although they appeared to recognize Fernão and the other two bearers, their faces turned wary at sight of the three Americans, and their suspiciousness did not ease until they saw Luís Quental, last to emerge from the jungle.

From behind Toni's shoulder his voice called some reassuring words to the youngsters, in the dialect of the Xara people. One of the older boys, spokesman for the group, called a greeting; and then suddenly, like leaves scattering in a storm, the whole collection of children scampered toward the village that lay on the other side of the tiny tributary, presumably to advise of the approach of strangers.

The Xara village, Toni saw as they crossed the shaky bridge and advanced to its edge, was a ring of huts that formed a great oval around a large well-trampled clearing. To be exact, it was more like one huge continuous hut with minimal partitions, completely open-sided where it faced onto the central core of the village; an arrangement that would seem to offer very little privacy for the inhabitants of the community.

A large number of men and women were gathered in the central clearing; the men standing to watch the visitors' arrival, the women squatting in small separate groups around homely household tasks. At first sight of the newcomers the tasks came to a halt, but it was easy to see what the women had been doing:

weaving crude baskets; minding small children;
pressing soaked manioc roots to remove the poison-
ous prussic acid; grating the pressed and now edible
roots into large troughs made of hollowed logs. Toni,
who had read something of these things, looked
around her with interest as she caught her breath, her
own ills for the moment pushed aside.

Each and every one of the adults, like their children, had short bobbed hair. The men were reasonably covered by sizable breechclouts made of bark;
the women were clad in no more than paint.

"Wait here," Quental ordered. "Don't enter the
village until I give the word. And whatever you do,
don't start filming until I give the go-ahead."

While Toni and the film crew remained at the
fringe of the village clearing with Fernão and the
other men who had been hired as bearers, Quental
moved forward into the thick of the tribesmen—a
tall, authoritative, alien figure surrounded by men
half a head shorter than himself.

The Xara men might have been handsome by
Western standards but for the mode of lip decoration
they favored. Pegged into place below each man's lip
was a large wooden disk that served to stretch it and
make it jut ferociously forward, whether for purposes of beautification or in order to frighten
enemies in battle. Toni had seen pictures of these lip
disks during preliminary research on various Amazon tribes, and so the effect was less startling than it
might otherwise have been.

There seemed to be a prescribed order to the proceedings. The standing men all watched Quental's approach impassively, saying nothing, as if each man were waiting for some other to make the first move. Following the direction of Fernão's gaze, Toni soon realized what they were waiting for. In one of the open-sided huts, a tall, strongly built man, about thirty years of age by Toni's reckoning, was in the process of donning a ragged pair of men's shorts. He then clapped a misshapen fedora over his neatly bobbed hair, shouldered a feathered spear and stepped back into the center of the clearing to greet his visitor, clad in what he apparently believed to be the accoutrements of a chief.

Fascination with the scene overcame some of her exhaustion as she watched. The headman, for so he appeared to be despite his youth, was a well-muscled man of handsome appearance. He alone of all the warriors was missing the ungainly disk; the scars on his lower lip suggested that his piece of wood might have been torn out by some misadventure.

Despite the touch of ludicrousness added by the chieftain's special garb, there was an impressive dignity in his manner as he greeted Luís Quental. He also displayed considerable warmth, and Toni received the distinct impression that the two men liked each other. The exchange of greetings seemed to follow a rigorous ceremonial pattern. Both men spoke loudly, as orators would, while the other Xara men listened in respectful silence.

Not understanding a word of what was being said, Toni spent a part of her time looking over the Xara women. With work for the moment put aside, they were not watching the greeting ceremony, which they had doubtless seen many times before, but were casting covert glances at the strangers who had come to their village. The faces of all the women were stained bright red above the cheek line. Toni had seen pictures of similarly painted women and knew that the shiny scarlet color was obtained from the oily seeds of a local bush known as *urucú*. The marks on their bodies were of a different, dark juice, *genipap*, which was used to create the most intricate of geometrical designs; a form of decoration that tended to distract the eye from the otherwise total nakedness of the Xara females.

Suddenly Toni's attention was caught by one particular young female of nineteen or twenty—not because this woman's appearance differed in any marked way from that of the others of her tribe, but because she alone appeared to be painfully self-conscious about her nakedness, a thing that gave not a moment's pause to any of her peers. Might that be the Xara girl who had been brought up by nuns? It seemed possible. She was about the right age, for one thing. Her arms concealed her breasts in a way that suggested shame; her eyes remained determinedly fixed to the ground; and Toni received the strong impression that the scarlet stain on the youthful face was in this case symbolic of a deep mortification not shared by any other woman in the village.

A burst of spontaneity from the Xara men called Toni's eyes back to the place where the headman and

Luís Quental had at last finished their ceremonial exchange. Now smiles and embraces replaced the formality of the earlier proceedings; although why the Xara should greet the dour doctor with such affection was a circumstance that remained beyond Toni's comprehension. But perhaps her brain was not in its best working order: the shortness of breath that had bothered her during the march still robbed her of her usual vigor, causing sensations of faintness that took every ounce of willpower to combat.

"Well, well," murmured Barney Evans into Toni's ear, "it looks as though one of them has a little modesty—besides the chief, that is."

She followed the direction of Barney's discreet nod to find that he was talking of the same young woman who had drawn Toni's interest a few minutes before. The girl, freed by the conclusion of the ceremonies during which she had not dared to move, now detached herself from the small group of females where she had been sitting and slipped almost unnoticed into one of the open-sided huts, still trying to conceal her youthful nakedness with her hands. She emerged seconds later, clad in a simple unbleached cotton smock that was oddly at variance with the shiny red paint on her face.

"That must be the girl Quental told us about," Barney whispered. "The one bred in a convent. Maria, I think her name is."

Toni licked her lips and tried to remember whether she had ever heard the girl's name before. Listening to Luís Quental talk of the Xara at mealtime the

previous day, she had heard him use various tribal
names, Bebgogti and Eketi and Bepkum and Mru-
prire and others even more unpronounceable. The
name Maria seemed quite out of keeping in that exotic roster. But of course it must have been given to
the girl by the nuns, which would account for its un-
tribal sound—yet another thing that set the girl apart
from the rest of the Xara women.

"Come on, Toni, what the deuce is the matter with
you?" Ty Chisholm gave her a gentle shove from behind. "Can't you see Quental's motioning for us to
come forward?"

Only a strong desire not to lay herself open to Luís
Quental's scathing criticisms prevented her from asking to forgo the welcoming ceremonies. How she got
through the confusion that followed Toni never
knew. The nodding, the smiling, the endless polite
speeches, most of them in a language of which she
could not understand a single syllable; and through it
all standing on two feet for which pain seemed too
small a word. Staying in one place helped the continuing shortness of breath, but that was about all.

Luís Quental introduced the fierce young headman
as Eketi, and after the introduction Eketi made an attempt to switch to broken Portuguese. He addressed
a few remarks to Barney and Ty and then gave up
when Quental explained that the American men did
not speak the language. It had not escaped Toni's attention that none of Eketi's efforts had been directed
toward herself, a fact that led her to conclude that in
this particular tribe women were creatures too lowly

to warrant masculine attention. And then Eketi turned to Quental again and reverted to the Xara dialect. Her bleared mind began to focus once again on her own physical discomforts.

All at once she became aware of the dark sardonic eyes that were directing a probing attention to her bosom. Luís Quental had said something that had not quite penetrated the haze of discomfort that seemed to have become a condition of life ever since she had arrived in this part of the Amazon basin.

"I beg your pardon?" blinked Toni, making efforts to pull herself back to the moment.

"I told Eketi you're a woman," he repeated in English, gesturing at her shirtfront. "He's not sure whether to believe me."

A glance at those standing around informed Toni that his were not the only eyes directed at the buttons of her shirt. The young chief, Eketi, and a score of other Xara, as well, were staring with open fascination.

Toni was too tired to care much, as long as they confined their activities to their eyeballs. "Then tell him again," she said.

"I've tried, several times," came the dry retort. "But he's never seen a woman wearing trousers before. As for the shape—he says shape can be changed when it's covered by cloth. He wants the demonstrable proof, and your hair won't do; the Xara make no sexual distinction by a person's haircut. He demands that you unbutton your shirt."

Quental's face was scrupulously expressionless, the

eyes hooded as they fastened on the soft swell of breast concealed by jungle khaki. However, instinct told Toni that he was enjoying this little scene—mocking her, perhaps, in some kind of perverse revenge for the riverside happenings of the previous day. Under his direct gaze a quivering self-awareness feathered over her skin, momentarily displacing the bodily aches and pains.

"Go right ahead, Toni," drawled Ty in his best tongue-in-cheek voice. "Do as the man says; unbutton your front. We'll be watching carefully . . . to see that you come to no harm, of course."

"You bet," added Barney, eyelids drooping in the direction of Toni's front. "We'll keep our eyes peeled for you, all right."

Toni cast a chilled stony look in the direction of her two fellow filmmakers. Traitors!

Luís Quental's quick scowl suggested that he thought the joke at Toni's expense had gone far enough. "It's all right, it won't be necessary to do anything in public," he cut in brusquely. "I've already told Eketi that you won't be willing to undress in front of the whole congregation under any circumstances. He suggests that it would suffice if you went into a hut with one person only, who can testify to the rest of the tribe. It's an imposition, I know, but a necessary one. You have to realize that the Xara are the very opposite of gullible. As I told you yesterday, they believe things only if they can see them with their own eyes."

Toni moistened her lips again while she tried to

think things through with her pounding brain. The open-sided huts did not seem very conducive to privacy, and the indignity of the request turned her hands clammy. She was accustomed to coping, but not with this kind of thing.

"It's best to go along with their wishes," Quental said, his voice for once grave and quiet, lacking its customary bite. "They wanted to seize you and perform the examination several minutes ago. It's taken some arguing to win this much of a concession. Naturally it will be one of the Xara women who accompanies you, not one of the men. Is that so very hard?"

Toni shook her head, thereby agreeing to the request. For some strange reason, considering that Luís Quental was at this moment behaving in less hateful fashion than he had ever done before, she found herself unable to look higher than the open collar where his strong throat rose. Her own throat felt tight—possibly because she sensed that he, of all men here, was probably envisioning that part of her body she would be required to bare.

"I have one request," she said. "Could it be the young woman Maria—the one who was bred in a convent?"

Quental turned at once and exchanged a few more words with the Xara headman. "Eketi agrees," he told her moments later.

Despite the respectful distance they kept, all women of the tribe who were within hearing must have been listening with extraordinary interest, because with no command issued they turned to look at their smock-clad companion. Those nearest her began to giggle and nudge her forward. Maria hung back at first, as painfully shy about having attention directed at herself as she had been earlier about her nudity. But when the strong fearsome young chief uttered a direct command, calling her by name, she moved diffidently forward and stood in front of him with downcast eyes.

She was quite beautiful, thought Toni. The scarlet stain that covered the upper half of her face gleamed on an intelligent forehead and fine cheekbones, setting off the smooth blackness of short bobbed hair. Although the young Xara woman's gaze was never once lifted from the ground while Eketi spoke a few condescending words to her, Toni imagined that her eyes would be dark and liquid, and very lovely beneath their sweep of lashes. And the intricate black patterns that stood out clearly on Maria's pale slender arms and legs might not be the North American ideal of beauty, but they were quite beautiful all the same.

Eketi dealt with the girl who stood humbly before him in a few curt offhand words, dismissing her with a gesture. Having issued his orders, he at once turned his back, presumably expecting a lowly woman to obey his directions instantly and to the letter.

"Go with Maria now," Luís Quental commanded, his voice becoming as dismissive as Eketi's had been. Then he, too, turned away and drew Ty and Barney into an exclusively male dialogue with Eketi.

Toni turned to Maria in time to witness a small but revealing incident. For one fleeting moment, the Xara girl lifted her lashes to look at the muscular shoulders of the man who was chief of her tribe; then lowered them just as swiftly. The expression in her eyes was veiled at once, but as Toni followed the young Xara girl she found herself wondering how any woman could display adoration, however well hidden, for a man who spoke to her in such peremptory fashion.

To Toni's gratitude, the girl Maria led her past the open-sided huts and the curious glances of the other tribeswomen and out of the Xara village altogether. She walked ahead with humbly bent head, not watching to see if Toni followed, silent until they reached the edge of the jungle.

"Come with me," she said then in Portuguese, darting the most timid of glances at Toni's face. "There is a place where we will not be seen. Sometimes, when I wish to be alone, I go there."

It seemed that Maria understood Toni's need for privacy. Toni smiled and murmured a word of appreciation for the girl's delicate sensibilities. She had no trouble understanding Maria, who spoke with a soft pleasing music in her hushed syllables.

The two progressed a short distance into the jungle. Although there was no well-beaten path in this place, it was an easy enough route, for the undergrowth was not particularly dense. Reaching a gigantic ceiba tree whose huge buttresses formed natural partitions at the base, Maria pushed some green creepers aside, revealing a hollow dark space like a small room, walled by the tree and curtained with vegetation.

"It is my private place," she said simply. "Wait while I make sure that no creatures have come here before us."

Within seconds a startled rodent about the size of a rabbit scampered into the open, and Maria indicated that it was safe for Toni to enter. "It is best to be sure," she said in her tentative unassuming way. "That animal was only an agouti, but once there was a very bad small snake."

Probably a fer-de-lance, Toni guessed, attempting to quell a moment of unease as she eased her way into the dank, dark, private enclosure. Here it was not possible to stand erect, and so both women sat, curled into the dimly lit space, facing each other. Toni's fingers started at once to fumble with her top button. Today, with every part of her body aching as it had never ached before, she wanted only to be done with this embarrassing procedure as speedily as possible.

"It is not necessary, *senhora*," came Maria's quick anxious response. "I do not need to see to believe, as others do."

Toni breathed a sigh of relief, and her fingers fell from their task. "That's what I was hoping you would say," she admitted.

"We will have to stay here a little time, in order that Eketi will think I have done as he asked. You will not mind?"

"Not at all," agreed Toni. It was good to be off her feet. In this dim cool enclosure she found some relief from her throbbing head, and her breathing seemed to come more easily. She felt a certain amount of curiosity about Maria, too, and that helped prevent total preoccupation with her own maladies. She considered loosening her bootlaces and decided against it: she had the feeling that once released from their confines, her ankles would swell like balloons.

"We do not need to hurry. I heard Eketi ask Dr. Quental if the men would join him for a drink of *kashiri*, a wine made from the sweet potato and other fruits. When men drink *kashiri*, women are not wanted. Besides, it is good to talk with someone who speaks my language."

The hesitant remark was wistful—but then Maria went on with great haste, as if she had forgotten herself. "But of course Portuguese is not my true language, although I was brought up to talk it with the nuns. My true language is the language of my own people. It is a good thing that the nuns arranged for me to learn my language as well as theirs. They brought me up in all things to be proud of my people, in case I might someday return."

Had they also told Maria the reason she had been handed over by her mother to an itinerant priest? As Toni could hardly ask Maria how much she knew about her birthright, she said instead, "I don't speak Portuguese as well as you do, I'm afraid."

"But you speak it very well, and we can under-

stand each other,'' said Maria. "It is good to talk
with someone who knows of the...the other world.
Dr. Quental knows, but if I spoke with him privately
others might think me...bad. I would not wish...
some people...to think me bad.''

"I don't see how anyone could possibly think
that.'' And then, hearing Maria's soul-deep sigh,
Toni used her sixth sense to add, "I imagine that
Eketi, for one, must think you are very trustworthy,
or he would not have asked you to come with me.''

Maria hesitated in a confusion of timidity and then
blurted out, "Did Eketi think to send me with you
because I speak Portuguese?''

Toni winced inwardly because she suspected Maria
was not going to like her answer. Maria was touchingly eager to know why Eketi had chosen her, but it
would be unfair to raise false hopes in the girl. "It
was because I asked that it be you, Maria,'' she said
gently.

"It was you that made the choice? Oh....'' The
timid optimism on Maria's face faded, and she
looked down at her fingers quickly, as if to hide her
disappointment.

Toni felt a surge of sympathy: it was clear that
Maria had thought the choice to be Eketi's own, and
perhaps it was the only sign of notice the lordly chief
had ever paid her. "I'm sure he thinks highly of you
all the same,'' Toni said, "or he would have settled
on some other woman.''

"Eketi does not think of me at all.'' Maria's diffident voice shook a little, and her twisting fingers,

too. There was a hopelessness in her demeanor that was not fully concealed.

Was Maria in need of a confidante? Her earlier words had suggested as much, and it took little imagination on Toni's part to realize that a young woman brought up away from her own tribe might find it hard to reveal her most personal hopes and longings to others who had been raised in quite different circumstances. In order to encourage Maria to talk if she wished to, Toni said, "Eketi is a very handsome man."

Maria's fingers faltered for a moment and then continued their twisting. She said nothing.

"He is very young to be such an important man in the tribe," Toni persisted. "How did he come to be chief?"

The direct question overcame Maria's reluctance. "Because he is stronger and braver than the other men," she said. Her voice trembled with a hesitant pride. "There is no test of courage Eketi could not pass. He can track a jaguar for a whole day without a rest. He can face a wild boar. He can take an electric eel into his bare hands and hold it without a quiver, when other men might scream from the pain. With his blowgun he can shoot a small bird high in a treetop, when it is so far that even Dr. Quental with his rifle might have trouble to take aim. And always Eketi brings it down, even when the bird is no bigger than a hummingbird, even when there is no curare on the tip of his dart...."

As if she realized she had admitted too much,

Maria fell into silence, in a state of some consternation. Her want of confidence put a new thought into Toni's mind: of course, Eketi must be married. Luís Quental had made some remark about monogamy that suggested such a possibility, and certainly Eketi was a man in his prime—old enough to have produced several children.

"I suppose there are women in the tribe," she said quietly, "who are envious of Eketi's wife."

"Eketi has no wife." Maria's voice was barely audible.

So the guess had been wrong: for Maria's sake, Toni felt relieved. "But surely he must have reached the age of marrying?"

"Oh, yes. A man of the Xara becomes a man, a real man, when he is very young, when the piece of wood is added to his lip. Eketi took himself a woman years ago, before he was chief, when he was even younger than I am today. But his wife died, and his children, too."

"What happened?" asked Toni gently.

"It happened in the time of the Big Sickness," Maria said simply in a sad voice. "That was before I returned to live with my own people. Dr. Quental, he told me that is when all of my own family died, when I had not even met them. But that...." A shadow passed through Maria's eyes, and she finished, "I cannot talk about that."

Toni bit back the question she had been about to ask. The Big Sickness? Perhaps it was cholera, or yellow fever, or some other jungle ailment? But if it was a painful subject for Maria, she had no wish to pursue it. There was also the distinct possibility that for Maria, discussion of her own background and her twinship was a taboo subject. Whatever the reasons for the girl's reluctance, Toni respected them.

"How long ago did Eketi's wife die?" she ventured, hoping to draw further confidences.

Maria sat with the cotton smock pulled modestly over her bent knees. Now she began to worry at the fabric that covered her legs, in a hesitant nervous gesture. "It is two years ago now. Eketi was very sad in the year that followed, the year Dr. Quental convinced me I must come back to live with the Xara. I think Eketi is over his sadness now and will soon pick another wife."

"Is there a woman he might pick, Maria?"

Maria's voice became a muffled whisper. "There are several young girls of marrying age," she said. "I think any of them would be glad to move into Eketi's hut. A man who is so strong, so fine, so handsome, so proud...."

Suddenly she broke off, and covered her confusion for again having confessed too much by saying, "Of course I do not think of such things. Eketi does not look in my direction. And I am past the age of marrying."

"You?" asked Toni, astonished. To her Maria seemed very young—no older than she herself had been when she married Matthew. And how young she had been then, how full of hope and promise, and how very much in love.... Why, Maria was hardly more than a child.

Maria explained a little more. "In this tribe most girls of fifteen are already mothers. And I...I will be twenty soon. Besides, I would be a very bad wife. Because I was not brought up with my people, I am not very fast or very clever at the things a Xara woman must do—the weaving of baskets, the working with bark, the grating of manioc, the drawing of designs with *genipap* juice—"

"You learned other things instead," Toni reminded her. "Portuguese, for one. Have you been teaching Eketi?"

Maria looked alarmed. "No, Eketi would not ask a woman to help him with such a thing. Dr. Quental has been teaching him, for he says that Eketi must learn, if he is to be a good chief for the Xara."

"What other things did the nuns teach you, Maria?"

"To read and to write." Maria overcame her timidity enough to raise her eyes, and in them was written a kind of anguish. "But those things do not make a good wife. What Xara warrior would want a woman such as I? I am ignorant in the ways of the tribe. And I am ...different."

Different? Yes, Maria certainly was different; and the miracle was that having been raised in a convent she had overcome her natural timorousness enough to return to the Xara at all.

Maria's eyes dropped again, and she plucked at her dress. "I am different because of ...this. When

others arrive from outside, as you did today, I feel I
must...."

"You didn't have to dress for us, Maria," Toni
assured her kindly.

The diffident voice slid down to the range of bare
audibility. "I dressed for me," Maria whispered.
Now her slender fingers came up to brace themselves
against her scarlet cheeks, as if in recollection of particularly painful memories. "It was very hard for me
at first, to...go naked as the other women do. But
I...learned, for I did not wish to be different. It
was...hard, but it did not...help. Oh, I have tried
to be the same, and still...."

All in hopes that Eketi would notice her, no doubt.
Poor, poor Maria. Her upbringing had prepared her
to be neither fish nor fowl. The nudity demanded by
life among the Xara would not sit well with the
modesty instilled by the nuns; the timorous girl must
have died a thousand deaths of mortification to find
courage to strip that very first time. And all to no
avail.

As for Eketi, he must be ten times a fool if he had
truly failed to notice this demure pretty girl! It was a
situation that awakened every sympathetic impulse
Toni possessed, but it was also a situation about
which she could do nothing. And considering her
own shaky relationship with Luís Quental, she could
not even broach the subject to him.

"We must go back now, *senhora*. The time is passing, and perhaps Eketi will begin to wonder. I would
not like to arouse his anger."

The time of sitting in a cool quiet place and thinking of another person's troubles had given Toni only temporary release from her intense physical discomfort. Waves of pain, this time accompanied by faint nausea, returned as she followed Maria's footsteps back to the Xara village.

She was relieved to see that the *caboclo* bearers, under Fernão's direction, were in process of pitching tents in the cleared fringe beside the river, beyond the ring of Xara huts. Perhaps before long she could excuse herself without losing too much face.

In the village clearing a score of small fires were now burning, and the women were tending their supper pots. In these duties the men seemed to have no part; their work of fishing and hunting must have been accomplished earlier in the day.

Eketi, perhaps mellowed by the powerful local wine known as *kashiri*, must have already given permission for some filming to be done. At the far side of the circle formed by the huts, Toni could see Ty at work with his equipment, the subject for the moment the young chieftain himself. For the benefit of the camera, Eketi was brandishing a spear and looking thoroughly ferocious; he had also donned a breechclout and a feathered necklace of beautiful design. With the ragged shorts gone and the fedora no longer on his head, he seemed to have grown in stature and nobility. How odd, mused Toni, that Eketi should think the trappings of civilization bestowed upon him any dignity at all. He was infinitely more impressive now—a healthy handsome man who might very well cause heartache in a young woman like Maria.

The other Xara males stood listening to their own voices on tape, so totally enthralled by Barney's Nagra sound system that they paid no attention at all to the whirring Arriflex camera—a ruse that must have been suggested by Luís Quental.

At Eketi's orders, the filming came to a brief halt while he heard Maria's shy-eyed and totally fabricated report, not one word of which Toni understood. She used the opportunity to speak quietly to Ty Chisholm, waiting until he had lifted his eye from the viewfinder.

"Where's Dr. Quental, Ty?"

Ty busied himself with changing lenses, not looking up for the moment. "In a hut over there, looking over the sick bay. There's quite a lineup. Last time I saw him, he was removing a plaster cast from someone's leg."

Toni glanced briefly backward and saw a cluster of Xara children surrounding an unmistakable tall figure. Quental was in process of demonstrating his stethoscope to a rapt young audience, and it appeared he might be tied up for a time. "Do you think you and Barney can get along without me for a while?"

"Sure." Ty at last looked up. "What's the matter, love—feeling under the weather?"

"I feel fine, Ty. Fit as a fiddle. But my feet are a little sore from the trek. I thought I'd go and lie down in my tent—but don't tell that to Quental!"

"What shall I tell him, then?"

"That I'm refreshing my makeup. But don't tell him anything unless he asks. He probably won't even notice I'm missing."

"But you will be around at suppertime, I presume," Ty noted, turning back to his Arriflex. "I'm told we'll be eating soon. Eketi has offered to let us share his meal. According to Quental, there's an old grandmother who cooks for his highness the chief. He says she's a hag to look at, but she puts together the best chow in the village. Turtle's eggs tonight, I hear. They tried to shoot a howler monkey in our honor, but didn't succeed."

"I'm glad of that," said Toni faintly, thinking of the almost human little faces she had seen in a distant tree early that morning.

Still bending over his camera, Ty drawled wickedly, "Quental says the Xara eat any damn thing that's edible, even grubs. Don't be surprised if you find a few in the pot."

Nausea climbed to Toni's throat and clung there, refusing to obey common sense. "Perhaps I'll pass on supper, Ty. I'm not hungry now, and if I get hungry later I have some dry biscuits in my kit, and some chocolate."

Ty glanced upward, his puckish face wearing the totally innocuous expression that told Toni he was up to no good. "If you don't fancy turtle's eggs, how about piranha? That's the other thing on the menu. Quental says it tastes very decent."

Toni swallowed a strong urge to make a fool of

herself. Desperate now, she longed only to stretch out in the privacy of her own tent and sleep until morning.

"And there are a few more specialties of the house—"

For once Toni didn't give a damn if Ty had the last laugh. "Don't bother going through the whole menu, Ty. This time you win. I confess I couldn't eat piranha if my life depended on it. Couldn't you make some excuse for me? Tell Quental any old thing."

"Tell him yourself," winked Ty, and turned back to resume filming before Eketi decided to take off in favor of the miracle show being offered by Barney.

Toni felt her elbow gripped strongly from behind at the very moment when she felt her legs were going to give out. "You'll eat whether you like it or not," came a low steely command at her ear. "It would be rude beyond belief to turn down Eketi's hospitality now. With food hard to come by, he's gone to great effort to put together a meal for so many visitors. Do you want to jeopardize your project just because your appetite rebels at the idea of piranha?"

Toni's senses lurched, but she voiced no further protest. Summoning the dregs of inner strength, she turned until all of that long lean body was in view.

Luís Quental's eyes fastened at once on her lips, and in them was a cold challenge. "As Eketi says," he mocked, "piranha eat us, we eat them. The Xara would not survive in this hard world if they had weak stomachs such as yours."

Ty overheard and turned briefly, frowning.

"Toni's never had a weak stomach before. Perhaps she's not feeling too well, despite what she says."

"I'm fine," protested Toni, pulling herself together by sheer grit force of will. "I suppose I can stomach piranha if I really must."

"Good." Luís Quental released his grip on her arm. "Because if there's the slightest indication that you're not feeling well, I'll have to get you away from this village at once. Otherwise. . . be prepared to eat with our host in half an hour."

Something told her it was not an idle threat. And so, because she could not allow the mission to abort on her behalf, she turned to help with the filming, all hope of a rest forgotten. Several minutes later, determined to provide visible proof that her physical condition did not warrant special treatment, she found herself helping Ty and Barney as they carried their equipment toward the tents on the fringe of the Xara village—a display of determination dictated largely by the fact that she knew Luís Quental was watching her.

At the tents she separated from her teammates in order to freshen for the evening. She was not alone in feeling hot, sticky and thoroughly disheveled after the long afternoon trek through the jungle. Ty and Barney voted in favor of a quick dip in the stream, in a spot that had been fenced off to prevent infestation by piranha; Toni decided in favor of a wet cloth and a small gourd of water provided by Fernão.

It helped to apply ointment to her skin and get into fresh clothes, and Toni's spirits had lifted somewhat before it was time to rejoin Eketi. She was peering into a small mirror, applying bright pink lipstick to give her face some color, when Barney appeared at the tent flap she had opened in order to admit more light. He was newly washed, brushed and shaved and had changed into a fresh shirt, a white one this time, in honor of the occasion.

"My God," exclaimed Barney with his eyes on Toni's lipstick tube, "that's just the thing. I forgot to bring a felt marker to make notations on my tape reels, and I've been looking all over for something to use. Is that stuff indelible?"

"Only when it's on something other than lips," Toni assured him with a last grimace in the mirror. The hair, smooth and shiny as licked butterscotch, was the only thing that passed muster in her eyes; her face was far too pale.

"Any chance I can borrow it from you?"

Toni replaced the cap of the lipstick, put down the mirror and tossed the small gilt tube in Barney's direction. "Be my guest. And no need to hurry about returning it. I have another."

Barney tucked the tube into his clean shirt pocket with a grateful grin. "Now hurry along, love. Quental's sent a Xara escort to bring us to Eketi's hut, and those warriors make me damn nervous. You know those curare-tipped spears of theirs? I almost backed into a nice sharp one when I was trying to get my Nagra away without losing it altogether. Quental warned me just in time."

Toni shuddered and eased herself out of her tiny

cramped tent to join Barney. "Around here it seems a little too easy to make a false step," she said more prophetically than she knew.

Somehow she managed to force herself into the appropriate behavior for the next two hours. The meal was made considerably easier because of the Xara attitude to women: Toni found herself eating at a respectful distance from the men. It was a silent meal shared with the old beldam who cooked for Eketi, who seemed toothlessly pleased to dip her fingers into Toni's bowl whenever she could. Somehow the bowl got emptied; and only Toni and the old grandmother knew how.

The men were occupied over drafts of potent fermented *kashiri* when Toni finally stumbled off to her readied tent. Hammocks could not be slung in tents as small as hers, so a thin lumpy mattress and a pillow of piassava fiber had been dragged into place—both, Fernão informed her, the property of Luís Quental himself.

She placed her flashlight on the mattress, lighted a hurricane lantern to leave burning in its stead, secured the tent flap with some care against the creatures of the night and dropped onto the mattress without even removing her boots.

Let the howler monkeys do their worst, she thought as she slid into sleep. Tonight she would not hear a thing. . . .

CHAPTER FIVE

IT WAS NOT LONG PAST DAWN when the commotion dragged Toni back to the land of the wakeful. Howler monkeys? No, those were human sounds, and there was an ugliness, a menace, in the very air.

She rolled off her mattress, feeling ill, wretched and all the more miserable because she had slept in her clothes. Her ankles above the tightly laced boots were swollen, she was sure, and so was every other part of her. But at least beneath the boots her feet were so numbed that she could feel nothing at all.

Her mind was still bleared with the long sleep when she stumbled to her tent flap, opened it—and froze. Like a scene out of a bad dream, two near-naked and utterly savage-looking Xara warriors were guarding the entrance to her tent. They wore no smiles to soften the intimidating effect of their lip disks, and their spears were pointed directly at her.

She inched her way into the open, moving with the utmost circumspection, and subsided white-faced into a sitting position in her tent entrance. The waving spear tips warned her to go no farther.

A quick appraisal of the situation told her that Ty and Barney were in similar dire straits, in the entrance of the adjacent tent no more than ten feet away.

"What's happened?" Toni asked in a hushed voice. The tightness of breath that had troubled her on the previous day had returned, but under the circumstances the condition seemed entirely natural. She kept one eye on the very tips of the spears, where a slick dark brown substance could mean only one thing.

"Ask Barney," said Ty dolefully.

"Practically nothing's happened," said Barney, sounding shaken. "All I did was go to the edge of the jungle about four o'clock this morning, only a few trees past the clearing. I was a little drunk, or I'd never have had the courage. We stayed up with Eketi, drinking *kashiri* until shortly before then. Ty was in pretty bad shape, too."

Ty put in his two cents worth of self-defense. "Hell, Toni, you know we don't usually overdo it. But Quental was giving Eketi a long lecture on the virtues of taking a wife and raising a family—or so we gathered, from the odd snatch we could understand. They were speaking Portuguese, a sort of weekly lesson, and it was pretty boring. We figured it would be rude to walk out on them, and as we couldn't understand more than the odd word...well, you know how it is. We indulged a little too much."

"Why on earth did you go into the jungle?" Toni asked, without taking her eyes off the spear tips.

"The howler monkeys had just started up their din," came Barney's miserable admission, "and I decided I might as well stay up and record some night sounds. It was a crazy thing to do, I know.''

"It doesn't sound exactly bright," Toni agreed dryly, "but it doesn't seem like a punishable offense, either. Why on earth would the Xara care?''

"There seems to be a strong suspicion that Barney had an assignation with a Xara woman," Ty revealed.

"My God, I wouldn't touch one of those dames with a ten-foot pole," Barney shuddered, "not after the stories we heard. There isn't enough *kashiri* in the world to make me do a damfool thing like that.''

A throbbing head and aching body were the last of Toni's worries now: the situation sounded far too serious for her liking. "Can't Dr. Quental do anything to help?''

"Quental's in the village now, trying to talk some sense into Eketi and the other men. Fernão here—" Ty tilted a shoulder at the tent on the far side of his own, and Toni risked a sideways glance "—Fernão and the other *caboclos* are in the same boat as us. Waiting for the verdict.''

At the third tent, Fernão sat with his head bowed, his face seamed with lines of resignation. Beside him, huddled in equal misery, were the two other men who had served as bearers during the jungle trek of the previous day. Although Fernão spoke the Xara dialect, he was making no efforts to converse with the men who stood guard. And because he spoke no English, his head had not even lifted at the present conversation.

Barney interjected a note of hopefulness. "Quental says this fellow Eketi isn't as hotheaded as the man who was chief before. In fact, we thought for a time that the whole thing was going to blow over, until someone identified the girl I'm supposed to have been leading down the garden path."

"Which girl was it?"

"The one in the dress."

"Maria," groaned Toni. Her heart sank another inch, if that was possible. Maria was doubtless somewhere inside the village circle, facing a fate similar to that now being brandished not two feet from her own face. "Perhaps you'd better tell me more about how it all came about," she said quietly.

"The Xara have a crazy little custom," Barney explained. "They all get up at about four in the morning, the whole damn village. It's one of the things that gave me the guts to go and start recording."

"They don't have clothes and they don't have blankets," Ty interjected, "so in those hours before dawn, when it gets really cold, they go and take a long dip in the stream. To warm up, if you can believe it. A hell of an icy place to warm up! We learned some of these things last night after you'd taken off to bed."

Barney took over the explanation. "Several people saw me coming out of the tent with a flashlight and heading for the edge of the jungle. They didn't pay me much attention at the time. But then, when they were all filing back from the river some time later, they spotted Maria coming *out* of the jungle. Someone remembered she hadn't been for the communal skinny dip, so...."

"The Xara always look for a quiet little nook in the jungle when they want to make love," Ty said glumly. "Partly for privacy, partly because it can't be managed too well in a hammock. That's another thing Quental told us last night, when we commented on the lack of walls."

"Maria claims she only wanted to be alone, but nobody believes her," Barney added.

"So they put two and two together and came up with two," Ty remarked in glum conclusion.

Toni reflected. After yesterday's conversation in Maria's private place, she for one believed the Xara girl. It was quite likely that Maria had gone to her private place to avoid the morning's communal nudity, especially with strangers around. But that, because it was a need the other Xara would not understand, would be very hard to prove.

"And where were you by the time the Xara came back from their swim, Barney?" Toni asked.

"Asleep in my tent. Good Lord, I wasn't two trees past the edge of the clearing when it came to me what a crazy thing I was doing. I hightailed it back to bed the first time something moved in the dark—and believe me, it wasn't a woman."

"And nobody saw you go back to your tent?"

"No. By then there wasn't a Xara within spotting distance."

"And they stayed down at the river for nearly an hour," Ty put in, "so there was plenty of time for the worst to happen."

"Except that it didn't," Barney gloomed. "Hell, I passed out without even taking off my clothes. At that point I couldn't have managed a button, let alone a broad."

A sidelong glance confirmed that Barney was still wearing last night's clothes, the white shirt now a little the worse for wear. Toni for one found every word of the story quite credible, but she was not the one that needed convincing.

"Oh, Lord." Her teeth worried at her lip as she considered the apparent hopelessness of the situation. All her continuing physical sufferings seemed unimportant in comparison to those threatening spear tips, which had not wavered by so much as an inch. There was no point expecting understanding from the Xara warriors who were standing guard. Their lip disks, their rippling muscles and the antagonistic expressions on their faces promised no quarter at all.

Luís Quental had said several times that the Xara tended to believe only those things for which they had the evidence of their eyes. And indubitably, with Barney's entry into the jungle and Maria's subsequent exit, they believed they *did* have the evidence of their eyes.

So why not inject some different evidence?

"Barney," she said slowly, "do you still have that lipstick tube I gave you yesterday?"

Barney patted his breast pocket. "Yes," he acknowledged.

"Can you manage to get a few traces of it on your shirtfront without those guards noticing? Not too much, and in an inconspicuous place. Perhaps under the shirt collar or on your chest. Maybe Ty can cover for you."

"Smart girl," murmured Ty, at once understanding Toni's intent. "Even Eketi admired our nice clean shirts last night."

He then coughed loudly and rose to his feet with one wary eye on the waving spears. In a loud obstreperous voice he started to speak to the guards, gesticulating all the while. For a few vital seconds no eyes but Toni's paid attention to the other American man still seated on the ground, crouching over his knees in seemingly innocuous fashion.

"Done," murmured Barney as he surreptitiously tossed something small into the tent behind him—the tube of lipstick, Toni was sure. He flashed a swift freckled grin at Toni. "Now it's up to you, sweetheart. If you can only get Fernão to translate...."

With Fernão's help it was not hard to convince the Xara guards that it had been Toni, not Maria, who had entertained Barney during those predawn hours. With the evidence of smeared pink lipstick on the underside of Barney's collar, and a little more that he had managed to stroke onto his chest, the facts seemed incontrovertible. Within moments the prisoners were being led to Eketi.

The Xara were observant if nothing else. Many people could testify that Barney had donned a fresh shirt before the previous night's feast. Many had seen him bathing in the river, his flesh unmarked by those traces of distinctive pink. Many could remember the exact color of the lipstick Toni had been wearing, and they all knew it was not the color of the *urucú* stain on Maria's face. And every single Xara tribesman, including Eketi himself, knew that Barney and Ty had stayed up until all hours drinking *kashiri*; that they had not returned to their tent until shortly before the howler monkeys set up their din. The only time Barney and Toni could have been intimate was during the period when the Xara were at the river; and the lipstick smears served as proof that they had indeed been intimate. And if Barney had been bedded down with Toni, how could he possibly have repeated the feat with Maria in such a short space of time?

"I would have mentioned it before, but I was trying to protect Toni," Barney insisted when asked why he had not revealed the facts before.

"Is she worth protecting?" Luís Quental muttered contemptuously through his teeth, before he turned to relay the latest developments to Eketi.

The whole charade put a sour taste in Toni's mouth, despite the reprieve from those threatening spears. But, she reflected with sinking spirits as she watched Luís Quental speaking persuasively to Eketi, the worst thing was that it had probably not been necessary at all.

By the time the Xara guards had herded their bunched prisoners into the village oval to display the new evidence they had been shown, Luís Quental had already been in process of leading a very frightened Maria into one of the huts, along with several of the

Xara men, among them Eketi himself. Maria's bent shamed head had told a part of the story; so had the stony expression on Eketi's face. At Quental's suggestion, Maria was to be examined for evidence of the virginity she persisted in protesting. But the doctor's word alone was not to be taken by the suspicious Xara braves; the tribe's vengeful males wanted to see for themselves.

At least, mused Toni, Maria had been spared the indignity of a public examination, something that would have mortified the painfully timid girl beyond belief. After much rhetoric among the Xara males, Eketi and his fellow tribesmen had accepted Barney's word, backed as it was by the evidence of the lipstick.

And Quental had accepted the story, too. On hearing it his eyes had glittered with disdain, not the relief one might have expected. Perhaps it was that, his icy contempt, which made Toni feel chilled to the bone for the rest of the morning, despite the growing heat of the day. Through a haze of happenings it was Quental's disapprobation that scored in Toni's consciousness; Quental's lean cynical face that loomed strong in her mind; Quental's taut mouth that told her the supposedly unseemly behavior did not meet with his favor. Each time his eyes touched on Toni, he pointedly turned away—but not before she had glimpsed his expression, one of the few things that seemed capable of penetrating her utter physical misery.

The rest of the morning passed in flashes. Xara

runners arriving with the enormously heavy sacks of gifts, only three hours after they had been dispatched through the jungle to fetch them—a burdened two-way journey that took less time than a single stretch had done on the previous day. Then Eketi distributing things: the Collins machetes and the aluminum cooking pots, and also matches, beads, magnifying glasses, combs and mirrors for the women, mouth organs, crayons, paper, sacks of salt. Ty filming; Barney recording—both scrupulous not to make a single false move. And through it all Luís Quental's scorn; and a cold, numb, heartsick feeling that Toni could not even blame completely on her physical wretchedness. Yet why should she care what he thought? And what right did he have to question her morals? Even if the morning's story had not been a total fabrication, Luís Quental was not the arbiter of her behavior.

Nevertheless, some inner voice told Toni that he did indeed judge her; that she had not yet heard the last of the morning's happenings; that she would be sorry, sorry, sorry....

In the final half hour before the slow, slogging return trek began, Toni was still wondering if the deception had been worth it. The farewell ceremonies now being celebrated in sonorous speeches seemed as endless as the welcoming ceremonies had been. Standing on her complaining feet on the outer fringe of a circle of men filled her with a numb envy for the women squatting elsewhere, largely excluded but at least comfortable in their exclusion. At the moment a little curare scratch might have been welcome; at least it sounded like a painless end.

"Senhora," whispered a timid feminine voice at Toni's ear. At the urging of a slender hand, she half turned to see who was plucking at her sleeve. Since Toni was standing on the very outskirts of the Xara warriors, a position dictated by her sex, her movements were unnoticed even by those nearest to her.

It was Maria, as Toni had known it must be. Creeping up from behind, the young girl had braved the possible wrath of the Xara males by advancing right to the very fringe of the circle in which they had gathered for the farewell ceremonies. All around the clearing, little huddles of women had halted their work and were watching through shuttered eyes, their scarlet-painted faces so still that it seemed they must be holding their breath as one, in expectation that Eketi's righteous fury would surely fall upon Maria's head at any moment.

"For you," whispered Maria, darting a swift nervous glance in Eketi's direction. She pressed something small, cold and weighty into Toni's hand and evaporated into a nearby circle of women as silently and as swiftly as she had come.

Toni quickly returned her attention to the grouping of men directly ahead, in order to assure herself that none of them had noticed Maria's lapse. Fortunately all eyes were turned in the direction of Eketi, who was in the act of declaiming a lengthy speech. And Eketi himself—had his eyes flickered briefly in Maria's direction? At first Toni thought they had,

but when the young chieftain continued his oratory
without a single pause, she concluded that Maria's
daring venture into male territory had not been
noted.

Surreptitiously Toni examined the thing that Maria
had placed in her hand. It was a green stone suspended on a thong. Although not a gemstone, it had been
inexpertly carved to represent a reticent turtle with its
head inside its shell. The stone appeared to be very
old; the marks of the carving were blurred by age.
Clearly it was a crude primitive piece and not likely
of great intrinsic value; all the same Toni was sure it
was one of Maria's most prized possessions. Perhaps
handed by Maria's mother to the priest who had
saved one of her twins from certain extinction so
many years before?

Toni was unutterably moved by the gesture. Her
throat grew tight as she considered what courage it
must have taken for the Xara girl to overcome her
natural timorousness, especially in full view of Eketi.
Because she sensed that Maria was watching her now,
and because she wanted the young Xara woman to
know that the gift had been accepted in the spirit intended, Toni quietly slid the thong over her head and
dropped the green stone into the valley between her
breasts, where her shirt would hide it from the possible curiosity of the Xara men. As the cold stone connected with her flesh, Toni had to fight back the
beginnings of tears.

For the first time since she and Barney had told
their fictitious tale, the knife edge of Luís Quental's

contempt seemed blunted. And all by the memory of the gratitude that had shimmered, briefly but unmistakably, in Maria's liquid eyes.

Perhaps the morning's pretense had been worthwhile, after all.

LEFT FOOT. Right foot. Left foot. Right foot. Forget the shooting pains. Forget the sweat. Forget the insects. Forget the difficulty of drawing every breath. Forget everything but the path and the plodding, plodding on. Left foot. Right foot.

"Perhaps you would be less weary, *senhora*, if you had taken more sleep in the night." The insidious murmur was so soft it was hardly louder than the steady shush-shush of booted feet on the floor of the damp jungle path. Oh, why didn't Luís Quental stop insinuating his verbal tortures in her ear?

Right foot. Left foot. Right foot. Toni was dry of lip, bleary of eye, weary of limb, sore of bone and numb of brain. She ached in every joint. To breathe was to suffer. She hardly knew what Quental was saying, and in her less lucid moments she wondered if Quental was really talking at all; if his voice was only a creation of her own mind. Perhaps it was just a jungle madness that had taken possession of her. The Green Hell of her own imagination.

"Is it growing difficult, *senhora*, to move your feet?" No, that scornful mockery was quite real. "I warned you this trip was too hard for a woman as soft, as yielding, as you. As I told you before, I'm prepared to carry you. Surely you can't continue to refuse?''

Toni managed to shake her head in concert with her numb plodding legs, in lieu of a verbal refusal. Her breathing was too shallow now to allow for a response; she felt decidedly asthmatic.

"Are you afraid to confess your weaknesses?" he murmured. "Or is it that you're afraid to be held in my arms? My arms are not so different, *senhora*, from the arms of any other man you've known. *Meu Deus*, but you are a silly woman. How can you pretend the idea of being carried offends you? It is a far less intimate embrace, you must admit, than the one you submitted to last night.''

Toni was too exhausted to respond to this renewed evidence that Quental still believed the prevarications of the morning. Ty and Barney had explained the truth to him shortly after the Xara village had been put behind, but Quental had only turned his back, his black eyes glinting with disbelief and scorn. What was it he had muttered then? "Like the Xara, there are times when I, too, believe the evidence of my eyes.''

"Give in, *senhora*," the inexorable murmur went on. "The burden on my back can be left behind; I can return for it later. Why are you so stubborn now? Last night you were not so loath to lie in a man's arms. Lie there and more. . . .''

Left foot. Right foot. And still the relentless murmur assaulted her from behind. "How many times have you been held in other arms? How many different men? And yet you refuse to be held in mine—in the most innocent of embraces. Why do you continue to refuse?''

The determined forward rhythm of her feet answered him. She moved like an automaton now, not wanting to think, because to think might be to stop the pistonlike thrust of her pained muscles; to think might be to submit to Luís Quental. And that she would never do.

Right foot. Left foot. Right foot.

At some point early in the trip those strong hands behind her had brought her to a forcible halt and removed the rucksack from her shoulders. She had not objected because she had not had strength to object; nor had she thanked him; nor had she even turned to face him. When had that been? So long ago. A thousand thousand steps ago. And having removed the rucksack, he had moved even closer to her in the line, so close that she could almost feel his breath stirring in her hair. All the better to torture her with his cruel insinuations.

Yet perhaps she should be grateful to Quental, for his taunts had kept her going long after every muscle in her body screamed surrender. As they kept her going now. Left foot. Right foot. Left foot. Right foot. . . .

''Thank God!'' came Barney's heartfelt exclamation a short time later, from two positions ahead in the line. His voice sounded very far away, but she knew it was not. She raised her head wearily and halted in her leaden tracks. Directly ahead, the late-afternoon sunlight of the hospital clearing hurt her eyes after the deep gloom of the humid rain forest.

"I thought we'd never make it," came Ty's exhausted answer from directly ahead of her. His burdened back was turned, and so Toni had trouble making out the words as he continued to move forward. She herself could not; her feet felt rooted to the ground.

"Move along," said a steely voice from behind, and when she did not do so, Quental added, "The time for giving in was half an hour ago. Surely now you can find strength to continue for a few more feet?"

Ty and Barney and all the *caboclo* bearers were well out of the jungle now. Out of the jungle was only about one step away. An eternity away. Left foot. Left foot. *Left foot.*

"C'mon, slowpoke, what's—" Ty half turned to look over his laden sagging shoulders. He stopped in his tracks. "Good Lord, Toni, what is it? You look *awful*!"

"Left foot." Her dry lips formed the words half to herself. Her knees seemed to have a mind of their own, wanting to move in every which way except the one way she wanted them to go. Why were they all staring at her? Barney, Ty, even the *caboclos*? And Getulio—he had emerged from the clinic building and hurried forward at first sounds of the party's return. And he was staring, too.

"Left foot," she wheezed to herself, and the extra expenditure of breath caused her to pitch forward.

She was hardly conscious of the hands that caught her from behind before she could make contact with the forest floor; hardly aware of the low curse that was ground out so close to her ear; hardly aware of the viselike grip that pulled her close against warm supporting strength.

"Getulio, go and prepare a bed. For now we'll put her on the daybed in my bungalow." The curt command was issued by the one man Toni could not see, the man who had helped make every step of this trip an exercise in self-inflicted torment. "The *senhora* needs to rest, and I think a hammock will not do."

"I'm...all...right," Toni got out in an unnaturally labored voice. The moment of blackness had passed, but she was still too far gone to realize that she would not be believed. Feebly she tried to free herself, but her weak efforts met with no success.

"Toni, you're white as a sheet," Barney said. "Why didn't you say something?"

Toni felt herself swept into a pair of muscular arms before her legs had another chance to buckle beneath her. *"Meu Deus,"* gritted the voice that had such power to cause distress. "You fool, you little fool! What were you trying to prove?"

He was angry, so very angry. She could tell by the ferocious tension in his sinewed arms; she could tell by the probing fury in his eyes, sweeping over her body, searching for the signs of her weakness. And somehow that, the terrible anger in Quental's face, seemed the hardest thing to bear. Tears over which she had no control sprang to her eyes and hovered there, swimming but not sliding over her ashen cheeks.

"Wait, Quental; you can't carry her with all that stuff on your back. Here, let me help...."

Quental evaded Barney's reaching hands with a bitter impatient oath. "Haven't you already done enough?" he rapped out, in the kind of voice that caused Barney to back away. "If you'd allowed her a good rest last night, she'd be in better condition to-day. Stand aside! She doesn't need a lover now; she needs a doctor. Leave her to me! If you so much as lay a hand on her, you'll live to regret it. Out of my way!"

As Quental started to stride toward the low bunga-low that was his own, Barney called after him, "What the hell's the matter with you, Quental? We told you we invented that tale! I was in my tent, not hers! And even if I had been her lover—which I haven't—it's none of your damn business! Toni's her own mistress!"

"And everyone else's," came a hiss through clenched teeth, the sound so low that it might have been just another figment of Toni's benumbed brain. Oh, damn. If her legs and her tear ducts had to betray her, why couldn't they have waited for just two more minutes?

Quental kicked open the screen door to his bunga-low with an impatient booted foot and stepped in-side. In her present state, Toni was in no condition to appraise the somewhat Spartan interior. With arms to support her and no need now for enough oxygen to support a strenuous march, her breathing had become marginally easier, but that was of little comfort. She remained mutely miserable about her state of appalling helplessness, and unhappily conscious of the tall grim-looking man who held her in an immutable grip while Getulio hastily applied sheets and a pillow to a daybed in one corner. From the close still way Quental held her, she knew he was listening with the professional part of his mind to every small rattle in her chest.

At last Getulio finished and stood back. "It is not so comfortable as a hammock, *senhora*," he apologized, looking concerned, "but as the doctor's bungalow has no bedroom, and no extra hooks upon the walls...."

Pulses suddenly unsteady, Toni glanced at her captor. All at once she was gasping again for the air that seemed not to want to enter her lungs. "I can't... take your... bed," she protested.

The daunting line of Luís Quental's mouth told her he would brook no arguments. "I never use it," he said in a quelling voice, then switched to Portuguese. "*Muito bem*, Getulio. Now lay an extra sheet over the foot of the bed, where the *senhora*'s boots will be."

Quental added a few more instructions in Portuguese, and Toni realized he was asking for his medical kit, which must have been abandoned on the path. Getulio dropped the second sheet and took off like a jackrabbit, banging the front door behind him. Toni found herself laid upon the daybed more gently than she'd expected. Unable to perform a proper examination until Getulio returned, Quental moved to the foot of the bed and sat on it, not troubling to pull up a chair as he unlaced one of her mud-caked boots.

"Too small," he frowned as he levered the boot from her foot and removed the sock. "I suspected as much from the way you were walking. Moreover, your boots were laced too tightly."

Pushing the leg of her trousers higher, he probed the ankle and the calf lightly, his strong sure fingers reflecting none of the anger that built in his face at sight of the flesh thus revealed.

"Meu Deus," he bit out under his breath, scowling as though he did not like the look of the ankle. Toni winced with pain and turned her eyes away. *She* did not like the look of the ankle, either. The little she could see was puffy and faintly pink with rash, as she had suspected it might be. She had not uncovered her body this morning, not even to her own eyes—partly from exhaustion and partly, she admitted now to herself, because she had not wanted to see. The glimpses she had taken while washing prior to supper the previous evening had been anything but reassuring; the rash had been spreading even then. How horrible that Luís Quental of all people should be able to witness the signs of her inability to withstand the rigors of the jungle!

"I was...all right...until today," she lied feebly through labored breaths.

Quental compressed his lips but did not comment on the prevarication. His voice was terse, urgent. "When did you first see this rash?"

"Tuesday...night."

"Your first night here," he muttered. "And this shortness of breath—have you ever been asthmatic?"

"N...no."

"When did you first notice that particular symptom?"

"That same...afternoon," she admitted reluctantly, air whinnying out with the effort of respiration. "It wasn't too...bad...at the...time."

"I'll do something about it as soon as I determine the cause." At the moment he seemed more interested in the cause than in the symptom, and the repressed anger in his face suggested very little concern for her as a patient.

As he unlaced the second boot, he asked a number of curt telling questions, many of them so incisive that Toni found herself admitting more of the truth than she had intended. "The rash...came... after...the *pium*...bites went down," she confessed at last.

He drew a chair into place beside the bed and pushed her sleeves high on her arms to examine the flesh that had been concealed beneath the cloth. His inspection was impartial and clinical, and his fingers moved over the surface no more than necessary.

"I told you that any medical problems were to be brought to my attention before the trip to the Xara village. Do you have some excuse for ignoring that order?"

Aware of the black criticism in his voice, Toni gasped out a miserable lie. "The...bites...improved," she said. "I was...fine...yesterday."

As he placed his hand on her forehead, there was disapproval in every tight line of his mouth. The hand felt cool, steady and reassuring in a way his expression did not. "Even if the initial symptoms vanished for a time, there's no excuse for taking into your own hands what should have been a doctor's decision. If this happens to be something infectious...."

That particular sentence trailed off on a note so dire that Toni had to clench her teeth for a moment in order to prevent them from chattering. "I'm not...that...sick," she struggled out at last.

"Perhaps not," he agreed grimly, finally removing his hand. "But the decision was not yours to make. Have you no conception of the consequences if...." He stopped, forced his scowl into a more orderly expression and started again. "There's no point second-guessing before Getulio brings my medical bag. There may be no problem. And as you were well enough last night to entertain your friend...."

"I...didn't," she protested in a gasp, but that only caused a deepening of the thunderous lines around his mouth.

At this point Getulio arrived with the medical bag, full of apologies because Fernão had carried it to the clinic, causing some delay. At a curt word from Quental, his assistant pulled a small table closer to the bedside, laid out towels and washcloths and vanished only to return with a shallow enamel basin of water. Moments later he left.

Through this minor flurry of activity, Toni submitted to the expected thermometer, flinching only slightly in the moment when Luís Quental's fingers seized her wrist to check her pulse rate. In the next few moments of enforced silence she was far too conscious of the strong fingers that captured her wrist; of the lean grim face bent in concentration; of the assured economical movement of his wrist as he shook the thermometer down. The tension in his face relaxed to a considerable degree after he'd read her temperature.

"How. . . is it?" she wheezed.

"Normal." His anger had subsided, and there was a note in his voice that sounded almost like relief. She might have been flattered by that if he had not added so coolly, "But that doesn't necessarily mean you are."

"I think. . . I'm a-allergic. . . to the Amazon," she confessed with difficulty, making a sorry stab at lightness as Quental moved from the chair he had been occupying and lowered himself onto the bed, only a few inches from her waist.

"I think you're allergic to something else," he contradicted gravely as he pushed her collar aside to examine her throat. Toni knew it was only the extremity of her own distress that caused the two fat waiting tears to leave her eyes and slide down her cheeks unchecked. Why did he finally have to look at her now, when she looked like this?

And why should an insane thought like that occur to her? It didn't really matter what he thought....

And then his hands moved to the buttons of her shirt. She knew better than to protest, any more than she would have protested with any doctor; but perhaps the reluctance she did not voice was apparent in the sudden twist of her mouth and in the way she turned her head to the wall.

"Try to remember I'm a doctor," Quental said with a strong element of sarcasm in his voice. But for the moment his hands hovered in the air above her breast, leaving the buttons alone.

It was the weakness, it must be the weakness that prevented her from behaving in a rational manner. Toni's fingers traveled to her face and stayed there, spread defensively, as if by hiding her cheeks and her eyes she could shut out the knowledge of what Quental's expression must be—scornful, cynical, impatient with this idiotic reticence she was showing. Being bitterly ashamed of herself for those two recalcitrant tears did nothing to help. She had not cried for years, not since Matthew's death; but pride prevented her from telling that to Quental now. Oh, damn, damn, damn.

"Surely you're not always so modest," he observed in an arid tone.

Her breath was ragged, and not just from the asthmatic effect. "I'm not...trying to stop you. It's just that... I don't want you... you or anyone... to s-see me like this. I look so... so *awful*."

And then, because that sounded like such a typically feminine thing to say, and one that would only cause a deepening of the disdain in those dark eyes, she stuttered on, "I'm s-sorry, Luís...." She choked for air and swallowed painfully as she realized what she had called him. "Dr. Quental," she corrected without opening her eyes.

He did not comment on her lapse. His hands returned to her shirt, and this time Toni managed to still her quivering nerves. As the top button succumbed to his authoritative fingers, he said in a quiet reassuring voice that held none of the scorn she had expected, and none of the sarcasm of a moment ago, "You see, *senhora*, it is not so hard when you think of me as a doctor and not as a man."

And yet it was impossible for her to think of him as anything else. How humiliating that any man should see her like this, but especially Luís Quental. As his fingers continued their slow journey to the second button and the third, she kept her fingertips pressed tightly to her lids. She did not need to see to guess that all parts of her body must look much as her arms and legs had done. Oh, why was she making such a fool of herself? And why did she have to pick this exact moment in time to start thinking of him as Luís?

He parted the shirt without releasing the clip that kept her brassiere in place, once again careful to make contact no more than necessary. Toni felt his fingers touch briefly on the crude green stone that rested in the hollow between her breasts. He muttered an incomprehensible foreign word, one that did not sound like Portuguese but more like the dialect spoken in the Xara village. "Where did you get that?" Then in swift succession he added, "Don't bother answering; you can tell me tomorrow."

His fingers, strong, cool, assured, moved for a moment at the base of her throat and the base of her ears, finding pulses, feeling glands. The touch was impersonal and professional and did not last long. Then the stethoscope: and that, too, was done.

"Don't worry, you'll survive," he informed her as he nested the stethoscope back in its case. "You should be all right by tomorrow. But at the moment your system needs a little help to shake off the effects of the *piums*."

"The...*piums*?" she croaked faintly, opening her eyes to ask the question.

He had moved back to the low chair at the side of the daybed, and there he sat—the broad shoulders inclined forward, the elbows loose on his knees, a dark forelock falling over his brow. His hard mouth was expressionless, neither stern nor smiling; his hooded eyes were fastened to the fingers she had just lowered from her face. Yet something told Toni that for some reason the diagnosis was to his liking.

"You're allergic to *piums*," he said dryly. "The *piums* on the river undoubtedly started the reaction, although from what you tell me you must have shaken it off at the time. But allergies sometimes have a cumulative effect, and I suspect that the *piums* at the

Xara village were the last straw. You must have
reacted to them violently the second time around.''

Piums at the Xara village? She stared, not com-
prehending, until he went on, ''There were quite a
few *piums* around this morning. Didn't you notice?''

''No,'' she admitted in a breathy gulp, not adding
that she had been too miserable by then to notice very
much at all.

''Hmm.'' He frowned at her, looking slightly puzzled. ''If you'd told me about the problem earlier, I
could have given you something to prevent this kind
of reaction. But as it is...I'm going to have to give
you a couple of shots. First Adrenalin, to get your
own defenses working. Then Benadryl—an antihistamine that should set you to rights. They won't help
your sore feet, of course. Only a new pair of boots
will do that.''

As he leaned over to rummage in his medical bag
Toni fought back a desire to burst into tears of weak
relief. So it wasn't merely inability to cope with the
jungle, after all.... She struggled to control the silly
impulse to cry as she watched the lean intent face
now frowning with clinical detachment at a syringe.
The cold swab of alcohol and then the sharp sting of
a hypodermic in her arm brought her back to her
senses, and after a quick gasp her expression became
more orderly. A second shot followed in quick succession, this time arousing no audible reaction.

After that there were two fuschia-colored tablets to
be swallowed, a feat Toni managed without trouble.
With an understanding of her problem bringing some

mental relief, a certain amount of strength was returning. Or had the shots already done their work? The impulse to cry had vanished, and although exhaustion remained, already her breathing seemed far less labored.

Luís Quental scowled in the direction of her hip as he at last rose to his feet. "Now I want you to undress and give yourself a sponge bath. I think you're capable. I've left you some ointment, too—something that will do the job a little more efficiently than whatever you may have been using."

Toni pulled herself up on the pillow, once more in control of herself. To her mild surprise, the exertion caused no trouble to her lungs. Gratefully she drew in a deep breath.

"Am I going to have this kind of trouble every time I see a *pium*?" So the instant relief had not been imagined: the sentence had come out with none of the difficulty of before.

"Not if you follow doctor's orders. That includes taking antihistamines whenever you're likely to have an encounter."

Toni allowed herself a deep sigh of relief; this next month or so in the Amazon jungle would have been quite impossible if the trouble had flared up continually.

"Doctor's orders also include staying off your feet until further notice. I think you'll be back to normal in a short time, but I intend to take no chances. In a little while Getulio will bring you a supper tray." Without explaining his intent, he moved across the room and through an open door, returning seconds later with one of his own shirts. "You can use this as a nightshirt—unless you'd prefer me to fetch your personal sleeping apparel."

"No, I...that won't be necessary." A quiver of weakness that had nothing to do with *piums* assailed her at the mental image of those lean long fingers pawing through her most intimate clothing. "Actually, I'd prefer to go back to my own place before bedtime," she said.

Quental had already reached the front door of the bungalow, his evident intent to leave Toni alone while she performed her ablutions. But now, with his hand on the doorknob, he paused and turned. For the first time in memory he looked at her directly, for a long searching moment. In the deeply set eyes there was something dark, burning, purposeful.

"No," he said, "I won't permit that."

"Then perhaps you should move me into the hospital."

"Absolutely not. You're allergic—not ill. Other than the *pium* reaction and a few blisters on your feet, there's nothing wrong with you that won't be cured by a good rest."

"But—"

"You'll sleep here as long as I tell you to," he said curtly, and walked out.

Toni's head fell back on the pillow, and she stared at the screen door that had banged behind him like an exclamation point to the sentence. Surely he meant merely that he intended to relinquish his quarters to her, as they were more comfortable than those she had been assigned? Surely he intended to move into the hospital with the other men?

Surely he had not meant those words the way they sounded.

Or had he?

CHAPTER SIX

TONI AWAKENED SLOWLY AND RELUCTANTLY, unwilling to abandon the warm pleasurable lethargy induced by a good sleep and a return of some bodily well-being. Her eyes feathered lazily open to encounter a darkness where only the faintest silver of moonglow revealed shapes and shadows. To her ears came a faint regularity of breathing—the sound of a quiet sleeper. Disoriented for the moment, she could not remember where she was.

And then she knew. Without alarm her eyes scouted the darkness again, finally discerning the dim silhouette of a hammock suspended not ten feet from her bedside. Its taut curved outlines told her it was burdened by a human weight, and she needed no guesswork to know whose weight it was.

So he had not moved to the hospital building with the other men.... But the fleeting sleepy thought was followed by a vague comfortable realization. Surely her imagination had been overactive last night? Surely his concern was only for a patient's well-being? His handling of her during yesterday's examination had hardly suggested intentions of a lascivious nature.

Normally Toni was alert and bright-eyed when she wakened. Still groggy this time, she concluded that the colored pills she had been given must have been sleeping medication of some sort. Certainly she had fallen asleep before her supper had arrived last night. She rolled onto one side, curious to see if the promised food had been left at her bedside. On the table where towels and basin had rested last night her eye encountered white dishes that gleamed like pale bone, luminiscent in the moonlight. She was not hungry at the moment, so she reached for nothing. She was sleepily distressed to discover that her strength had not completely returned. The stresses of the past few days had taken their toll, it seemed. Although medication had freed her breathing and relieved that swollen sensation, it had not yet restored her to her energetic self. All the same, she should be grateful for the merciful relief offered by the shots. And the sponge bath, too, had certainly. . . .

What sponge bath? Jangles of alarm tingled her to full wakefulness as she remembered that she had done no more than wipe her face and her throat. She had tried to remove her shirt, going so far as to get one arm out of a sleeve before falling back against the pillow, exhausted. She had intended to start again after a moment's rest. And that was the last thing she remembered.

Yet her searching hands now told her that she was very definitely out of her own clothes, every last stitch. The loose man's shirt she wore, twisted around her midriff, was several sizes too big. And below that there was nothing—nothing but skin that felt soothed, cool from the Amazon night and unmistakably clean. At some point a sheet and blanket had been drawn up to her waist, possibly not so very long ago, because the real chill did not usually set in until halfway through the night.

She had been sponged clean since yesterday's jungle trek, and very thoroughly, too; and she had certainly not done it herself.

At the very thought of what must have happened, peculiar feelings assailed her lower limbs, turning them shaky. Luís Quental might avoid looking at her when she was aware of his attention, but had he been so circumspect when she was asleep?

No, drugged, corrected Toni, with a touch of anger that helped alleviate that feeling of abject helplessness. She needed only the memory of Luís Quental's terrible tension by the riverside to tell her that, given the circumstances of last night, he must have succumbed to the temptation to look at her, and very thoroughly, too. No doubt that dark burning gaze had possessed her flesh without a qualm; and perhaps the hands that had been so impartial yesterday had been less so during the intimate ablutions required. Oh, Lord, how long had he fed his fierce hungers?

Certainly, in light of this new and unsettling development, it seemed unwise to remain in this bungalow for any longer than necessary, despite all doctor's orders to the contrary.

The sudden explosion of howler monkeys into the

darkness shattered the sequence of Toni's thoughts, but only momentarily. The unearthly din that had been so terrifying two nights ago was far less so by now. She cast a brief glance in the direction of the hammock: that long lean body had not even stirred at the sound. Wryly she reflected that it might be possible in time to accustom oneself to the Amazon— *piums*, in her case, excepted.

Surely if the howler monkeys had set up their caterwauling it could not be so many hours from dawn? And if she could stay awake until then and gather her strength, she could certainly manage the trip across the compound to her own shelter. The prospect of undertaking the journey on her shaky legs was daunting, but less daunting than staying here with her unnerving host.

A pink dawn was barely staining the sky when Toni slid her naked legs out from under the covers. She remained seated, not putting her feet on the floor, while she looked around the dim room to see if she could spot her own clothes. They were nowhere in sight; perhaps they had been given to Getulio for washing? They had certainly needed it! Her boots, too, were gone, perhaps for cleaning, but a pair of moccasins—her own—were on the floor beside the bed. Automatically she reached over and shook them out, as she had been warned she must always do. Less than three days in the Amazon and already she was becoming an old hand!

She took some brief pleasure in noting that her limbs were once more normal in appearance: long, slender, shapely and, as far as she could see in this uncertain light, no longer bearing traces of an unsightly rash.

But if the legs were normal in appearance they were normal in no other way; they almost buckled when she put her weight on them. A moment passed before her equilibrium was restored, and she realized the effect was only momentary—the result of muscle strain and possibly medication. She made a face at the shirttails flapping about her thighs. But its owner was a tall man, and the shirt covered her adequately if not elegantly. Well, it would have to do. She set one precarious foot out to begin her journey.

"I told you to stay off your feet until further notice," said a cool authoritative voice.

Toni gasped softly; she was certain she had not made a single noise. As her knees gave way completely, she collapsed back onto the bed and sat there staring at Luís Quental. How could he possibly have heard her over the incessant chorus of early-morning jungle sounds that filled the air?

He had not stirred except to turn his head. His eyes were totally wakeful, alert and darkly enigmatic. She had not yet grown accustomed to the new directness of that gaze; it filled her with wobbly sensations.

"Moreover, I told you you were sleeping here until I permitted otherwise. In this compound everyone obeys my orders. Where did you think you were going?"

"To my own quarters. I feel fine now."

"What quarters?" came the sarcastic rejoinder.

He reared himself up on one elbow, without once taking his eyes off her face. The growing light in the bungalow revealed that he was clad in pajamas of a pale cream color that emphasized the depth of his tan, with a light blanket thrown over his lower limbs. "Getulio and I looked that shelter over yesterday, to see what could be done about repairing the chinks. We decided the whole structure was too unsteady to be worth the effort, so Getulio dismantled it altogether."

Toni gasped, this time audibly. Those dark eyes had turned decidedly derisive, and even the normally grim mouth had curled into the beginnings of a taunting smile.

"Getulio found nothing strange in my order. A hut like that can be rebuilt in an afternoon, with the help of a few *caboclos* from the village. Getulio will see to doing it. . .later. Believe me, by the time I permit you to lie under your own roof, the structure will be very much sounder."

Toni's poise was still shaken. "And when will that be? Surely you don't expect me to stay here with you!"

His incipient smile vanished with the abruptness of a switchblade being sheathed. He settled back on his hammock once more, and rested the back of one loosely curled hand over his eyes. Only his mouth was visible now, and it was expressionless but for the bitter lines that seemed permanently molded into place. "Only twenty-four hours ago you had no such qualms about sharing quarters with another man," he pointed out cynically.

Annoyance caused Toni to bite her lip so forcefully that it hurt. "You really aren't going to believe me, are you?" she said, putting a caustic ring into her voice.

"No," came the aloof answer, followed by a full ten seconds during which Toni steamed in silence.

"Nothing happened at the Xara village," she stated at last, her voice well chilled to conceal the fact that she had reached boiling point. "But even if it had, you have no reason to think I'd be willing to stay under this roof."

"Surely you don't believe," came the arid observation, "that I would take advantage of the situation. I am a doctor, *senhora*, and you are my patient. As long as that situation persists you are quite safe with me. You will move out when I allow it, and not before. And I will certainly not allow it before I decide you're cured! Which, if you continue to exercise your childish emotions, may be longer than you think."

Every atom of Toni's body quivered, partly because she was sure she had managed to conceal her emotions very well. Force of habit helped her to hold her tongue until she could control it again. "And exactly when, in your medical opinion, will I be cured?" she asked, with admirable control, considering her continuing state of anger.

He reacted to the touch of sarcasm not at all. "I'll decide...later. After yesterday's exertions, a day's rest is probably in order, although I may allow you out of bed for a few hours later on. I can hardly give an informed opinion until I've examined you again."

"Which you did last night," Toni snapped, all caution suddenly flying to the winds. "And very thoroughly, I'm sure! I might have known when you gave me those sleeping pills that you only wanted to look to your heart's content. What did you see, Dr. Quental? What did you *touch*?"

The bronzed hand at once vanished from his eyes. The gaze that once more turned in her direction was cold, proud and disdainful. "Is that your opinion of my professional ethics?"

"Yes!"

"Then form a new opinion at once." His retort was so positive and scornful that Toni sensed he could only be telling the truth. "Those were not sleeping pills, but the oral antihistamine you'll continue to take whenever there's a prospect that you might encounter *piums*...in order, *senhora*, that I do not have to prick you full of so many holes that you feel like a pincushion. If you didn't wake, it's because your body told you not to wake—just as it should be telling you now to lie down and stop this foolish feminine behavior."

Toni stared. Was it possible she had been mistaken about Luís Quental? It could very well be that the pills had not been a sleeping medication, as her suspicious mind had suggested earlier. If so, she had only herself to blame for not waking.

All the same, how thoroughly had he feasted his eyes?

"Antihistamines do make a person sleepy," he went on shortly, heaping more coals of fire upon her head. "In any case it was Getulio who bathed you and changed you for the night. He's used to orderly duty; he's been doing it for many years."

The shakiness that assailed Toni this time was due to reaction, not to rage. It was evident that upon finding herself clean and clad in the nightshirt, she had come to some very wrong conclusions, and these had to be quickly revised. Oh, Lord, why had she issued those wild accusations?

She hated having to apologize to Luís Quental, but she was mature enough to know she must do so at once. "I'm sorry," she said quietly, her long lashes fanning downward to shield her eyes. "I seem to have misjudged you. I thought—"

"It's very clear what you thought." The scornful sardonic voice discounted her low apology. "Your encounter with the Amazon, *senhora*, appears to have affected your powers of reasoning. Even if I had ulterior motives, how could I possibly pursue them under the circumstances? If I tried, your American friends would surely leap to defend your—" again that marked, mocking hesitation "—your honor. Now lie down and rest; it's still very early."

Toni felt about as large as a *pium* herself as she settled back on the bed. Already the air was growing too warm for the blanket, and so she pushed it away with her foot, intending to use only the top sheet to cover her lower limbs. In the process the nightshirt shifted, revealing for one brief instant too much of her thigh. She glanced upward quickly: Luís Quental was no longer even looking in her direction. Clearly it was not he who had the nasty mind; it was she herself. Chastened by his reprimand and ashamed now for her unjust suspicion, she wanted to say something to mend fences—if such a thing were possible.

"I really am sorry. It seems you've had only my welfare in mind, and I . . . I've been churlish. It's very good of you to ask Getulio to rebuild the shelter. When will it be ready?"

There followed some moments of silence during which his only comment on her second apology was to put on a sour expression. As to her question about the shelter, he did not answer it at all. Well, thought Toni without pursuing the matter, he probably found it hard to forgive her for her ill-warranted accusations.

During this time of silence he threw off his blanket, revealing the rest of his cream-colored cotton pajamas. The move delineated the powerful musculature of the long legs a little too clearly, and Toni turned her eyes to other parts of the room. This bungalow certainly was more sturdily built than the small structure she had been assigned earlier: its ceiling as well as its walls were of a cool white stucco that would allow no rain or insects or horrible creatures of the night to penetrate. The furniture, bamboo for the most part, was simple and spare and not unattractive. Much of the bungalow appeared to be one large room, which might account for the lack of a bedroom. Possibly that one open door led to a dressing room or a study?

Yes, it had been thoughtful of Luís Quental to

allow her to sleep in here, and to put Getulio to work on rebuilding. With that curious pendulum effect that sometimes comes after misjudgment of another person, Toni began to wonder if she had been unfair in other ways. Feelings bordering on warmth started to stir as she remembered other things—the affectionate respectful way the Xara had greeted the doctor; the way he had relieved her of her burden during the jungle trek; the way he had respected her reluctance to undress during last night's medical examination.

It could not be said that her attitude to him had undergone a complete reversal, but it was certainly in the process of being reassessed. ˙

"I promise I'll follow doctor's orders from now on," she said to the ceiling.

"Good," came the curt clipped answer, "because you have no choice."

Toni sighed. It was too much to expect that a dedicated woman hater like Luís Quental would accept her tentative gestures of friendship. "Where did Getulio put my things?" she asked on a sudden thought. "I had a suitcase full of fresh clothes, and I'll be needing them later—provided you permit me to get out of bed."

"Why don't you ask Getulio what he did with them?" The irritable retort offered no encouragement to continue the conversation; it suggested that he was growing decidedly fed up with her chatter. "He's always up and about before dawn. At some point he'll turn up with your breakfast."

Toni braved another question. "When?"

"When he's able," Quental returned in a short voice. "There are a few people here who are sicker than you. Getulio will be attending to them first."

It was immediately after this quelling exchange that Luís Quental rose from his hammock. At the sounds of rising, Toni angled a swift glance in the direction of the man who had just levered himself onto the floor; then looked away swiftly as she realized that the thin cool cotton of his pajamas allowed disturbing shapes and shadows to be seen a little too clearly for comfort.

Other than that, his concern for her sensibilities could not be faulted. In order to change into his day-time gear, he vanished through the open door. This, Toni later learned, led to a small utilitarian dressing room and a cluttered study; farther along a short hall was a tiny functional bathroom with sink and toilet only. These extra rooms formed a wing at right angles to the main bungalow, with the vine-shaded veranda she had noted on arrival set into the L shape of the building.

During his absence in the dressing room, Toni's sense of humor reasserted itself as she reflected on the conclusions Ty and Barney might have drawn when they saw Getulio at his house-wrecking task last evening. Or had they seen? The small abode was so effectively screened by bushes that the others might not have been aware of Getulio's actions at all. And no doubt if they *had* noted they would have been reassured by their sardonic host that the situation was only temporary. Otherwise Ty and Barney would most certainly have asked some telling questions!

Moments later Luís Quental emerged from the dressing room, his hard-muscled height once more restored to full decency. As always, his khaki shirt was open at the throat and rolled at the sleeves, revealing the powerful forearms darkly tanned by many years spent under a tropical sun. The jungle garb suited him—emphasized the lean fit body on which not an ounce of flab resided. It occurred to Toni fleetingly that if it were not for the cynical personality he would be a very attractive man...and in that moment her eyes locked with his. She colored and looked away quickly, feeling unaccountably young and immature at that moment.

"I'll be back to have a look at you later," he said coolly. "Even though there aren't too many patients in the clinic right now, I can't neglect my morning rounds. When Getulio arrives, he'll see to your more personal needs. Don't worry, you'll be perfectly safe in his hands. And don't bother trying to convince him to let you out of bed before I've checked you over. Getulio always follows my instructions—to the letter."

"I wasn't going to try anything of the kind," she protested without raising the lashes that fanned over her cheeks. Oh, damn. Why did her eyes have to turn as evasive as his once had been? It was because she had lowered her defensive guard, she knew. The morning's brief altercation had forced her to take stock of her attitude toward Luís Quental. If he was prejudiced against women—well, no doubt it resulted from some compelling reason long buried in his past. Just because Garcia knew of no reason did not mean that no reason existed. And Quental did have honorable instincts; of that she was now sure.

She had taken a new measure of him as a man, and that had made her aware of his virility as she had never been before.

Even after he vanished through the swinging screen door the tang of him tantalized her nostrils: that clean male scent not fully concealed by the clinging aura of soap and antiseptic common to his profession. Pictures flashed through her mind like images on a screen: the shadows of masculinity seen through flimsy cream cotton; the corded muscles; the dark disturbing eyes; the mouth with its hint of firmly controlled sensuality.

Not since Matthew's death had she allowed herself to think of any man in such terms. If she allowed it now, perhaps it was because Quental's abiding hatred of women, his scrupulous examination of the previous evening and her own ill-founded accusations of the morning had assured her that she was quite safe from his advances.

And so her mind misbehaved, playing dangerous games, until Getulio arrived a short time later. *"Bom dia, senhora,"* he grinned, cheerfully wagging his brick-colored head. "So, I attend once again to your needs. But I think you will not remember that I was here last night!"

"I'm afraid I don't, Getulio," Toni admitted.

Getulio removed last night's uneaten food from beside the bed and set down a fresh tray. On it rested a little glass containing two pills similar to those Toni had taken the previous evening. "It is true, *senhora*; you were very far from awake when I gave you the bath. Now first the temperature, just in case, and then the tablets...."

During the next few minutes, while Getulio attended to his ministrations, Toni turned her mind to wondering what messages Senhor Garcia might have imparted three days before. Getulio still wore that aura of a man fairly bursting with good news. Luís Quental, on the other hand, had not seemed pleased at all; yet Toni had received the distinct impression that the two pieces of news were somehow linked. Not that she could satisfy her curiosity in any way: it would be impertinent to ask Getulio outright what Garcia had told him.

Sketchy ablutions performed and face freshened with a damp cloth, Toni accepted the breakfast Getulio handed her, a bowl of porridge laced with great slices of fresh fruit. There was more fresh fruit on the tray, and two boiled eggs.

"You seem very cheerful this morning, Getulio."

"It is because my son, Braz, will be arriving soon, *senhora*, and his wife, Ana."

"Where does he sleep when he brings his wife?"

"That other time, they slept in the little hut, the one I took down last night."

That sidetracked Toni, and for the moment questions about Braz and Ana were put aside. "When will you be rebuilding it, Getulio?"

He shrugged. "When I have time, and when I can get a few men to help. A little building like that can be put up in a single afternoon. It will be better then, for the rain will not come through the roof."

So Luís Quental had not been lying about that, either. So much for her wretched suspicions!

For a time, as she devoured her breakfast with a relish she had not experienced for several days, Getulio moved around the room, folding blankets, unhooking Quental's hammock to store it for the day, dusting and tidying. As he worked he asked some questions about the trip to the Xara village, effectively preventing for the moment a return to other topics. At last he came back to the bedside and perched on a chair to watch Toni finish her meal.

"You must be very proud of your son, Getulio. When did he graduate as a doctor?"

"Only last year, *senhora*. But he is not so young a man as you might think. He is past thirty, and he has been married for four years. But then, he was already twenty years old when Dr. Quental sent him to be educated."

"Dr. Quental sent him?"

"Assuredly. If the doctor had not decided to do something to help, Braz would be no more than a poor *caboclo* like me. I have the education of the convent and some medical training, too, but I could not have sent Braz for all those years of special learning."

A laden spoon paused in front of Toni's mouth. Oh, Lord, her opinion of Luís Quental would have to undergo some drastic revision!

"Dr. Quental said that Braz was clever, although he had had no more than a little education from the nuns along the river. So he sent Braz to school in Manaus. That was eleven years ago, when Dr. Quental first came here—the year he himself had become a doctor. Then, when Braz learned very fast, he sent him to medical school. And after my son finished at school, he went to intern in a big hospital in Rio de Janeiro—and that, too, Dr. Quental arranged. It is only last year that Braz has set up a practice of his own in Rio, and again the good doctor helped with the cost. Oh, yes, he could not have been kinder to Braz if he had been his own father!"

Perhaps that was one of the reasons Luís Quental had himself been in Rio eight months before? It might very well have been about that time that Braz O'Hara needed help in setting up his practice.

"It is good to have a clever son like Braz," Getulio sighed. "If only he would produce some grandchildren, to bring me comfort in my old age."

"Perhaps he and his wife have been waiting until he finished with his training," Toni consoled.

"Perhaps," Getulio answered, but in voicing the wish he turned temporarily pensive.

Toni put aside the empty shell of the second soft-boiled egg. "Where did you put my things, Getulio, when you pulled down the little shelter?"

"In there," he said with a wave in the direction of the dressing room. Toni's swift unease subsided when she heard Getulio's next words: "Dr. Quental said to leave them in the suitcase, so that is what I did. Would you like me to unpack something for you?''

"A mirror and a hairbrush, and...." Toni bit back the request for her cosmetics case: surely there was no reason to care that much about her appearance? Despite her wayward dreams of a few minutes ago, she had no intention of letting down her guard as far as men were concerned. "And anything else you think I might need," she finished.

"Muito bem," agreed Getulio, and while Toni dug into a banana he vanished into the dressing room, to emerge a few minutes later clutching not only the requested items but also a small zipped floral bag that she recognized as the unasked-for cosmetics case. It contained little more than face cream, a compressed foundation and a tube of lipstick; even her perfume had been left behind in Manaus.

Getulio laid the requisites near Toni's lap and returned to his chair.

"Nearly four years ago, it was," he mused, "that time when Braz brought his wife, just after they were first married. The little shelter has not been slept in since; that is why the rain was coming through the roof and the insects through the walls. Since then when Braz comes he has been alone, and so he sleeps in the big building, in the room where your friends are now staying. But then, at that time he could not. *O, Deus!* In those days a person could not have found a place to sling an extra hammock. The little hospital was always busy then.''

And that raised a number of other unanswered questions, leftovers from Toni's first day there. The discomforts of her body had pushed many things from her mind, among them Luís Quental's inexplicable revelation that the Xara no longer slept in the hospital when they were ill, as they once had done.

"Why is it seldom busy now, Getulio? It seems to me it would be better if the Xara who are seriously ill stayed here rather than in their own village."

Getulio scratched his astonishingly colored hair. "But Dr. Quental says it is better if they do not," he said. "Sometimes, if there is a sick Xara who must be watched day and night, he will be brought to sleep here, in this bungalow. But others come only as far as the edge of the clearing, and the doctor goes to see them there. He says it is better."

Toni's brow fretted with the question. "Why, Getulio?"

"He wishes to keep them away from the other patients—the *caboclos* who live nearby and those who come from the other settlements along the river. To let those people come close to the Xara—oh, mother of God! That can be very dangerous."

Toni came to the seemingly inescapable conclusion that the dangers stemmed from the Xara's hair-trigger tempers and their fierce possessiveness about their womenfolk. With other things she had been told, and especially after her spine-chilling personal experience of yesterday, it seemed a logical assumption.

"You see, *senhora*," Getulio went on, "in the old days when there was a patient who should be kept away from the Xara, the doctor would bring that patient in here to share his own roof. Always that patient was ordered to stay away from the big building. Then one day one man disobeyed, and that is when the trouble started. It happened two years ago."

"Trouble?"

Getulio poured a mug of dark steaming coffee from the pot on the breakfast tray and added copious amounts of sugar without asking Toni's preference, which fortunately did include sweetening. "Yes. You see, although the man had a broken arm, he also had influenza, just a very little case. He was not very sick, but it was enough. Within a week nearly every Xara in the hospital was dead."

Shock froze Toni's arm just as she had been about to reach for the proffered mug. "What?" she whispered.

"But perhaps Dr. Quental could not have prevented it, even if he had tied the man to his bed. You see, the man had been searching for gold when he broke his arm—there are always stories of gold to bring men to the back rivers of the Amazon. The man had been found and brought here by some people of a Xara village. Within one week the people of that village were dying, too. And then the next village, and the next, and the next...."

The time of the Big Sickness. Influenza? Toni had thought Maria had meant some strange tropical disease; but then, perhaps the Xara had worked up immunity to such things. Thoroughly shaken, she listened as Getulio went on to confirm this guess.

"For the Xara, the diseases of the jungle are not so much, for they are used to them. But the sicknesses that come from outside...oh, it was very very bad. Like flies they died. And Dr. Quental, he could do nothing to prevent it, even with the newest of medicines."

No wonder Quental was so paternalistically protective of the tribe! No wonder he had threatened to leave her here if she showed any signs of illness! No wonder he had left the table so abruptly that first day when the touchy topic had been broached! To Luís Quental, the doctor who had been unable to prevent so many deaths, it must be the most painful of subjects.

Getulio went on, adding to the horror story, "In that time there were five Xara villages. For two months the doctor hardly slept. Mother of God, it is fortunate that the man has the strength of a bull! Each morning he would walk to one of the villages. He would work there all afternoon and all night, sleeping only when the howler monkeys started. Then he would rise with the sun and walk to the next village. And the same the next day, and the next, and the next. I do not know how he did it. I myself, I was tired all the time, and I slept each night. Those weeks, they were very terrible. And when they were over, some were saved, the strongest only. Dr. Quental, I think he blamed himself for not being five men, but I tell the truth when I say that not one Xara, not one, would have survived without him. And when that bad time finally came to an end, the doctor came back here, and he sat like this...."

Getulio hunched over in his chair and dropped his head into his hands in a posture of abject despair. When he raised his eyes again, they were visibly moist from the mere memory of what had transpired two years before.

"For many hours he sat like that with his head in his hands, not eating, not sleeping, not answering when I spoke. When a strong man has strong feelings it is a thing to turn the heart big in the chest. Perhaps you will think me a weak man, but I confess there were tears in my eyes to see him that day."

Toni felt her own tears very close to the surface. "Oh, Getulio. If that's a weakness, then perhaps we should all be weak."

Getulio blinked and rubbed one eye as if it contained a speck of dirt. "But the doctor, he did not cry. He sometimes...choked, but he kept it all inside. And then, when it began to grow dark, he raised his head. His eyes were very black and very old and very deep. His mouth was...." Getulio cast about for a word to describe what he had seen and came up with none. "It was the way it often is today, but more. Much more."

Closed, bitter, brooding, and doubtless scored with exhaustion and scarred with the haunting marks of a deep tormenting memory that could never be erased. Yes, Toni could imagine, and every sympathetic chord in her heart suffered for the mental anguish Luís Quental must have undergone.

"And then the doctor said, 'Go to bed, Getulio. There is work to do tomorrow.' He has never spoken of this matter since. But the next day he began again to walk to all the Xara villages, each in turn. It was then that he told them they must come to sleep in the hospital no more. And he talked to them of gathering into one village, so that there would be men and women enough to make more children, for many had lost their husbands or their wives. And he told them to stop using the bark of trees, and roots, and other things that stop the making of babies. And he told them that the children they bore would be stronger because of the things their parents had suffered. And he talked to them of planting crops that would help keep them strong, for he said that in the years to come it was the strong who would survive. And he talked to them of learning, for he said that they must learn if they were to understand what was happening in the Amazon."

It explained so much: why Quental gave Eketi lectures on the subject of remarrying; why he admonished the Xara chief on the virtues of starting a family; perhaps even why he had convinced Maria to return to her decimated people. It also gave a new, bitter edge to the disturbing story of what could happen to twins born into the Xara tribe.

"Once there were three thousand Xara and now there are only three hundred. It is so with most tribes in the Amazon. It is a very sad thing. My own grandmother was a Xara, taken away from her people by bad men in the big days of rubber, when such things were common. Then men used guns to take the women they wanted, and the Xara could not stop them. I remember her when she was an old, old woman and I was a little boy. She told me that when she was young there were ten thousand Xara."

So the decimation of the Xara had been going on for some years. During those years, how many twins had died because of Xara custom and ignorance and fear? It was an irony in its very bitterest sense, and one that must tear at the moral fabric of Luís Quental's very being. And yes, he did have moral fiber; Toni was now sure of it. If the happenings earlier that morning had started a reversal of opinion, Getulio's revelations had completed the job.

Luís Quental might be a hater of women, but he was not a hater of mankind.

And if he was a hard man—well, that too could be forgiven. Only a hard man could have done what had to be done during the time of the Big Sickness. And, thought Toni with a curious wrench of the heart, perhaps under that impenetrable shell he was not so very hard after all. . . .

"Mother of God, what have I done?" Getulio muttered, shaking away the past to return to the present. "I put your coffee back on the tray, and now it is cold as a stone. Wait, I will empty this, and then I will pour you another."

After Getulio had dumped the contents of the mug

outside the screen door, he bustled back to the bed, the old cheerfulness fully restored.

"The river has risen," he observed brightly as he refilled the mug and once again laced it with sugar in the Brazilian fashion. "It rained again in the night. The season of flood has started, and in a few days there will be something for your camera to take pictures of! Ah, the jungle will bloom soon—perhaps even before Braz and Ana arrive. I tell you, it will be good to have my son living here again."

"*Living* here again?" While her eyes cast the question in Getulio's direction, Toni tested the coffee. Fresh from the steaming pot, it was still too hot to drink. She lowered the mug and looked at Getulio with dawning comprehension. No wonder he had found Senhor Garcia's news pleasing!

"Ah, did Senhor Garcia not tell you? But it is no secret, and Senhor Garcia arranged it all himself. Braz will be returning to live here and be a doctor in this place. The Brazilian government will be paying him for the job."

"That's wonderful news, Getulio!" Then another thought occurred to Toni, causing puzzlement to replace the warm pleasure on her face. "But does this clinic need two doctors? It seems to me there's only enough work for one."

"It is true," nodded Getulio. "Since so many Xara died, there are not too many patients now. Even old Manoel is not really needed. If he were not so old, with nowhere to go, he would have been sent away for lack of work."

Toni made a helpless gesture. "Then why—"

"Did you not know? Dr. Quental is to go when Braz arrives. Next Tuesday, when the plane comes to the river, the doctor will be leaving this place—forever."

CHAPTER SEVEN

MIDWAY THROUGH THE MORNING, after a cursory examination no more intimate than yesterday's had been, Luís Quental pronounced Toni virtually recovered. "By tomorrow you should be entirely back to normal," he declared as he put his stethoscope away. "This afternoon you can get out of bed, as long as you don't overdo it. And you'll need an early night, of course."

Toni breathed a sigh of relief; she disliked the enforced idleness. "I feel entirely back to normal," she said. She pulled herself to a sitting position against a propped pillow. "I suppose I'll be sleeping in my own shelter tonight, after all?"

"Not tonight; it won't be ready."

"But I heard hammering outside. I thought Getulio must have started working on it."

"He's started something else," Quental told her, giving her another of those direct searching looks to which she had not yet grown accustomed. "I told him to construct a wooden tub, so that you'll be able to bathe in privacy whenever you wish. It seemed a more urgent requirement."

Swiftly Toni looked away from his gaze as the

memory of his arousal during her riverside bath intruded into her unruly thoughts. At the moment, with old dislikes undergoing revision, she regretted ever having tried to cut him down to size. True, Quental had been arrogant and unmannerly; he had heaped her with scorn; he had misjudged her in many ways; and perhaps in the future she could expect little better at his hands. But Toni was not inclined to vengeance, and she could forgive a person's faults—particularly if that person also had redeeming qualities.

The bathtub was a thoughtful gesture: another small proof that Luís Quental was not quite the monster she had originally thought him to be. Again Toni was inundated by a warm glow of gratitude. The gesture was one she would never have expected, and it certainly relieved her mind to think she could put both sponge baths and river baths behind her forever.

"That's very considerate of you," she said, lashes dropping in a way that was fast becoming habit.

"Unfortunately the carpentry involved in building a tub is somewhat demanding, because the chinks can't be filled with clay or mud. The task will take Getulio several hours. The shelter will have to wait."

When Toni continued to stare fixedly at the bumps in the sheet made by her own knees, he added sardonically, "Surely by now you have no fear about spending another night under this roof."

"Oh, no." Toni's answer came a little too quickly. For some odd reason, although his abrasive mockery no longer troubled her too much, she was finding it harder and harder to maintain a cool surface in his presence. Despite the direction of her eyes, she saw far too much of the muscular legs seated on the chair beside the bed. His hands especially were in view— the strong capable fingers that looked so hard and yet could be so gentle; the wrists with their light dusting of crisply textured hair; the thin gold watch that nestled there. "I have no fears at all."

"I take it you've decided you're quite safe in my hands," he concluded with a distinct trace of irony.

She turned her face slightly to the wall, putting those lean bronzed fingers out of view. The very mention of being in Quental's hands, whatever the reason, aroused a train of quivering speculation that was best left alone. Perhaps she should not have indulged her erotic fantasies earlier that morning.

"I know I'm safe," she said. "I'm sorry I ever thought otherwise. It's only because I didn't. . . know you very well. I trust you completely now."

"How touching." His voice was deeply sarcastic. "But in case you have lingering doubts, let me reassure you further. As I won't need to keep an eye on your condition tonight, I intend to sleep in the hospital."

And that brought a new wash of sensations that, for lack of a better description, Toni decided must be relief. From the sounds now, she could tell he had risen to his feet; seconds later he moved into her line of vision again as he headed for the door. Suddenly she wanted very much to have him stay.

Quickly, and without analyzing her need to keep

him talking, she said, "Getulio told me some things about you this morning, Dr. Quental."

"Really."

The response was discouraging, but at least Toni's words had brought him to a halt with his hand on the doorknob. For some reason she felt as nervous as a schoolgirl beneath that probing black gaze. Her fingers curled into the sheet for strength. "I heard that you supported his son through medical school, and—"

"Getulio talks too much," came the cutting reply, effectively reducing that avenue of conversation to a dead end. Toni quickly cast about for a new direction to take. Instinctively she knew she should not bring up some of the more bitter revelations Getulio had made.

"I didn't know you were planning to leave this place, Dr. Quental. I was so surprised when Getu—"

Quental clipped across her words. "If you're so starved for male companionship, I suggest you avoid topics that will only serve to drive me away," he cut in.

A slow warmth rose to Toni's face. "I'm not starved for male companionship," she protested.

"Oh?" His eyes narrowed with insolence as they slid over her face, taking in every detail of her appearance, lingering on the curve of her mouth with open scorn. "In that case, why did you apply your makeup so carefully this morning? In order to make a conquest of yourself?"

Oh, Lord, thought Toni. Had she been that transparent? Her fingers rose to her cheeks, pressing the heated flesh. "I thought you might allow visitors," she improvised. "I'd like to see Ty and Barney."

He hesitated perceptibly, then agreed with his usual curtness. "I'll send them in right away."

What had ever made her think she could try to be friends with this man? And of course that was all she wanted: to be friends. As she watched him turn his back and go out the door without so much as a parting word, Toni reflected that the barriers he had erected against women were far too formidable to be broken down by any overtures on her part—especially since he would be leaving in a matter of four days, while she herself would be staying on for a month. If she so much as asked where he planned to resettle, he would undoubtedly be as dampening as ever. It was very likely that in four days she would be saying goodbye to him for all time. Not that she really cared, but. . . .

"Was that a deep sigh I heard from over there?" asked Ty as he came through the screen door, closely followed by Barney. The sight of their familar friendly faces brought a warm smile to Toni's lips.

"I'm afraid it was," she answered lightly. "I was just expressing my woe at being confined to this bed, even for the morning. I'd much rather be up and about. I feel quite like myself again!"

"And you look like yourself, thank goodness." Ty beamed with satisfaction at her improved appearance. "Amazing what a good night's sleep will do."

"Very decent of Quental to let you share his quarters,'' Barney observed, looking around the large, sparsely furnished room. "We had no idea how bad your other hut was until we saw Getulio taking it down.''

"Where does Quental sleep?'' asked Ty curiously, eyes traveling toward the area of the dressing room. "Along that corridor?''

"No, in this room,'' Toni said quite evenly, although once again her eyes were a little less than direct.

"Oho,'' said Ty.

"Don't get the wrong idea, folks,'' Toni came back swiftly. "Dr. Quental slept in a hammock.''

"A likely story,'' scoffed Barney amiably. "That daybed looks plenty wide enough for two.''

Ty chimed in, "And now that you have no other place to sleep. . . .''

Toni reacted by stiffening, and her tone turned unusually rigid. "Really, I wish you wouldn't joke about it. Dr. Quental wouldn't dream of taking advantage of the situation! Why, he's even moving into the hospital tonight. He couldn't have been more considerate.''

Barney and Ty exchanged glances of exaggerated bemusement, then looked back at Toni.

"An about-face if I ever heard one,'' said Ty.

"First good word she's ever said about the man,'' Barney threw in.

"I wonder. . .'' mused Ty.

". . .what really happened last night?'' finished Barney.

Ty looked at Toni judiciously, as if measuring her. "She does look a little different about the eyes," he observed.

"They're merely glazed from listening to the two of you," Toni said with unusual asperity. "I'm beginning to be sorry I asked for visitors."

"My, my. Toni the Tigress. Are you sure you really are feeling quite yourself?"

Toni forced herself to relax and laugh. "Of course I am. Now tell me, have you decided on a short holiday while I recover, or are you planning to proceed with the shooting schedule I drew up?"

"We're working," said Ty. "We do sometimes get along without you, sweetheart. We've revised the schedule, though, at Quental's suggestion."

"Oh?"

"Yes. We'll leave the jungle shots for a week or so; Quental says it really blossoms during the rainy season. So we've decided to shoot something else today."

"Something else?"

"Rapids." Ty smirked, looking pleased with himself. "Quental says there won't be a better time to do that than right now. When the river's low, there are too many rocks jutting up. But it's not so high yet that it's a raging torrent. Quental says we'll be safe with Getulio, who knows the river like the back of his hand. Should make a nice sequence, if I can keep my lenses dry."

Toni's eyes sparkled; she was never averse to a little adventure. "If you wait until tomorrow I could come with you," she suggested eagerly.

"No, you positively couldn't," contradicted Barney. "Not after what you've just been through."

"Dr. Quental says that with proper medication the *piums* won't trouble me so badly again, at least no more than they trouble both of you."

"All the same, we're not taking you straight from a sickbed to a rocky river cruise."

"On Sunday, then," she suggested. "That's only the day after tomorrow."

"Uh-uh," Ty objected. "Our goal is the mission just a short distance along the river, and Quental says Sunday is a bad day to land in on them. And on Monday he'll be needing Getulio to help pack up his belongings. Did you hear Quental was leaving for good?"

Toni's heart repeated the small plummet it had performed on first hearing the news earlier. "Yes, I heard. Well, maybe you can put off filming the rapids until after he goes."

"Not a chance," Barney cut in. "Getulio won't want to be bothered once his son, Braz, arrives. But that's not the only thing. There wouldn't be room for you *and* our equipment in the boat, no matter when we go. Quental pointed that out as soon as we suggested waiting a day or two. So you see, love, you're just out of luck this time."

"I hate to miss out on the excitement."

"Excitement?" Ty snorted. "You saw those little rapids when we first landed...they're practically nothing! Hell, Toni, you'll probably have just as much excitement staying here."

Which, as a forecast of things to come, was truer than Ty knew.

WHEN TONI WOKE on Saturday morning, she was startled to find herself looking directly into a pair of dark sardonic eyes. Luís Quental was sitting by her bedside, fully dressed, and she had the odd impression that he had been there for some time, waiting for her to wake.

"Did you sleep well?" His voice was mildly mocking, and it contained a new timbre she had never heard before.

"Yes," acknowledged Toni, telling herself that the leaping of her pulses was due only to the sudden awakening. She pulled herself up in bed, first confirming that no nightshirt buttons had come loose during the night. Quental watched her fingers at her breast, seemingly amused by the quick checkover.

There was something different about him this morning. The directness of the gaze was not new, so what was it? With a little shiver Toni realized that the half twist of his mouth emphasized the sensual quality that had only been hinted at before. And that timbre in his voice—that had been sensual, too.

Moreover, his clothing was different. He no longer wore the drab jungle khaki he had worn so unfailingly that only the crispness of a fresh shirt or the knife crease of trousers advertised a change of clothes. Today he had chosen close-fitting linen trousers and an Italian sports shirt, dark in color and loosely laced at the neck, revealing hints of firm olive-bronze flesh.

Paradoxically, although these clothes were more urbane than his usual apparel, Luís himself looked more uncivilized. Or perhaps just more dangerous....

Luís: oh, damn, why had she started to call him that in her mind? Toni's eyes skated uneasily toward the door. "I suppose I can get up for breakfast this morning," she suggested.

"Yes, you can get up, once I've assured myself that you're really...ready."

"You said I was all better yesterday," she reminded him.

"I prefer to be doubly sure," he came back in cool professional fashion. "Open your mouth, please."

The inevitable thermometer was promptly tucked into place, and her wrist was seized in a no-nonsense grip while his sure fingers felt for her pulse. So he had only been waiting by her bedside for the brief morning examination, and no doubt impatient because he had better things to do with his time. Relieved and disappointed all at once, Toni submitted halfheartedly to the swift silent examination that was as impartial and as carefully unintrusive as every other examination he had given her.

"You look pleased, Dr. Quental," she remarked as he leaned over to replace the tools of his trade in his bag. "Does that mean good news?"

He rose to his feet beside her and gave her one of those long unsettling looks. "I can't think when I've ever been so happy to lose a patient," he observed with the closest approximation of satisfaction she had ever seen on that lean face.

"Then I can get up for the whole day?"

"Yes. Now aren't you glad you followed my instructions and went to bed early yesterday?"

"Er, yes," said Toni, although he had insisted on such an early bedtime that she had been restless late into the night, a circumstance that accounted for her tardy awakening today.

Those dark enigmatic eyes were still mocking her in some strange way. There was a mute challenge in the air, and Toni was not certain what it meant. Quental went on, "You'll be glad to hear that Getulio finished constructing the tub, and although it's not elegant it holds water. You can have a bath before breakfast if you wish. The tub's out on the porch, and it's already filled. The water's good and hot, because a few kettles full of boiling water have just been added."

On the porch? It didn't sound like the most private of places. "Getulio shouldn't have bothered," she said. "I really prefer a tepid bath." But it was not the water temperature she was thinking about.

As if in answer to her thoughts, Luís added in a dry voice, "I also asked Getulio to string up a canvas curtain, in case you're worried about your privacy. Unfortunately, short of building a bathhouse it's the best that can be arranged."

"That was very thoughtful of you."

Faint mockery crossed his lips. "Well, which will you have first—bath or breakfast?"

"I think I'll eat first," Toni decided.

"In that case you might as well breakfast in here. There's no point in getting dressed twice."

Toni glanced toward the small table flanked by a single chair, where she had eaten a solitary supper the previous evening. When Luís Quental had appeared with her tray the night before, he had told her he was filling in for his assistant. "Shooting the rapids is exhausting work," he had said in that two-edged voice of his. "Getulio—and your friends—will be heading for an early bed tonight."

Toni had asked a few questions about the success of the trip, but the replies she had received had been so daunting that she had been discouraged from asking further questions. Not that it mattered; she knew Ty and Barney would be bursting to recount their experiences today.

"I don't want Getulio to have to bother with a tray," she protested now. "He went to quite enough trouble to prepare one last night, when he must have been tired from his trip."

"Getulio didn't prepare last night's supper; I did."

A by now familiar pulse started to tick in Toni's throat. So, another example that proved Luís Quental to be a far cry from the arrogant, self-centered creature she had once considered him. How thoughtful of him to take over kitchen duty when Getulio was in a state of exhaustion! "Then I owe you a double thanks," she said. "It was a delicious meal. But this time round there's no need for a tray. I think I'd rather eat where I can have company for the meal."

"As you wish," came the cool reply, accompanied

by a smile that caused a deepening of the sardonic lines on his face. But it was a smile, very definitely a smile, and as he angled toward the door Toni found herself warming to him once again, despite the cynical manner he wore like a suit of armor.

As soon as he had departed, she slipped out of bed.

She was a little surprised, when she entered the tiny dressing room, to find that her suitcase had been emptied at some point—possibly early in the morning, since Getulio could enter this part of the bungalow from a door that led directly onto the veranda. Perhaps he had decided her clothes would crease less if hung up? A quick glance behind doors and in drawers ascertained that all her things were there. She dressed for breakfast quickly, choosing an ancient pair of work trousers and her oldest shirt, because she knew she would only have to change again after her bath.

She had just finished stroking her hair to silky caramel smoothness when she heard sounds of someone entering the main room of the bungalow. The banging of the screen door was followed by the tiny discernible noises of cutlery clinking on a tray. She made a face in the mirror, put down her hairbrush and headed for the sounds.

"You didn't have to do that, Getulio. I—"

She was driven into a surprised silence as she reached the large room and saw not red hair, but black.

"I thought you were Getulio," she said somewhat

redundantly, stopping in her tracks. Her heart performed a brief erratic tattoo.

The tall masculine body straightened from setting down the tray. Luís's eyes swept Toni from head to toe in an open appraisal that did things to her pulse rate. His lean saturnine face turned decidedly derisive. "As you see I'm not," he said.

Off balance, Toni fingered a shirt button near her waist and wished she had buttoned one more at the upper end of the scale. "I thought you agreed that I wouldn't have to eat alone," she said.

He turned his attention back to the tray and began unloading its contents. "You don't have to," he said. "I've decided to accept your invitation. I finished my morning rounds early today, and I imagine I have a half hour or so before the first of the day's patients start to drop by. I'm eating with you."

Toni examined the table and saw two of everything: two cups, two bowls, two plates, two knives, two forks, even two raffia place mats. Perhaps the other men had already eaten? She was not displeased to have company: last night she had spent some unaccountably yearning moments over her unshared dinner.

"I suppose I overslept the breakfast hour," she concluded out loud. "You should have eaten with the others."

"Would you rather I had?"

"No," she admitted; and in fact to herself confessed that she was inordinately pleased. She slid into the proffered chair, murmuring thanks. Fingers brushed against her shoulder—an inadvertent contact, perhaps, yet her flesh leaped in instant response. By the time Luís Quental lowered himself into his own place at the table, her fingers and her eyes were very determinedly occupied in dissecting a mango.

It was a tiny table, which perhaps made the next contact inevitable. Reacting too strongly, Toni snatched her ankles back beneath her own chair and glanced upward in ill-disguised alarm, her customary air of cool competence totally disrupted. A pair of dark brows tilted into a sardonic question.

"Why the violent reaction? Do you think I did that on purpose?"

"Of course not." Toni let her ankles make a tentative return to their former position, stopping only when her overly acute senses told her that her trouser cuffs were making the slightest of contact with another pair.

"Scrambled eggs?" While he ladled some onto her plate, he added coolly, "I haven't noticed you jumping from anyone else's touch. Should I be flattered...or offended?"

"Please don't be offended; it was just a reflex on my part—quite involuntary."

Even though Toni's eyes were turned to her plate through most of the meal that followed, she was far too conscious of the man across the table—of the measured movements of lean long fingers manipulating knife and fork; of the shirtfront where the disturbing texture of crispness could be glimpsed through the loosely fastened laces; of the muscular forearms where a like dusting of hair darkened the firm teak-tanned skin. But above all she was agonizingly and exquisitely aware of every stirring of those long legs beneath the table, and once or twice she could not conceal her reflexive reaction.

"Perhaps you're not used to breakfasting with such a long-legged man," he remarked when the last of several inadvertent body brushings had caused Toni's knees to jerk too markedly.

"I suppose that's it," she agreed, dabbing her mouth with a napkin, as much for purposes of concealment as anything. Damn this unaccountable lack of poise!

He poured two cups of coffee from a heavy metal pot. "But you are used to breakfasting with a man— or perhaps I should say *men*."

Toni glanced up; his observations seemed to have taken a somewhat derogatory turn. From personal experience she knew she could not disabuse him of his misconceptions, but some deep need impelled her to try. "Look, Dr. Quental, I—"

"Luís," he corrected emphatically. "Have you forgotten you called me Luís the other day?"

Toni felt her throat turn dry at the unreadable expression that met her from across the table. "And you told me to call you Dr. Quental," she reminded him.

"You were my patient then."

The curtain of pale hair swung forward as she lowered her head to sip her coffee. "It's hard to change. I still think of you as a doctor." Which, she admitted to herself, was very far from the truth.

"In that case, I'll give you one more order—as a doctor. From now on you're to call me Luís. I insist."

Toni was far from displeased, despite her earlier protest. But...oh, damn, why did she have to keep hiding her eyes like a teenager on a first date? Luís Quental had not made a single advance, except in her imagination. She looked up again and put a light tone in her voice. "In that case I have no choice but to obey, Dr. Quental."

"To obey...Luís," he corrected. Although his eyes were dark pools too deep to fathom, there was a small smile playing about his lips. A decidedly sensual smile.

And there went Toni's misbehaving pulses all over again. "Luís," she repeated.

"I notice you didn't manage the whole sentence."

"I've forgotten what it was," Toni lied.

"In that case I shall have to remind you...later," he murmured. Before she could think of a fitting reply to that somewhat two-edged remark, he had leaned forward and reached one hand across the table. Startled, she pulled back in the moment before his fingers connected with the opening of her shirt.

"I was going to look at your stone. Surely you don't object?"

"I...no, of course not." Damn, damn, damn. Why did she have to keep overreacting? All the improprieties were in her own mind, stimulated no doubt by the searchingly direct way Luís had been looking at her ever since yesterday. She pulled the thong free without removing it from her throat and held Maria's stone forward for his inspection. As she watched his practiced fingertips stroking the crude markings, her imagination did a little more overtime.

"I saw it around your neck when I examined you, but I didn't take time to look at it well. I'd have to say it's genuine. Where did you get it?"

"Maria gave it to me."

One dark brow notched upward. "Really? A gift of gratitude for preserving her modesty, I suppose?" He inclined forward a few inches, far enough to drop the heavy stone back into the valley between her breasts. His withdrawing fingers made a momentary contact with curved flesh, a touch so fleeting it could only have been accidental. Or had it?

Toni's upward darting glance found only those illegible black eyes and a mouth with a sardonic twist. Luís's lids drooped briefly as he said with perfect coolness, "You do know what the stone is, don't you?"

"I—no."

"Surely you have some idea how the Amazon got its name? You must have done homework on the region before coming to film here. You seem to have come well enough prepared in other ways."

"I do remember reading something about that," she acknowledged, studying the edge of the table where Luís rested one elbow loosely. "From the legend of the Amazon women, wasn't it? As I remember, the first explorers saw some warrior women who...." She paused, too distracted by his flexing fingers and the negligent bend of his arm to recall the exact details. Where was her vaunted competence now? "Women who...." Her voice trailed off.

"Fought beside the men," he filled in dryly. "Those first explorers—Spaniards, not Portuguese— came to the conclusion that they had done battle with a tribe of Amazons as in Greek legend, especially because some of the less hostile tribes along the river had already told tales of a race of tall, fair-complexioned warrior women. According to stories the Spanish leader Orellana had been told, these women lived alone, deep in the jungle, but appeared at times to fight beside their chosen lovers. The tribes along the river called them the Cunhas-teco-imas— the Women Who Live without Law. Perhaps it would have been more fitting to call them the Women Who Live without Men."

Toni stopped herself in the act of worrying the tablecloth with a fingernail, the kind of nervous mannerism she never indulged in normally. For her, after these past lonely years, the descriptive name seemed to hold a special significance. And yet it had been her own choice, hadn't it? She forced a light laugh that sounded too self-conscious for her liking. "If they had mates," she pointed out, "they didn't live without men entirely."

"They did most of the year. In any case the term I used was lovers, not mates. And that brings us back to your stone. There's another native word used to describe the Amazons: Icamiabas, or Givers of Stones of the Forest. Legend says that the Amazons formed those stones of green clay and gave them to the men they wanted for their lovers—lovers on a temporary basis, of course. They became involved in no permanent unions. The men would be taken back to the city of the Amazons long enough for the ladies to satisfy their mating urges, and then set free. It was considered quite an honor for the man, or so the legend goes.''

"Legend?" Toni touched the very real stone just visible in the vee of her neck. "This seems quite three-dimensional to me.''

"Your stone, and other carvings found in museums in Brazil—not always turtles—are the closest thing to proof that there's any substance to the story at all. For generations beyond counting, green stones like that have been handed down as prized possessions in certain Indian families, always with a retelling of the legend, always with pride that some ancestor was the chosen lover of an Amazon. Perhaps there's some grain of truth in it, after all. Tribes a thousand miles apart, speaking different languages altogether, tell remarkably similar tales and treasure remarkably similar stones.''

During the recitation Toni's face had fallen, and her eyes had forgotten to be evasive. "I wouldn't have taken this from Maria if I'd realized. I did guess she might value it, but I had no idea it was such a rare family treasure.''

"Perhaps she wanted you to have it." Luis had spent most of these past minutes in contemplation of the stone's resting place, but now his gaze rose to

Toni's face. "But I do wish she had given it to Eketi instead. He could use a little encouragement."

"*Eketi* could use encouragement?" Toni punctuated her astonishment with a surprised little laugh. "Good grief, if he's interested in Maria why doesn't he just say so? She's head over heels in love with him!"

"What?" Luís leaned forward, clearly riveted by Toni's disclosure. Then he subsided, still staring at Toni as if he did not believe his ears. "On the contrary," he disagreed slowly. "It's Eketi who's crazy about Maria. Why do you think he was so upset when it seemed she'd taken a lover? Eketi has far more sense than the previous chief. If Maria's name hadn't been mentioned the other day, the whole affair might have been settled without incident."

Toni stared back. "I can't believe he loves her! Why, he treats her like the dirt under his feet."

"Dirt?" A harsh little laugh punctuated the amazed word. "You're very mistaken. Eketi is terrified of Maria because of her education. For months I've been trying to talk him into working up courage to approach her, but he's very stubborn about it. He says he has reason to know she's not interested in him. And I'm inclined to agree with Eketi. Maria won't even look in his direction."

Toni shook her head vigorously. "It's just the other way around! Maria thinks the sun rises and sets on him, but she's afraid to lift her eyes in his direction. And she's almost given up hope that he'll ever look at her."

"Did she actually *say* so?"

"She didn't have to say for me to know!" Toni hesitated for a moment, trying to remember how much Maria had revealed and how much had been guesswork on her own part. "She was very evasive, but I'm absolutely sure that's why she worked up enough courage to take off her clothes. She's painfully shy, you know, so that first time must have been total anguish for her. But somehow she managed it, because she wanted to be like the other women—so Eketi would notice her."

"Notice her? *Meu Deus*, he notices nothing else!"

Suddenly they both started to laugh in a shared moment of delight as the truth became clear. It was the first time Toni had ever seen Luís Quental's face break completely out of its cynical mold, and she found herself liking what she saw. How warm, how handsome he might have been if laughter lines had scored that mouth instead of the marks of a lifetime in bitterness! Once again she found herself turning weak inside in ways she had not expected.

The laughter, because of its very intimacy, ended in an awkward moment of silence. When Luís's sobering eyes darkened without leaving her face, Toni's dropped to contemplate the remains of the breakfast.

"Well, I'll have to speak to Eketi again," Luís said after a moment. "I'll pay another visit before I leave on Tuesday. Perhaps I can convince him enough to overcome his reservations. He's more than ready to marry, I know, and he's only been putting it off because of reluctance to propose to any of the other girls when Maria is the one he wants. He's in total awe of anything he considers civilized, and he considers Maria civilized. He's sure she'll reject him because she thinks him an ignorant savage."

"Is that why he's been learning Portuguese? To impress Maria?"

"That's added incentive, I imagine. But Eketi is really learning because he wants to be a good chief."

"Surely if you tell him how Maria feels. . . ."

"I'll try," frowned Luís. "But I can't promise I'll succeed. Eketi's pride is a very tender thing; he wouldn't want to be turned down. It might help if Maria so much as batted her eyes in his direction."

"And she'll never do that," sighed Toni. "Isn't love silly?"

"Yes, isn't it," murmured Luís, and he shot her a dark glance that set the air to twanging with invisible vibrations. "And so often confused with sex."

Toni rose to her feet quickly and started to stack the breakfast dishes. "I'll take these to the cooking shack. Isn't that where Getulio washes them?"

"Yes, but Getulio isn't around at the moment. I gave him a. . .a small job to do." Luís also came to his feet and moved around the table until he was standing behind her. An arm reached around from behind, and a restraining hand touched Toni's arm lightly. "Just leave these; I'll look after them. You go and have that bath."

Once again she reacted as if stung, snatching her fingers away at the moment of impact. His body was not touching hers, but the lean height of him crowded her against the table closely enough that she could not move without connecting. Her knees seemed to turn to jelly.

"Reflex again?" he mocked, raising his hands to her shoulders and forcing her to turn and face him. His mouth, at Toni's eye level, wore a knowing sensuous downward twist. "Or is it a case of nerves? Perhaps I should have examined you more thoroughly."

She closed her eyes briefly as she uttered a silent prayer for strength. Caught in a web of sexual tension, she could not have moved away from him if she had tried.

"What, afraid to look at me, too? Surely Maria's modesty isn't catching."

The taunt was one that could not be ignored. Her lashes fought their way open just at the very moment when those cruelly carved lips murmured, "If you want to be kissed, say so. I care very little for coyness."

He had moved no closer, but the overpowering heat of his body communicated itself across the single inch between them. Toni already felt her limbs melting toward that heat, no more resistant than candlewax close to a strong flame. Mesmerized by the strong tendons of his moving throat, she swayed briefly, helplessly forward and then pulled back again.

A hard knuckle skimmed upward to tilt her chin higher, so that she could no longer evade those smok-

ing dusk-dark eyes. They were readable now: and the
message was a derisive one. "Are you trying to rouse
me to a frenzy—perhaps because you prefer to pretend you've been touched against your will? You
refuse to ask for a simple kiss, yet by your actions
you ask for much more."

"No, I...I'm not asking for anything." But her
eyes were glazed and feverish, and her mouth was
soft and moist for the kiss she was already tasting in
her imagination. Try as she might, she could not increase the inch between them. The strength of will
that had kept men at arm's length for years seemed
totally shattered now, but some vestige of habit kept
her from closing the gap. She wanted the kiss—but
she wanted him to kiss her.

When she neither moved away nor moved closer,
the mockery faded to be replaced by open contempt.
"A woman who deliberately does this to a man de-
serves nothing but scorn," he muttered. "You're trying to make me want you; why don't you admit it?"

There was an arrogance in the way he waited, as
though he knew very well he could force her into
making the first move. Despite his very palpable
reaction to her nearness, the whole unyielding length
of him was a rejection of her soft surrendering plian-
cy. She might have fought him, but at the moment
she could not fight herself; and so Toni threw the tat-
ters of her pride to the winds.

"Please kiss me," she whispered.

At her request, a slow smoldering passion took
possession of his face. "You're flirting with fire,"

he murmured. "But I think you already know that...."

He took his time, hurrying nothing. One hand rose, and his fingers sank into her hair, holding her head in stillness and readiness for the surrender to come. Then the other hand: its warm imprint moved upward to her mouth, tracing the moist trembling outlines as if to memorize them. The fingers traveled lower—delving into the indentation of her chin, describing the curve of her jaw, taking detours into the little hollows of her throat, finally sliding down to the topmost button of her shirt. For disturbing seconds his fingertips insinuated themselves beneath the heavy stone that lay there and tested the silken valley of her skin. Had he moved to the fastenings then, she could not have stopped him; but instead, with a caressing expertise gained in no Amazonian rain forest, his thumb moved over to stroke her sensitized breast, teasing it lightly without thrusting the fabric aside.

Long before his fingers brushed her nipples, a wildfire readiness had turned them to traitorous trembling peaks of desire, and nothing could stop his stroking fingertips from discerning that revealing fact, even through the heavy cloth of her shirt. Even passion's heat did not blind Toni to the brief gleam of contemptuous triumph in his pagan heavy-lidded eyes. And yet she could do nothing to stop him: there had been too many years of self-denial. She caught her breath on an unsteady note as her sensitive flesh succumbed to a soft skillful feathering; then bit her lip as his entire palm curved over the full sweet swell of her breast.

And then, unhurriedly, his lips descended, and the smoke-dark eyes closed in. For exquisite moments his mouth moved lightly, brushing back and forth against hers, teaching her the tastes and textures of roughness and smoothness, hardness and softness, moistness and manliness. It was a taunting, tempting, deliberately arousing technique that probed no command—as light, as enticing, as maddeningly erotic as the slow expert caressing of her breast.

She closed her eyes as a great wave of wanting flooded upward from her lower limbs. Her hands crept unbidden around his neck and clung, finding more stimulation in the vitality that met her fingertips. Her whole being begged for a deepening of the kiss. Desire washed its way through her racing blood, until at last—heady, half-drunk on the masculine flavors that had seeped through her slightly opened lips, and eager to offer a more complete submission—she parted her lips more fully and sought his mouth with an ardor and eagerness that betrayed her inability to hold back anything.

He stopped at once, pulling apart with a suddenness that left her dazed, limp, confused and hurt. It took a moment to adjust to the sudden interruption of passion.

A curious cruel half smile played about Luís's lips. His sardonic gaze trickled over her lips, still parted as if to invite the deeper plunder of his tongue.

"Odd...I have a feeling you didn't want to stop," he murmured derisively.

Toni struggled to regain lost dignity. Turning quickly, she spent some moments regirding her defenses. The disruption of her senses was reflected in the disorder of her expression, and that was what she did not want him to see.

"Am I right?" persisted the mocking voice from behind her. "Are you disturbed that I stopped? Would you have preferred...more?"

"Of course not." Her lightness was not badly feigned, considering her system was still reeling from the unexpected self-betrayal and Luís's subsequent rejection. "I don't deny I was enjoying the experiment. But that's all it was—an experiment."

A low smoky chuckle sounded somewhere near her ear. "And what was the verdict?"

Toni took a deep, deep breath. There was no point pretending she had not been affected by what had happened during the kiss. "You passed on the self-control test," she said lightly. "But I'm afraid I didn't."

"Good." He sounded too amused for Toni's liking. She was still trying to dredge up the wit to deal with the situation when she heard him go on, "Because I'm looking forward to the moment when I *do* kiss you properly—as I promise I will, as soon as I can be sure of no interruption. And that's one promise I look forward to keeping."

It sounded more like a threat than a promise; nevertheless the words set a thousand butterflies as big as blue Amazon morphos to fluttering in Toni's lower stomach. That Luís's kiss would probably be a punishment as much as anything—perhaps to demonstrate his invulnerability to her charms—did nothing to calm her quivering sensibilities.

"In that case," she said somewhat shakily, "it's just as well you're sleeping in the hospital now."

"Oh?"

And with that he gathered the stacked dishes on the tray and walked out the door. And that one little word hanging in the air could have meant anything at all.

Toni stared at the screen that still trembled from his passage, experiencing a crazy tumble of sensations. Of course this thing would never go further than a kiss. Luís's pride and his hatred of women precluded that. All the same, anticipation filled her with an intense sexual excitement, despite the lingering humiliation because he had not completed the kiss. How had he found the willpower to break away? She could still almost feel the intimate press of those thighs, the power of them, the warmth of them, the wanting of them...and yet he, not she, had brought the kiss to a halt. And this in spite of the deep frustrations that must torment a man who had forsworn women years ago.

And her own vow to remain faithful to Matthew— what had happened to that? It seemed very hard to think of Matthew now. And yet was a kiss so very disloyal?

By the time she finally turned toward the dressing

room in order to choose fresh clothes to don after the bath, she had managed to quell all small guilts by reminding herself that nothing much could happen in the few days that remained before Luís left this place forever. Certainly not with Ty and Barney near at hand, and with her duties as producer to claim much of her attention. But oddly, those thoughts brought little comfort; instead they filled her with a fever of restlessness....

Sifting through her clothes in the small cupboard, she started to pull out a nondescript cotton shirt, man-tailored, as were all the shirts she had brought for the month. And then, almost of its own accord, her hand reached for a somewhat more feminine piece of apparel. The flimsy white silk shirt was not exactly frivolous, even teamed with close-fitting scarlet slacks that would hug her hips in ways the baggy jungle trousers had never done. Well, why not, she thought defiantly. They were the only halfway decent clothes she had brought to this place, and she might never have another opportunity to wear them. Ty and Barney were sure to tease her unmercifully, but it was really none of their business. Just because she took a notion to look like a woman didn't mean she was doing it for a man!

She slipped out of the morning's unshapely clothes and into a terry-cloth robe of such unerotic design she hoped no one would see it. As she had noted earlier, a door from this wing of the bungalow opened directly onto the secluded vine-enclosed veranda where the tub stood. A large low oblong construction with plank sides like barrel staves, it was set into the L of the building, enclosed by two walls so that the canvas curtain Getulio had hung would form a sizable private triangle. Soap, towels and her own shampoo bottle had already been laid beside the tub—by Getulio, no doubt.

She laid her fresh clothes on a small table that had been placed at hand for that purpose. There was a small stool, too, and this she pulled close to the tub to serve as a stand for her towels and her soap. She tested the tub with her fingers and found it luke-warm, by now a reasonably comfortable temperature for this climate.

And then, with a sigh of pleasure that sponge baths and chilly river immersions could be abandoned for-ever, she pulled the canvas curtain that completed the enclosure, stripped off the terry robe and stepped into the water.

For a minute or so she simply soaked, aware of her own body in a way she had not been for years. Vanity was not a part of her nature; all the same she was pleased to see that all signs of the *pium* ordeal had vanished, leaving her long slender limbs and her firm full breasts as silky smooth as the water that now caressed them.

And then, scolding herself for the unaccustomed preoccupation with self, she turned to the business of cleansing herself. Wanting to shampoo before the water grew too soapy, she started with her hair. She worked it to a vigorous froth and rinsed it by plung-ing beneath the water, holding her breath for thirty seconds while her fingers worked the lather out of her scalp. She came up gasping, eyes tightly closed, hair streaming over her face. Blindly she reached for a towel in the direction of the stool she could not see. Her fingers connected with nothing but air.

Had she grown disoriented underwater and misjudged the placement of the stool?

"Oh, damn," she muttered, trying to wipe the last traces of shampoo from her eyes.

"I'll be glad to hand you a towel," said a deep mocking voice, "as soon as you say 'please.'"

CHAPTER EIGHT

SHOCK WAVES reverberated from tip to toe, sending splashes over the side of the tub. Toni tried to do everything simultaneously—open her eyes, push her hair aside, wrap her arms around her exposed breasts and sink right through the bottom of the tub, all at one and the same time.

"Luís!" she gasped, having managed at least the feat of recovering her vision.

"At least you got the name right." The derisive taunt was followed by a tempting shake of the towel that dangled just out of reach. He had moved the stool a little farther from the tub, far enough that to reach the towel she would have to abandon the undignified huddling of arms.

She opened her mouth and took a deep breath, ready to howl for help.

"Scream if you like," he said unconcernedly. "You'll get no answer, except perhaps from the howler monkeys. Old Manoel is half-deaf, and all the patients in the clinic are far too sick to come running to your aid. In this part of the world, people don't check in with minor complaints."

Every pulse and every pore in her body jangled

with an overflow of conflicting alarms. But gradually, as she stared wild-eyed, and as those openly insolent eyes stared back, the scream she had intended to voice seemed to die in her throat.

"That's better," he said coolly "As you have very little choice in the matter, you may as well accept the situation."

The situation? He could only be implying that the other men had left the compound this morning, perhaps to do some filming on the river, possibly even sent on a wild-goose chase by Luís himself. Was that why he had put a deliberate end to the kiss—because he knew she would be more vulnerable once she was in the bath? So much for her short-lived admiration of Luís Quental!

Anger restored some equilibrium, despite the continued pumping of adrenaline through her system. "Please may I have the towel," she requested frigidly, hunching her knees to her breasts.

"I don't like the way you say 'please.' If you want it, come and get it." With a short harsh laugh he laid the towel across his lap, where she could not possibly reach it unless she got out of the tub altogether. "Aren't you going to ask me why we're alone? Well, relatively alone. Patients excepted."

Toni compressed her lips, pushed her streaming hair out of her eyes and replied tautly, "At least I know we're not alone for long. Ty and Barney would never go out on a whole day's shoot without consulting me."

"There's one flaw in your logic," came the soft

dangerous drawl. "Doesn't it occur to you that they might not have returned from *yesterday's* shoot?"

She stared, disbelieving, while Luís allowed that distressing piece of information to penetrate. The previous afternoon, during the period when she had been allowed out of bed, she had gone down to the dock to see Ty and Barney take off with a boatload of equipment, and Getulio as guide. Two or three hours later Luís had ordered her back to bed; at the supper hour she had accepted his word that the others had returned. Or had he actually said so? She remembered now that he had discouraged her questions.

But if Ty and Barney weren't back, where were they? A whole new kind of concern washed through Toni, displacing some of the dismay at her own predicament.

"They're quite safe." An arrogant twist hardened Luís's mouth. "I think I told you about the mission downriver. It's not so far—only a half-hour trip. But shooting the rapids is hard exhausting work, so whenever Getulio does it he always stays overnight. Your partners would be welcomed there, too." He glanced at his watch, a thin gold wafer nestling on the strong wrist. "I imagine they'll be starting on the return voyage anytime now."

A half-hour trip? Then surely, at the risk of a little waterlogging, she could stall; if Ty and Barney had made a reasonably early start, they could arrive at any moment. The tub was not much protection, but it was better than nothing—and nothing was what she would have if she stepped out to get the towel. Logic helped to disperse the worst of her fears, and she recovered several extra measures of spirit. "You might have told me all this last night," she said, glaring.

"I wanted you to sleep in peace—" he paused for dramatic effect "—while you could."

For the moment the implication of his words escaped her; her mind was furiously occupied in thinking of other things. Why would Ty and Barney desert her like this? Why would they not object when they realized Getulio intended to stay overnight?

"As your friends could hardly take to the river without a guide, I imagine they had very little choice in the matter. And Getulio had direct orders from me not to start the return trip until today. Now come, out of the tub. I'll dry you off if you like."

Toni pressed fingers to her throat to subdue a moment of hysteria. "You must be out of your mind!"

He shrugged, unconcerned by her reaction, and viewed her with faint scorn. "Then dry yourself if you prefer. I merely thought it might be an interesting preliminary."

"If you think I'll permit you to kiss me now, you're quite mistaken!"

"Kiss you?" His insolent gaze shifted to the knees squeezed against her breasts, mentally dispensing with the protective layer of water. "That's an interesting euphemism."

The last of Toni's shaken self-possession shattered as an expression of total outrage took over her face.

To her further anger, the loss of poise seemed only to amuse Luís.

"Why pretend to be insulted now? All through breakfast you were wondering what it would be like to have me make love to you."

"I was doing nothing of the kind!" she denied, all the more hotly because she had been doing just that.

"Oh?" A brow notched upward, above eyes that glinted skepticism. "You were sending out signals like a bitch in heat. Need I remind you who asked for a kiss?"

"You tricked me into it!"

"So innocent, Antonia?" he scoffed, his use of her full name adding a disturbing note of suggestiveness. "You're as ready for an affair as I am."

"You're mad!"

"You've had affairs with other men," he pointed out contemptuously. "Why not with me?"

There was no point issuing heated denials on that particular score; Luís had long ago made it clear that he disbelieved everyone's explanations. Nevertheless she snapped, "Barney is just a friend."

His eyes glittered with disbelief. "Perhaps it's time you made a new . . . friend." With those softly spoken words he left the stool and came to the foot of the tub with the towel in one hand. He spent a moment enjoying Toni's consternation as he looked directly down into the limpid water where she sat crouched forward to conceal her breasts. Then, kneeling, he reached into the tub and seized an ankle with a firm powerful grasp.

Toni could stop nothing without risking far worse. She tried to kick—a futile effort, for the ankle was held in a grip of soft steel. In her precarious position she could not even use the last resort of physical resistance, as she had once done with Barney. She continued to struggle as best she could, but her flailing seemed only to amuse Luís. Contrary to all logic, wild and unwanted sensations began to shiver upward along the captive limb.

Ignoring her infuriated protests, he insinuated the towel between each toe as though it were an object of love. "Such a wild little foot," he murmured. "It wants to kick... or does it want to be kissed?"

With that his tongue drew a leisurely liquid trail over the instep. There was a deliberate experienced eroticism to the gesture that sent little rivers of molten fire racing along her veins, chasing all other sensations out of mind. Toni gasped and shuddered visibly. Watching her reaction with smoldering eyes, Luís moved his open mouth over an ankle, and the moist imprint seemed to burn all the way to her breasts. She closed her eyes, stifled a moan and clutched the sides of the tub.

A soft scornful laugh restored her wits. "Can you still deny that you're willing?" he mocked cruelly as he released the foot, letting it sink back into the water. "You're a weak quivering creature, no more capable of resisting your passions than any other woman."

Toni made a quick recovery, sloshing water over the sides of the tub as she regained some degree of modesty with her hands. "I can resist *you*," she blazed.

"I intend to have you, whether you resist or not," Luís warned arrogantly as he rose to his feet and hooked his thumbs into his belt, drawing attention to the masculine contours of his thighs. "In any case, I don't believe your resistance will last past the first kiss." He looked at her piercingly and added in the softest of voices, "Need I remind you that's something you have yet to experience—from me?"

"Never!"

His smile was sardonic. "You'll be willing enough when nightfall comes. I could soon make you willing now, but frankly I prefer not to have the act of love interrupted by some *caboclo* in the throes of a malarial attack. We'll proceed at the end of the day, when I can be sure no more patients will arrive."

Nightfall? Luís's threats were idle; by nightfall the others would most certainly be around to protect her. And after this morning no power on earth could force her to go willingly into those arms where she had longed to be not so many minutes before. Not after his duplicity; not when he treated her in such cavalier fashion!

"Out of the tub," he commanded brusquely, at last holding a towel within her reach. "I retract the offer to dry you, but I have no objection to letting my imagination run riot. Today I've made no promises to turn my back. I'll watch."

Toni snatched the towel without thanks. Luís settled himself once more on the low stool, his gaze direct and disdainful in a way that curled her toes and sent indignation tingling up and down her spine.

Fortunately it was a huge fluffy outsize towel, and she managed to hold it in such a way that it concealed most of her as she stepped out of the tub with a great deal more haste than grace. The towel remained wound around all vital parts as she hurriedly pulled her scarlet slacks over still dripping legs, scorning the simple briefs that would mean only one more delay in restoring decency. The dampened slacks clung too closely to her skin, but there was no help for that. Under cover of the towel she tried to propel the zipper fastening upward, with little initial success. More haste, less speed; and using only one hand did not help.

"This time it seems your difficulties are not pretended," he taunted. "Can I help?"

"Certainly not!"

"Your manner of dressing leaves a great deal to be desired," he noted sarcastically, leaning over to seize the silk shirt and brassiere that remained on the small table. "But I expect the clothes will come off with rather more panache. If not, I shall enjoy teaching you...."

At last Toni managed to close the zip to the waist, making the towel a necessity only for her upper half. "You'll teach me nothing!" she vowed through clenched teeth.

"I hadn't imagined I'd have to," came the cynical retort. "But I see you could use some lessons in the art of donning garments provocatively, in the way that pleases a man. However, I find no fault with the choice of clothes you've made this morning—except for this."

He stretched one long limb to make a hip pocket available to his hand, and with sick horror Toni saw her unprovocative brassiere go into it. That done, he held out the silk shirt with a deliberately mocking smile.

"Ah, Antonia, you are a transparent woman—as transparent as this silk. You chose the clothes to please me, and it pleases me to see you in fewer of them, that's all. I happen to find brassieres unerotic."

Although the shirt was not completely sheer, it was enough of a see-through that without an undergarment it would leave too little to the imagination. "I can't be seen in public like that!" she protested.

"Exactly," came the cool reply. "But then, I'm not asking you to go in public with it on. In fact I suggest you stay away from the *caboclos* who come to the hospital today. If a rough river dweller saw you in this flimsy silk, he would be sure to think the worst of your...virtue. And believe me, my cool American beauty, most of the river dwellers are very rough men. So please, today, save yourself for my eyes alone."

Speechless with outrage, Toni snatched the silk shirt and turned her back to finish dressing. Was it possible Luís was only trying to humiliate her, to pay her back in kind for whatever anguish she had put him through that day at the river? Yes, it could be, she decided wildly. Hating women, he must have hated her for witnessing his weakness that day. Now he wanted to witness hers. A man who had lived the embittered life of a hermit for so long might very well brood about such an incident, might very well decide to take a twisted revenge.

Certainly, with Ty and Barney returning soon from their overnight trip, Luís could not really expect to follow through on his threats. Perhaps he just wished to enjoy her mortification: and that he would most certainly be doing, she realized with dismay as she looked down at the erotic delineation of her breasts. The nipples over which she had no control were taut, erect and visible as dark shadows through the silk. Dampened by rivulets of water running from her dripping hair, the shirt clung like a limpet exactly where it should not cling, revealing too much of the full pale curves and making no secret of her unwilling arousal. She hoisted the towel over her shoulders, intending to use it as a shawl, only to find it whisked away by one very determined hand. With his other hand Luís seized her shoulder, forcing her to turn.

His fingers freed her at once, and he retreated by a few paces. Well, if he wanted to see her humiliation, he was certainly seeing it now! She did not wish to give him the satisfaction of knowing how thoroughly shamed she felt, and so pride prevented her from making undignified attempts to cover what she knew he must have already noticed.

"Very revealing," he concluded, letting his eyes

trickle with maddening insolence over the finished effect.

"How long does the punishment go on?" she asked coldly, thrusting defiant hands into the beltline at each hip.

"Punishment?" His dark brows lifted quizzically in pretended surprise. "What I have in mind is not punishment but pleasure."

Damn his lean, sour, cynical face! "Look, Luís, your little joke has gone far enough. You've turned the tables and you've made your point. I apologize for setting out to...to shame you that day by the river. Believe me, I'm sorry. Now may I get into something decent before the others return?"

"Certainly."

But when she swiveled, thinking to enter the bungalow and heaving a sigh of relief that the ordeal was now over, she found herself stopped by a forceful arm.

"I said before the others return. That doesn't mean today." A twist of cruel amusement curled his lip. "Don't you understand, Antonia?"

She stared at him in renewed alarm, a pulse ticking erratically in her throat. "But a half-hour trip—"

"A half hour going," he corrected softly. "Two days coming back."

CHAPTER NINE

WHAT WAS SHE TO DO—run? Not into the Amazon rain forest, where people could vanish without a trace, hopelessly lost within five minutes of penetrating those gloomy cathedral depths that had been called Green Hell for good reason. Not by taking to the piranha-infested river without a manageable craft of some kind. The two large dugouts that remained down by the bank had no motors of any kind, only those odd circular paddles; and Toni knew she had neither the skill nor the strength to maneuver the heavy boats through the swiftly running river.

And she could hardly impose her troubles upon the few deathly ill patients in the clinic, or upon the ancient half-breed Manoel, who was too old to help and who in any case spoke neither English nor Portuguese.

Several ragged riverside *caboclos* stopped by for medical aid during the day. Toni considered and discarded the prospect of approaching one of them for help: as Luís had said, they were a rough-and-ready lot. Would she be any safer in their hands than she was in his? Possibly not. And she could not approach the strangers closely enough to determine whether any of them looked trustworthy. Through the day Luís made a point of meeting each incoming river-craft at the dock, leaving Toni no opportunity to approach the outsiders in private. Moreover, this morning Luís had locked her out of his bungalow with a mocking flourish, so there was no possible way for her to acquire a change of garment. And without a change of garment, she could hardly approach a total stranger.

Damn the man for his outrageous behavior! He must have been planning this very scenario ever since yesterday; and possibly with Getulio's full conniv-ance. Or had he even needed to take Getulio into his confidence? Getulio spoke no English, and he might very well have set off expecting that Ty and Barney knew exactly what they were letting themselves in for.

It was Luís himself who had engineered the film team into making the trip yesterday; she remembered that perfectly well. The subterfuge was unforgivable. And he expected her to fall into his arms? Well, damn him, she would not! How ignominious it would be to turn helpless and spineless in the arms of a man who professed for her and for all womankind nothing but deep disdain. How mortifying to let his unloving hands have their way, while she lost wit and will and reason and pride and every shred of re-sistance. How humiliating it would be to let him brand her with kisses while murmuring words of hatred in her ear. . . .

And yet the memory of the exquisite weakness that

had earlier shivered upward from her toes, against her wishes and against all reason, filled her with dismay and apprehension for the coming night. She knew that despite the best of intentions it was possible she might be weak—if she once let Luís touch her. She spent the day in a fever of apprehension that increased apace whenever he drew near. Those mocking, darkly scornful eyes gleamed with a masculine triumph that promised no reprieve and set the blood to pounding nervously in her veins.

Without Getulio the meals relied heavily on the canned goods that seemed to be available in considerable quantity and array, thanks to the weekly supply flight.

"Not exactly the fare of a fine Rio restaurant," Luís noted dryly over the noon meal, for which they sat on the veranda of his bungalow at a safe distance from prying eyes. "But you seem to have a hearty appetite today. Perhaps you're less apprehensive about this evening than you pretend?"

Toni compressed her lips and bent her head over the food. Boiled sweet potatoes, canned peas and canned corned beef were not her idea of gourmet fare, but at least they were a change from the inevitable black beans and fish that were Getulio's stock-in-trade for this time of day. And there was a good supply of nuts and fruit to fill up the chinks as soon as the canned goods palled. As Luís had remarked, her untenable situation had done nothing to interfere with her appetite. "I'm merely building my strength for later on," she said coldly.

A low suggestive laugh was the answer she received, along with a murmured, "Good."

At the end of the day, shortly before sundown, he insisted that she accompany him to the river while he bathed, a ritual he reserved until after the patients had been fed and settled for the night, with the old half-breed Manoel left to watch over them. Despite Luís's derisive taunts, Toni stonily avoided watching him strip to the skin. She cast a fleeting glance at the water only after she had heard the distinctive splash of a dive, long enough to ascertain that he was stroking strongly out into the swift current, as he had warned her not to do.

He dressed swiftly when he emerged from the water, commenting on Toni's determinedly averted gaze with no more than a deep throaty chuckle of such arrogance that she felt her hackles rise. She had not turned her back completely: that would have been too reminiscent of another occasion. But she stood stiffly, straight as the flagpole itself, staring stonily toward the far riverbend and hoping against hope that by some miracle Getulio's craft would put in an unexpected appearance before the last light of day.

"Come for a stroll," Luís said, moving into view. His hair was still damp from the swim. A dark unruly forelock fell over his forehead, emphasizing the uncivilized qualities in his face.

"No, thank you."

"I insist." Obdurate fingers reached for her wrist to enforce the command.

She snatched her arm away before contact could be made, an action that merely brought a superior satirical lift to his dark brow. He dropped his hand, but his manner said more clearly than words that her efforts at resistance were no more than an exercise in futility.

"I always go for a stroll along the riverbank at this time of day—at least until the river gets so high that there is no riverbank. Seeing an Amazon sunset in the proper setting is good for the soul."

"Then by all means go," Toni retorted tautly. "Your soul could use a little improvement."

"I'll call a truce for the duration of the walk." The offer came in a cool unfriendly voice. "Hands off; eyes off, too."

Toni nibbled imperceptibly on her lip as she considered that. The sun was very near the horizon. Twenty minutes or so of relative safety? At least it put off the moment when she had to start fighting off his advances, a moment that was approaching much too swiftly for her liking.

"Naturally my promise doesn't hold if you throw yourself into my arms," he added with unflattering sarcasm. "There are some limits to my self-control. Well, are you coming? If you don't I can only assume it's because you're impatient to get into bed with me at once. We can do that if you like; I've already turned down the bed and switched on some low romantic lamps."

The unmitigated arrogance of the man! Toni cast a cool withering glance at the lean supercilious face, swung her long scarlet-clad legs in a new direction and started to walk away from the dock, along the riverbank, without looking to see if he followed.

Moments later he moved wordlessly into the lead. The river was not yet so swollen as to touch the bases of the trees that fringed it. Nevertheless it was a narrow precarious passage between the green water and the green trees. Strips of damp grass alternated with the soggy mossy mudbank that squished beneath the light slippery moccasins she had worn in preference to the temporarily discarded boots. They moved slowly, with Luís pacing his longer stride to her slow uncertain progress.

"This tree is a capirona." He pointed upward as they moved beneath an umbrella-shaped specimen. High above, Toni heard the sibilant buzz of wild bees, but she was too engrossed in finding safe footage to follow the sweeping direction of his arm. "And that's a calabash—the one hung with fruit like green footballs. Brazilian chestnut...babassu.... Nowhere else in the world will you find so many different species of trees growing so closely together. In fact, you seldom find more than a handful of any one kind of tree growing in one place."

He came to a halt, and because his tall body blocked the way, Toni also stopped perforce. "Perhaps it's nature's way of protecting them from the spread of disease, which can be a problem when too many trees of one species grow together—in the Amazon, at least. The *hevea*, the best rubber tree of all, is a native of these parts; until less than a hundred years ago it grew nowhere else in the world. Then one man managed to transplant a shipment of seedlings elsewhere, and soon it was growing in nice, neat, manageable rows—except in the Amazon. When Henry Ford tried to start a plantation in this part of the world, it failed because of disease. And yet the solitary rubber tree thrives deep in the jungle. There are a few plantations now, but in the Amazon most of the rubber still has to be collected the same old way—deep in the jungle. Which should,'' he finished dryly, ''explain to you why the great wild-rubber boom collapsed. In its own home territory, rubber couldn't be produced cheaply enough to compete with those nice neat rows in Malaya and other tropical countries.''

Toni professed interest in no way. Why give him the satisfaction? The lean-featured face turned to her quizzically for a moment, and then he started to walk again, not commenting on her silence.

''There's a carnauba tree—it's famed for its wax. And this is a cow tree. Slash it and it yields a milk that sometimes serves as a substitute for the real thing.''

They pushed past trees whose unfamiliar names were as exotic as the air-feeding flowers and decorative vines that draped them, often in exuberant streamers that drooped to the water's edge. Luís moved with the surefootedness of a man who knew exactly where he was going, avoiding the pitfalls and roots that seemed to turn Toni's every step to a hazardous slippery gamble. Therefore she was not unhappy when the short walk came to a halt, when they had progressed no more than fifty yards from the docking area.

"We'll stop now," Luís decreed as they reached a place where a great fallen tree, uprooted by last year's flood, lay parallel to the bank, its massive root system already a home to climbing vegetation of all kinds. Directly ahead a sharp arrow-leafed palm overhung the river.

"It's too hard to push past that yacitara palm. Those spiny leaves are capable of impaling passersby on the river and lifting them right out of their boat—so you can imagine what they would do to that flimsy top of yours. We'll watch the sunset from here."

Issuing no invitation to Toni to join him, he dropped onto the tree trunk, outstretched his limber limbs and crossed his feet to wait for the moment when the sinking sun reached the horizon. She, too, sat down—at a safe six-foot distance.

"That's a floating island—one of the first of the season," Luís noted as a great bed of greenery and hyacinths swept swiftly past. "Or perhaps in this case I should say a floating flower garden. I doubt that particular island could hold a person's weight, but in the height of the flood people sometimes do use floating islands for free transport down the river. Some are acres in size—twenty feet thick and covered with trees."

At Toni's determined lack of curiosity, a glint of amusement appeared on his face. "People usually ask why the islands don't sink. The reason is that there's very little topsoil in the Amazon—only a thick matting of jungle growth.'' He glanced at her mockingly. "But I suggest you don't try to escape that way, if a large chunk happens to float by. The transportation is free, but the destination is somewhat uncertain. The Indians say that all rapids are the home of Quaquilmaneh, the spirit who eats boats... and sometimes islands, too. And if you happen to make it to the Amazon itself...well, in flood you might wash right out to sea without seeing either shore. At its mouth the Amazon is ten times as wide as the English channel.''

Toni had resolved not to ask questions, but his words touched on worries that still nagged at the back of her mind. "Are you *sure* Barney and Ty are safe?''

"Yes, I'm sure. The rapids on this particular tributary are not particularly difficult, and no one knows them as well as Getulio does. With a couple of old river hands to help him haul the boat back upstream, he could easily manage the return trip in a day. Usually he arranges for two *caboclo* friends to accompany him for that exact purpose. But this time—''

"You decided Ty and Barney could do the hauling!'' Toni glared as the full extent of Luís's treachery became apparent. "How thoughtful!''

"They'll be a little sore,'' he admitted in a disingenuous drawl. "Towing by pulling on a piassava rope is hard work for someone whose hands are not callused, and as Getulio will be too busy on shore to stay in the boat and help with the hauling...somehow, I think your partners will remember this trip.''

Toni muttered something unprintable under her breath as Luís went on sardonically, ''Don't feel too sorry for your friends. Someone has to move the rope from tree to tree, and Getulio risks as many discomforts or more on the shore. Hornets with stings like scorpions, trees with spines like swords, hungry alligators lying like logs at the water's edge. And then there are the anacondas—they always stay close to the riverbanks and nest in the shallow waters where Getulio will sometimes have to walk. I imagine your friends would prefer to do their work in the boat.''

Toni's gray eyes sparkled with unconcealed anger. ''Somehow I can't work up sympathy for Getulio,'' she flashed, ''especially as he's aiding and abetting your schemes.''

''Oh?'' Luís muttered with feigned nonchalance, just as the river turned to an incredible red blaze under the lowering sun. ''Perhaps you'd have more sympathy for Getulio if you turned your eyes back and looked upward. There's a tree behind you I think you should look at.''

Toni did—and was instantly reduced to a quivering mass of gelatin. She stopped the scream that rose to her throat only by throwing herself directly and forcefully into the very arms she had sworn, with all the best intentions in the world, to avoid.

''What, surely not afraid?'' The amused sarcasm did not reassure her at all. The two muscular arms that had received her shaking body, almost as if expecting it, now closed around her in an inexorable grip. "It's only a small anaconda," Luís mocked, "no more than twenty feet. And he couldn't possibly hurt you. He's still too busy digesting his last meal to pay you any attention whatsoever. Now look once more and you'll see there's nothing to be afraid of. He won't eat again for a month or so."

With her head impelled by firm fingers, she found her unwilling eyes forcibly turned to a treetop some twenty feet behind the water's edge. The anaconda was sleeping. The serried coils of its thick grayish brown body, camouflaged by its own markings and by the late shadows cast by the foliage, were draped sluggishly over a stout branch just visible through the trees.

"Any fool can see he's already bloated with a meal," Luís scoffed. "Perhaps it's the horns projecting from the head that alarm you? I admit they do look a little strange. That's a part of his meal the anaconda can't digest. He's been up there for the past couple of days, waiting for them to drop off—which they will, as soon as his digestive processes finish their work."

Shuddering sickly and with no thought now of evasive tactics, Toni turned her head toward Luís's chest. Her voice was muffled by the warm close press of his shirt. "Please let's get away from here," she said.

"I'm not ready to go," came the cool retort. "I told you there's nothing to be afraid of. *Meu Deus*, do you think I would have allowed you to set off in this direction if there were? I have no love of female hysterics.''

Despite the touch of scorn in his voice, his words were reassuring. Only the suddenness of the apparition in the trees had caused Toni's momentary panic; unreasoning fear was not one of her failings. It evaporated now in the realization that she had been well and truly tricked into doing exactly what Luís had wanted all along.

"I warned you not to throw yourself into my arms," he mocked. "You fool, you little fool. This is all I've been waiting for. . . ."

He forced her face to turn to his, and his dark desirous eyes closed in. In the instant before his mouth took hers by storm, she closed her lips tightly and started to struggle against his encompassing viselike arms.

His head jerked free as her fingernails raked his shoulders, scoring even through the fabric of his shirt. His grip tightened, turning hurtful. In the black eyes little pinpoints of the sunset reflecting from the river's surface were like tiny red embers—flaring danger signals that warned of anger aroused. His mouth thinned to a cruel bow.

He made no more move to force his kiss, but waited while she wore herself out with futile efforts to fight free of those muscular arms. And then, as his superior strength finally brought her resistance to a halt, his eyes softened and began to smolder, and a new expression took possession of his mouth.

"Must you fight?" His voice was low, intimate,

husky with desire. "You threw yourself into my arms, remember."

"Only because you tricked me into it!" She remained stiff, stifled by his overwhelming embrace. "You knew the anaconda was here!"

"True," he breathed, the expelled air so close it fanned her mouth. "But given my choice, I would have set off in the opposite direction. Need I remind you that you led the way?"

"You could have stopped me," she asserted wildly, as his lips deposited a little line of kisses along her rigid jaw and into the pulsing hollow of her throat.

"Why would I? This is a romantic place, a beautiful place... the kind of place to start an affair. If you fight, you're only fighting yourself. You asked for a kiss earlier, but what you really asked for was something else altogether... something you want, something I want, something we've both been thinking about ever since we first saw each other."

Suddenly every ounce of starch deserted her. Perhaps it was the unsuppressed passion in his smoking eyes, the soft wooing warmth of his voice, the heavy sensuality of his mouth that overcame her resistance. Whatever the reason, the fight ebbed from her body and a great helplessness welled up inside, turning her soft, pliant, compliant. His strength and his purposefulness and his nearness turned her weak and dizzy. The male aura of him filled her nostrils and the male warmth of him overpowered her reason. Perhaps she had spent too many years trying to be strong, trying to forget she had a woman's needs, a woman's heart, a woman's weaknesses....

And if this was a weakness it was a sweet one, like the molten sweetness that had stolen through her limbs during that one uncompleted kiss. What she saw now in his eyes was what she had then wanted to see; what she felt in the heat of his arms was what she had then wanted to feel; what she heard in his voice was what she had then wanted to hear. Powerless to resist, she melted, soft as warm butter in his hands.

"Let me love you, Antonia," he murmured. "Let me do the things I want to do, the things I must do, the things you want me to do...."

Gently a thumb traced the outline of her lips and then probed, softly commanding. He stroked the full lower lip away from her teeth—and then, even as her lips parted in helpless obedience, his fingers moved away, leaving only the man taste of his hand to tell her he had violated her mouth in any way.

"Let me kiss you," he muttered. It was a command, not a request, for he waited for no answer; and in any case the answer was already in the tremulous expectancy of her parted lips. She groaned a feeble denial, but his lips descended, taking what she could not refuse to give. His breath mingled with her own as she submitted to the insistent exploratory invasion of his tongue, his easy mastery making a mockery of her intentions. She clung to him, trembling, shamed by her weakness but imprisoned by it all the same. Her own aching hunger prevented her from fighting the mouth that possessed hers so expertly, so thoroughly, so passionately, so deeply. For this wild uncaring moment she surrendered to the tastes and textures of temptation, captive of her own unreasoning responses.

At last he lifted his head. "Let me do with you as I want to do," he breathed hoarsely into her hair. And with that he swept her shuddering unresisting body into his arms. Surefooted, strong armed, he carried her along the riverbank, close against the wall of his chest. The last red blaze of sunset paled beside the black blaze of wanting in his eyes. The lean bronzed face was consumed with a pagan need to possess, a terrible smoking intensity that made all remembered emotions seem small. There was no mockery now, only a naked desire, a burning purposefulness that was matched by the impatience of his long strides.

Not once taking his eyes from her flushed face, Luís negotiated the narrow treacherous margin between river and trees, ascended the rise, covered the ground to his bungalow even as rose red sunset gave way to purple dusk. A faint glimmering of willpower flickered back into being as Toni heard the bungalow door being kicked closed behind his heel. How could she respond with such complaisance in the hands of a man who held her in contempt? To surrender so abjectly to someone who despised her was a betrayal of everything she believed about love, and she knew she must not do so without making some effort to stop him.

No fight remained in her limbs, only a fluttering helplessness, but she managed to utter some stran-

gled cries of protest as he laid her where she had slept
for the past two nights.

"No, Luís, please, I beg of you...."

He stroked several errant strands of smooth hair
away from her moist brow.

"Let me tempt you," he breathed, and his thumbs
laid their male imprint upon the secret sensitive
places of her ears—the shells, the lobes, the little hollows hiding there, each place a harborer of sweet sin-
ful impulses that caused her to gasp with a pleasure
she did not want to feel.

"No," she moaned, turning her head away. But
her clinging hands, her parted lips, her melting hips
sent different messages to the virile body that had
come down on the bed beside her. He twisted downward to touch a nipple with his tongue, moistening
the silk of her shirt. There was no need to tease a
response from her body. The pointed trembling taut-
ness of dark flesh visible through the semitransparent
silk gave the lie to all her low moans of denial. "No,
Luís, no...."

"Let me undress you," he murmured, and the buttons of her blouse succumbed one by one to his fingers, freeing the deep swell of her breast before he
captured it with the palm of his hand.

"Let me touch you." The thickened urgent words
were no request, but an accompaniment to what his
hard imperative hands had already done. "Let me
taste you...."

She moaned as his masterful mouth possessed her
breast with no barriers of fabric now. Beneath the

feathering touch of his lips the weakness turned to wildness. There was a madness in her now, a wanting that coursed through her like a forest fire out of control, burning upward and downward from the very place where his tongue and his lips and his teeth were taking command of a nipple—toying with it in expert ardent ways that told he knew very well how to arouse a woman.

Then her hips, too, were freed, and his hands blazed a searing trail over her flesh even as he stroked the clothes away.

"Luís, stop," she whispered as he stood up to shed his own clothes. But this last fevered plea might as well have remained unuttered, for it gave him no pause, and she herself had long since passed the point of no return. His tanned hands were impatient on his shirt buttons, as they had not been on hers. The square powerful shoulders came free, and then the fit flat stomach, darkly tanned against the lean-hipped linen trousers. The hard toned biceps of his upper arms contracted with haste as he unfastened his belt buckle, propelled the zip downward, bent to free his legs from the last of his clothes. And then the naked virile length of him came crushing down on the bed beside her, removing much from her view. But still the impressions were indelibly imprinted on her mind: the hard smooth flesh; the dark disturbing dusting here and there; the paling of suntan on firm flanks; the masculinity of that well-muscled body.

"Let me take you," he murmured as his arms gathered her close against the warmth of limbs whose potency robbed her of the will to resist physically, even if she still tried to deny her own needs. She fought to remind herself that it was sexual drive, not love, that motivated Luís; that he wanted her only to assuage the urgencies of long self-denial; that he scorned her, hated her, held her in contempt. She would not, could not, must not respond.

"No...oh...."

And then there were no more protests. Hard fingers laced themselves into her hair, holding her face in readiness for his onslaught. His lips reverted to the most primitive of languages, parting hers with a forcefulness that left her no choice but to submit. As his mouth took possession of the innermost softness, her senses spun crazily. Only the most desperate of reminders to herself kept her arms from stealing around his shoulders, her hands from exploring the feel of him as she longed to do, her mouth from responding to his deepening kiss.

Matthew, Matthew, Matthew, she told her mind to say, trying to conjure up visions of her husband to protect herself against what was most certainly a travesty of everything she believed about love. But her mind betrayed her, and the name that rang in her body and her bloodstream and her brain was Luís, Luís, Luís....

Heavy against her bared breasts lay the matted texture of his male chest; heavy against her waist was the tense corded stomach; heavy against her hip lay the demanding contours of his male body, which would find its peace only at the expense of hers. His kiss was abrasive, urgent, intrusive now—not asking but demanding, not giving but taking. It was her ultimate submission he wanted, and he told her so with hands that burned their way over her breasts and her waist and below. Her legs resisted parting only feebly, and the movement of dissent was brushed aside by fingers too strong to resist.

That insistent masterful hand now seeking and finding did so only as a precursor of a swift loveless possession for which she ached and against which she strained. Surely the writhing of her hips was the last protest of a lost cause... surely the wild tremors deep in her core were fear, as his touch grew too intimate... surely the little animal sounds low in her throat would have been denials if they had not been silenced by the domination of his mouth.

She was unprepared for the suddenness with which he jackknifed away. All at once she was freed and staring with glazed uncomprehending eyes as he jerked to a sitting position beside her, black eyes smoldering at her with an emotion that now seemed very like anger.

"Would you please tell me," he said in a voice hoarse with unslaked passion, "why in the name of God you're still a virgin?"

CHAPTER TEN

"ARE YOU TRYING to rob me of my sanity? You might have told me before I went so far."

She stared at him, voice clogged in her throat, still not able to believe that he had actually stopped—that he had been *able* to stop. As reason slowly reasserted itself, and she remembered that she had not wanted to surrender herself to a man who treated her with such contempt, she reached for a sheet to cover her breasts and her uncontrollably shuddering limbs.

"You were married for two years; you told me so. Or were you lying about that?"

The response Toni managed to make was uneven and half-swallowed, but audible. "No, I wasn't... lying. I was... married."

Luís looked at her as if he could not believe his eyes. Beneath the jut of those strongly delineated cheekbones, the muscles in his face worked as he attempted to control some strong emotion. After a few starkly silent moments he rose from the bed and walked to the dressing room, his muscular frame unnaturally rigid. He emerged a few minutes later wearing a black cotton dressing gown of kimono design, loosely tied around the waist. Still too shaken by what had happened to raise her eyes to his face, Toni watched the still uncovered calves of his legs advance toward her. Decently covered now, as was she, he sat once more on the edge of the bed.

"I've examined enough virgins in my lifetime to make no mistakes," he stated in the most peremptory of tones. "I think you'd better explain."

"My marriage was never consummated," Toni said in a low voice.

"That much is self-evident," came the faintly sarcastic rejoinder. "Now be good enough to tell me the reason."

"I don't owe you any explanations," she said without raising her eyes.

"Well, then, I must start making assumptions. As your responses seem quite normal, despite your... reservations, shall we say, I have to assume that your husband's were not. Was he impotent, or was it because he simply wasn't interested in... women?"

Some defense of Matthew was called for, and perhaps that was what impelled Toni to give the explanation she had claimed not to owe.

"There was an accident," she said with a lack of inflection that told nothing of the churning, yearning heartaches of those years. "Matthew was a quadriplegic."

The memories were painful even today, nearly five years after Matthew's death, and perhaps that showed in the bleakness of the eyes she now raised to the man who had almost taken what her husband had never been able to take.

Luís remained silent. As his understanding grew, so did his compassion, and then some other, even deeper emotion—remorse, perhaps, for his misjudgment of her character. And because for once there was no contempt, no condemnation, in his silence, Toni went on, revealing more than she had intended to reveal.

"It happened the day of our wedding," she whispered. "That's why I...."

Her tightening throat cut off the rest of the sentence, but there was no need to spell out again that her marriage had not been a normal one. After a thoughtful moment Luís spoke. "Tell me about your husband," he said softly, in the kind of voice she had never heard him use before.

She was not sure why she obeyed, and yet she did—hesitantly at first, talking of that painful part of her life that had colored her whole existence. How she had gone from Spain to New York, planning to work her way through college. How she had found a temporary job searching land titles. How she had met the young, eager, vital law student and fallen in love. How the college plans had been put aside when Matthew proposed.

"We were both very young, and we didn't have much money, so we had decided to honeymoon just outside of New York. After the ceremony we checked into a small old hotel. There were some yellow roses in the lobby, and I...I happened to say how lovely they were before we got in the elevator. Our room was on the seventh floor."

Room seven-seven-seven. "I asked for it because it's my lucky number," Matthew had said, laughing as he swung her into his arms and carried her over the threshold into the room. It had been the seventh day of the month, and July, the seventh month of the year. She had been nineteen and he had been twenty-four and they had been very much in love.

"He left me in the room and went back downstairs—to buy some roses, although he didn't tell me that until later."

"Seven yellow roses. God, Toni, I only wanted to tell you I loved you, and look what a mess I've made of my life. Of our lives. Of me. Damn those yellow roses!"

"There was a faulty elevator." Toni took a deep breath, but her level voice faltered in no other way. "Something gave out right after it stopped at our floor to pick him up. Two others were killed. Matthew was... luckier."

Or had he been luckier? "Let me die," he had pleaded so many times. "Let me die. Kill me, Toni. If you love me, give me something and let me die. For my sake, for your sake... oh, God, I'll grow to hate you, Toni, if you don't let me die."

"After that he had no use of his limbs, except for a few muscles in one arm," she finished dully.

Luís broke the silence in a quiet grave voice. Toni was grateful that he kept his pity, if any, to himself. "And you. Tell me about you."

"There's really nothing to tell."

"Yes, there is," he insisted evenly. "For one thing,

how did you survive for those years? The medical bills must have been enormous.''

"It wasn't so hard.''

But it had been hard, and perhaps Luís guessed at some of the financial struggles of that time, for he added quietly, "Did your parents help?"

"My parents are both retired, living in Spain. They survive on a small pension. But Matthew's mother is a widow, and at the time she had a small house about forty miles out of New York. When Matthew got out of the hospital we were able to move in with her. I managed to get a good job I could commute to in the city, as a girl Friday with the production house that still employs me. Matthew's mother cared for him during the day while I worked.''

There was no pretty flesh to deck the bare bones of that story. But perhaps Toni's silence said more about the drudgery and dreariness and hopelessness of those two years than any words could have done.

"And you found in your career what your husband couldn't give you,'' Luís stated after some moments of absorbing what she had told him. "Some kind of fulfillment.''

"That's not so,'' she denied, but for the first time she seemed uncertain, her eyes turning a troubled smoky gray, like wind-ruffled water. With one finger she traced a restless pattern on the sheet and then smoothed it quickly, as though she knew the action betrayed too much. "It wasn't always easy, but it worked out all right. I was...content.''

It was not a total lie. After the worst of the shock

had passed there had been bittersweet moments—times when she had known herself to be needed; times when she had found a poignant satisfaction in her growing ability to support herself and a crippled husband; times when Matthew had been touchingly grateful that she had not annulled the marriage. In the beginning. It had been like that in the beginning.

And then there had been the first seeds of suspicion. *"Why were you late today, Toni? What did you do?"*

"And your husband," Luis asked, touching the finger that still wore Matthew's wedding ring. "Did you love him?"

"How can you say you love me, Toni—a man who's no man at all?" The eyes that had been so bright had grown bitter, the eyes of a stranger imprisoned in a familiar face. "Look at me when you say you love me, so I can see the lie in your eyes! Look at my arms! Look at my legs! How can you love me when I'm no more than a parody of a man? You'd be happier if I were dead. Oh, God, curse those roses. . . . "

"Yes, I loved him," she said simply.

"Who is he, Toni? I don't believe that! What's his name? Does he work in your office, Toni—does he? I know you take a lunch hour. Is that when you've been seeing him? In some seedy little hotel? Oh, God, do you really expect me to believe you? What does he give you that I can't, Toni? Does he give his life for you as I did—as I still would if I could? Or does he just give you roses? My God, yellow roses. . . . "

"How did he die?" came the next slow question.

It took Toni a minute to formulate her reply. This,

too, was a painful memory, perhaps the most painful of all, and she wanted her answer to betray no more than necessary. "I saved enough money to buy Matthew a special wheelchair," she said. "It was one of those things with all sorts of gadgets. It could be activated with the few muscles he could use. It was a little hard for him to get used to it. At first he was always setting off in the wrong direction." She swallowed and finished in a strained voice, "I should never have bought it. There was another accident—a fatal one this time."

"Describe the accident."

"I don't think—"

"Tell me," Luís said in a voice so authoritative, so measured, that she began to tell despite herself.

"I was at work. His mother went out one day on a short errand. When she came back, he was dead at the bottom of the basement stairs. The wheelchair had fallen—I suppose because Matthew activated the wrong command."

"Suicide?"

"Of course not!"

A hand like a band of steel closed over her wrist. "Call a spade a spade, Antonia. If he committed suicide, say so."

She cast a wild trapped look at the somber-faced man who seemed to see too many things with those dark incisive eyes. "If it was suicide, how could I possibly know? Matthew couldn't write. He left no note. Even his mother was sure it was an accident. And I . . . I have no reason to believe it was anything else."

"Are you sure?"

Her gaze turned defiant. "It's better that way, isn't it? Let the dead rest in peace."

"And their mothers, too?" he murmured, a little too intuitively. Then with a frown he freed her wrist, as if he had just realized that his grip was too tight.

"I'm not a fool, Antonia. I'm familiar with those mechanical contraptions, and also with the narrowness of stairs in small houses. Even to maneuver to the head of the stairs—which presumably had a door, as most basement stairs do—would be a complex task for your husband. Why don't you admit what you must know in your heart?"

Tears sprang to Toni's eyes, because in her heart she did know, had always known. And there it was in the open—the deep bottled knowledge, the ache of guilt that had tied her to Matthew in a way mere love could never have done. Her hands covered her face, trying to press back the tears and with them the admission that was so hard to make, even to herself.

"The truth this time," Luís said gravely. He was the complete professional now—not aggressor but confessor, not lover but listener. He reached forward and pulled the fingers away from her eyes; and the unwanted tears began to spill in earnest. Shamed by this exposure, Toni let out a deep sob and tried to turn her face away.

"Let it go," he ordered; and she did.

And through the strangled sobs, the truth she had told to no other person at last emerged.

"He. . . had sent his mother out on the errand. He

said nothing to her to suggest what he intended...
but I knew, I knew from the first. When I saw what
she had bought, I knew...."

"Go on."

"It was roses, seven roses...*yellow* roses."

"SUICIDE IS A SPECIAL KIND OF TYRANNY," Luís said
later, much later, after the tears had finally choked to
a halt. Two hours had passed since sunset, and still
lights burned in the low bungalow lost in the Amazon
night. For much of the time the tears had flowed
against Luís's black dressing gown, but there had been
no passion in the arms that held her, only compassion.

For Toni the wrenching sobs of remorse had at last
given way to a kind of cold despairing exhaustion.
Some minutes ago Luís had left the bed altogether,
dressed himself properly in daytime clothes instead
of the well-dampened robe, and without comment
handed Toni a clean shirt, which now covered her
nakedness more effectively than the sheet. He had
moved halfway across the room and turned his back
while she donned the shirt, and there he still stood—
his hands jammed into his pockets, his head slightly
bent as if in brooding contemplation of the patterns
in the grass matting that served as a rug.

"Suicide is a kind of tyranny from the grave," he
went on, "because of the burden of guilt it puts on
those who are left behind. Among other things, you
feel guilty because you bought him the chair, the
suicide weapon. But you shouldn't. The decision was
his."

"'Should' and 'shouldn't' don't help much," came the low despondent answer. "His mother felt guilty, too, and she thought it was an accident."

"But I imagine she manages to live with her guilt, and possibly even transfer some of it to you because *she* didn't buy the chair. Whereas *you*...."

"I've managed, too."

"Have you?" Luís turned to face her, his strong mouth straight but no longer cynical, no longer scornful, no longer accusatory, as it had been through so much of their acquaintance. "I don't think so. You're a beautiful woman, Antonia— young, vibrant, desirable, in the prime of your life. Your husband died when you were only twenty-one, five years ago. Yet in those five years there's been no man. Don't you see what your husband deliberately did to you?"

"Not deliberately," she protested. "Matthew wanted me to be happy. He was bitter about himself, I don't deny it, and sometimes suspicious during the last year. Who wouldn't be in his situation? He lived a living death, able to do nothing for himself. He hated that. He grew to hate himself. His body was useless, his limbs were wasting, his mind was twisting."

"Oh, I can understand the agonies he must have been going through. I find it harder to forgive him for trying to ruin your life, too."

"You're mistaken," she said.

"You might also try admitting that he grew to hate you."

"That's not true."

"Then why," came the soft question, "do you think he committed suicide?"

Toni tensed her fingers, steepled them together and studied the arch they formed. "Because he couldn't bear living like a vegetable. And also for my sake. He wanted me to be happy."

"Are you sure he didn't do it so you *couldn't* be happy? I think he wanted to ensure your loyalty—and for all time."

"That's nonsense!"

"Then why," came the swift retort, arrowing to the heart of the matter, "did he send you such a clear message? It wasn't your anniversary; there was no reason to buy flowers. Yellow roses meant nothing to his mother, but they did mean something to you. He couldn't write a note, but he wanted you to be in absolutely no doubt that he had killed himself—and that he had done it for your sake. If he still loved you, really loved you, he didn't have to leave that... suicide message. Don't you see he wanted you to feel guilty?"

For some more moments Toni continued to avoid those eyes that were like dark mirrors, reflecting truths she had long evaded. At last she said bitterly, "I suppose you're right. I think he did grow to hate me."

"Why?" Then, after a pause, "Talk about it, Antonia. Get it out of your system. What reasons did he have to hate you?"

"For going out every day, all in one piece. For seeing him every night as his limbs wasted...washing him, dressing him, caring for his needs. He hated that I had to see him that way." She hesitated, and then it came out in a rush. "And maybe he hated me most of all for never having allowed *him* what he was sure I must allow some other man sooner or later."

"Then he knew you had the needs of a normal woman."

"Yes, he knew," she said tiredly. "We had shared a number of very passionate moments. But I had some odd old-fashioned notions, and Matthew had respected them."

How many times she had punished herself for withholding from Matthew that small measure of content. How many times, in the darkness of night, she had regretted not having given herself freely and fully, in the first flush of young love. In retrospect it had seemed a very small thing to give—but a very great thing to withhold.

"I think you really did love him," Luís said in the quietest of voices.

Two tardy tears sprang from a source that had seemed quite spent. "Yes, I did," she whispered, and then went on unsteadily, "He was so warm and understanding before his accident. When I...resisted, he managed to maintain a sense of humor about it— wrote me silly little notes, gave me funny desk signs. *My Mind Is Made Up; Don't Confuse Me with Facts.*" Her voice lowered to an anguished whisper as she went on, "You see, at that time Matthew...loved me, really loved me. Old-fashioned notions and all."

"And your old-fashioned notions also included some other rare commodities—scruples about fidelity and loyalty to your husband, even a husband who could never satisfy your need to be a woman."

"Yes, I suppose that's so," she agreed dispiritedly, at the moment finding little comfort in the strict moral code that had been instilled through the years of growing up in straitlaced Spain. "I would never have been unfaithful to Matthew, although he didn't. . . see it that way."

"There's no reason to be faithful to him now. You can't remain tied to a dead man forever." He paused, then continued, "Or are you by now so dedicated to your career that you don't care about things like a home and a husband and children of your own?"

"Yes, I. . . care."

"Then isn't it time you let go of that part of your life?"

Toni sighed, not with sorrow but with a vague formless sense of release. Although all barriers had not yet been broken down, Luís's persistent questioning had been like a battering ram at the strong door of old guilts. Her thoughts were still too disorderly to produce actual relief, but she recognized that it had helped, somehow, to put so much into words. The knowledge that Matthew must have grown to hate her: that had been the inadmissible, the unspeakable, the unvoiced and unvoiceable thought. And now that it had been voiced, the gate between past and present had been partially breached.

The silence between them grew, accentuated by the night sounds of the jungle—the cricket chirpings, the bird cooings and callings that were so seldom heard in the heat of the day. At last Luís swiveled on his heel and went to a small corner cabinet. Without asking Toni's wishes he poured a measure of neat brandy and came back across the room. Bending over the bed, he eased it into the grasp of the slender fingers that were now beginning to relax, as they had not done during the previous two hours.

"Medicinal in purpose." He smiled the kind of smile he had never bestowed on her before. There was a warmth in the dark eyes, a caressing reassuring quality that had nothing to do with desire. "It's not intended as an aphrodisiac, I assure you. Perhaps it will help you sleep."

"Thank you." The brief unflirtatious glance Toni directed upward held a strong measure of gratitude; and then the expression was swiftly hidden as she lowered her eyes to the glass. She sipped at the brandy, welcoming its sting in her throat, watching wordlessly as Luís found a flashlight and thrust it into his hip pocket without switching it on. Then he prowled silently around the room, extinguishing lights. He left the last lamp burning until the brandy had been downed, and then that, too, was turned off. In the darkened room she could hear a door opening; could feel a slight draft of night air on her shoulders. She shivered.

"I'm sorry, very sorry," he said into the blackness. There was a quality of rue and humility in his low husky tone, in sharp contrast to his usual self-assured cynicism.

For trying to force her into having an affair against her will? To Toni it seemed the apology could mean only that. Anger at his duplicity had long since been replaced by thankfulness for his eleventh-hour continence; by gratitude for his instinctive perceptiveness about her marriage; and by a warmth engendered during the two hours when he had held her in a close, comforting, undemanding embrace that must have put considerable strain on his self-control.

"It doesn't matter," Toni said, suddenly exhausted by the excess of emotion she had expended since the morning. "You didn't do anything, in the final analysis."

"I'm not apologizing for trying to have an affair," he replied gruffly. "I'm apologizing because of something I forgot. Something I have...forced myself to forget for eleven years. Perhaps because I didn't want to remember."

There was a hoarseness to his voice, a trace of harshness, as if he found the words very difficult to say. His admission seemed to call for some question, and so Toni voiced a low, "Oh?"

She could hear the unsteady catch in his breath. "I'm sorry I assumed all kinds of things about you. You see, Antonia, I had forgotten there were still a few women in the world like...like you."

CHAPTER ELEVEN

VERY LITTLE HAPPENED before Monday morning, when the misbegotten river trip drew to an end, bringing two sorer but wiser members of the film crew stumbling back into the jungle compound. Or perhaps it would be more exact to say that what did happen—the important thing, the beautiful thing, the wild thing, the wonderful thing—happened so imperceptibly that Toni was not aware until later that it had happened at all.

Before the return of the others she did, however, learn a startling fact from Luís, one that provided a rationale for much of his initial reaction to her and his cynicism thereafter. And while it did not exactly lessen the impropriety of his behavior since, perhaps it explained that, too, in part at least.

He revealed the fact on Sunday morning, while he was back in his own bungalow, picking up some personal possessions. Toni was to continue to sleep alone under this roof, an arrangement that reassured her, with no more specific words said, that Luís had abandoned all designs upon her person.

"That night I saw you at dinner," he said suddenly, turning to face her, "it wasn't the first time. I'd seen you earlier that day—at my brother-in-law's house.''

At Garcia's house? Toni stared numbly, assimilating this new and surprising fact.

Luís went on, ''I know where Diogo keeps his spare key, and I had reasons for going there that day. I let myself in, went upstairs and walked out on a balcony. I saw you. You were sunbathing.''

In the nude: she remembered. She had thought herself alone for the afternoon, as Barney and Ty had gone off on a prearranged double date with two Carioca girls. But Barney's date had failed to materialize, and he had returned unexpectedly, coming upon Toni as she dozed in a state of undress at the poolside. And that had been when Barney had made his move. Drugged with sleep, Toni had almost responded, not fighting Barney off until it was nearly too late.

A few days earlier telltale color might have risen to Toni's face upon discovering that she had been watched, but today, in the aftermath of a long night's reckoning, her face remained ashen beneath the light golden tan. ''Then you saw Barney kissing me,'' she stated.

''Yes. But that's all I saw, because I left. I couldn't. . . didn't *want* to see any more.''

''But you thought you knew what would happen.'' No wonder Luís had thought her well versed in the ways of having affairs!

He acknowledged that with a bitter self-deprecating nod. ''Yes, I thought I knew. And when I saw you with another man that same night—''

"You don't have to explain," Toni cut in, too enervated to pursue the topic. "It doesn't matter. It really doesn't matter."

In the afternoon, a relatively free one for Luís, it rained rivers. They sat companionably on the shel tered veranda, talk drowned by great thunderclaps, until the roar changed to a slow steady downpour. The rain, Toni mused, would slow the return of her teammates. Today she did not care.

After that they talked of innocuous things. Toni heard a little about the pitfalls of growing up with six older sisters—the dry, often humorous anecdotes sometimes causing her to laugh, which was perhaps why Luís told them. And she found herself telling of the small village in Extremadura where her parents had settled in her preteen years, in order to enjoy the low cost of living in Spain.

That evening, under skies rinsed clean, they went together to watch the sunset, this time from the relative neutrality of the riverside dock. Then she learned a little more about what Luís planned on doing upon his return to civilization. In no way did he give her any clue as to what had occasioned the change of heart.

"There's a research post I could take in connection with the school for tropical medicine," he told her. "It's a special unit, looking for solutions to the medical problems faced by Stone Age Amazon tribes when they come into contact with civilization. I considered going there a few years ago but decided against it. Now...."

"Surely the post won't still be open?"

"It should be," he said dryly, "as I've been funding the research unit myself."

As the last rays of the sun turned the river to a red radiant bath, there was a silence so companionable that Toni felt emboldened to ask softly, "What made you decide to return to civilization?"

Something in Luís's face closed as swiftly as a window blind being yanked down. His mouth turned taut as he answered evenly but aridly, "If I stay here there's very little more I can do for the Xara. Perhaps the answer to their problems will come from research. Medicines, vaccines, more knowledge about the body's immunological systems—these are the only things that can really help them now."

Toni waited, thinking he might want to talk about the things Getulio had told her; but evidently he did not. At last she said simply, "It's such a change for you."

"No, it's not," he contradicted. "When I first started studying medicine, my original intention was to get into research. Perhaps you're not aware that there's a serious problem in the Amazon. The pure-bred primitive tribes are vanishing—in fact, some have already vanished. The *caboclos*, the half-breeds, are ridden by malaria, but with the help of modern medicine they're a hardy enough lot. The same can't be said for the undiluted strains. With more settlers coming to the Amazon every day, tribes like the Xara are being killed off because they have no immunity to very ordinary ailments—colds, influenza, measles, that sort of thing. They're being killed off by the diseases of civilization, as surely as their ancestors were once killed off by mine.''

Toni darted a quick look at the grim set face bathed in the sun's dying light. "By yours?''

"Yes. My forebears were rubber barons—didn't you know? They became rich on the lifeblood of Amazon Indians and *caboclos*, too. It was a killing thing to work the rubber trees, for as I told you they don't grow in rows. The rubber workers—*seringueiros*, they're called—had to rise two hours before dawn. They walked miles through the jungle every day, first slashing the trees, then collecting the sap. Long into the night they would still be crouched over choking smudge pots, smoking the rubber into huge hundred-pound balls fit for transportation. A man who eked out an existence in that way died a miserably early death. Some men still do it, but at least those who do it nowadays do it of their own free choice. In the old days they didn't.''

"But how—''

"Brute force.'' Luís's voice was devoid of emotion, but Toni sensed that the sins of his ancestors sat strong upon his conscience. "There were laws against the tactics my ancestors used, but in those days there was very little protection for a remote tribe on a remote tributary. The Indians didn't want to work the rubber—why should they? It didn't make *them* rich, and in any case they had no need of money. Working the rubber long into the night meant they couldn't even feed themselves properly. Do you wonder that the Xara have so little trust in outsiders?''

"No," Toni said quietly.

"Such things could never happen nowadays; the primitive tribes are very well protected by the Brazilian government. Ironic, isn't it, that diseases like the common cold are finishing what my ancestors started."

Was it a grim morality, then, that had brought Luís to bury himelf in this remote place—a desire to expiate the wrongs perpetrated by his forebears? It seemed likely. Unwilling to reveal that Getulio had already told her so much of the story, she asked no more questions about the Xara's population problems.

"Where will you be living when you leave here?" she asked as they trudged up the hill to return to their separate sleeping quarters.

"In Manaus—that's where the research unit is located. My ancestral home," he finished on a note so bitter that Toni felt constrained against asking too much.

She made one more remark. "I suppose we'll see you next month, then, when we're filming in Manaus."

"No. Next month I'll be far too busy," he said in a harsh discouraging voice.

A moment later they reached the parting of the ways—Luís tall, dark, brooding, now silent, moving scrupulously away from Toni's slender frame. Inexplicably hesitant, she paused and turned to him before setting off in the direction of the bungalow. She had the feeling there was something she wanted to say, or wanted him to say, but she could not think what it was. Nothing in Luís's lean expressionless face suggested that he shared her hesitation.

"Good night," he said in a remote voice.

"Good night," she echoed after an awkward pause, and turned toward her solitary bed.

It was not until the following morning, after the others had returned in a righteous display of blistered hands, injured egos and frayed tempers, that she knew what it was she had wanted to say; what she had wanted him to say. It came to her in a great flash of understanding when she saw Luís kneeling down to help secure the *lancha*, a dark forelock falling over his brow, the fabric of his khaki trousers taut over his bent knees. And in that moment she understood the thing—the important, beautiful, wild, wonderful thing—that had happened over these past few days.

She had fallen in love with Luís: desperately, deeply, head over heels in love. She had fallen in love with the bones of his face and the shape of his ears and the set of his mouth and the dark disturbing eyes. She had fallen in love with the long, lean, virile body and the skilled sure hands. She had fallen in love with the way he walked and the way he talked and the way his crisp black hair curved over the nape of his neck. She had fallen in love with the warmth of his skin and the indefinable tang of him—that clean, masculine, marvelous something that filled her nostrils when he was near.

But most of all, she had fallen in love with the man.

To Toni's relief, Ty and Barney joshed her not at all about the events of the past few days—at least not at first. In answer to an outraged question from her two cohorts, she informed them that Luís had slept in the hospital and been a perfect gentleman. They took her word as to the sleeping arrangement, but not as regarded their host.

"I'd like to get my hands around his neck," Barney said murderously.

"Your hands don't look up to it," Toni noted dryly, with a glance at the liberal bandages Luís had applied to his blistered palms.

Ty brandished a similarly swathed fist in the air. "I swear he wrapped us up like a pair of mummies just to protect himself," he grimaced.

"I expect he didn't realize the return trip would take so long," Toni suggested, mentally crossing her fingers. "He told me it's usually done in a day. Did you get some good footage?"

"Dynamite," Ty conceded. "All the same, if I'd known what we were letting ourselves in for...."

"Perhaps that's why Dr. Quental didn't tell you," Toni smiled, oiling troubled waters as best she could. "I'm sure when you see the rushes you'll decide it was all worthwhile."

"You can hardly call them rushes when we won't see them for a month," grumbled Ty.

The muttering eventually came to a halt as Ty and

Barney went off to throw their exhausted bodies into hammocks for the rest of the morning. Toni breathed an inward sigh of relief: at the moment, hugging the newness of her discovered feelings to herself, she felt unable to cope with her two longtime buddies.

Getulio did not share the ill effects suffered by his fellow travelers, and so Luís directed him to gather together some fellow *caboclos* to see to the rebuilding of the small shelter. "As Braz and Ana will be taking over my bungalow," Toni heard him say, "it will have to be done before tomorrow. Tonight, of course, the American *senhora* can continue to sleep in my place."

The American *senhora*: it sounded so cold, so polite, so impersonal. After what had happened between them, how could Luís possibly be so detached? Was this the same man whose lips had seared her, whose hands had scorched her, whose eyes had blazed over her nakedness with such an intensity of passion that her flesh still burned at the memory of his touch?

It seemed that now the emotion was all on her side. Throat tight, and not wanting to listen to more of the overheard conversation, she swiveled on her heel and walked away from the place where Luís and Getulio were conferring.

Some instinct told her to turn when she had covered no more than thirty feet. Her heart leaped, skipping several beats, to find dark tortured eyes trained on her retreat. They were quickly wrenched back in Getulio's direction, but in that moment she knew that the flames burning in Luís were banked, not extinguished.

He still wanted her; and he wanted her with a fire so fierce that it was consuming him, body and soul.

She spent the rest of the morning, the last before Luís was to leave for Manaus, in a ferment of sorting out her own emotions. And when the morning was through she knew that she could not watch love walk out of her life—even if it meant putting aside the last of her outmoded loyalties to Matthew; even if it meant shedding the scruples of a lifetime; even if it meant risking hurt and heartache.

But if she had hopes of any romantic encounters in the brief time remaining before Luís's departure, they were dashed at noon that day. Over the communal meal he announced that he intended to undertake another overnight trip to the Xara village—to speak to Eketi, Toni surmised. He would not return from this trip until Tuesday morning, prior to the *Catalina*'s arrival. He discouraged Toni's suggestion that the film crew might accompany him for the trek, pointing out that Ty and Barney might be better served by a day's rest.

"Getulio will be here to look after all of you," he said. "It will be time enough for you to go back to the Xara village when Braz arrives. He's quite capable of taking care of you there: Braz grew up on this river. He speaks the language of the Xara, and he speaks English, too, so there'll be no problems of communication. Moreover, the Xara trust him. Remember, like Getulio, Braz has a strong strain of Xara blood."

Toni's suggestion seemed destined to die a natural death when the two other members of the film crew confessed they were still numb from the grueling physical ordeal of hauling a heavy boat through the rapids. Luís nodded, seemingly oblivious to the pointed injured glances that accompanied Ty's and Barney's descriptions of their present physical discomforts.

"I'll be leaving late this afternoon," Luís said, rising from the table. "Come to the dispensary in an hour, both of you, and I'll have another look at those blisters."

"There's no reason I can't make the trip with Luís," Toni said as soon as he had departed. There was no need to analyze her motives: she knew what they were.

"Oh, it's Luís now, is it," came the wise comment, as Ty and Barney exchanged one of their knowing looks.

"What on earth would you *do* at the Xara village, Toni?" There was a wide-eyed innocence in Barney's face. "Turn yourself into a one-woman film team? There's no point in your going there without us. Or is there?"

"One tent or two?" asked Ty laconically.

Damn that pair for being so perceptive! "It would just be in the interests of establishing a better relationship with the Xara," she fibbed quickly. "I'll distribute a few small gifts, talk to some of the women through that girl Maria, gather some more background material. It could be useful, Ty. By the next time we all go together, we'll be dependent on this other doctor, Getulio's son. Perhaps he does have a good relationship with the Xara, but after all, he's been living in Rio de Janeiro for some years. I doubt if he's held in such high regard as Lu—er, Dr. Quental.''

Ty put on a benign expression. "High regard," he repeated thoughtfully.

"Taken the tumble, Toni?" asked Barney, bland faced.

"No, I haven't." Toni's voice was tart, unlike her usually soothing tones. She knew she was protesting too much, and the stain of color that rose unbidden to her face was not helping matters at all. She decided on a frontal attack—the only way to deal with this impossible pair once they started their unmerciful hounding. She glared at them icily.

"And what if I did? You're not my keepers, either of you. I'll tumble if I want, when I want and with whom I want. I don't give a damn whether you like it or not."

"Oho," said Ty, idly rubbing the tip of his nose. "This is a change of heart. Perhaps we should have asked more questions about the sleeping arrangements these past couple of days."

"With Manoel to stand watch in the clinic," mused Barney, "there'd be no need for Dr. Que—er, Luís to bunk there, too."

Toni compressed her lips. "Think what you want about me, but don't involve Luís in your nasty little suspicions! He hasn't made a single pass!"

Two enragingly expressionless faces stared back at her flushed and flustered countenance without uttering a single comment.

"Which is more than I can say for the two of you," Toni added with vicious intent. "Both of you might cast your evil little minds back to a certain day in Rio. Maybe there are some things you *don't* know about each other! If you want to accuse anyone of making passes, accuse yourselves! Both of you were quite ready to ask me for a . . . a tumble, as you so inelegantly put it! And it took a black eye to stop one of you!"

Again the two men looked at each other, not a single flicker betraying their reaction. "Odd she never gave me away before," said Barney at last.

"I never did believe that tale about walking into a screen door," said Ty. "But never mind. She put me through the wringer, too."

"I wonder . . . ."

"Do you think . . . ?"

"Yes, I do," said the other.

"There are tumbles and there are tumbles," Ty said enigmatically, as he and Barney turned to look at Toni again.

"Oh . . . oh . . . damn you, both of you!" Frustration turned Toni's eyes too bright. "I told you, Luís hasn't tried anything! And even if he did want to, now—how could anything *possibly* happen at the Xara village? By the time I've tramped six miles in boots half a size too small, I won't be fit to fall into bed with anyone! You must be mad if you think anything could happen there!"

The faces of her two teammates remained perfectly straight; they exchanged another conspiratorial look. "She's right," said Barney. "Sore feet and sex don't mix."

"I think it's time we took a hand in this," judged Ty.

"Can you think of a solution?" asked Barney.

Ty contemplated for a moment. "Only two," he said. "One for each foot."

"Too bad she can't buy any around here," Barney sighed.

In concert they turned to Toni, their faces grave and pompous in a way that might once have made her laugh. "We've decided," Ty pronounced, "that you'd better fly to Manaus tomorrow. You need a new pair of boots."

"You've got to be joking! I can't leave in the middle of the job."

Ty lifted his brows. "Do you think you're indispensable? Besides, I need some more of that film stock we put into refrigeration in Manaus. Most of what I have got wet."

"Impossible," Toni said, glaring. "You didn't take most of what you had on the trip through the rapids—and what you took was all in rubber bags."

"Rain," came the glib retort, "dripping through the roof of the supply shed. And leaky cans. The damage is irreparable."

"I could use some more of the tapes I left at the hotel," Barney mused as if deep in thought. "Can't think how I managed to go through them so fast."

Patently they were lying: Toni continued to give them her very best evil eye for several belligerent moments. And then it welled into the forefront of her consciousness that she really *did* want to go to Manaus; that she could not bear to have Luís walk out of her life; and that she really did not give a damn what Ty and Barney thought. Her eyes fell away from the dueling match that had been going on. "I couldn't be back in less than a week," she said, "because the plane only flies here on Tuesdays."

Ty smiled indulgently. "Exactly. . ."

". . . what we had in mind," finished his partner in crime.

BITTER DISAPPOINTMENT altered with bouts of crushing self-doubt during the flight to Manaus. Had she been wrong about Luís after all, Toni wondered. He had seemed displeased, almost thunderously so, upon learning of her intentions. But as he had not been informed of her plan to visit Manaus until Tuesday morning, shortly after he had emerged from a jungle that still dripped from the night's torrential rains, there was very little he could say or do.

By then sounds of the nearing *Catalina* had warned of its imminent arrival, and Getulio had left in the *lancha* to ferry his son and daughter-in-law back to the compound. To save overloading the boat later, he had also taken most of Luís's possessions on this first trip—and also, as it happened, Toni's scant luggage for the week. Since she had left a suitcase full of city clothes in Manaus in the care of the hotel, she required very little for the trip.

It had been arranged that the pilot would return in several hours, after he had made his other weekly calls, in order to pick up Luís and Toni. It was a short delay but a necessary one; Luís needed time to confer with the man who would be taking over his work at the jungle clinic.

Getulio's son, Braz, turned out to be a surprisingly handsome man. Out of his amalgam of Portuguese and Amazon Indian blood—with some Irish thrown in, if his name and his coloring gave any clues—Braz O'Hara seemed to have inherited the best features from each race. He had his father's startlingly burnished hair; the golden bronze skin of the Xara; a compact muscular frame; a fine profile and quick intelligent face; and dark liquid eyes. It was also likely, Toni decided somewhat skeptically, that he had a very polished bedside manner; he had that look of a Lothario about him.

But there was an easy charm to Braz O'Hara that inspired liking if not trust, and Toni found herself wondering why there seemed to be a certain amount of reserve in the air when he and Luís Quental exchanged greetings. From what Getulio had told her about Luís's educating Braz as if he were his own son, she would have expected more warmth between the men. Or perhaps, to be more exact, more warmth on Luís's part.

Braz's young wife, Ana, the schoolteacher, gave every appearance of worshiping the ground her handsome husband walked upon. In the space of a few hours' acquaintance Toni found herself wondering idly whether Ana—a nice, dumpy, homespun woman who would never outshine her husband—might not have encouraged this move to the Amazon in order to escape feminine competition in Rio de Janeiro.

But if Toni had speculations along those lines, it had been impossible to pursue them, for she had seen very little of Braz and Ana in the time before the plane returned. On this occasion the pilot had few other calls, and so it had been quite early in the afternoon when the drone of the plane advised of its return.

Not long ago, with last goodbyes said, Getulio had ferried her and Luís along a turgid river whose waters now lapped at the very base of the trees. The river in flood: it seemed symbolic of her own emotional level, which for good or for bad seemed to be rising toward some kind of high-water mark.

Her first opportunity to speak privately to Luís came after the plane was aloft. Perhaps to discourage conversation, he had closed his eyes, which today looked very deep and tired, the tiny telltale lines that fanned out from the edges telling her that he must have been up most of the night.

"Did you speak to Eketi?" she asked quietly, deciding she must take this opportunity to establish communication.

"Yes, I did." His voice was expressionless and his eyes remained closed. "Most of the night, in fact. I couldn't convince him."

"Oh," said Toni, disappointed—and not only for Maria's sake. The course of love seemed to be a rocky road indeed. She studied her fingers for a moment and noted that they were decidedly unsteady. This time it could not be put down to *pium* attacks during the river trip. In addition to taking antihistamines in advance, she had been well slathered in insect repellent and covered all over by a heavy net of suffocating weave. Perhaps it was the scent of insect repellent that caused the tight taut set of Luís's nostrils.

"Eketi doesn't choose to believe that Maria removed her clothes in order to attract him," Luís went on wearily. "He says there's nothing provocative about a woman without clothes. In fact, as the evening wore on, he even admitted to some crazy notion that Maria has been flirting with outsiders—myself included."

Toni stared, nonplussed, as Luís's dark eyes feathered slowly open, wearing discouragement like a stamp. "Why on earth would he think that?" she asked.

Luís sighed heavily. "Because Maria puts her clothes on whenever an outsider arrives. To Eketi, clothes are erotic and nudity is not. He believes she's almost advertising her wares—putting herself on display, so to speak. If he weren't in such awe of her education, I suspect he would be very stern about her laxity."

"Good grief," said Toni with a little half laugh of dismay. It was hard to believe that Maria's agonizing bashfulness could be interpreted as a sign of forwardness, but with the Xara anything was possible.

"I simply couldn't shake Eketi's logic. To him it's very simple. If Maria wanted to catch his eye, he says, she would never have removed her clothes in the first place."

Toni turned her eyes to the window and sat in silence for a moment, watching the colors of the rain forest unfold like a tapestry far below. As Eketi could not be convinced, perhaps she could speak to Maria the next time the film crew went to the Xara village. For Maria, possibly a simple thing like leaving her dress on in Eketi's presence would do the trick.

As if Luís understood what she was thinking, he said in a dry voice, "Don't bother suggesting that Maria remain clothed all the time, either. She's been going naked for too long, and the rest of the Xara would consider such a sudden cover-up quite immoral. They already look askance at Maria for her occasional use of clothes. It's probably why they were all ready to believe the worst of her the other day."

"Oh, Lord," muttered Toni. "In other words, she's damned if she does and damned if she doesn't." Then she added on a sudden thought, "And yet Eketi himself puts on clothing when outsiders arrive. Nobody seems to consider that immoral. Where's the logic there?"

"In his case the clothes are used to denote rank."

"Then if Maria were Eketi's wife," Toni reflected,

"I suppose she'd be allowed to cover up with impunity?"

"Perhaps—but she'll never be Eketi's wife," Luís returned. His hand rubbed the back of his neck in a gesture denoting weariness. "Unless Maria makes some direct approach, and soon, there's absolutely no chance for her."

"Soon?"

"Eketi's come to the conclusion that he's been without a woman for too long. I'm afraid my own persuasions had something to do with the decision. Only a few days ago he made a vow to his tribal gods that he would take a wife by the time of the next full moon. He's looking over the marriageable girls—not with enthusiasm, but because he knows he owes it to his people to start producing children."

"Oh, Lord," groaned Toni, feeling sick for Maria's sake. "If I'd known all this I would have put off my trip to Manaus. I might have been able to—"

"If your errands in Manaus aren't urgent," Luís sliced through her words, his voice peremptory, "you most certainly shouldn't have come."

And then he turned away and closed his eyes, signaling an abrupt end to the conversation. Toni's heart curled into a small hurt ball, and she made no effort to continue an interchange that was not wanted.

Why did Luís seem so decidedly hostile to the idea of her coming to Manaus? Did he think she was chasing him? From his discouraging manner, it seemed humiliatingly likely that he did. And, Toni admitted wryly to herself, that was exactly what she *was* doing, with a kindly push from Ty and Barney. What arrogant extraordinary creatures men could be: so ready to pursue, yet so unwilling to be pursued. And they talked about women being hard to understand!

Darting a covert glance at his set averted face, she wondered if he had mentally stowed her back in the category of women for whom he had nothing but scorn. A misogynist of long standing could hardly be expected to undergo a complete change of heart overnight. Doubtless Luís was something of a male chauvinist, too, and as such considered the hunt purely a man's prerogative. And he was also the type to whom marriage would be pure anathema. Perhaps, knowing of her resistance to Matthew's overtures, he thought she might make demands along those lines?

Feeling decidedly unsure of herself, Toni settled back for the flight and closed her eyes. Oh, damn. If she had to fall in love after all these years, why had she picked a difficult man like Luís?

It was midafternoon when they reached Manaus. In the week of absence the Rio Negro had broadened to a breathtaking degree, and the great floating docks had risen more than Toni would have believed possible, despite everything she had been told.

Luís saw her settled in a taxi and said a distant goodbye, not even inquiring as to which hotel she would be patronizing. After he had already closed the taxi door, Toni swallowed her pride enough to lean out and ask where he himself would be staying.

"Diogo—my brother-in-law—has arranged for a hotel suite." Automatically Toni knew it would not be the modestly priced hotel used by the film crew.

"Oh? Perhaps you could tell me which hotel, in case—"

"It's only a temporary arrangement, until renovations are done on the old Quental place."

"I see." Toni paid minute attention to the sidewalk, but what she really saw was the long legs standing there, as if impatient to be off. "Well, then, I suppose we won't meet again."

"I suppose we won't," he concurred, and swiveled to go.

"Luís!" It was a cry so involuntary, so desperate, that it was uttered with no thought for what she was going to say next. While those dark enigmatic eyes were turning once more in her direction, Toni cast about wildly for some excuse, any excuse, to keep him from walking out of her life altogether. "Last time I was in Manaus, I was...very busy, and I didn't have a chance to see the city. If you could spare a little time during this next week...."

And then, because the negative expression on his face suggested that he was about to say no, she added quickly, "I'm not suggesting a whole day of sightseeing, for I know you'll be occupied in other ways. But perhaps you could spare an hour."

After a moment of hesitation he nodded curtly. "I'll see you in exactly two hours, then. After today I'll be too busy for such things. I'll meet you in the square in front of the Opera House. Don't be late, for I have to meet an incoming flight." A small pause produced a sentence that was more of an after-thought than anything: "I can't offer to take you to dinner; I'll be dining with Diogo and Constância—provided their flight comes in on time."

It was not much of a promise, but it was better than nothing; and as the taxi finally pulled away from the waterfront Toni determinedly tried to mold her thoughts into more optimistic patterns. She was discouraged to find that Luís was meeting Diogo Garcia, but remembering Garcia's parting words a week ago she realized that such a possibility should have occurred to her before now.

A whole week lay ahead, and surely Luís would not have to spend all his spare time with his sister and brother-in-law? There must be ways to rekindle his desire enough that he would arrange for further en-counters. More feminine clothes for one thing, she decided as she cast a rueful glance at the plain slacks and tailored cotton shirt she had worn for the flight. And perfume....

It took Toni all of the two hours that followed to prepare for the late-afternoon rendezvous, and much of the time was spent in a lather of wondering what to wear. The valet service at the hotel, encouraged by a healthy tip, managed to press and freshen a half dozen dresses that emerged from the long-checked suitcase in a severely creased state. By the time these were returned to her hotel room, her skin had been soaked in a delicious cologne-scented bath; her hair had been shampooed and blow-dried into a gleaming caramel curtain; her makeup had been applied with more artfulness than she had used in years.

From the skin out she chose every garment with ex-aggerated care—trying on, turning in front of the mirror, discarding only to try on once again. Wistfully she remembered the lacy feminine underthings that had gone wasting on her honeymoon; she had not bought such impractical garments in years. On an impulse she flung on some clothes, snatched her purse and dashed out, catching a taxi and having it wait while she raced into the Credilar Teatro, the main department store of Manaus, to rectify the omission.

What to wear over the almost transparent and utterly feminine underthings created another atypical flutter of indecision after she returned to the hotel. She finally settled on a silky sleeveless cotton print, partly because its toffee-and-cream tones enhanced the sleek shine of her hair; partly because the swinging pleated skirt did nice things for her long shapely, nylon-sheathed legs; partly because the high buttoned front did not *have* to be buttoned all the way to the top. It looked simple enough for late-afternoon sightseeing, yet not so simple after all. Satisfied, she dabbed a refresher of perfume behind her ears and on her wrists; took one last turn in front of the mirror—and then, in another sudden spurt of decision, unbuttoned the top of her dress long enough to whisk off the brassiere that had cost a small fortune, considering the wisps of nothing that had gone into its making.

Not that this lack of proper underpinning was at all apparent once the dress top was back in place. But Luís had said he found brassieres unerotic, and if he happened to brush against a woman's body . . . and if, and if . . . .

"I'm sorry, I'm five minutes late," she apologized as Luís greeted the taxi that had taken her within hailing distance of the Opera House. He thrust a bank note of large denomination through the window, forestalling Toni's attempt to pay the driver. Then he opened the rear door and held it for her. A long silken leg emerged seeking the sidewalk, and then another, brushing briefly against the trousers of a cream linen suit. Toni's stomach muscles tightened with an anticipation that traveled all the way upward from the skin surface where the brief contact had been made. As she leaned forward to accept his helping hand, the neckline of her dress—one extra button undone during the taxi ride—disclosed not only Maria's stone but also a not very subtle view of curved tempting flesh, visible only to the eyes of a man in position to see.

Breathless but unable to blame this on anything but the knowledge of where his eyes were trained, Toni added as she came to her feet, "Will you forgive me?"

"I will, but only because I don't have to meet that flight after all. I called to check on the arrival time and found it had been canceled until tomorrow." His voice, too, sounded huskier than usual, but his fingers were firm as they gripped her elbow, steadying her to her feet.

"Oh? Then I suppose your dinner plans have—" But that was a little too blatant, and Toni halted abruptly, sorry that she had ever started the sentence.

"Is that an invitation?" Luís asked dryly.

"No, really, I—it was just a casual thought."

A brief flame leaped in his eyes. "Between some people," he murmured, "there are no casual thoughts."

But the innuendo was followed by no invitation, and the disturbing increase of pressure on her arm changed back to the lightest of touches as he guided her up the broad vista of balustraded steps that led to the truly extraordinary Opera House of Manaus.

As always, Toni experienced a sense of awe as she paused before the building. The magnificent structure, recently restored to the blue-and-gilt opulence of its heyday, would not have looked out of place in Paris or Versailles. Here, overlooking the black flood of the Rio Negro, the exuberant jungle and the red-roofed patchwork of the city, it was an astonishment. What incredible lives the rubber barons of another era must have led here in the middle of the jungle!

"This is the most expensive opera house ever built," Luís remarked, shading his eyes to scan the castellated walls. "The tiles for the dome came from Alsace-Lorraine, the marble from Carrara. But really the whole building came from England. It was constructed there, taken apart and then brought across the Atlantic piece by piece."

In the sumptuous reception foyer, tall vases of Sèvres porcelain and rich golden draperies enhanced the effect of soaring cream and coral marble pillars.

"Jenny Lind sang here once," Luís told her, all impersonal guide as they entered. The presence of a tour group, as well as a number of solitary sightseers, militated against any intimacy at this moment. "The Ballet Russe performed, too, and Pavlova. Sometimes you hear it claimed that Sarah Bernhardt also appeared, but in truth she refused the invitation, even though she was offered a king's ransom. It was not always easy for the rubber barons to find takers for their offers. In those days it took six months out of a performer's life to come here, most of it spent in traveling time. The chorus girls always came willingly, though—and other women, too."

"I've heard Manaus wasn't unlike the Klondike in that regard," smiled Toni, who knew that at one time two out of three Manaus homes had been houses of ill repute.

"Women came from all over the world hoping to make their fortune. The rubber barons—my great-grandfather among them—used to throw jewels at the stage. It must have been an extraordinary scene: rustling brocades, rouged ladies of the night, laughter and love...."

Surrounded by sumptuous French ironwork and vistas of marble, by heavily carved chairs of jacaranda wood and chandeliers of awesome dimensions, Toni did not find it hard to imagine the glittering bygone era Luís was evoking with his words. But as she had seen it all before, she spent more time in watching Luís's lean face than in looking over the splendors of the Opera House.

"The rubber barons wanted this to be the grandest opera house in the world—grander even than those in Paris, London, Rome, Vienna. And it was. Look at that ceiling mural—pink angels communing with some very angelic-looking humans, probably intended to depict the rubber barons. I imagine that's about as close to heaven as any of them got," he finished on a sardonic note as his eyes slid downward, leaving heaven behind.

"They acquired the trappings of civilization, those ancestors of mine, much as they acquired the chorus girls—for a price. Everything for a price. They sent their laundry to Europe to be done as readily as they sent their sons and daughters to be educated abroad. Can you imagine how many shirts a man would need in order to send his dirty linens on a six-month round trip?"

Luís's attention was directed at the tiers of ornate opera boxes adorned with angels and cherubs, but Toni sensed he was seeing something else: the vision of the suffering *seringueiros*, the poor rubber gatherers, Indians and *caboclos* both, whose lives had been bled in order to make such extravagances possible. But if he was reminded of such things he did not speak of them now.

"And in the end," he went on, "they acquired nothing but grief. By the time this building was completed the end was already in sight. Within a couple of years Manaus was virtually a ghost town...the brothels closed, the rubber barons ruined, the chorus girls gone, and only the ghosts of lost glory inhabiting the boxes and the stage.''

His gaze left the opera box on which it had been trained and fell on Toni. "Are you sure you're interested? I don't believe you've looked at a single thing."

After some mental fumbling, Toni decided on the truth. "I've seen it before," she admitted.

Luís was silent for a moment. "If you'd told me I would have picked something different. What haven't you seen?"

"What else is there to see?" she countered.

"The Market Building, for one. That's very colorful—parrots, caged animals, fruit and vegetable stalls...."

"I've seen that, too," she sighed. "And the Salesian Mission Museum. And Taruma Falls. And the excursion to Monkey Island. I don't think there's a thing I didn't do, for we'll be filming in Manaus when we finish with the Xara. I had to look everything over."

"How about The Church of the Poor Devil? That's so tiny you might have missed it, even with the best of intentions."

"Yes—in fact, I went there three times. It was my favorite place."

Pobre Diablo, the Church of the Poor Devil, was a minuscule edifice in a suburb of Manaus. It had been built by one poor man alone, laboring with his hands and his heart to create a crude church no larger than a small room. Toni had found it more touching than all the magnificence of the rubber barons' transient dreams.

Luís nodded, not mocking her preference. "Have you eaten since breakfast?" he asked abruptly. "I saw you didn't take anything at lunch."

"No," admitted Toni, feeling a sudden pang of hunger in concert with the quick joy his words awakened.

"It's far too late in the day for lunch, but still somewhat early for dinner. Nevertheless, come along. We'll find something."

Leaving the Opera House, they walked a route Toni scarcely noted for the thunder of speculation in her head. It had not sounded exactly like an invitation to a slow intimate dinner; all the same it was a start. And as Luís was not meeting his sister and brother-in-law until tomorrow. . . .

On a crowded street lined with dozens of the shops that marked Manaus as a free port, he came to a halt beside a dark-skinned woman clad in a colorful dirndl skirt, a street vendor of some sort. Toni watched, disappointment gathering into a hard ball in her throat, while Luís negotiated the purchase of two gourds full of steaming soup.

"It's called *tacacá*—very nourishing, very filling and usually very palatable."

Toni bent her head to the gaily decorated gourd in which the *tacacá* had been served, covering her abysmal disappointment as best she could. Hunger overcame hurt as she found that the spicy savory soup was a palatable replacement for the lunch she had skipped in her state of high tension at noon.

"Well, what's the verdict?" Luís asked after she had downed the gourd's contents.

"I liked it."

"Still hungry?"

"A little."

"Then you shall have another," he decreed, and turned once more to the street vendor, declining a second helping for himself. It was not until he had finished this new round of negotiation that Toni's spirits began to lift.

"This time I've bought the gourd, too, not just the contents. Come, you can drink it in my car."

"Car?" With a leap of the heart Toni obeyed the hand that was already urging her along the street, maneuvering skillfully to avoid other pedestrians.

"I rented one this afternoon. Not much to look at, but it runs. I'm going to take you on one sightseeing tour I know you can't have done. Now don't ask questions, for I'll tell you nothing until we get there."

"There" was not so very far. Ten minutes later, just as Toni was finishing her second *tacacá*, Luís braked the car on a quiet cul-de-sac in front of a high ornate wrought-iron fence that enclosed an estate of impressive dimensions. Marble pillars fronted a facade scarcely less ornate than that of the Opera House, and not so very much smaller. The stately sumptuous architecture suggested a French château, and in the lengthening of late-afternoon shadows, ghosts of the past seemed to inhabit the place. Despite its grandness, it had a clammy closed look, as though it had not been inhabited for some years.

"What is it?" asked Toni, curious.

"Surely you can guess."

"Your great-grandfather's home?"

"One of them. Well, what do you think?"

"It's . . . imposing."

"A halfhearted comment if I ever heard one."

"On the contrary, the place takes my breath away. I can't imagine anyone living in such grandeur, that's all."

"Come along and I'll show you around." Luís reached across to unlock the door on Toni's side, bringing the inevitable contact as his arm brushed briefly across her breast and was as quickly withdrawn.

"Unfortunately, most of the furniture's under wraps. Nobody has lived here since my mother died, about four years ago. But there are some fine frescoes and a superb marble staircase, and other things to see. Perhaps your imagination can dispense with the dustcovers. . . ."

An enormous entrance hall with a floor of marble inlaid in two shades of green opened onto rooms that were palatial by any standards. Even the spectral dustcovers that shrouded everything seemed lost in these vaulted spaces. Since the rugs were rolled and wrapped in white like the mummified furniture, their footsteps rang on bare floors, adding to the sense of ghostly unreality.

"And this is where you're planning to live?" Toni asked with more than a little awe.

"Yes."

"It's such a...dramatic change."

"Is it? Yes, I suppose it seems that way. But perhaps I'm a more civilized man than you give me credit for. I grew up in this house, after all. To me it holds memories of my parents, my sisters, my cousins, my childhood friends."

"Where are all your sisters now?" she asked, realizing she had not put that question the other day during Luís's recital of family anecdotes.

"All married and all scattered. I have no relatives left in Manaus." He came to a halt in a vaulted space where a grand piano suggested onetime use as a music room; then slowly started to retrace his steps toward the entrance foyer, guiding Toni without touching her. "There are some rooms less overwhelming than these—the nursery, the bedroom where I slept when I was a boy, the games room, the conservatory. I was happy here once. I can be happy here again."

It sounded more like a resolution than a conviction. Beyond that, Luís seemed disinclined to allow a closer examination of his motives for choosing to live in this enormous mansion. It was a decision that seemed astonishing to Toni, and not one in keeping with what she knew about the man.

"Aren't you going to show me the upstairs?" she asked when it seemed that he was leading her to the front door again.

Luís tilted a quizzical brow, but he changed direction and started up the ornate marble staircase without comment. As they ascended, Toni ventured, "You said this was only one of your great-grandfather's residences. Where were the others?"

"Paris, Newport—and one other here in Manaus. It's smaller, less...what was the word you used? Less imposing. If you had some heart for the Church of the Poor Devil, I'm sure you'd prefer that house. It's more intimate, more livable. I can't show it to you because it's rented at the moment. As you can imagine, it's easier to find tenants for a small house than for a white elephant like this."

"Two houses?" puzzled Toni as they attained the top of the great circular staircase. "It seems odd that your great-grandfather would keep two in one city, especially when one is as enormous as this."

Luís came to a halt halfway along a corridor where dust motes reflected the slanting languishing light of day. With his hand on a doorknob, he turned to face Toni, holding her with unsmiling eyes. "Surely you can guess why? It would take a very naive person not to know that two houses could mean only one thing—two women. Only one of them was his wife."

The moment disturbed Toni unduly because of the strong tide of magnetism that sent currents through the air, as if carried by the hovering shimmering dust motes. A piercing sexual awareness traveled over her skin and arrowed into the pit of her stomach, but she had no way of knowing whether Luís, whose face remained impassive, shared her feelings.

He went on as he turned to open the door, "Yes,

my great-grandfather kept a mistress, and not very discreetly. She was a great beauty, a ballet dancer, a rising star in a modestly famous troupe. For a time she was touted as another Pavlova.''

"And she gave it all up...for love?" Perhaps, with her inner yearnings longing to be expressed, Toni was thinking more of herself than of a long-ago courtesan. "That's rather romantic."

Luís smiled cynically. "She didn't give up very much. My great-grandfather's wife lived in the little house. His mistress lived here."

Toni did not need to be told that the room into which Luís was now ushering her had been the personal bedroom of that long-ago demimondaine. It whispered illicit passion. The Louis Quinze furniture, the velvet-covered Récamier couch from which the dustcover had partially fallen away, the gilt-framed oils of lush naked women on the silk-lined walls— and the bed. The enormous canopied bed. Ornate entwined cupids decorated its heavily carved posts. Dustcovers were draped over the spread and the upper part of the canopy, but these did not conceal the great swaths of cut-velvet bed hangings.

Toni hardly dared to breathe. The bed held her eyes; and suddenly, on a certainty, she knew it held Luís's eyes, too. He was looking and she was looking and they were both thinking the same thing; and although they were not looking at each other, both knew what was in the other's mind. . . .

She expected Luís to make some move now: the tension between them had grown unbearable. But he did not. He merely waited until Toni turned her eyes in his direction, and then he smiled sardonically.

"I think you've seen enough of this floor." He held the door for Toni and then closed it firmly behind them. "Everything else is an anticlimax. Come, I'll show you the gardens. They were quite grand in their time—exotic birds, tropical fish, flowering trees, even a maze. They're overgrown now, but. . . ."

Toni hardly heard his words as he followed two paces behind her down the great circular staircase. She was conscious of only two things: the bed she had seen, and the proximity of that lean virile body, so near that she could almost taste the aura of him in the musty air, so close that she could feel his warmth with every pricking cell on the surface of her skin.

"Luís." She halted and turned, putting a hand on his arm as they reached the halfway mark of their descent. "Please. . . ."

He tensed and came to an immediate halt, still two steps above where Toni had stopped. His face was carefully wiped of emotion; hers was not. Her eyes asked the question and her mouth gave the answer—its moist tremulous softness telling him he need only take to be given.

"Luís, please," she repeated, trembling because nothing in his face encouraged her now. And then, because words were hard and because what she wanted to say could be said without them, she reached for the thong that hung around her neck. Wordlessly she pressed the green stone into his hand.

Luís spent a silent moment looking at its crudely carved surface, turning it between those long fingers whose touch she ached to feel. Now strong emotions chased each other across the harsh planes of his face, drawing deep indentations around the mouth and nose, setting an erratic pulse to ticking in his forehead, causing the hollows beneath his high cheekbones to work as if with some terrible tension.

"You're not the type of woman for a liaison that has no future," he said at last with difficulty, not taking his eyes off the stone. His voice was hoarse, shaken. "Not you. Never you. Now that I know that, I can't—"

Her throat hurt. She looked not at the stone but at Luís's well-loved face, so high above because of his elevated position on the stairs. What he had said was only the confirmation of what she had guessed: that for a man like Luís, marriage was out of the question.

"I'm going in with my eyes open, Luís. I don't expect anything you can't . . . offer."

"Antonia," he breathed in a ragged voice, "don't. . . ."

She managed a brave smile as his tortured eyes rose from the stone, finding hers. In his face was a dark purgatory, a battle raging for possession of his faculties. "Didn't you tell me these stones were given to procure a . . . a temporary lover?" Her lightness was pretended at considerable cost. "I'm nearly twenty-seven years old. I want a lover, Luís, and I want it to be you. What was it you said the Amazons should have been called—the Women Who Live without Men?''

Luís nodded, seeming not to trust speech.

''Oh, Luís,'' Toni whispered, abandoning every last shred of pride as she stepped upward to end the small separation between them. ''Don't you see, I've done that for too long?''

CHAPTER TWELVE

How THEY CLIMBED THE STAIRS Toni never knew. Whether he led her, whether she led him—it seemed a small thing beside the possessive light that leaped into those night-black eyes. No words were needed now. As they climbed they clung, abandoned in their hunger. She was aware only of the ardent lips, of the kisses on her hands, in her hair, on her throat; of the urgent hands that coursed over her breasts and her hips as shamelessly as her own hands were discovering him.

"Wait," Luís said thickly as they reached the bedroom. Despite his towering needs, he put her momentarily aside. Walking to the bed, he wrenched the dustcovers aside, revealing a counterpane over silken sheets. Then he strode back across the room and stopped forcefully a foot from where Toni stood. He lifted his hands, sinking them in her hair, while he possessed her with his eyes. A thin line of color darkened the high arc of his cheekbones.

"Heaven help me," he breathed unsteadily. "I can't do this as I should. I've waited too long and I've wanted too long and I can't be patient now...."

"Oh, Luís," she said, trembling, "you don't have

to be patient with me." As she spoke she reached for the buttons of his shirt—undoing them, pushing the shirt from his shoulders, touching the hard corded textures of him, making love with every exploratory movement of her hands. His heartbeat drummed against her fingertips, telling her that desire was a thunder in his blood, too. Eager to wait no more, she reached for his belt.

"Oh, God," he grated harshly, and his kiss exploded against her mouth, a dam burst of need so violent that no power of will could have contained it now. She cared not that his lips were bruising in their deep possession, that his hands were less than gentle as they tore the clothes from her limbs, that his arms were almost punishing in their impatience as they swept her toward the bed. Pausing only to divest himself of the last of his clothes, he came crushing down beside her.

And then his mouth was moving hungrily over her body, sparing no part of her as he awoke the sensations she had longed to feel. But his soul-deep groan as he bathed her breasts with his lips warned that his continence had been strained too far. "Make love to me, Luís," Toni whispered, lacing her fingers into his hair.

He pulled her into his arms, his entire being shaking from the violence of a passion too long contained. "Forgive me," he rasped as his mouth and his black burning eyes descended once again. "Oh, my darling, this won't be as it should be for you."

But it was as it should be for her. The roughness of

his chest against her bared breasts, the poised power of him, the naked hunger in his face—these were what she wanted in her heart.

"Oh, yes, it will," she whispered, wrapping her arms about his neck in the moment before his mouth sealed off further words. And then, in a single bitter-sweet second, the hard forcefulness of his passion at last took full possession of her body.

Although the moment was swift, her rigidity was an involuntary reaction to the terrible urgency with which he had claimed her. Fighting her own tense-ness, she clung to him, desperately wanting to give her heart and herself with no reserve, no restraint. She wanted to rise with him to heights where she had soared only in her imagination; wanted him to wait, to be patient with her until she could capture the rapture she had never known.

But perhaps for Luís there had already been too much waiting. After a last fierce deepening of his kiss, the driving gave way to a shuddering, and the shudder-ing to a stillness that told of spent desire. As his mouth released hers and moved to her throat, he groaned deeply, as if he knew that the final surge of his love-making had brought no answering surge from her.

After a time he rolled away altogether, freeing her from his weight. He pulled her into his arms and stroked her hair so tenderly that she knew it was a wordless apology for the importunate way in which he had taken her. And at last, as a brooding darkness gathered beyond the windowpane, he spoke, his voice husky with emotion.

"I'm sorry. I was too impatient."

"That's not so." She turned to smile tremulously into his eyes and reached out her fingers to stroke the lean loved contours of his face. She explored the hint of stubble just beneath the skin, the angular bones, the pulse beside his ear that was invisible to everything but her seeking touch. And then her hand traveled down to his chest, where the green stone of the Amazons lay against a tangle of dark crisp hair.

"Have you forgotten, Luís? I asked." She touched the stone and then stroked the skin around it, discovering the vital sensations that were like aphrodisiacs to her fingertips: the warm firm blend of muscle and bone and man.

"But the first time...*O, Deus.*" His eyes darkened with a regret so deep it touched her to the core. "It should have been right for you, so very right. Next time I'll show more self-control."

He left the bed and moved to the window, his lithe muscular frame a magnet to Toni's eyes. A man's nakedness was not new to her; there had been too many months of caring for Matthew's most intimate needs. But this was different, so different. Seeing Luís moving naked in the dusk-dim room, her throat grew tight with longing for what she had still not known. He was a superb male creature, a man of powerful physique in the prime of his strength, and because she saw him with the eyes of love she understood the driving urgency that had prevented him from fulfilling her long-denied needs.

With soft lights switched on, he returned to the bed

and sat on its edge. Elbows on knees, he stared fixedly at the floor. "It's no real excuse for my lack of continence, but perhaps you'll understand when I tell you I've wanted you ever since that day I saw you in Rio de Janeiro. After I returned to the Amazon I couldn't put you out of my mind. The sight of your softness, the smell of your perfume... I used to wake in the night remembering those things. It was a kind of torment wanting you. I began to think of ways and means from the first moment we met." He made a self-deprecating gesture. "I wanted you badly—but even at my lowest ebb I never intended to be the animal I was tonight."

"Luís, you weren't that! You've lived the life of a hermit for too long. Don't you think I know what frustration does to a man? Eleven years—"

"I haven't even that excuse," he said in a hollow voice, and buried his face in his hands. "At least, not completely."

"Oh, Luís...." And with love and need and forgiveness clamoring to be expressed, she pulled him down to the bed beside her and began to tell him with her hands of the love that she held in her heart. And soon, with a slowness and sureness he had not shown before, he began to make love—tenderly, expertly, ardently. With kisses bathing her breasts; with hands coursing slowly, knowingly, over the secret wellsprings of her womanhood; with sensuous caresses and soft words of love, he brought each part of her to a singing readiness.

"This is how I wanted it to be... for you, for me. I love you, Antonia. I love you more than I can tell."

The husky words awakened a swift joy, for they gave her more of Luís than she had expected to receive. And now she could make her own admission, a confession of the deep emotions that had led her to give herself with such abandon. "And I love you, Luís," she whispered as she raised her lips to return the gentle imprint of his. "I love you so. . . ."

This time as his powerful body levered into place, her readied flesh sprang to receive him. Nothing could stop the flood tide now. From deep within it rose—sure, deep, swift, a torrent of desire that sent her hips straining upward to meet the most marvelous moment of all. . . .

After, a long time after, when they lay twined together in a darkened room, she murmured, "Oh, Luís. I'm glad it was you. So glad."

They talked long, long into the night—the little exploratory nothings of lovers, important and unimportant all at once, to do with the shape of a nose or the curve of a mouth or the taste of warm skin to the lips. They made love again, lingeringly. They talked of many things, but Luís did not speak of taking her back to her hotel, nor did she speak of going. He did not talk of the future, nor did she. And at last, warm with love and sleepy with surfeit, they slid into a night world where Toni dreamed impossible dreams of sleeping always in those strong enfolding arms.

Sometimes through the night—that long memorable night spent so intimately wrapped in his embrace—she woke. Once, to find him touching her lips as if to remind himself they were there. Once, when Luís pulled a light covering over their naked limbs to close out the chill of the predawn hours. Once, when glimmerings of dawn crept through the curtain cracks to lend a pale luster to the scene. But because it was too early to rise, and because she did not want to wake from a dream so beautiful, she inched closer into the curve of his body and drifted once more. And because the lovers' discoveries of the previous night had kept them awake so late, and because neither had rested much the night before that, both slept long beyond their usual waking time.

The click of the chandelier switch and the full blaze of light brought her instantly awake. When she felt Luís's arm tighten involuntarily around her, she knew he had awakened, too.

"So," purred a strange feminine voice in the language of this country, "my pure, pure Luís is not so pure after all. How amusing."

Rigid with shock, Toni snatched the sheet to her breast and stared at the intruder. Luís uttered a low guttural curse, speaking Portuguese as the woman had done. Putting Toni firmly aside, he levered himself to a sitting position in the bed, not trying to conceal the nakedness of his lean muscular torso. For a moment, the stone of the Amazons swung strongly on its thong, then settled into slow motion against its bed of crisp chest hair.

"Perhaps it's amusing to you, Constância," he said wearily, "but not to me. Where did you come from? I thought your flight had been canceled yesterday."

"It was canceled, but Diogo begged a ride from a friend with a private plane. We arrived late yesterday and checked into the hotel. When you didn't appear, Diogo thought perhaps you'd broken your promise."

"You know I wouldn't do that," growled Luís.

Constância laughed lightly, poise intact as her cool eyes traveled to Toni. "I know you wouldn't. That's why I came over with a decorator, to start talking about renovations."

To her utter dismay, Toni now realized that a strange man stood in the doorway, some few feet behind the woman who must be Luís's sister. The decorator, no doubt. Even as Toni noted him, he gave a soft apologetic smile and backed away, vanishing altogether from a scene that seemed to disconcert him a great deal more than it did the woman Constância.

With an arch smile that suggested no embarrassment whatsoever, Luís's sister walked farther into the room. Despite the high-waisted Empire dress that revealed a state of advanced pregnancy, her walk was sinuous and self-aware in the way of a woman who knows herself to be utterly, extravagantly lovely. Her face was an angelic oval, her sleek cap of hair exquisitely coiffed. Like Toni's, it was a pale caramel color—tinted, perhaps—but there the resemblance ended. Her eyes, her dark winged brows, her graceful hands. . . all proclaimed a purely Latin descent.

Constância stopped half a dozen feet from the bed and smiled at Toni with a sweetness that suggested no chagrin or censure at finding her in such a compromising position. "A pretty little thing," she murmured with only the faintest hint of condescension. "How did she snare you, Luís?"

Luís clicked his teeth with an audible snap and spoke through them. "*Meu Deus*, Constância, is this...*adult* behavior necessary?"

"Oh, Luís, don't be childish." Constância made an airy dismissive gesture in his direction, without taking her eyes off Toni. "I'm curious, that's all, to see who finally engineered your fall from grace. I approve; she really seems quite sweet and unspoiled."

"Get out, Constância," Luís hissed in a tight steely voice. "I'll see you downstairs."

Two plucked brows arched upward, and a shapely mouth pretended a pretty pout. "So eager to get rid of me? In that case I'll leave as soon as you introduce me."

"Must you have your pound of flesh?" gritted Luís. "All right, then...Constância, this is Senhora Carruthers."

"How do you do," Toni managed through frozen lips, the long habits of self-control coming to her rescue despite the state of her nerves and the strong desire to sink right through the sheets.

"American?" Constância guessed from the accent. "How quaint."

Luís cut across the sophisticated little observation with evident impatience. "Go back to your decorator, Constância. Haven't you seen enough?"

"You haven't introduced me properly, Luís. Or

does the pretty *norte-americana* already know I'm your wife?''

Wife: the word was like a body blow, and Toni went white from the impact.

CHAPTER THIRTEEN

THE CHURCH OF THE POOR DEVIL: perhaps here there would be peace for her troubled soul. It was in a suburb of Manaus, this humble place of worship, and Toni had to ask the taxi driver to wait while she went inside, dashing through a sudden seasonal rainstorm in the light plastic raincoat she kept in her capacious purse for just such contingencies.

Under today's bursting clouds the already swollen river would be rising, but now it seemed symbolic only of tears. In the humid tiny enclosure of the church, she removed the raincoat and knelt, wishing she could weep those tears.

Luís's wife. His wife. *His wife.* The discovery had been shattering. Why had it never occurred to her that he might be married? Just because a man immolated himself for eleven years did not mean that he had left no worldly ties behind. Did not mean that he had abandoned the things of the flesh altogether. Did not mean that he had become a true hermit in every sense of the word. Did not preclude sex. Did not mean that he might not desire a woman, sow a seed, sire a child.

She had not talked of these things with Luís. Immediately after Constância had left the room, he had dressed, in grim silence and without apology, while Toni watched him with huge shock-dilated eyes. At that point she had wanted only to escape, to be alone, to think—and of all the sick thoughts that warred for possession of her mind, the need to escape had been strongest. As soon as Luís left the room, she had thrown on her clothes, hardly able to do so for the shaking of her fingers. As she descended the stairs she had heard muffled sounds from one of the larger salons: an amused feminine voice; the deep, controlled, resonant voice that could only belong to Luís. Within view of the cavernous entrance hall, the decorator had been peering under dustcovers, taking notes. He had studiously avoided looking at Toni.

She had left the mansion on foot, almost running and not looking to see if anyone followed, too choked and wild-eyed at first to know where she was going. At length sheer exhaustion had slowed her; and then the taller buildings of downtown Manaus, sighted in the distance, had given her her bearings. In time she had regained her hotel, still in a state of deep shock. Later in the morning there had been several phone calls from Luís, which she had refused to accept. In time, because she feared that he might appear in person at the hotel, she had hailed a taxi to bring her to this place. The tiny room-sized chapel, so touching in its simplicity, might give her strength to face the knowledge of what she had done.

That Constância was pregnant with Luís's child— that was the worst. Could she ever forgive herself for what had happened? Swept on a tide of desire, she had abandoned so many of the values by which she had lived her life. Some of them she had abandoned willingly, in the full knowledge that Luís had not offered marriage. But other principles she had abandoned unwittingly: and that was what seared her soul, ate at her insides, filled her with horror and self-hatred and a sense of deepest despair.

Perhaps she could have suspected, should have guessed, should have *asked*. There was more than one way to make a brother-in-law: Constância was most surely Diogo Garcia's sister. Her name had been bandied about often enough in conversations between Luís and Senhor Garcia; but the conclusion that Constância was Garcia's wife had seemed such a natural one that Toni had never questioned it.

Was it to see Constância that Luís had been in Rio so many months ago? Toni had surmised that his visit was in some way connected with Getulio's handsome son, Braz, who had been living in Rio, too. But that had been pure speculation on her part. Now a different conclusion seemed inescapable. Eight months ago... yes, he must have seen his wife on that visit to Rio. Constância's condition was evidence enough, and if Toni wanted more proof it could be found in something Luís had admitted last night. "You've lived the life of a hermit for too long," she had said to him. "I haven't even that excuse," had been his choked answer. "At least, not completely...."

That Constância seemed to find amusement in her

husband's infidelity did not permit Toni to forgive herself. Adultery, adultery, adultery. It was not a nice word. Was there any nice word for what she had done, what Luís had done? The strong guilt that had stained her existence after Matthew's suicide seemed diminished and blanched by comparison with this new guilt—a guilt she must live with for the rest of her life, just as she must live with the knowledge that for her there would be no more stolen moments, no more nights spent folded in strong arms, no more love, no more Luís.

How could she bear a life so empty? And yet she knew she should, and could, and would.

The recognition that she was at least strong enough to forswear future assignations restored some small measure of calmness. Only ten minutes had passed since her arrival at the Church of the Poor Devil, but she knew she could not keep the taxi waiting for much longer; she must leave. There must be someplace to escape Luís's persistence.

She emerged from the tiny church. The downpour had passed, and already the sky had cleared to a brilliant cloudless blue, as is so often the way with equatorial storms. Everything looked wet, sparkling, different: most of all the empty space by the roadside where she had told the taxi driver to wait. Why would he leave without collecting his fare?

She had had no time to adjust her thoughts when a hand gripped her arm and a deep urgent voice said, "I hoped I might find you here when I was told you had caught a taxi in front of your hotel. Why did you leave this morning without saying anything?"

She died a thousand small deaths in the moment before her reeling mind adjusted to his presence. Her skin tingled, but her spine stiffened. "Surely you can imagine," she answered in a tortured voice. "Let me go, Luís."

"Antonia, we must talk."

"There's nothing to talk about. Please. I don't want to talk."

"Then at least listen!" His insistent grip urged her toward the rental car parked a short distance away. "There are things I have to say. Important things. That's why I came here, why I sent your taxi away—after receiving your description from the driver. I decided it was time we talked of the things we didn't speak about last night."

She came to a forcible halt, resisting those steely fingers. Her eyes, too bright with unshed tears, sparkled at him angrily. "Such as the fact that you have a wife—and a child on the way? Spare me the revelations, Luís. I discovered those things for myself this morning. In the school of hard knocks!"

His hand fell away from her elbow, but his somber searching eyes held her as surely as his fingers had done.

"But I thought you already knew," he said slowly, his voice quiet but shaken in that moment of realization. "Diogo and I talked of Constância in front of you; I remember that well. He introduced me as his brother-in-law. And you said you were entering the relationship with wide-open eyes. It never occurred to me that you might not know."

She knew it must be the truth, but it dispelled none

of her inner anguish. She looked away at the rain-washed streets, escaping those dark probes that searched her face. "And that condones everything in your mind?" Her voice was embittered, transferring a part of her own great guilt to him. "I'll admit I enticed you last night, perhaps made it impossible for you to refuse. But you were ready to be unfaithful to your wife days ago, at a time when I had given you no encouragement whatsoever."

"I don't deny that. Moreover, the only thing that has stopped me since is scruples about *you*—not about my marriage. When you hear the whole story you'll understand. You're upset now, Antonia, but perhaps you'll be less so when you hear about my wife. Now come to my car. We'll drive someplace quiet and talk."

"So you can ask me to continue this illicit affair?" The question was low but fierce, a cry from the soul. "So you can take me in your arms and tell me there's no sin as long as there's love? So you can hold me. . . kiss me. . . comfort me. . . make love to me. . . oh, God. . . ."

She buried her shamed face in her hands because deep in her heart those were the very things for which she ached.

Luís put an arm firmly around her shoulders and with his free hand forced her face to tilt upward toward his own. "I'd be lying if I told you I don't want to do those things. I wanted you before, I want you now, and no power on earth can change that. I don't deny I'll ask—but I'll force nothing on you. Have you forgotten so easily that I stopped trying to have an affair once before—when I came to the conclusion that your code of behavior didn't include that sort of thing?''

He took a pained harsh breath and then reached to the collar of the open-necked sports shirt he wore. Moments later, Maria's green stone was lowered over Toni's throat. "Perhaps when you hear what I have to say you'll give me this again. Without it I'd have tried nothing last night. And without it I'll. . . .'' Here his voice turned unsteady. "I'll try nothing to-day."

Toni's breath in her lungs seemed bottled to bursting point; the wish to weep bitter tears against Luís's broad shoulders had become unbearable.

"Is it so hard to trust me?" During the short conversation, his eyes seemed to have aged, the cynical lines etching themselves into a deeper mold. "Yes, I suppose it is," he answered himself bleakly. "I know how it must look to you, for I know how it looks to myself. An adulterer, a man of no honor. . . . All right, I won't drive you out of the city. Get in the car and I'll take you back to your hotel. You can trust me for that long, as I'll have my hands on the wheel."

This time when he pressed she submitted, knowing even as she did that she would have to listen to his persuasions on the drive. If she had any fears that he might go back on his word and aim away from the city core, they were soon set to rest. Slowly negotiating the rain-rinsed suburban streets, he headed on a route that Toni knew would lead in time to her hotel. He talked as he drove, without taking his eyes off the road. And if these were persuasions they were strange ones, for at the moment he spoke in a flat unemotional monotone.

"It's hard for me to talk about my marriage, perhaps because like yours it started with high hopes. Although it was virtually an arranged match, it was an arrangement I never tried to get out of, because the first time I met Constância I fell head over heels in love. My wife was very young, very naive, when I married her. She was just out of convent school and had only turned eighteen. As her family was exceedingly strict and old-fashioned, she had had no experience of men. In those days she was touching and eager and...."

He stopped and started again. "I was young, too, only twenty-six at the time, and about to set up practice. We had an idyllic honeymoon, a month in Europe. I agreed to join a clinic in Rio because Constância had school friends there. At her request I put aside the research I wanted to do... at that point I would have given her the moon on a platter. We bought an estate just out of the city, and for another month we lived as though the honeymoon would never end."

Only the whitening of his knuckles on the steering wheel betrayed the depth of pain in those memories. But there was something in the very bleakness of his voice that fleshed out, in Toni's imagination at least, the story he was telling in such swift skeletal strokes.

"We were called back to Manaus because my father died. Constância returned to Rio directly after the funeral. I myself couldn't. There were family matters to be arranged, the will and legal tangles and property settlements, the complex business of the family foundation—it was a large estate, and by then my mother was in poor health, too. It seemed I might have to stay in Manaus for several weeks. The separation wasn't to my liking, but there was very little help for it. After the first two weeks I decided to take a quick flight to Rio and surprise Constância one night. I did—but it was not a pleasant surprise for either of us. Perhaps you can imagine why."

There was no particular need for Luís to describe the scene that must have transpired. Toni could imagine it very well—the ardent young husband, still in the flush of first love, arriving to find his once innocent wife in the arms of another man.

"There's a word for women like my wife, women who cannot live without men, even for a night. I used to flay myself with wondering what went wrong. Perhaps if I had taught her less well... perhaps if there had been no separation... perhaps, perhaps, perhaps. So many sick thoughts went through my mind when the worst of the shock was over. I didn't realize then that it was an illness with Constância, not so very different from alcoholism or drug addiction. I couldn't forget—no man could forget such a thing—but I tried to... forgive.

"That was the first time. It would be pointless to tell you of the others. Even after the estate tangles were settled and I had returned to Rio for good, I soon found that there were... others. At first when such things happened, Constância would weep prettily, make promises and in time entice me back into her bed. And again I would try to forgive. A weakness on my part? Perhaps—but then, I have the needs of a man, the passions of a man, the weaknesses of a man. And hope dies hard—it took a time before I realized that no one man could possibly satisfy her appetites.

"When I finally recognized that it was a kind of sickness, I managed to find some pity for my wife. She devours men as voraciously and indiscriminately as a piranha devours flesh. And like a piranha, she does so with no sense of sin. Despite the convent upbringing, Constância has very few moral scruples—and very little use for religion; she abandoned the church years ago.

"My pity ended when she put aside even the pretense of remorse. Pride began to keep me from her bed, and after that she took her lovers with no hint of discretion, sometimes staying openly at hotels, sometimes inviting men to her bedroom in the hearing of the servants. She found some excuse for this in saying I had failed to satisfy her by staying away from her bed. Divorce? Yes, I considered it—it is permissible in Brazil. But I'm moving ahead of myself; I'll come to that in a minute."

Of course he could no longer consider divorcing the woman who was expecting his child: there was no need for Toni to put such a question into words.

"Let me finish telling you about those early months," Luís went on, his face now a mask. "One day my wife suggested that I might be happier, less bitter, if I took advantage of the freedom she was prepared to allow. She suggested an open marriage—pointed out other people we knew who had similar modern arrangements." The deep bitterness that had dictated so many years of Luís's life now turned his voice to gall. "It was the final insult, the thing that drove me to the Amazon. I refused to live that kind of life. I left Constância when we had been married for no more than six months."

The cynicism, the brooding, the disillusionment, the attitude toward women—it explained so much about Luís. Toni's heart contracted as she considered the depth of suffering that had driven Luís to bury himself in the jungle eleven years before. Perhaps, after all, it *was* moral principles that had sent him there: not the same ones Toni had once imagined, but moral principles all the same.

"I thought I could learn to do without women altogether. Unfortunately, I found it wasn't so. There were trips to Rio over the years, more trips than I care to remember. I'm not proud of this. But hope has a way of clinging, of reasserting itself during the long empty nights. . . .

"And for all those years there was only one woman I wanted: my wife. You see, Antonia, in spite of everything, I still . . . loved her."

And did he, to this day? It seemed possible, despite the words of love Luís had murmured into her own ears last night. Dying a little inside—for herself, for him—Toni listened with a full heart as more of the tortured story poured out. She hardly noted that Luís had brought the car to a halt on a quiet cul-de-sac only two blocks from her hotel. Although he was not driving now, he kept his face turned to profile, as if the windshield held all of his attention.

"The arrangement suited Constância very well: I in the Amazon, she in Rio. She wanted no divorce. The Quental name, the Quental fortune—these things assured her entrée into the social strata she liked and was accustomed to. And at those times when I was in Rio, she professed love—something she still claims to have given to no other man."

Luís waited for a time before he went on, as if in silent remembrance of the past that had so soured his existence. "There comes a time when a man's pride will no longer allow him to make a fool of himself, and for me that time came a little less than four years ago. Attached to my estate in Rio there is a small house—a gatekeeper's house, not very grand. I'd allowed Braz to move into it when he married Ana, and I had warned Constância that Braz was one man she must leave alone. It won't take a great leap of your imagination to guess what happened."

"No," came the low response from Toni. So her guesses about Braz O'Hara had not been without foundation. Moreover, Luís's story explained the indefinable tension she had sensed in the air during the short time he and Braz had been talking together. What a doormat Ana must be, to have put up with such cheating for so many years! Had love so blinded her that she didn't see? Or did she deliberately close her eyes?

"In Brazil it's not necessary to prove infidelity to secure a divorce. A separation of three years is sufficient. And so I...stayed away from Constância for three years. It was hard but...necessary. Eight months ago, when the time was up, I returned to Rio and...."

There was a pause during which the pained inhalation of Luís's breath told of past torments. "I told Constância I wanted a divorce—despite her tears and pleas, despite her embraces, despite everything. For once I was able to say no. I walked out—not the easiest thing for a man who has been three years without a woman. And not the easiest thing when the woman starts to...."

But here his voice choked to a halt. A moment passed before he started again, his face now suffused with color, but his voice once more under control. "I knew I would need to stay in Rio to consult a lawyer, but I didn't want to stay in a hotel because I was afraid Constância would find me and take advantage of my...weakness. I knew Diogo's house was empty—or rather, I believed it was—and I knew where he hid the spare key. I went there. And then, when I walked out on the balcony and saw *you*...for one terrible moment I thought you were my wife. To lie there naked, deliberately tempting—it's the sort of thing she would do. It was the hair color, Constância's color. Oh, not her real color, but the one she's been using these past few years. I stared, flabbergasted. Then you turned your head—and I realized you weren't my wife. But by then... *meu Deus*, do I have to spell it out? For the first time in many years I found myself looking at a woman who was not my wife. Looking... and desiring.

"I should have turned away, but... I couldn't. At least not at first." Now Luís half turned until he had Toni in view. One arm still rested on the steering wheel, but the other he laid along the back of the seat, not touching but so close that she could feel the clenching and unclenching of his fist stirring the back of her hair.

"That night in the restaurant wasn't pure coincidence. I had a compulsion to see you again. All day visions of you making love by the pool kept running through my mind like a refrain—not so extraordinary if you consider the state of frustration I was in. For once it wasn't thoughts of my wife that tormented me: it was thoughts of you. In the early evening I returned to Diogo's house and waited in my car until you came out, this time with a different man. I followed you to the restaurant. I fought a terrible battle with my frustrations that night, and my frustrations won."

Toni's head was bent low, allowing her hair to swing forward. Had he always wanted her only as a substitute for Constância, the woman who had been a fever in his blood for years? "So you went to your wife," she said aloud, turning the knife in her own wounds.

"Yes, I went to Constância. I make no excuses for myself. I wanted a woman and I took my wife... but by then the woman I wanted was you. Only you. *You.*"

Toni scarcely dared to breathe for the tamped-down vehemence that had entered his voice. But soon he subsided again and readjusted his long legs to a more comfortable position in the driver's space.

"I stayed with her that night," he told her as unemotionally as if he were reading a weather report, "and for another three days after that. I brought up the matter of divorce again, and this time she pretended she was agreeable enough. It didn't occur to me that she might be fighting it in a new way—by ceasing to use the birth-control methods she had always used. Despite our short interlude together I saw a lawyer before I left Rio and instituted proceedings. As we had lived apart for many years, and as I had more than enough evidence against her, I didn't anticipate trouble. At the time you arrived at my clinic I was expecting news from Rio... but not the kind of news Diogo brought."

Although Toni was staring blindly out the window, she could feel his face turning toward her now, could feel the tormented eyes coming to rest on her mouth. "That's when I learned about the pregnancy—the day Diogo flew in to the compound with your film crew. He brought a letter from Constância. She had written me several times in the intervening months, pleading with me to come to Rio, thinking it better to confront me with her condition face to face. As she had said nothing about pregnancy, I suspected other...motives. Finally she became desperate and enlisted Diogo's aid.''

All the little mysteries of a week ago explained. Toni closed her eyes and in one moment saw a procession of memories flash subliminally by, memories that had not been painful at the time but now were unbearably so. Had she only known Luís for a week—eight days? It seemed a lifetime. An eternity.

"Constância wanted Diogo to extract a promise from me, you see—that's why she asked him to deliver that final letter in person. For her part, she offered to move to Manaus, to put her Rio friends behind her, to start afresh. For the sake of the child I agreed." Then, after a pause, Luís added quietly, "Look at me, Antonia."

Obeying the command out of compulsion as much as compassion, she did. Meeting hers were dark eyes in which a deep mixture of emotion could be read: pain, remorse, desire and more, much more.

"It took you to make me realize that my feelings for my wife faded years ago, that only sheer frustration was keeping them alive. It wasn't love that took me to Rio from time to time, it was sex. I used to accuse Constância of using me, but the truth is that I was using her. For many years she's been an expensive whore—no more."

Toni's face was stiff with the effort of showing nothing. "You mustn't say a thing like that." She succeeded in forcing the words through a throat that felt as tight as newly scarred flesh. "She's your wife, Luís. She's bearing your child."

"Is she?" That old cynicism crossed his face, shadowing his eyes. But if he had more doubts on the subject, he kept them to himself. "Yes, I suppose the child is mine. My wife never wanted children, and she'd never have allowed herself to...." His voice trailed off, and he added grimly, "I'll do what I must for Constância, and for the child, too. But I owe her no love, no marital fidelity. If I want to take a mistress I will."

Toni reached for the car door. "I don't want to hear this part. Goodbye, Luís."

"No!" The single word thundered with disbelief. He reached for her, almost pulling her arm from the socket as he wrenched it away from the door handle. Struggling, Toni placed her hands defensively between them as he gathered her into his arms. His strength overpowered her, but she managed to turn her mouth away in time to prevent the kiss. His lips instead seared her throat, causing a return of weakness that robbed her fleetingly of resolve.

"Be my mistress, darling. I love you, Antonia... oh, God, I love you. It seems I've waited all my life for you, you, only you.... I'll make you happy; I swear I will." His scorching breath burned her with the messages she did not want to hear. Beneath her palms braced against his chest, his heart raced out of control, in unison with hers. "The other house I own in Manaus...as soon as the tenants go it can be yours. It won't be wrong; there's nothing wrong when there are vows written in the heart, in the blood—"

"Luís, no," she gasped, fighting against herself as

much as she fought against him. "You promised you'd force nothing. And what you're suggesting is, wrong, wrong, wrong."

"You can't deny me now," he said thickly. "I've already had my share of denial in this life. I won't let you say no."

"Stop, Luís!" She shoved at his chest with all her might. "You're hurting me! You're behaving like a brute. . . a madman!"

For a time his grip only tightened hurtfully, the fingers digging into her shoulders so deeply that she cried out in pain. Then he released her as roughly as he had seized her, thrusting her aside with a deep anguished groan and returning to his own position in the car. Toni belatedly grew conscious of the several curious Brazilians who were staring openly through the car windows. The glass was partially lowered, and although it was unlikely that the passersby spoke enough English to understand what she and Luís were saying, the emotion in their voices must have told its own story.

Luís seemed not to care who listened. He slammed a fist against the dashboard with such force that the car shook. "Perhaps I am a madman—but who would not be half-mad after the things I've endured? I've told you little of what happened because I thought you might be feeling enough to fill in the rest. In the name of mercy, Antonia, how can you condemn me?"

Toni tried to take hold of her shattered willpower by seizing the door handle once again. Her hand shook, but her voice was steady. "I do condemn you, Luís, just as I condemn myself. I can't forgive... either of us. Don't try to stop me, and don't try to see me again."

This time he made no move to halt her escape forcibly, but she was nearly stopped all the same—not by his hand, but by his voice. As she left the car, the one anguished word he strangled out was the cry of a soul in damnation: "*Antonia...!*"

"Goodbye, Luís," she said, and ran down the street as if chased by the very hounds of hell.

LATER, surveying the wreckage of her life, Toni wondered how she found the inner strength needed for the next few days. Stung by her condemnation, Luís had allowed a temporary escape, but his impassioned pleas had not come to an end. It was hard to refuse his phone calls, hard to walk unseeingly past him when he waited in the hotel lobby, hard to pretend indifference when his persuasions followed her along a street.

And it was hardest of all to make the decision that there was no safety for herself in staying anywhere Luís could find her. She supposed that Diogo Garcia had left Manaus, and that Luís had again assumed full responsibility for his wife, but even that circumstance seemed not to halt his pursuit, which day by day became harder to evade. Even on the day she left Manaus, after the awful week came to an end, he was there—watching with anguished smoke-dark eyes as she boarded the *Catalina*. She knew he expected her to return to Manaus in three weeks; and it was then she made the decision that she must leave the Amazon altogether.

As soon as she returned to the jungle compound, she told Ty and Barney of her intent—and that was hard, too.

"You can't call it quits," Ty groaned, aghast. "Good Lord, Toni, we're a team."

"Think what we've been through together!" echoed Barney, his honest freckled face disintegrating with dismay. "Why, Toni? Why?"

"Quental," swore Ty, slamming one fisted hand into the palm of the other. For once there was no puckishness in his expression as he examined Toni's face, drained by the toll the past week had taken. "My God, Toni, what has he done to you?"

"Nothing." Inadvertently Toni's fingers traveled to the valley of her shirt, reaffirming that the stone of the Amazons still rested there, heavy as her conscience. "Nothing."

Barney's eyes narrowed. "That's not true. You look as though you've been crucified."

"I told you, it's nothing to do with Luís!"

"I'll kill him," said Ty.

"Line up," said Barney, flexing his fingers.

They were not going to believe her, so at last Toni told them a part of the truth to give credence to her very large lie. "Nothing happened between Luís and me—not really. Yes, he wants me to have an affair, and no, I don't want to give in...not now. That's why I *must* leave."

"What really happened, love?" asked Ty, becoming suddenly gentle.

"I found out that he's married, that's all. And his wife's pregnant—very pregnant." In the stunned silence that greeted this news, Toni's whisper was aching. "I...I'm afraid I fell a little too hard. If I stay I might...oh, please try to understand."

At last her sorry state of mind communicated itself enough that their objections came to a halt. No more was said, although sometimes during that last week in the Amazon she found Ty and Barney looking at her sadly, as if they saw the slow death she was dying inside. It was a difficult week, with memories of Luís flourishing like jungle creepers on the decay that was her life.

Knowing of Braz O'Hara's liaison with Constância, it was impossible for Toni to establish a comfortable relationship with him during that one last week. For his wife, Ana, however, she felt more warmth, and perhaps under different circumstances a friendship might have developed between them. Clues in several brief conversations suggested to Toni that Ana was well aware of her husband's infidelities and chose to ignore them. It appeared that in Ana's worshipful eyes Braz could do no wrong.

"Perhaps I could start a little school for the Xara children," Ana suggested somewhat wistfully on the first day of Toni's return. It was during the evening meal, when everyone was gathered around the rough picnic table. An English conversation was taking place at one end of the table, and a Portuguese con-

versation at the other; and because Toni was partic-
ipating in neither she overheard snatches of both.
The remark had caught her halfhearted attention,
and so she stopped listening to the morose efforts
coming from Ty and Barney and started to watch
Ana covertly instead.

"There is little for me to do here, Braz, on the days
when you go to the Xara village. Tomorrow I could
come with you instead of staying here."

"Oh, my little Ana, are you so afraid of letting me
out of your sight?" Braz teased, confident in his
virility and in Ana's devotion. "Believe me, you can
sleep with no worries tomorrow night. For me there
is no temptation at the Xara village. Remember, I am
part Xara myself. I know too well what can happen
to a man who casts his eyes in the wrong direction."

"I wasn't thinking of that," Ana denied quickly,
her lids dropping as a flush rose to her plain face.
"You know I trust you, Braz. I always have."

"Oh, my loyal little wife." Braz laughed affection-
ately and squeezed her arm. "It is good for a man to
have a woman like you, so gentle, so uncomplaining.
There is nothing that makes a man feel so much like a
man! I thought you were pleased to come and live in
this place. Are you already so lonely for your little
pupils in Rio that you talk of starting a school?"

Getulio broke in with a none too subtle criticism.
"If you started a family of your own," he censured
his son, "she would not be lonely at all. And if you
want to feel like a man, produce a child! Then perhaps you can stop trying to prove it in other ways."

Quick to her husband's defense as always, a flustered Ana leaped into the fray like a lioness defending her cub. "If there is no child, you cannot blame Braz! It is my fault, mine alone. There have been tests. Braz has done everything a man can do, everything a doctor can do. And he has even forgiven me for causing him this great sorrow. Braz is man enough for any woman, and as to proving it—"

"Stop, Ana," Braz ordered sternly, bringing Ana's dramatic outpouring to an immediate halt. "My father wants to hear no more. Now, about this matter of a school for the Xara children. How could you run such a thing? You don't speak the dialect."

"But you told me of the young Xara woman who speaks Portuguese." Ana had been jolted back to her usual soft accommodating manner by her husband's censure. "Maria, is that her name? Perhaps she could help me, once a week, for one day. Of course, Braz, if you don't think it's a wise idea...."

Braz smiled indulgently. "I will think about it and perhaps speak to Eketi tomorrow. Then we will see."

A school for the young Xara children did seem an excellent idea, Toni reflected the following day as the difficult jungle trek neared its end. This time, with new boots, and with antihistamines to fortify herself against chance *pium* encounters, the march had been exhausting but not impossible. In view of her previous difficulties, and because she would in any case soon be leaving the team, Ty and Barney had urged her to forgo the trip altogether and stay at the compound with Ana. But Toni had personal reasons for wanting to visit the Xara village. It was Maria who had brought her here again; and she hoped to speak to the girl privately as soon as the lengthy welcoming ceremonies had been dispensed with.

Today the ceremonies seemed inordinately long. By now familiarity had conquered much of the original suspiciousness, and Eketi allowed all of the proceedings to be filmed—a concession that seemed to double the time required for speechmaking and posturing.

But at last the ceremonies came to an end. Braz O'Hara vanished to start treating the day's lineup of patients. Ty and Barney went off to film a sequence involving curare—not the actual preparation of the poison, whose recipe remained a closely guarded secret, but something to do with the dipping of spears and arrow tips into the noxious pitchlike mixture. Toni was not wanted at this man-only ceremony, and so she was at last free to seek out Maria.

It was not hard to spot Maria's cotton smock, donned as usual for the advent of outsiders. In a cluster of naked, giggling, *genipap*-decorated women, it was Maria who looked to be the outsider, despite her shiny scarlet face and the intricate black patterns on her arms.

"Can we talk, Maria? Perhaps in your private place?"

Bashfulness kept Maria's lashes lowered over the *urucú* stain on her cheeks, but she murmured agreement, and Toni sensed she was glad of the opportunity to talk again. Soon, with silent footsteps, Maria was leading Toni to the hidden buttress of the ceiba tree. Upon Maria's quick inspection, a huge ugly *mygale* spider leaped out and scuttled off to a safe haven. Half a foot across and venomous, too, it startled Toni only briefly. Although she had been told that the *mygale* sometimes ate small birds, her short experience in the Amazon had taught her that not many creatures—insects and piranha excepted—attacked unless hungry, provoked, trodden upon or surrounded by others of their species.

As soon as they were settled for conversation, Toni removed the green stone from around her neck. "I wanted to return this, Maria. I thought it was best not to do it in sight of the tribe, in case there were questions."

"But I wanted you to have it," protested Maria, at last risking a tentative upward glance. "It is a very powerful stone. The thing you did for me...I had no other way to tell you I was grateful."

"I'm glad if I helped you in some way, Maria, but I really can't take this."

Maria eyed the dangling stone and shook her head. "Perhaps for you it will bring luck," she said wistfully.

Toni's sense of desolation grew briefly acute. And then she fought remembrance away and tried to concentrate on Maria's problem. "Not for me, Maria, but perhaps for you. I've learned that this is one of the love stones of the Amazon women—the stones they gave to the men they wanted for themselves. Why don't you give it to Eketi?"

Maria's eyes reflected a confusion of alarm. "But I could not do that! Why, it would be just like telling him that. . . ." She bit her lip and halted.

"That you love him?" Toni finished gently, holding the stone on her lap until such time as she had finished persuading Maria. "Oh, yes, Maria, I know that you do."

Maria's face fell and she whispered, anguished, "Is it so easy to see?"

"In front of Eketi you hide it very well," Toni assured her gently. "Perhaps too well for your own good. You see, Maria, I have reason to believe that Eketi loves you."

Maria looked dazed. "Loves me?" she repeated stupidly, and for reasons that Toni understood very well, tears sprang to those dark eyes, not falling but shimmering in competition with the gleaming *urucú* juice.

"Dr. Quental told me so. He also said that Eketi is afraid of you because of your education."

"Afraid of *me*?" Maria looked down quickly and shook her head. "Eketi is afraid of nothing. And he is a wise man himself, far wiser than I."

"Even wise people are not always wise in love." Toni experienced a return of the sinking sensations that had become a part of daily life. "Take the stone, Maria. Give it to him."

"I. . .I couldn't. Eketi would think I was too bold. And—" her voice lowered to a whisper "—it would never work."

"For you, Maria, I think it might." Toni smiled a

wry regretful smile and tried once more to press the green stone into Maria's hands.

Maria still held back. "Nothing else has worked," she said in an agony of despair.

The removing of the clothes, of course. Toni knew it would be unwise to tell Maria that that particular sacrifice had been in vain, and so she maintained silence about some of the things Luís had told her. But there were some hard facts she could not hide. "Dr. Quental says that Eketi has vowed he will take a wife by the next full moon, Maria. Did you know that?"

"No," came the muted answer, after a short agonized pause.

"You must give him this stone, Maria. It may be your last chance. I can't guarantee it will work, but I do know that if you make no move he's sure to choose one of the other marriageable girls. You see, Maria, he's convinced you would refuse him."

Without another word, Toni placed the stone in the lap formed by the unbleached cotton smock. This time Maria did not protest. She bent her cropped hair low over the carved green turtle so that Toni could not see her eyes, and started to twist the thong in her fingers in a fever of indecision. With a great heaviness of heart Toni saw that the two quivering tears had left their home and were streaking a slow path over the scarlet urucú.

"Can you go back to the village alone, *senhora*?" Maria asked, trembling. "I would like to stay by myself for a time, to think."

As Toni trudged the short distance to the Xara village, she had no particular faith that Maria would overcome her painful timidity enough to approach Eketi, especially in the milieu of the village where the constant ebb and flow of humanity left little opportunity for privacy. For this reason, as soon as the curare filming was finished, she sought out Eketi himself.

Today, at the behest of the filmmakers, he had not donned the shorts and hat that he patently believed to be symbols of civilization. In colorful feathers and brief breechclout, he looked every inch the magnificent tribal chief, with his rippling muscles and healthy bronze skin. Toni addressed him without preamble, drawing some disapproving looks from the other Xara males nearby.

"Maria wants to see you," she said, blessing the fact that she and Eketi had a common language in Portuguese and that the other Xara men could not understand it.

A light glimmered in Eketi's eyes, but in the presence of his fellow tribesmen he put on an indifferent lordly expression. "If she wants to see me, I am here."

"She. . . can't come here right now. But it is important. I can take you to where she is."

"Oh?" Eketi's nonchalance, Toni was now sure, was pretended for the sake of his peers. She grew even more certain when he added, "And where is she?"

"There's a big ceiba tree, and—"

With seeming boredom, Eketi interrupted. "There is no need for you to explain. I know it well, that secret place where she goes when she wishes to be alone." And with no more words, he turned and started an animated conversation with his fellow warriors.

Toni's spirits sank to think her efforts had been in vain. Perhaps Luís was right; perhaps it was too late. Eketi must have made his decision for another wife.

But ten minutes later the empty ache of futility was replaced by a wry satisfaction, when she saw Eketi's tall solitary figure leaving the village and heading toward the jungle. And somehow she knew that this time the love stone of the Amazons would work its wonders well.

CHAPTER FOURTEEN

NEW YORK IN NOVEMBER. A chilly, rainy, blustery morning that warned of winter's advent. Garbage men on strike. Old gum wrappers and dog-eared cigarette packs, caught by the gusting wind, swirled around Toni's feet like autumn leaves as she hurried along the street, dodging endless streams of pedestrians and great piles of broken green garbage bags that spilled their contents on the sidewalk.

She was breathless by the time she turned in to a utilitarian office building that had seen better days and spotted the clock over the bank of elevators. Oh, damn. Five minutes late for the Friday-morning budget meeting. Lateness was becoming a bad habit, and one that was hard to break when sleep so often eluded her long into the empty nights.

And she'd be another few minutes late by the time the elevator reached the seventh floor. The ride would be interminable, stopping at every single floor as it always did at this time of day, to discharge passengers. It was the worst part of working in tall buildings: standing in slow elevators gave a person too much time to think. In the old days she would have been reminded of Matthew; at least those memories had now been put to rest.

Moving to an inconspicuous corner in order to allow the elevator to fill, Toni jammed her hands into the pockets of her belted tan raincoat and stared at the lighted floor display above the elevator door, willing it to speed quickly through the numerals that would indicate she had reached her goal. As the great metal doors finally slid closed and the upward journey from the main floor began, the *M* light flicked off to be replaced by the illuminated numeral two.

Second floor. Two. Two was a pair, a couple; two was what she and Luís would never be.... But no, she mustn't think of that. She mustn't think about the two letters that had arrived from Luís shortly after her return to New York, both marked Please Forward because Luís believed she was no longer working for the production company. Toni had opened neither of them, and she had returned both of them marked simply Address Unknown. And after that there had been no more.

There were other ways to think of two...Maria and Eketi, for instance. And the two hours they had both been missing from the Xara village, after Eketi had gone to find Maria in her secret place. Afterward Maria's lowered eyes and scarlet-painted cheeks had given away no secrets, nor had Eketi's feigned unconcern; but Toni had seen him fingering the green love stone that hung around his neck. By now Maria and Eketi were surely two, an indivisible pair....

Third floor. Three. The threesome of which she had once been a third. Ty and Barney had long ago finished with the Xara sequence, and also with the Manaus segment. At this point her former buddies would be filming in Tierra del Fuego, down around inhospitable Cape Horn. Dear Ty, dear Barney. It would be nice to be with them now. But having left them in the lurch on the Amazon episode, it was impossible to ask for a return of the assignment, which in any case had been handed to another producer—another female producer. And a very attractive one, too.

Fourth floor. Four. Four programs in the miniseries she was working on now. The work she had been assigned to, filling in for that pretty producer who had been sent to South America in her place, was to do with desert wildlife; Toni had only recently returned from a month in New Mexico. Considering the way she had let her employers down, she was lucky they had not fired her outright. Excuses about not being hardy enough for the jungle didn't hold much water when she had survived conditions as bad or worse on other assignments. Grateful not to have joined the ranks of the unemployed, Toni had no complaints about her current assignment, except that at the moment, with a break in the shooting schedule, it was not demanding enough: it gave her too much free time. Thinking time.

Fifth floor. Five. Five, five...for a moment Toni's mind stuck at that, until she remembered that fifty feet or more was the annual rise of the Amazon in flood. But it would be the dry season there now—the river no longer swollen; the jungle no longer in full bloom; the passion and the promise passed.

Sixth floor. Six. Luís's child would be six months

old now.... Toni knew that because the one and only letter Ty and Barney had sent from Manaus, a joint effort, had been written six months ago. "We'll be doing some filming in the Quental mansion," Ty had written. "As soon as I saw it I knew it was just the thing. Quental invited us there the other day, I think in an effort to soften us up, for he's been trying to worm your address out of us ever since we returned to Manaus. (Never fear; Barney and I have mouths like clams, and your word is our command. I think we've convinced Quental you're no longer working for the company. He believes you're in Spain, with your folks....)"

Barney had added his own inimitable touch to the letter. "Ha!" he wrote. "It was us that softened Quental up, in getting him to agree to the filming of his family mansion. Unfortunately we can't shoot until the lady of the house is available to play hostess on our footage; Quental himself still refuses to appear on film. That means a short delay, because we hear she just gave birth last night. However, we should be able to wrap up Manaus in another couple of weeks, three at the most...."

Seventh floor. Seven. It was seven months since she had seen Luís. *Seven.* . . .

She turned her eyes away from that numeral and fought her way out of the still crowded elevator. Sixty seconds later, raincoat shed and apologies said, she had joined others around an inelegant boardroom table where numbers a good deal more complex than simple integers were being discussed. Budgets weren't Toni's favorite subject, but they were a vital part of TV production, and at least they chased the mean blues from the mind. And Toni's boss—Ralph Anderson, the head of the production house—usually managed to chair the meetings with a minimum of fuss.

"Coming to the screening, Toni?" Anderson asked as the meeting began to file out nearly an hour later.

"Screening?"

"Yes, we're having an interlock. The sound track still needs some work, but it'll give you an idea." Toni must have looked particularly nonplussed, because Anderson added with a frown, "Didn't you get my memo? I asked my secretary to be sure you got it yesterday, so you'd try to keep this afternoon free. Damn that girl; if she makes one more mistake I'll—"

"Of course I kept it free," Toni said quickly. Ralph Anderson's secretary was not the most reliable employee in the company, but she was sole support of two children since her husband had deserted her. And possibly the memo was sitting on Toni's desk, along with other papers she had not had time to rifle through on account of late arrival. "I'm a little dense this morning, that's all. I must have been thinking of something else."

"You do look a bit under the weather," Anderson conceded. "But then, I can't say you've been looking yourself for some time. I've been meaning to ask, Toni: have you had a checkup since you returned from South America? You might have picked up one of those nasty tropical bugs."

"Yes, I have; and no, I haven't—picked up a bug, that is."

Anderson nodded, although he still looked dubious. "See you in the screening room at three-thirty, then. I'll be interested in your opinion of the thing."

If the memo was buried in the avalanche of other internal documents that had arrived recently, it managed to elude Toni's attention. And as it turned out, Ralph Anderson's secretary was absent—again—because of a child's illness. So it was later that day that Toni entered the screening room no wiser than she had been in the morning. She settled herself in a seat and exchanged pleasantries with a film editor, with her boss and with several other men who were present for the viewing. The chatter ceased as the lights were extinguished.

"Okay, roll it, Charlie." Almost at once the screen went bright, and bold numerals flashed past in swift succession, this time in reverse, as the leader on the film went through its countdown.

No titles or credits had yet been added, but Toni knew at once what it was. She stiffened in her chair, hands digging deep indentations into the armrests.

It started with a long aerial shot of the river, low in level and silted in places, against green vistas of jungle. Dissolve to the inky Rio Negro pouring its black tribute into the mud-yellow Amazon. Then the camera panned over the great floating docks of Manaus....

The announcer track had been added to Barney's sound effects and the voice tracks on Ty's film. It was all there on the screen: the bugs; the beautiful flamingos and parrots; the great glittering morpho butterflies of the bluest blue ever devised; the jungle compound; the tumbling white-spumed rapids; the howler monkeys; Getulio grinning in his *lancha*; the exuberant tangles of vines and other vegetation; the exotic flowers; the tapirs and the *mygales*; Eketi brandishing a spear and looking suitably ferocious; huddles of scarlet-faced women shot from modest angles; even a well-fed anaconda sleeping in a tree.

It was like being kicked in the stomach after a major operation. *This is your life, Antonia Carruthers.* Even the footage shot after her departure, because much of it reminded her of things Luís had described, seemed to open up the half-healed incisions. There were scenes of miserably ragged *seringueiros* slashing rubber trees, gathering the sap, smoking it into huge hundred-pound balls by laborious and unhealthy methods that had not changed in a century. There were scenes of the river at the high-water mark, lapping halfway up the trunks of towering trees. There were scenes of floating islands like great green flowering rafts, drifting down the swollen river. There were scenes of still waters suddenly boiling as the carcass of a dead tapir was thrown into a sluggish piranha-infested *igarapé*. There were scenes of the return to Manaus....

The announcer's mellifluous voice, telling of the days of the rubber barons as the camera toured the Opera House, was an unnerving echo of memories best left alone.

"But if the Opera House was an expensive white elephant of culture built to impress the world, it was by no means the only vanity of the era. The great mansions of the Amazon could stand comparison with those of Fifth Avenue in its heyday. Although many of these pretentious marble palaces became crumbling monuments to folly, stripped of their treasures in the aftermath of the bankruptcies that followed the rubber boom, a handful survived to testify to that era of wealth beyond avarice. Of these we were fortunate to film one of the finest. . . ."

Toni turned completely numb as the Quental mansion came on the screen, and moments later Constância. Smiling, serene, beautifully coiffed, she was lovelier than ever now that restored slenderness, along with a seductive emerald green hostess gown, showed off her graceful figure. After that all became a blur of solid gold dinner services, gilt-framed Monets and Manets, Sèvres china, Aubusson carpets, Louis Quinze period pieces. And then the bed.

Toni closed her eyes. She could not bear to see that bed of beautiful dreams and bitter awakenings, of raised passions and dashed hopes, of love found and love lost. The bed that was now undoubtedly shared by Luís and his wife. It helped that she could not see: but she could not shut out the announcer's voice. It droned on, telling of the mistress who had once slept here and of the rubber baron who had kept her. . . .

And then, at last, the announcer started to speak of gold taps and Roman bathtubs and gardens reminiscent of Versailles. The camera must have left the bed, but still Toni's eyes remained closed, her face drained of blood.

"But in the Amazon, man's vanities seem destined for an evil end. Several weeks after our film crew finished shooting, a fire destroyed this, one of the last great testaments to the wealth and power of the rubber barons. And so the charred Monets, the blackened cracked china, the melted gold are buried forever, or scattered with the ashes of its onetime occupants. *Sic transit gloria mundi.* So passes the glory of the world."

Deep shock had sent Toni's eyes flying open, but the screen showed no fire, no smoking ruins: only the humble tiny structure of the Church of the Poor Devil. If there were scenes after that she saw none of them. If there were words she heard none of them. Ashes of its occupants? Whose ashes? Those of the long-ago rubber baron and his mistress, or. . .?

Was Luís dead? Had he been dead for months? Would some inner voice not have told her—some snapping of the invisible cord that tied her to the Amazon? Luís. . . .

"Well, gentlemen—and Toni—what do you think?" The lights were on and several people had risen to their feet.

"Personally I find the announcer a bit pompous," commented someone. "And as for burying melted gold—hell, no one in his right mind would do that."

"The footage is fantastic, though. And those howler monkeys! My eardrums still hurt."

"Toni, I don't hear your voice in all this. Toni. . .?

Good Lord, you're white as a sheet! You'd better sit down again.''

A hand reached out to support her, then several hands. But Toni, unseeing and unhearing, had already reached the door. Without a word she opened it and walked out.

"What do you suppose got into her?" asked one of the men.

"She said she couldn't stomach the Amazon when she was there," Anderson said, looking puzzled. "At the time I didn't believe it, but... hell, maybe it was seeing the piranhas at work again."

CHAPTER FIFTEEN

"I'M AFRAID DR. QUENTAL is not in at the moment."
The voice on the other end of the telephone was
pleasant and impersonal, but the words started an
avalanche of relief that released the pent-up emotions
of three days. "Not in at the moment." Luís was
alive, alive, alive.

It had been Friday evening, after business hours in
Manaus, when she had started trying to find out
about the fire. A dozen frustrating calls that evening
had produced no results whatsoever. Toni's Portuguese was a little rusty from lack of use, and perhaps
that accounted in part for the fact that she had been
able to get no coherent answers by long-distance telephone. The former Quental phone number was no
longer in use; there was no new listing under that
name; Senhor Garcia could not be located either in
Brasília or in Rio; various other numbers in Manaus
were on answering service for the weekend; yes, the
newspaper had filed stories on the fire, and perhaps
if the *senhora* could call back at the beginning of next
week....

To do nothing was to die inch by inch, and so Toni
had caught a flight first to Miami and then to Ma-

naus, arriving on the Sunday. It was now Monday morning, and for the first time since the screening she had the news she had wanted to hear.

"But he does... work there?" she asked the switchboard operator.

"Assuredly, Dr. Quental works here, in the special-research unit. But as I told you, he is not in. Would you like to speak to one of his assistants?"

"No, I.... Can you tell me where he is living now?"

"I am not at liberty to give that information," said the operator. "Would you care to leave your name?"

"No, thank you." And there the call ended, with little news beyond the all-important news Toni had longed to hear. A visit to the newspaper office produced more results: no one had died in the fire, and only one person, an elderly servant, had been hospitalized for smoke inhalation. Senhora Quental, the story said, had been in Rio de Janeiro at the time; Luís had been absent for the week, visiting the clinic he had founded in the Amazonian jungle. There was no mention of an infant. At the time of the fire, Luís's child would have been about two months old, so Toni surmised that Constância might have taken the child to Rio in order to visit old friends.

The newspaper story expanded at some length on the historic interest of the home, on the value of its contents, on the Quental family and the fortune they had built in the days of the rubber boom. And it also provided a clue as to where Luís and Constância might be living now.

"Such effects as were saved from the fire will be moved within a few months to a second home built by the founder of the Quental fortunes back at the turn of the century. This home, although considerably more modest in dimensions, is also a site of historic interest to students of that great era in the annals of Manaus."

The story gave an address. Toni did not need to read on to know that the house was the one in which the rubber baron's wife had lived so many years before. Luís had mentioned tenants, but there had also been some implication that the tenants would be moving out; this story seemed to confirm it. By now it was quite likely that the house was once more inhabited by a Quental wife.

Toni now knew everything she had come to Manaus to find out; it was time to go home. She left the newspaper office and hailed a taxi to take her to the ticket office where she could book a return flight. In an odd way she knew that the scare of thinking Luís dead for these past days would help her adjust, in the long run, to the emptiness of her life in New York. Living without Luís seemed a small thing now, in comparison to living in a world where he did not even exist. For the first time in months, peace washed through her soul, cleansing it of some of the guilts. She could even hope wholeheartedly that Luís might find happiness with Constância—and if not happiness, then some sort of peace with himself.

At the airline office, no immediate bookings were available. Toni reserved space on the next possible flight, which would take her out of Manaus on Wednesday. Two days were far too long to spend in a city where she risked seeing Luís at every turn, but there was no other recourse. And if she took care, their paths would not cross.

The balance of the day was spent in the safety of a dark movie theater and in the hotel room, except for one long taxi trip taken under cover of night. The route she instructed the driver to follow took her past the ornate gates where the charred skeleton of the Quental mansion still stood; past the humble Church of the Poor Devil; and finally to the house where Luís must be living now. It was a handsome, unpretentious old Victorian house of native red stone, situated on a quiet tree-lined street. Toni asked the driver to stop for a minute. After a short halt during which she wondered which of the lighted windows might be the bedroom shared by Luís and Constância, she told the taxi driver to take her back to the hotel. A pilgrimage to expiate past guilts, perhaps? A need to sound the death knell to the last of her hopes? Or simply self-torture?

Or it could be that this compulsion to visit the scenes of heartache served some worthwhile purpose—like pulling folders out of a filing cabinet in order to destroy them. Whatever the motive, it must have been a strong one, for it also decided her course of action for the following day. Tuesday was the day the floatplane went on its weekly trip to the place where Luís had spent so many embittered years. From previous experience Toni knew perfectly well how to make arrangements to be on the flight; she also knew she could fly back the same afternoon, as Senhor Garcia had done.

From Getulio, who loved to gossip, she would doubtless hear news of Luís more personal in nature than anything she could learn from strangers in this city. His health, his frame of mind, his child: these were the things she wanted to know about, and could ask no one in Manaus. She was aware that Luís would find out at some point in the future that she had made the trip—but by then she would be long gone.

The hour-long flight passed quickly, in a mood that was poignant and painful but no longer as unbearable as it had been during her last days here. Out the window of the plane Toni surveyed the endless panorama of the Amazon basin, lush green threaded with the distinctive ocher of the river, until the plane began its descent over waters of quite a different hue.

By the time the *Catalina* had landed on the green water and taxied to the raft in mid-river, Getulio was already approaching in the *lancha* in order to pick up the weekly supplies. At once Toni spotted the distinctive brick shade that set his hair apart from the uniformly dark thatches of the riverside *caboclos*.

Getulio's astonishment at seeing Toni emerge from the hatch evaporated quickly, to be replaced by a warm genuine pleasure.

"Ah, it is good to see the *senhora* again!" he smiled. "But we did not expect you."

"I'll only be staying for a few hours, Getulio. I've

made arrangements for the pilot to pick me up on his return flight.''

"Ah, well. Even a short visit is better than none. Wait, I must load the supplies before I help you into the boat.''

As Getulio loaded crates and cartons into the *lancha*, he exchanged news and views with the flight crew and the village inhabitants, as was the weekly custom. Toni listened keenly as she stood waiting on the great raft where all this took place, but heard no mention of Luís Quental. And then the *lancha* was loaded, and it was time to climb in.

"Oh, no,'' she agonized moments later as the boat approached a bend in the river and she remembered.

Getulio looked at her in puzzlement. "There is something the matter?''

"The *piums*,'' Toni said, trying to brush the precursors of the coming black cloud away from her arms, her face, her ankles, her sandaled toes. "I forgot about the *piums*.''

With so many matters of moment on her mind, the need for antihistamines had been forgotten—not that she had any of the prescribed medication on her person. Nor had she thought to dress for insects today. The jungle wardrobe had long since been tucked into mothballs; in her haste to leave New York she had not even packed it. Today she had thrown on totally unsuitable clothes: a full cotton skirt with a short-sleeved blouse. They were pretty and they were practical, but not with *piums* around.

"I didn't even bring insect repellent! Oh, Lord, I'm going to be a mess."

"Ah, well, if you are to have trouble, a hospital is the place to have it," said Getulio philosophically.

It was too late to do anything but roll into a ball and pray. Politeness dictated that she should be asking for news of Getulio's son, Braz, and of Ana, but at the moment Toni was far too occupied in removing as many target areas as possible from the coming *piums*. Taking pity on her vulnerability, Getulio threw her an old tarpaulin, and gratefully she buried herself under it head and all, shutting out the worst of the barrage before it arrived.

She did not uncover again until the cutting of the motor and the bumping of the boat against the dock told her that the landing had been reached. As she struggled out from under the tarpaulin, the first thing she saw was the lower half of a man's body on the dock—the bend of knees as he hunkered down to steady the gunwale; the capable tanned hands with fingers that were long, strong, sensitive, familiar....

"Luís," she whispered as the tarpaulin was pushed away far enough to confirm her guess, and her eyes connected with the eyes whose dark torments had troubled so many of her dreams.

If surprise had turned Toni to a quivering mass of nerves, it seemed to have frozen Luís into position at the edge of the boat. Beneath the tan, his face was drained of color, the sockets dark and deep-set over the high cheekbones, the loved face far too thin.

At last he recovered enough to take the painter that

a patient but somewhat puzzled Getulio was holding out. Scarcely taking his eyes off Toni, he attended to securing the piassava rope to its mooring. His none too steady fingers fumbled the simple task; it was easy to see he had been strongly affected by Toni's arrival. At last he came to his feet and studied her with almost hurtful intensity, drawing a deep and uneven breath.

"The *senhora* says she has come to visit for only a few hours," Getulio interjected hastily. His apologetic tone suggested that he had misinterpreted the loaded silence and the look on Luís's face. "I thought this time you would not mind, doctor, as she is not staying. Please do not be angry. She has already been attacked by *piums* on the river."

Clearly Getulio believed that Luís's old hatred of women had reasserted itself. And Luís, who evidently could not yet trust himself to speak, was not ready to disabuse Getulio of the misconception.

"The *senhora* will need something for the *pium* bites at once, doctor," Getulio noted, still sounding worried by his employer's reaction. "Would you like me to attend to that? Or—"

"No." Luís's voice sounded unreal, strained, laden with emotion. He swallowed, forcing himself to continue. "No, Getulio. I'll do it."

He reached to help Toni from the boat, and she accepted his hand after a visible quiver of hesitation. A slight shortness of breath assailed her, and with Luís's strong fingers holding hers it did not even occur to her that this might be due to *piums*. As she came to her feet on the dock beside him, her throat caught at the closeness, the unchanged height of him—the remembered aura that turned her senses dizzy. And then she won one small battle with herself and removed her fingers from his grasp.

Slowly he let them go, still holding her with his eyes. "You've come because you heard," he stated in English, in the timbre of voice so often heard in the secret places of her heart.

She took several shallow breaths, using oxygen to fight the sensations that overwhelmed her. "I wouldn't have come if I'd known you were here," she managed to say. "Oh, Luís. This makes things very difficult. I'm sorry."

"Sorry?" His unsteady laugh held echoes of deep emotion.

She made her face behave, muscle by difficult muscle, and schooled herself to remember the ugly truths of her relationship with Luís. "Your wife and your child—are they here or in Manaus?" Somehow she succeeded in making the question sound like mere politeness, but in truth her stomach muscles contracted into knots as she waited to hear the answer.

"Then you don't know," Luís muttered, his voice almost cracking. He took a ragged breath and added, "No, they're not here."

"But they are . . . well?"

Luís nodded, "Yes."

Toni could not bear to ask more. It was enough to know that she would not have to face Constância in person; that she would not have to see the living evidence of the passionate embraces Luís had shared with his wife. Still ashen and casting about for something to break the terrible and wonderful intimacy of Luís's gaze, she turned her eyes to the top of the riverbank where no others stood.

"Why are you . . here?" she asked, speaking with difficulty because of the effort required to restore the conversation to normalcy. "I expected. . . Braz and Ana."

Luís must have heard the question, but he did not answer it; his dark eyes were occupied in devouring Toni like a man too long starved for the sight. And so it was Getulio, who had not needed English to understand the names, who finally inserted the information into the electric silence that seemed to embarrass him—possibly because he was still misinterpreting the meaning of this scene.

"Braz and Ana will return in one week, *senhora*. Dr. Quental has agreed to be here for a short time only, in order that they may visit Ana's parents in Rio and show off their fine little ones. Ah, such handsome babies!"

In light of the conversation she had overheard some months before, Getulio's statement should have triggered question marks in Toni's mind. But at the moment it was Luís she wanted to know about: Luís and nothing else.

With an almost shuddering effort, Luís dragged his eyes away from Toni's lips and said unevenly, "I'll explain, but not here. Come with me." Gripping Toni's elbow as if he had no plans to let her go,

he turned to his aide and spoke in Portuguese. "Today you'll have to unload without my help, Getulio."

"Sim, doutor."

"First to the dispensary." Luís steered her up the
riverbank, his hand trembling only slightly as it made
contact with Toni's forearm. Her overly sensitized
skin reacted like a geiger counter in the presence of a
uranium strike.

"The dispensary?" she croaked, making an unsuccessful stab at withdrawing her arm.

"Because of the *piums*," Luís reminded her, reaffirming his command of her elbow, and also of himself. "And there's a patient I should check on, because
I don't want interruptions when we talk. Once I get
you alone in the bungalow, I'm likely to forget altogether that I'm a doctor."

He led her through into the main entrance and
spoke a few words in the local dialect to the ancient
half-breed Manoel stationed there. Through the open
door into the ward, Toni could see several patients lying leadenly in the ubiquitous hammocks of the
Amazon. One was moaning and fevered, in the
throes of a malarial attack.

"I'll have to attend to that man," Luís said, guiding Toni toward the curtained area where he treated
outpatients. The curtain swung closed behind them,
shutting out Manoel's eyes if not his ears. Luís settled
her on a chair and devoted a moment to finding the
required antihistamines. "Here—some salve for
those bites. And take these pills."

Toni accepted the fuschia pills and a glass of water

with hands that shook more than she might have wished. Her voice was not too much of a wheeze as she asked, "Will I . . . need a shot this time?"

"We'll see," Luís said—all medical man at this moment, brisk and efficient and noncommittal. "I'll look you over and decide. Just sit there; I'll only be a few minutes."

The space where Toni waited was not unlike doctor's examination rooms everywhere: less grand, perhaps, but orderly and efficient, with an examination table and locked metal cabinets containing supplies and medications. The usual complement of medical implements was lying around—rubber tubing and probes and tongue depressors and cotton swabs and various pieces of gleaming stainless steel. There was also a desk flanked by two chairs, and it was on one of these that Toni sat, occupying her still shaky fingers in applying the special salve. It soothed with such speed that, had her thoughts not been unraveled now, she might have spared a smile to think that pride had once prevented her from asking for it.

With *pium* bites attended to, there was only Luís to occupy her mind. Luís, Luís, Luís. To see him, to hear his voice, to know he was only a matter of yards away: these things were like drugs to an addict. And like an abstaining addict, she must not allow herself to indulge. Even a small lapse—a kiss, a caress—might lead to more than she could handle. There was only one cure for her hopeless case: total abstinence.

The few minutes alone gave her time to marshal her defenses and don her suit of emotional armor.

She could do nothing about the quivering nerves in the pit of her stomach, but she did manage to put on a pale mask of composure, her determination firmed by fixing her mind resolutely on the wife and child who waited for Luís in Manaus.

And so when he came back through the curtain, reaching Toni's side in two purposeful strides, she raised the palms of her hands in a gesture of rebuttal. "No, Luís."

He had been reaching for her, and Toni knew from the smoking of his eyes that he wanted to kiss her, intended to kiss her. "Antonia," he breathed raggedly when she stopped him, but he did not complete the move to gather her in his arms. His face fought a brief tug-of-war, and the professional half of him won. He retrieved the chair from the other side of his desk and set it down beside Toni's.

"I'll have to look at your arms and listen to your breathing. Bear with me, darling. I won't do a thing until we're alone in the bungalow."

And that was a statement of intent that Toni could not even find strength to dispute, with Luís reaching out to seize her arm. Then an ankle: and his touch evoked exquisitely painful memories of another occasion when he had laid his lips on the very same flesh. She submitted to the stethoscope with trepidation, knowing that she must but fearing that this part of the examination would tell Luís too much about her internal state. Luís's fingers shook slightly when the device neared the swell of her breast above the brassiere, but he made no untoward move, and Toni buttoned swiftly as soon as the stethoscope was withdrawn. And then he turned his attention to the glands hidden behind her ears, each area so sensitive to his light probing touch that Toni felt faint from the contact.

"This time the pills should be enough," he smiled, coming to his feet and returning his chair to its usual resting place. He walked back to Toni's side and reached for her elbow. "Now come along to the bungalow. We need to be alone."

"No." She jerked her arm away as if she had been burned. This was the moment she dreaded: the moment when her inner fortitude must be put to the test. "Don't touch me, Luís. You've finished your examination now."

He stood tall above her—lean, reassuring, caressing her with his eyes. A deep smoking need had replaced his smile of moments ago. "Believe me, your conscience doesn't need to give you a moment's twinge," he said huskily. "Now come along. Once I've explained, you'll understand."

"You've said that before," she reminded him, digging in on her chair. "If you have anything to explain, explain it here."

"Everything's changed; trust me."

Changed? Hope poked its head up like a first spring flower, only to be trodden on by a skepticism born of too many months of despair. She defied him with her eyes. "Tell me what's changed, then. Until you do, I'm staying right here."

Annoyance grew on his tanned, lean-featured face.

"Are you really going to force me to go through this in a semipublic place? We could be interrupted at any minute. When I tell you, I want to be where I can take you in my arms. It's torture for you to keep me here, Antonia. You can't be so cruel. Now let's go."

"No, Luís! Tell me here and now, and tell me everything."

Anger built briefly in his face and then changed to a disturbing exasperated expression, as though he were considering sweeping her forcibly into his arms and carrying her off to the bungalow with no further ado. At length he said disparagingly, "Women," and walked back to his chair. He sat down and looked at her in a decidedly challenging way.

"If you insist on keeping me waiting, expect some waiting in return." His voice was cool and mocking, all the ardency of moments ago stamped out of existence as though it had never been. The ascetic Luís was once more in control. He sat with elbows resting on the desk, fingers splayed and steepled beneath his chin: an utterly professional posture. "Perhaps you've forgotten that I *can* be patient when I must. Now tell me what you've been doing for these past months, and what brought you to the Amazon. You've already made it clear you didn't come with intentions of seeing me."

Secure in having the desk between them, Toni leaned forward tensely and dropped one layer of pretense. Her voice was urgent with the need to know. "First tell me what's changed, Luís."

His eyelids drooped, and for a brief moment his

lips turned as cruel and arrogant as they had been in the early days of their acquaintance. "After you," he drawled in a dry sardonic tone.

"Luís, that's torture!"

"Exactly," he said. "Now start talking."

Their eyes dueled until Toni subsided into her chair, thinking. "Everything's changed." What could Luís mean? That he had abandoned his responsibilities? Forgotten his promises? Divorced Constância? She did not want to be the cause of a marriage breakup, especially when there was a child involved. Perhaps she would not like Luís's news.

And until she heard it she had absolutely no intention of putting herself within the reach of temptation. To go with him alone to the bungalow was something she was not willing to do—at least not yet. If Luís intended to prolong the agony of the wait, there was very little she could do about it short of acceding to his wishes. And so, with what grace she could muster, she started to tell of where she had been and what she had been doing. Luís thwarted her efforts to shorten the tale by interrupting with maddening frequency, questioning every small detail until she thought she would scream.

"Didn't it occur to you to at least steam my letters open before you returned them?" he taunted at one point.

"Yes, it occurred to me," she answered hastily. "I've told you everything now, Luís. Please—"

"I'll decide about that," he cut in. "Perhaps you could have saved yourself some moral anguish if you'd read the second letter. In it I told you of the decision I had reached not long after you left—at some cost, I admit. It was the decision to do everything in my power to make my marriage work. Now tell me more about the apartment where you've been living."

"Luís . . . !" she protested, her tone anguished.

"Go on," he directed in the most pitiless of voices.

And there was more after that. Had she heard from Ty and Barney? What was this miniseries she was working on? Did she enjoy the assignment?

"It doesn't much matter if I do," she said, beginning to grow desperate. "When I get back to New York I'll probably find I've been fired. I took off without asking permission, and they have no idea where I am. Now please won't you tell me your news?"

"There are some other questions that have been eating at me for many months," he started in again; and so began the next round of questioning. What had she done with her evenings? Had there been other men? Dates? When, where, with whom; and most important—what had happened on those dates? Had the men been invited back to her apartment? Had she fallen in love with anyone?

And yet his mocking expression told Toni that Luís was asking the questions only in order to retaliate for her stubbornness, not because of any real need to know. Perhaps he had picked up some bad habits from Ty and Barney.

"I don't think you have any right to ask," she

retorted defiantly, "until you tell me what you have to say. What I do with other men is my own business. I'm not your wife, Luís; I'm not answerable to you."

His eyes flickered with a light that could only be amusement and then grew opaque again. "Well, then, I'll save that question for now. Tell me one more thing, and this time I want the whole truth. Have you been happy?"

Toni looked away quickly. "Not very," she admitted, her heart tightening like a fist as she remembered the pain of these past months. It was a lie only by omission of the full awful truth. "That's why I made the trip here today. A pilgrimage of penance, I suppose. I thought I could take one last look and then start forgetting."

"I see you've managed to forget something else, too," Luís said softly, casting a glance at the slender, tightly fisted hands that rested in Toni's lap. No gold band encircled the ring finger on her left hand, nor was there any change of skin color to indicate that it had been worn recently in that particular place. It had been moved to another finger, not with acrimony, but with a lingering wistfulness because she had never been able to give her first husband the happiness or the union that should have been denoted by the ring. Worn on a different finger, it had not been forgotten: only put into a different place in her heart. To wear it on the ring finger had seemed a travesty when she had put her love into another man's keeping, and her body into another man's hands.

"Yes, I—"

A rustle of curtain and the "Hem!" of a voice warned that Getulio was asking for admittance. "Would you like to take a coffee with the *senhora*?" he asked of Luís, peering around the curtain. "I have prepared a tray."

With the tray safely deposited between them, Getulio poured two mugs and placed them on opposite sides of the desk. The short interruption and the brief change away from English was like a punctuation mark separating Toni's disclosures from those Luís was about to make.

"Do you know what Brazilians say about coffee?" he asked after the moment of silence that followed Getulio's departure.

"No." Toni stared into her mug, sick with apprehension caused by the wait. At least Luís's procrastination had told her one thing: the coming revelations were sure to be important ones. She hoped, and yet hated herself for hoping.

"I'll change the order of the saying in translation, as being more appropriate for the occasion." His voice was an infuriatingly slow drawl that kept the suspense unbearable. "Coffee, say my countrymen, should be four things: hot as hell, black as night, sweet as a kiss, and... strong as love."

"Luís, don't," she whispered, pleading. "Please just tell me what you have to say."

"Where shall I start?" he asked dryly, perhaps in revenge for the tortures she had once put him through. "From the day I found you had left the

Amazon altogether, causing my whole world to come crashing about my ears? From the struggles of conscience that kept me from following you at once? From the day I decided to try to make my marriage work, despite everything? Or from the day of my... fatherhood?''

Toni risked a glance at the darkly shuttered face, wondering what had caused that cynical note to return. ''I never heard whether it was a boy or a girl,'' she said.

''Both,'' said Luís.

''Twins?'' Toni puzzled, only to receive a nod of confirmation. She produced a hollow excuse for a laugh and dropped her eyes to stare at the floor. A double reason not to destroy a marriage. With a purposefully light voice she remarked, ''It must be catching in the Amazon.''

''I take it, then, that you do remember about the frequency of twin births among the Xara. Did you know they now accept the phenomenon? And it's just as well they do. One set was born last week, and there's another set on the way a few months from now—for Maria and Eketi.''

''Oh, Luís, that's wonderful!'' Toni briefly put aside her own impatience in order to respond to news of such a joyful nature. ''Then Eketi and Maria are now man and wife?''

''Yes, and very happy, too.'' A small smile played over his strong mouth, wiping away all traces of cynicism. ''And I hear it all started with a stone. Odd, what a little stone can do....''

The words were too evocative, causing Toni to fall silent. Luís went on, revealing more. "From that you may have gathered that the Xara women now permit themselves to be examined when they're pregnant. But the really important thing is that the Xara men now accept the phenomenon of twins. It should do wonders for their population."

"What changed their minds?"

"Once upon a time I told you that the Xara believe only what they can see. I was never able to convince them that twins were in the genes, but seeing twins—another man's twins—did convince them."

It took very little puzzling to produce the answer to that. "Your twins," Toni guessed.

"Go back a moment and think that through again." Luís's voice was sardonic but not discouragingly so. "Surely after all I've told you in the past it can't be too hard for you to reach the right conclusion."

And when she remained silent too long, guessing but not stating her guesses aloud, Luís added, "Red hair is a very distinctive trait that's only in certain genes. Anyone could see at a glance that the father was Braz. And Braz has some Xara blood in him, so. . . ."

He allowed some time for that to sink in before proceeding softly, "Constância admitted as much—not that she could very well deny it. She knew she was expecting twins, but she was as shocked as anyone when they turned out to have red hair. It seems that she had no idea Braz was the father. Evidently there had been several other contacts after I left Rio—deliberate ones, because she knew that my short interlude with her could not possibly have resulted in pregnancy; the timing was wrong. Braz just... happened... at some point during her efforts to get pregnant. You see, Antonia, Constância was altogether prepared to foist another man's child upon me. She wanted to save the marriage by fair means or foul."

"Luís, tell me—"

"Don't be so impatient," he said, fixing her with a stern eye; and Toni forced herself to subside again in her chair. Luís was telling this in his own time, in his own way, and she knew that to pester him with questions might only cause him to become even more circuitous in his revelations.

"The red hair, that was the thing. The Xara have seen only two red-haired men in their lives: Getulio and Braz. They *know* hair color is inherited. Why, even the smallest Xara child looking at those twins can tell they're Braz's children, both of them. From there to accepting the twin phenomenon was a very small step. Of course, the entire Xara tribe trooped over to the edge of this compound to see the evidence, as soon as they heard the news about Ana's babies."

"*Ana*'s babies?" Toni repeated faintly. Her head whirled from following all the disclosures that were tumbling out so fast.

"They are now. Braz and Ana are adopting them. There are a few formalities to go through still, but basically it's a *fait accompli*. Ana's very happy about it, all things considered. She knew about Braz's infidelity, so that part was no shock to her. In fact, she can almost forgive Constância now that she thinks of her as a surrogate mother, not as a rival.''

As if she knew that Luís was reaching the denouement of his piece, Toni remained silent, holding her breath for his next piece of news.

"When Constância abandoned the babies they were only about two months old. I had a fairly good notion that Ana would accept the babies and love them as extensions of Braz. I decided to risk presenting the evidence in person. And so I flew here—the babies, too, and the nursemaid who had been minding them. It was during that week that the Quental mansion burned down.''

Luís now stood up and walked around the desk to look gravely down into Toni's eyes. "I'm divorced now, darling. Perhaps, despite everything, I would have lived up to my promise if Constância had lived up to hers. But I was still struggling with the unhappy prospect of acknowledging another man's children when she left. As I was refusing to share a bed with her. . . need I tell you that motherhood didn't change certain things about Constância? If I wasn't willing to satisfy her, other men were.''

"Divorced," whispered Toni. It was what she had suspected; and yet her whole world was still rocketing and reeling with the realization that, in the event, her own part in the past had not been the deciding factor.

"The divorce proceedings had never been fully dropped. It was easy enough for the lawyer to proceed. Constância could have fought it, of course, because of my one...lapse. But under the circumstances...." He paused and went on softly, "It's all done, darling, finished. Constância is out of my life now—forever."

"Oh, Luís...." Tears started to Toni's eyes and shimmered on her lashes—the tears she had been unable to shed for these past few months, except in her heart.

"I hope you're not about to tell me you don't approve of divorce," he said with a return of the old sardonic dryness.

She did not, in many cases. But for Luís—Luís, who had suffered a purgatory of many years; Luís, who had lived through infidelities faced by few husbands; Luís, whose marriage could never have succeeded—for Luís there should be a second chance.

"I'm a free man now, Antonia, and I have been for several weeks." A smile warmed his eyes, turning them as deep and rich as soft black velvet. "If I hadn't wasted so much time looking for you in Spain...."

"You went to Spain?" she asked, her throat suddenly dry again.

He nodded, possessing her with his gaze but not yet with his hands. "And met your parents," he said.

"Oh, Luís—"

"Do you have any idea how hard it is to find people when you don't know their last name? If you recall, you had told me the general area where they live, but very little more—and you had certainly never mentioned your maiden name. I knocked on a lot of doors. You'd be surprised how many expatriate Americans live in that part of the world."

Toni was still staring up at him, tears of happiness shimmering on her lashes, when he went on softly, "I approve of them, although I'm not sure they return the sentiment wholeheartedly. But they do have your happiness at heart. They know you've earned some joy after the difficult years you've had, and so they gave me their blessing—along with your address in New York. I'd be there right now, looking for you, if I hadn't promised Braz and Ana to fill in here for a while. *Meu Deus*, when I discovered your old film crew had been lying about your whereabouts I could have throttled them. If your parents hadn't relented...well, I would have found your two former friends and choked the truth out of them somehow."

Laughter bubbled through Toni's tears of happiness. "Ty and Barney would never have told you. They thought you were a cad of the worst sort."

"And do you think that, too?" he asked huskily, pulling her to her feet. "You did once. You called me a madman. And perhaps at the time I was."

Her soul and her love trembled in her eyes. "I didn't think that in my heart, Luís. Never in my heart."

The fires that had been so well banked now rekindled in Luís's eyes. An emotion that was desire but far more than desire worked across the planes and angles of his face, softening the mouth to a sensual loving line. "Then perhaps I can hope for the right answer," he murmured smokily. "Now don't you

wish we were in a less public place? When I propose,
I want to do it where we can't be interrupted."

"YES, LUÍS...yes, yes, yes," she whispered not so
many minutes later, in the privacy of the bungalow.
Luís, importunate to know her answer, had urged the
question upon her as soon as they closed the door behind them, shutting out the rest of the world.

He had taken her in his arms before he asked. Now
the lips that had occupied so many of Toni's bitter-
sweet dreams descended to seal the pact. There was a
fierceness and a tenderness in that kiss, a meeting not
only of mouths but of hearts. Their lips sought each
other with a hunger born of the months apart, tasting
the deep heady tastes of love even as their hands traveled in an urgent rediscovery of its textures. They
drowned in that kiss—deeply, wholly, exquisitely.
Desire swiftly became a flood tide of need, invading
the haunts of passion in his body and in hers.

If Luís had not broken apart before they reached
the daybed, Toni would certainly not have done so.

Pulling abruptly away, he put several feet between
them. Dazed and disappointed, Toni looked at him
without understanding. What had been happening
seemed so natural, so right, so free of guilt—two
parts of a whole joining only to remain joined by
stronger bonds for all eternity.

Luís had stopped. And yet his hands still shook
with strong passion held in check; his eyes still hun-
gered; and there was no visible lessening of the
powerful need that had flamed into life in those

moments when they had stood so closely clasped to each other.

"I have to prove to you that I can be less than a madman when I know there's a lifetime of sanity ahead. I want to put no more strains on your scruples, Antonia. If you'd prefer to wait, I can be... patient."

At those words, spoken in a voice choked with effort, Toni's brief disappointment evaporated. Emotion she had thought could rise no higher welled higher still. That Luís, despite his imperative needs, loved her enough to put aside the frustrations of these past months: it sent her heart spilling shamelessly into her eyes.

There was no love stone now to say what she wanted to say. And so she closed the space between them and started to unbutton his shirt.

"Luís, darling," she murmured as she slid her fingers through the opening to caress the warm firm flesh where the stone had once rested, "you don't have to be patient with me."